Dear Readers:

Please, come and join us at the beautiful, Victorian-style Seascape Inn, a magical bed-and-breakfast nestled on the Maine coast. A short walk from the graceful and alluring inn lies Sea Haven Village, where Fred and Lucy will welcome you to the Blue Moon Cafe, a picturesque eatery where you can dine in summer by the gentle ocean breeze and, in winter, be intrigued by the shroud of mystical fog and crisp, cool sea mist.

After your meal, stop across the street at The Store, a fairly modern grocery and gas station owned by Mayor Horace and Lydia Johnson. There you can pick up most any incidental you might have forgotten in your haste to pack. Should you arrive by car, rest assured it'll be in good hands with Jimmy Goodson at Jimmy's Quick Service Garage.

Other residents ready to welcome you to the peaceful village include Pastor Brown, a handsome, young minister; Miss Millicent Thomas, the elderly owner of Miss Millie's Antique Shoppe; Sheriff Leroy Cobb, who stops in at the cafe every afternoon for a slab of Lucy's homemade blueberry pie; Hatch, who maintains the lighthouse; and, of course, the ever-nurturing Miss Hattie, caretaker of Seascape Inn. Oh, and do try to ignore the rantings of Miss Hattie's neighbor, Beaulah Favish, insisting that strange things are going on at Seascape Inn, mmm? She's reportedly a touch eccentric—even when it comes to relaying the Seascape Legend.

Please, come join us by reading the fifth *Seascape* series novel, *Beside a Dreamswept Sea* by Victoria Barrett, and let the magic of Seascape Inn work for you as it is rumored to have worked for those special few who've dared to . . .

Live the Legend

From the *Seascape* Creators,
Victoria Barrett and Rosalyn Alsobrook

The Seascape Romance Series from St. Martin's Paperbacks

BEYOND THE MISTY SHORE by Victoria Barrett
THE PERFECT STRANGER by Rosalyn Alsobrook
UPON A MYSTIC TIDE by Victoria Barrett
FOR THE LOVE OF PETE by Rosalyn Alsobrook
BESIDE A DREAMSWEPT SEA by Victoria Barrett

TOMORROW'S TREASURES by Rosalyn Alsobrook
(*coming in December 1997*)

Beside a Dreamswept Sea

A SEASCAPE ROMANCE

VICTORIA BARRETT

St. Martin's Paperbacks

BESIDE A DREAMSWEPT SEA

Cover photograph by Steve Terrill, courtesy The Stockbroker.

ISBN: 0-312-96251-7

Printed in the United States of America

St. Martin's Paperbacks edition/June 1997

10 9 8 7 6 5 4 3 2 1

Beside a Dreamswept Sea

Chapter 1

The child was going to drown.

The truth slammed into Tony Freeport with the force of a sledge. A stunning truth, considering she lay tucked safely in bed in the Shell Room of Seascape Inn and, in his fifty years as a ghost working with his beloved Hattie in assisting others here to heal, he'd never before seen anyone come to harm under the inn's roof. But in Suzie Richards's dream, all the signs of real-life drowning were evident: panic, an inability to breathe, and fear. So much fear . . .

Dream or reality, if Tony didn't do something quickly, the nine-year-old daughter of Bryce Richards and the deceased photojournalist, Meriam, *was* going to drown.

What could Tony do? What *should* he do? Suzie taking on the burdens of family no child should ever have to carry had been the catalyst insisting he intercede this far. But to intercede into her dreams? Did he dare?

This had to be a near-miss warning. Had to be.

He looked through the closed bedroom door, out into the upstairs hallway. The paneled walls deepened the night's shadows and the only light was that seeping through the bank of mullioned windows centered inside a small vaulted alcove at the far end of the hall. Tall hand-carved mahogany bookshelves flanked those windows. Tony couldn't clearly see the books in them, but he didn't have to see them to know each book's title, to know each spine stood straight. Nor did he need to see the pillows on the thick cushions of the window seat nestled between those shelves to know they'd been fluffed. Hattie Stillman nurtured everything in her care, which included all of Seascape Inn, most of Sea Haven Village, and, at one time, him.

He scanned the polished plank-wood floor from the far end of the hallway back toward the end where he stood. On the left, facing the Atlantic Ocean, was the master bedroom, dubbed the Great White Room years ago, and the bath. On the right, the L-shaped staircase leading down to the first floor, and the Cove Room where Bryce Richards should have been sleeping but wasn't. Instead, the man dozed slumped on the hallway floor, his head lolled back against the paneled wall, his slippered foot rumpling the edge of the white Berber rug that stretched from the stairway's landing nearly all the way down to the Shell Room, about a yard from Tony's feet.

Bryce was a man on a mission. Two sets of his friends from New Orleans, T.J. and Maggie MacGregor and John and Bess Mystic, had found "magic" at Seascape Inn, and Bryce had come here with doubts but hopes that enough magic remained to grant his daughter peace from the emotional demons haunting her sleep since her mother's death two years ago. But even in sleep, Bryce was despairing; Tony sensed it. Despairing that, though armed with its angelic innkeeper, Miss Hattie, the charming old inn couldn't hold *that* much magic and, without it—God knew Bryce had tried everything else—Suzie's nightmares would be an endless source of her suffering.

And Bryce despaired that she'd dream and, asleep in the Cove Room across the hallway, he'd not hear her cries, not know to come and comfort her. For reasons of his own, he had forsaken sleeping in the comfortable stuffed chair in her room or in the luxury of a soft king-size bed and had chosen to stand guard on the hallway's oak floor outside her door, listening, waiting, and praying he wouldn't be needed.

The agony of the situation had broken Tony's heart, and he'd aided the quiet of the house in lulling the reluctant Bryce to sleep, agreeing with his darling Hattie's assessment that Bryce was worn to a frazzle. But who wouldn't be? Worried sick about his three children overall, Suzie and her nightmares in particular; fighting a constant battle of wills with that dour-faced Mrs. Wiggins, whom Bryce's wife had hired to care for the children when Jeremy had been born four years ago; and then—right on the heels of the narrow-miss divorce between John and Bess Mystic—that blasted Tate divorce case. It was a wonder Bryce Richards was still upright!

In the days since their arrival at Seascape Inn, Hattie had mumbled repeatedly that no more a devoted father than Bryce ever had graced the earth, and Tony wholeheartedly agreed with his beloved on that appraisal, too. Bryce was a fine father, a fine man, and a fine attorney.

Yet that hadn't spared him from challenges.

As if he hadn't had enough on his plate already, he'd been tossed a moral dilemma on the Tate divorce case that would have brought even the most avid believer, the most confident man in the world, to his knees. A shame he had represented Gregory Tate. Not only disagreeable, the man had proven himself unscrupulous and coldly calculating. Though the divorce had been granted and the case was behind Bryce now, it had left him weary, his opinion even more jaded about the odds for successful, happy marriages—and it'd left him admittedly curious about the mysterious Mrs. Tate.

So was Tony. He leaned against the doorjamb, propped the toe of his shoe against the floor, then rubbed at his neck. Why had the woman never once appeared in court? Never once attended the attorney/client meetings with Bryce, Gregory, and her own attorney? Her behavior was curious.

Tony grimaced. Now, because he had given Bryce this brief but much-needed respite of sleep, Suzie fought the fiendish nightmare alone. Tony shouldn't intercede further—dream intervention was expressly forbidden—but she was suffering uncomforted, and that was his fault. He couldn't deny responsibility and condemn her to this. Hattie would never forgive him. Worse, he'd never forgive himself.

Protocol be damned. Tony shoved away from the wall. Rules and regulations, too. What more could be done to him? Already he lived in the house with his beloved Hattie and yet he couldn't talk directly with her, couldn't hold her, couldn't love her as a man should love a woman—as he *would* have loved her had he been given the chance. What could be more challenging? And a child's life hung in the balance. Likely her father's, too—if anything should happen to her.

Theoretically, people didn't actually die just because they died in their dreams. But what if Suzie did? In Tony's experience, dreamers *always* had awakened prior to actual dream-state death. So why wasn't Suzie awakening? Soaring heart rate. Gasping something fierce. She might not drown, but she could have a heart attack. Drowning or a massive coronary, dead was dead.

He tried several tactics to nudge her into awakening.

Nothing worked.

Now what?

Having no idea, Tony scowled, feeling inept and agitated. The bottom line was Bryce Richards had little more left to lose. Tony *had* to intercede.

He stepped into Suzie's nightmare, into a raging storm.

The wind stung, bitingly cold, whistling through crisp brown leaves that had fallen from the poplars and oaks near the shore. Familiar poplars and oaks. Familiar low stone wall running along the rocky ground to the pond. And familiar white wrought-iron bench, north of a familiar, freshly painted gazebo.

Criminy, Suzie was in the pond behind Seascape Inn!

Did she realize this yet? That her recurring dream actually took place here?

Odd. Before three days ago, Suzie never had seen Seascape Inn or its pond, and yet she'd suffered this same nightmare for the past two years.

Agitated by the blustery wind, Tony squinted against the darkness and glimpsed the shadow of a little rowboat—the very boat he himself with his lifelong friends, Hatch and Vic, had fished from as boys. Rocking on turbulent waves, the boat dipped low, took on water. And—sweet heaven, it was empty.

"Suzie?" *Where was she?* "Suzie?" The wind tossed Tony's words back to him. Nearing the water's edge, he called out again and stumbled over a giant oak's gnarled roots.

His foot stung.

Startled, he winced. Physical pain? How peculiar. It'd

been half a century since he'd felt physical pain. . . .

He frantically scanned the dark water. Later, he'd think about the pain. He had to find Suzie now—before it was too late.

Midway across the pond, something flashed white. Her nightgown? No. No, it wasn't. Just froth from a wave. Fear seeped deeper, into his soul. *Where was she?*

Straining harder, skimming, probing, he spotted her. Near the bow of the boat, floundering in the water, arms flailing, head bobbing between the waves.

Oh, God, she really *was* going to drown. Unlike her other dreams, this one wasn't a near-miss warning!

He cupped his hands at his mouth. "Suzie! Hold on to the boat. I'm coming. Just hold on to the boat!"

"I can't!" she shouted back. Swallowing in a great gulp of water, she choked.

The sound grated at his ears, tore at his heart. Why in the name of everything holy did she feel it vital to hold on to the oars? Though wooden, they wouldn't offer enough stability in the turbulent water to keep her afloat. Still, she held them in a death grip.

He had to find out why. Though dangerous—fear of him, in addition to the fear and panic she was suffering already, could worsen her situation dramatically—to help her, he needed to understand her rationale.

She screamed. A shattering scream that pierced his ears and reverberated in his mind. A chiseled hollow in his chest ached. Whatever the risks, damn it, he *had* to take them.

Focusing, he tapped into the child's thoughts.

You have to get both oars in the water and keep them there, Suzie.

Not her voice. A memory. Something she'd been told by a woman. Someone older—twenties or thirties maybe. And that accent—definitely not anyone from Sea Haven Village, or from Maine. Southern. Distinctly Southern.

The child took a wave full in the face, sputtered, then coughed.

He hurried toward her, resenting that in her dreams he obviously lacked his special gifts, his abilities and talents with the physical, that would allow him to fish her out without getting so much as a toe wet. In dreams, it appeared he was as weak or as strong as a normal man. And while at times he'd love to again be a normal man, when Suzie was clinging to life by an oar wasn't one of them.

What did it all mean?

He returned his cupped hands to his mouth. "Suzie, let go of that oar right now and grab hold of the boat. Do it! Do you hear me? Do it!"

Her wet hair swept over her face and clung to her tiny cheek in a clump, her eyes wild with fear. "I've got to keep both oars in the water! I've got to, or I'm not gonna get better."

This was new ground, and Tony waffled on what to do. His heart told him to go get her. His logic warned if he touched her, with her body temperature as low as it surely was already from the frigid water, the cold could result in pneumonia and she'd die. But if he didn't physically get her out of the pond quickly, she'd die, too. Simply put, he was in a lose/lose situation here. Damned if he did, damned if he didn't.

He had years of experience. He just had to not panic. Had to think about this. He cleared his mind, then weighed the pros and cons, mentally searching for alternatives less risky to Suzie.

There were none.

He hated any but win/win situations, yet the core in this one rested right where it had before he'd begun his search: She had a fighting chance with pneumonia. She didn't with drowning.

Tony dove in. Hit the frigid water that sucked out his breath, then stroked furiously toward her.

The lack of true physical exercise for too many years had him winded and tiring quickly. Soon, his arms and legs felt like lead and he couldn't seem to get enough air to feed his starving lungs. They throbbed and ached, and the physical sensations of weight and gravity and oxygen deprivation had him sluggish, tired, moving about as quickly as a hypothyroid snail. Without his special gifts, could he get to her in time?

"Please, don't let her die. Please, help me help her." She was so close. So close. . . . *"Please!"*

He dug deep, scraped the remnants of his reserves and pulled a mighty stroke.

His fingers snagged the collar of her nightgown.

He tugged, grabbed her more securely with his left hand, the boat with his right, then curled her tiny body to his and hugged her to him. She latched her arms around his neck, squeezed so hard he sensed she was trying to crawl into him. And then she began to cry. Deep, heart-wrenching sobs that jerked viciously at his heartstrings. "Shhh, it's okay, little one. I've got you now. I've got you now."

She breathed against his neck, her voice a rattled whimper of sound. "Promise?"

This crisis, she'd weathered. This time, she'd survived. Awash in gratitude and relief, he swallowed hard. "I promise."

Water swirled, tugging at his clothes. Awareness stole into him and he recalled stubbing his toe on the gnarled oak's root. His foot actually had stung. And now, more awareness of the physical dragged at him. Her moist, warm breath at his shoulder. Cold as she was from the frigid water, the warmth of her tiny body. The feel of her fingers digging into his neck. His own need for oxygen, for rest. The weight of his uniform. Sensations.

Lifelike . . . sensations.

His hands began to shake. Awed, humbled, he shook all over. He'd not felt any physical sensations since he'd returned home from the battlefield for burial back in World War II and, because he hadn't, now he couldn't be sure which of them, he or Suzie, groped with greater emotional turmoil.

She was alive.

And, for the first time in half a century, he was feeling the actual touch of another human being.

His eyes stung and a tear—a tear—slid onto his cheek.

An uneasy niggle nagged at him. He'd been in many situations in the past fifty years and had felt nothing physical. So why now? True, he'd never before entered anyone's dreams—and he fully expected to pay a steep penalty for trespassing into Suzie's now—but there had to be some deeper reason for this. His sixth sense screamed it. And it screamed that something about these particular "special guests" made this intercession, and their situation, different from the hundreds of other special guests he and Hattie had assisted at Seascape Inn.

Suzie wheezed. Feeling the rattle against his chest, he prayed Seascape would protect her from almost certain pneumonia. Over the years, many had called the inn the Healing House, and how fervently he hoped its reputation proved prophetic for Suzie.

These special guests are different. A woman's voice echoed through his mind. *This situation is different.*

She sounded urgent, yet calm and dispassionate. Who was she?

Who I am doesn't matter. My message is what is important, Tony.

Why?

You'll have to find the answer to that yourself, I'm afraid.

I see.

No, you don't. That's part of the problem. But you will, Tony. I'm rather, er, persistent.

Just what he needed. Another stubborn woman to contend with. *Well, I'll have to figure it out later. Right now, I need to get Suzie out of this water and wind before she freezes to death.*

Ah, I'm encouraged. The woman sighed.

Excuse me? Kicking his feet, he steered toward the shore, holding on to Suzie and the boat for fear his strength would fizzle.

You're mired in a quandary yet still putting Suzie's needs first. I'm encouraged by that. And, yes, I expect you will figure it out—eventually.

Terrific. Stubborn and snooty. A barrel of sunshine. *I'm encouraged that you're encouraged.*

Save your sarcasm, Tony. The woman laughed, soft and melodious. *You're going to need your energy.*

He wanted to kick something. Actually, he wanted to kick "Sunshine." Wicked of him, but did she have to be right about the energy bit, too? His muscles were in distress; he didn't have the energy for this verbal sparring—or the time for it. Not right now. Suzie had stopped crying, but she still clung to him as if she feared he'd forget and let go of her. He'd promised, but promises didn't hold much value to Suzie Richards; that much was evident. At least not those aside from her father's. In the chaos of what had been their family life, Bryce somehow had retained his children's trust. That in itself, considering the circumstances, was a miracle.

To reassure her, Tony smoothed her frail back until her shudders eased. When they subsided, though vain, a sense of satisfaction joined those of relief and gratitude inside him. He'd catch hell for breaking protocol, but feeling Suzie inhaling and exhaling breath made whatever price he had to pay worth it. The last thing she needed was more tragedy in her life. It wouldn't do Bryce any good, either. The man had suffered his share of challenges and then some.

Unfortunately, from all appearances, he was fated to suffer a few more, but at least those challenges wouldn't include the death of his oldest daughter.

They might, Sunshine commented.

Tony's skin crawled. *Not if there's any way in the world for me to stop it.*

You might want to recant that statement, Anthony Freeport.

No way.

We'll see.

A shiver rippled up his backbone. Images raced through his mind. Images of Suzie again in the little boat, trying to do something with the paddles and falling into the pond. Images of her in the water during a storm, gasping. Drowning. And images of Tony standing alone on the shore, his hands hanging loosely at his sides, his shoulders slumped, watching and yet powerless to help her.

Powerless? Shock streaked through him. But he'd never before been powerless here. Never . . .

Until now.

Sunshine's softly spoken warning thundered through his mind. His knees collapsed. He locked them, stumbling and shuddering hard. God help them all.

This wasn't an ordinary dream.

Chapter 2

The more things change, the more they stay the same.

Sitting on the sun-dappled ground in a Biloxi, Mississippi, cemetery, Caline Tate swept that thought from her mind, her hair back from her shoulder, and looked at the weathered headstone of Mary Beth Ladner, the stranger buried next to her grandmother.

Mary Beth didn't feel like a stranger to Caline. For as long as she could remember, after Sunday services at First Baptist Church, she had visited here with her father. And nearly as long ago—the winter she turned seven—it had dawned on Caline that Mary Beth Ladner's grave never had flowers on it. Not on Christmas. Not on Memorial Day. Not on any day. And why it remained barren perplexed Caline as much now as it had the first day she'd noticed.

Someone once had loved Mary Beth. Someone once had mourned losing her. They had to have mourned losing her to have had chiseled into the stone: *She was the sunshine of our home.* Where had they gone that they couldn't bring a woman so special to them so much as an occasional flower?

Biting her lip, Caline placed one of two yellow carnations near the base of the stone. Years ago, the florist had told her carnations meant joy and, considering it only right that a woman who'd brought joy in life should have joy brought to her in death, Caline had made a tradition of bringing Mary Beth a carnation every Sunday and pausing to whisper a few kind words over her grave. Before she'd realized it, those pauses had grown to visits, and those few kind words had lengthened to chats. And, somewhere along the way, those chats had become her refuge, her safe haven to discuss her hopes and dreams, and her troubles. Troubles far too private to discuss with her parents or even her best friend.

Now that Caline was thirty-two, married and recently divorced, little had changed. She still came to Mary Beth's grave to talk through her troubles.

"Life's funny, isn't it, Mary Beth? We set our sights on what we want and we make all our decisions with our wants in mind, and just when we think we've got it all figured out, life slips us a curve ball and—*wham!*—we end up with everything we *never* wanted. Why is that?"

Caline stared off into the branches of the winter-barren oaks, the twisted pines that were a familiar sight in hurricane country. "I just don't get it. I knew what I wanted the first time I saw your headstone. I wanted to be the sunshine of my own home. And I thought I'd have that with Gregory, eventually, but . . ."

An empty ache seized her chest and a lump swelled and blocked her throat. He'd made promises to her. Sacred vows. And he'd broken them all.

Why had he done that? *Why?*

Tears gathered on Caline's lashes and the oak limbs distorted and blurred. "I loved him, Mary Beth. I might have been a terrible wife—God knows he told me I was often enough that I have no choice but to believe him—but I did love him with all my heart. My love just wasn't . . . enough."

A squirrel scampered up the trunk of the oak then leapt from one barren branch to another. The time had come for her to leap, too.

"I came to tell you I'm going away for a while," she said, rummaging through her purse for a tissue. "The divorce is final now and I need to decide what to do with my life."

Pulling a crumpled tissue free from the clasp on her wallet, she stiffened her shoulders then swiped at her eyes. "I'm going to drive up to a friend's cabin in Nova Scotia and stay there for a few months. My parents think the change of scenery might do some good. I'm hoping they're right. I'm about as scared as scared can get, Mary Beth. I never thought I'd be starting over at thirty-two with nothing I ever wanted."

Gregory had given her no choice. He'd given her even less. Sometimes she hated him for that. Sometimes she hated herself for it.

A streak of hopelessness snaked through her stomach. Fighting it, Caline stood up, then brushed angrily at the blades of dead grass clinging to her skirt. "Dad will bring your carnation on Sunday when he visits Grandma Freemont's grave. I didn't have to ask him. He knows it's important to me that you know you're not forgotten." Tears again welled, and Caline traced the edge of the worn stone with her fingertips. "You'll never be forgotten."

She shouldn't say it. Shouldn't even think it. But she couldn't hold back from Mary Beth. Caline never had. "This trip is kind of a pilgrimage. The truth is, I'm sorely lacking courage and a whole lot more right now. With the divorce final and Gregory already remarried to that woman, I'm thinking that for fourteen years I let him rob me of the things that make me who I am. All except one. I don't want to lose it, too. It's weak. Just a flicker of a spark. But it's still there. And I'm not sure if I've got the guts to nurture it. I can't hurt like this again, Mary Beth. I just can't."

Caline drew in a deep, steadying breath. "That's why I need the courage. Because that tiny spark inside me still craves being what you were—the sunshine of my home." The tears shimmering in her eyes splashed onto her cheeks. "And I don't know if I'm strong enough anymore to go after it."

She dabbed at her eyes and sniffed, irritated with herself for soggying up yet again. "I know I have to try. If I don't, I'll hate myself. I really don't want to hate myself, Mary Beth. So if you've got any pull up there, I'd really appreciate some help."

What he wouldn't do for a little help here.

Leaning against a small desk, Tony raked a hand through his hair, took one last look through the window at the gardens outside the inn and the forest beyond them, then glanced back over his shoulder across the Shell Room to Suzie. Sitting Indian-style on the spool bed and surrounded by plump, ruffled pillows, she brushed at her hair in long, smooth strokes. Nearly dry, it gleamed glossy brown. She'd refused to lie down until it had—she'd catch pneumonia, she'd said—but she had compromised and tucked to the knees beneath Hattie's colorful patchwork quilt.

Suzie liked the Shell Room. The hodgepodge decor appealed to Tony, too. Old and new blended with the painted white antique dresser, chest, and desk that somewhere along the way had been stenciled around the edges in blue. Suzie liked blue best.

Tony didn't like much of anything right now. Hattie would give him hell for his attitude, but he was in the same royal snit he got into every year as Thanksgiving inched closer. And this year, considering Suzie's situation, his snit could be even worse because, no matter how much he'd prefer to think it, Suzie's *couldn't* be an ordinary dream.

Wet hair from a dream? Him feeling lifelike sensations? Her drowning, and him powerless? It *had* to be a premonition.

He glanced at her reflection in the window to the left of the bed. Through a copse of wind-blown trees, lights from Sea Haven Village winked in the distance. Could he countermand a premonition? Were his special skills and talents enough? His physical gifts didn't exist in dreams, yet that's where her troubles resided. How could he help her without his special gifts?

She sighed, and he sensed more than heard the weak rattle in her chest. Hopefully by morning the pneumonia scare would pass. Not that he could do anything more about it. He couldn't.

Powerless.

Shivering, he let his gaze slide back out the window into the night.

Tony?

Recognizing Sunshine's voice, he again wondered who she was and why she was here. He could ask, but she'd already said her identity didn't matter and innately he knew she wouldn't answer. She might even take off again. *Yes?*

Hasn't it occurred to you yet that I'm here because this challenge isn't just about these special guests?

The thought has crossed my mind. His feeling physical

sensations proved something was different. The question was, What? *So why are you here?*

To bring you a message.

A message? That too was odd. Not unprecedented, but unusual enough to give him the willies. *Okay. I'm all ears.*

Actually, you're about eighty-percent attitude. I'm just hoping I can lasso the other twenty percent long enough to do my job here so I can go home.

I didn't ask for your help.

No, Tony. You didn't. But you need it. Is that what's grating at you? That you need my help?

It was, but he wouldn't admit it. He could blame it on the Thanksgiving thing, but the truth was it was a matter of pride. Seascape Inn was his domain, his and Hattie's, and Sunshine was an interloping trespasser. He didn't like it, would be lying if he said he did, so he said nothing.

The message is that your challenge in this case isn't only with the emotional demon haunting Suzie's sleep and with Bryce's trials, though you must assist with both of those, of course. Your challenge is with you.

Thanksgiving is always a challenging time for me. Tony looked down to the floor where it met the white baseboard, fearing this had nothing to do with Thanksgiving but figuring it was worth a shot to not have to admit that, either.

True, but I'm afraid that isn't the challenge.

He'd known, and yet he'd foolishly hoped she'd let him slide by with it. He stuffed a hand into his pocket. *It's about me fearing and doubting my ability to help Suzie alter her personal history—if in fact her nightmare is a premonition of her personal history.*

In a sense, yes, it is about fear and doubt. But you'll have to dig deeper, Tony. Otherwise, you're in major trouble here.

Why am I getting the feeling that if I fail myself, I'll also fail Suzie and Bryce?

I can't answer that.

Can't, or won't? He asked, but wasn't at all sure he really wanted the answer.

Can't.

Suzie's dream has to be a premonition, doesn't it?

That too you must determine. This is your turf. I'm just a . . . temporary guest.

She knew his feelings about her being here. And, while she might prove persistent and/or contrary, she'd been gracious; he had to give her credit for that. Though he'd be wasting his time asking, he had to do it anyway. *What exactly is your mission?*

You'd best focus on your own challenges, hmm?

Whatever her mission was, it couldn't be as vital as Suzie and Bryce, and Tony did have troubles enough of his own to resolve without worrying about Sunshine's, too. *Okay, consider your message delivered.*

Very well, Tony. Good-bye.

Thoughtful, he rubbed at his lip with his forefinger and thumb. If Suzie's nightmare wasn't a premonition, he didn't have a clue what it was, or what it'd take to help her. And that sorry truth would scare the socks off a saint, much less him, a mere ghost.

He should be asking Suzie questions, gaining her insight on the background material he already had about her family, but he couldn't make himself do it. Not yet. Though children readily accept oddities—and as much as Tony hated to admit it, he was an oddity—in Suzie's current state, he just couldn't take the risk she'd wonder how he'd gotten into her dream, and then wonder who he was, which inevitably would lead to that godawful question he most hated: *What* are you?

"You didn't lie." Suzie looked up at him, her eyes wide and curious but no longer riddled with the fear they'd held in the dream.

He paused pacing near the foot of her bed. "I won't ever lie to you, Suzie."

She wanted to believe him; it radiated from her. But she couldn't let herself. Not yet. She reached over to the nightstand beside the bed and set down her hairbrush. "What's your name?"

Resilient. A damn shame she'd had to be resilient to survive this long. Feeling tender, he smiled down at her. "Tony."

"I've seen you before, haven't I?" She looked at his Army uniform, at his jacket's shiny brass buttons, then focused on the carnation at his lapel. "You were the man at

Uncle T.J. and Aunt Maggie's art gallery. I saw you when I looked at the picture of that house."

"That's right."

"Did you come here for vacation, too?"

"Not exactly."

"We did. Daddy says me and him and Jeremy and Lyssie, my baby brother and sister, need quality time together. I think Daddy mostly needs a nap."

"I think you're probably right." Tony chuckled. "I live here all the time."

"Seascape Inn looks like the house in Uncle T.J.'s painting."

A test, pure and simple, to see if Tony would tell her the truth. "That's because it is the same house. Your uncle T.J. has visited here a couple of times."

"He likes it here. He tells Daddy so all the time." Looking pleased by the truth, she grabbed up the covers bunched at her knees, then lay back against the pillow. Soft light from the bedside lamp slanted over her feet. "I do, too."

"I'm glad." Would she keep on liking it here? Once she realized the pond was the one in her dream, she'd probably hate it. And the thought of anyone hating his beloved home turned Tony's stomach.

"I like you, too. You help me here. At home, I'm by myself." She dipped her chin, again focusing on the flower at his lapel. "I don't like being by myself in the water, Tony."

"I know." His insides twisted. "But I'm here now. That's a promise."

She had that look in her eye; the *Doubting Thomasette* in her had reared its ugly head. With a we'll-see lift of her brow, she half covered her mouth with her hand, then yawned. "Nobody except me could see you then—at Uncle T.J.'s. How come?"

Surprise streaked up Tony's back. Evidently, even after her harrowing experience, she was more ready than he for questions and answers. "I'm . . . different. That scares some people."

"I don't like being scared."

"I doubt anyone does."

"Do you get lonely?"

Tony thought of Hattie. Of seeing her day in and out and yet never getting to really live with her, of the lifetime of love and memories they would have shared, of the Christmas wedding they'd planned that never had come to pass. And he thought of the children, the blessings they'd dreamed of raising together which destiny had denied them. Oh, they'd reconciled themselves and compensated as best they could—and he was grateful for all they did share. Yet, at times, and especially now when feeling the physical, he ached for all he'd lost. And a part of him hurt even more deeply for Hattie because he now knew she had suffered these physical pains he'd been spared until today each and every day of her life.

"Yes, Suzie." His voice cracked. "Sometimes I get so lonely I don't think I can stand it."

"Me, too," she confessed in a whisper. "But taking care of Jeremy and Lyssie and Daddy makes me feel better." Solemn and serious, she looked up at his eyes. "Do you take care of anybody—besides me?"

Caring. His salvation. Hattie's, too. A touch of serenity returned and a smile skimmed over his lips. "Yes, I do. I call them special guests." When he saw the question in her eyes, he went on to explain. "Sometimes people who are hurt inside come to visit Seascape Inn and Miss Hattie and I try to help them. That makes us feel better—like you with your family."

"Does Miss Hattie see you too, then?"

His heart plunged to his stomach like a hollow rock. "No. I'm afraid that would just make us both sad."

"You loved her."

Gazing at Suzie's fuzzy pink slippers beside the bed, Tony looked up.

"My daddy is sad." Suzie shrugged. "He loved Meriam and she died."

Meriam. Not Mom, or Mother. Meriam. Was Suzie still that angry at her mother for dying? It would explain the nightmare—if it were a nightmare and not a premonition.

Tony picked up Suzie's brush then moved it to the dresser. Its hard bristles grating against his thumb felt good. He'd loved Hattie Stillman heart and soul for sixty years. "You're very observant."

"I'm nine."

Despite feeling depressed to his toenails, he grinned, then turned to face Suzie. "Only you can see me—at least for a while."

She mulled that over, then cocked her head. "Why?"

He leaned back against the dresser, crossed his legs at his ankles, then rubbed at his temple with his forefinger. "That's kind of hard to answer."

"My friend Selena says difficult stuff is always hard to answer—she's a grown-up—but I don't think it is. I think you just have to say the truth. If you lie, stuff's hard, but the truth is easy."

Out of the mouths of babes. "I agree. But sometimes people have the devil's own time accepting the truth, especially if they don't understand it."

Weak winter moonlight slanted in through the window and over Suzie's face. Her lips weren't blue and her teeth weren't chattering anymore. He was glad to see it. He straightened up, walked over, then tucked the quilts up under her chin. "And on that fine note, I think it's time for you to go to sleep."

Fear slammed through her, made her pale cheeks pasty white. "I—I don't want to sleep."

When she slept, she dreamed. A tender knot hitched in his chest. Being alone in the dreams frightened her. "You don't have to be afraid anymore, Suzie. I'm here to help you now, and you won't be alone in any more nightmares—not at Seascape."

She frowned up at him. "I was."

"But you won't be anymore."

"How come?"

"Because I'm going to be with you. I didn't know enough about your dream before, but now I do." He debated, then went on. "Seascape is a healing house. That's why you're here. Your dad and Jeremy and Lyssie, too."

"Seascape *is* magic," Suzie said with the authority only a nine-year-old can muster. "Aunt Maggie said so, and

Jimmy told me, too. But I didn't think they meant it *really* was magic, but now I think it must be."

She wanted to believe yet, as with the promises, she feared being disappointed. "Who's Jimmy?"

She reached down for a little yellow flowered quilt. One not quite big enough for a bed, but perfect for dragging on the floor behind tiny feet and cuddling, one clearly made by Hattie. Tony recognized her stitching, and the yellow carnation she'd appliquéd on its corner.

Suzie tugged it close. "Jimmy Goodson. Don't you know him? Miss Hattie says Jimmy's the bestest mechanic in the whole world, and Daddy says Jimmy's kind of like Miss Hattie's son. I helped him plant a yellow tea rose bush in the garden today. He showed me how to not cut my foot with the shovel."

"Ah, I see. I wasn't sure if you meant a Jimmy from home or from here." Tony smiled. So the bulletin board bets on Seascape Inn's special guests continued down at the Blue Moon Cafe, Jimmy continued to win them, and he had indeed bought Hattie the yellow tea rose bush with his winnings on the John and Bess Mystic bet, just as he'd planned. "Well, a girl nine, I would say, surely does need to know how to use a shovel."

"Uh-huh." More relaxed now, Suzie's eyelids grew heavy. "Do you think Seascape is magic?"

"In a way, I suppose it is."

"Daddy took me and Jeremy and Lyssie to the Blue Moon Cafe for ice cream and I asked Miss Lucy, the lady who works there, and she said Seascape is magic, too. She said it's a place where people come to heal broken hearts or spirits or dreams because the lady who built it loved everybody so much, and love fixes broken stuff."

Tony's mother, Cecelia Freeport. A healer, she had loved well. And, yes, far stronger than death, love lingers. His very presence here proved that. "Lucy told you all this?" Tony rubbed at his neck. A born romantic, Lucy usually just went on and on about the legend, or tried to draw others into her family debate on whether angels were spiritual beings or humans passed on. Likely she'd spared Suzie both because of her tender age.

Suzie nodded.

"If Lucy Baker said so, then I guess it must be true."

"That's what Mr. Baker said. He said Miss Lucy can't abide lying." Suzie blinked slowly as if puzzling something out. "I'm not sure what 'abide' means but I guess it's that she doesn't like lying. No grown-ups do. Do you know Mr. Baker? He's got a gold ring that looks like a lump. I asked what it was and he said a nugget. I'm not sure what that means, either, but it's pretty."

A scrape on the floor out in the hallway claimed Tony's attention. Bryce had awakened. "We'll talk more tomorrow. You need to rest." Tony drifted his hand down over her face. "Sleep, little one."

She clenched her jaw to resist, but by the time his fingertips touched her chin, her expression had gone lax and she slept peacefully.

Tony slipped into the hallway with a lengthy list of questions and too few answers, then tapped into Bryce's mind. Generally men weren't as sensitive as women to the intrusion. More often than not, they thought Tony's comments or suggestions were their own consciences. But this time Tony's invasion wasn't to guide, it was to explore. Why was Suzie having this dream? Why was it always the same—her falling out of the boat, then drowning? And Bryce had been coping, so why now was he seemingly at wit's end?

Wading through Bryce's thoughts, Tony sensed intense frustration. Futility. Feelings of failure ran rampant through the man. He loved his children—that emotion burned deeper and stronger than all the others combined—and he wanted the best for them.

Tony opened himself further to the man's pain, to his longings and desires. And, staggering from the intensity of Bryce's inner conflicts and feelings, Tony concluded one simple truth: Bryce Richards believed heart and soul what he most needed was a mother for his children.

Tony agreed.

And disagreed.

Suzie, Jeremy, and Alyssa did need a mother—a special one who'd love them unconditionally. But, immersed in focusing on his children, Bryce didn't realize he was also in dire need. Nor did he seem likely to realize it anytime soon. Meriam had been dead for two years, yet he still loved her as if she were alive—or thought he did.

Tony sighed. The man had yet to face some hard truths about their relationship. And those realizations, Tony well knew, wouldn't come easily. Learning life's lessons rarely did. But he and Hattie would do all they could to make the challenge easier.

A woman began crying.

Deep inside his own mind, Tony heard her clearly. Yet all the leaf-peepers had gone home. Bryce, his children, and Mrs. Wiggins were the only guests at the inn. Perplexed, Tony let his thoughts drift from Bryce toward the distant sound.

The vision hazy at first, he focused on a woman driving a rental car, a white Chevrolet Caprice. She was pretty, petite and blond, and crying. Not deep, racking sobs. Silent tears. Ones that sprang from a wound so deep inside her, just looking at her was painful. She was on a highway—Tony scanned the area—near Bangor. The map on the seat beside her had a snaky pink-highlighted path drawn to Nova Scotia—from New Orleans.

Bryce and the children were from New Orleans.

Tony tapped into her thoughts. Though scattered enough to make him dizzy, he soon pieced together that she was recently divorced and mourning someone. Not her ex-husband. Someone important to her, though. A yellow carnation was pinned to a floppy hat that lay on the passenger's seat beside her and, for some inexplicable reason, a phrase ran through her mind time and again: *She was the sunshine of our home.*

It seemed associated to someone named Mary Beth. So close to the name of Tony's own deceased sister, Mary Elizabeth. Was this Mary Beth the woman's mother? The woman mourned?

Mary Beth.

The carnation.

She was the sunshine of our home.

The divorce . . .

Criminy, this was Bryce's mysterious Mrs. Tate! And she was here in Maine.

To meet Bryce? Was that why Tony had heard her crying?

As she drove, Tony checked the street signs. Sea Haven Highway. The road to Sea Haven Village from Bangor. Well, that clinched it. Where it'd lead, he hadn't a clue—never before had he been lured like this to a potential special guest—but already he'd been warned these special guests were different, so he'd follow through and see to it that the mysterious Mrs. Tate would have the opportunity at least to come to the inn and meet Bryce Richards.

Concentrating hard, Tony urged her to turn, mentally luring her to the inn as he had so many others—and he met with surprisingly strong resistance.

Wonderful. Just wonderful. Not only mourning. Not only wounded from the divorce. Caline Tate faced even more challenges. Thanks to that ex-husband of hers—Bryce's client, no less—the woman was sure to be reluctant if not in downright refusal mode. With Bryce's realizations about his marriage to Meriam yet to come, and Cally's own emotional demons to be confronted, this was going to be a doozy of a case. But, by gum, Tony and Hattie had faced challenges before, and Suzie was worth the extra effort. Bryce and Caline, and Jeremy and Lyssie, too. Tony just prayed his and Hattie's guidance would be enough. Though they always tried their best to aid special guests, unfortunately, they weren't always successful. And he couldn't shake that image of himself from Suzie's dream. The one of him as *powerless*.

"Tony?" Suzie called out. "Tony, are you here?"

The *Doubting Thomasette* had awakened. He paused a second longer, and glimpsed Caline Tate taking the turn to exit onto Sea Haven Highway. Ah, she had chosen to come to the inn. Good. Good. He could lure, encourage, but the special guests had to make their own decisions, and he wouldn't have it any other way.

"Tony?"

Smiling, he returned to Suzie. "I'm here."

"I *know* Seascape has magic." Sober-eyed, she nodded against her crisp white pillowslip.

Just this moment, he was happy to agree. "Why is that, little one?"

"Because I called and you came—and because I smell your carnation even though I see right through you."

His smile fell to a frown and his skin knitted between his brows. "I won't hurt you."

"I know that." She clicked her tongue to the roof of her mouth and rolled her gaze ceilingward. "You came to help me."

Acceptance. Sweet acceptance. He savored it for a long moment and, when he answered her, his voice sounded unusually gruff. "Yes, I did."

"Well, then, what I want to know is if you can get us a new mom. Selena says . . ."

Joy bubbled in his chest. God, but he loved children. A pang of longing, of wishing he and Hattie had had the chance to have their own, slid through him. He shunned it. Their situation wasn't perfect, but at least he was here with his beloved—more or less. "Who's Selena?" Suzie had mentioned her earlier.

"My grown-up friend. Uncle John's little sister. Do you know John Mystic and my aunt, Bess?"

"Yes, I do." Boy, had those special guests given Tony a run for his money. They'd narrowly escaped divorce. He and Hattie had been thrilled with the outcome of that case.

"Selena's old. At least twenty-five—maybe more."

Tony repressed a smile by the skin of his teeth. "Twenty-five. Well, that's old, all right. So what does Selena say?"

"My dad says time makes things better. My doctor does, too. We talk and talk every week but I still keep having the dreams, anyway. That's how I know time won't work. They're not lying though, just wrong." Suzie fidgeted. The covers under and over her crinkled. "But Selena says the only way to get better is to get and keep both oars in the water. I think she's right. If I can get Jeremy and Lyssie a new mom who'll love them, then maybe that'll fix things. Lucy Baker said love fixes broken stuff, and not having a mom is kind of being broken, don't you think?"

Tony wanted to hug the child. To wash the hurt away. But he couldn't. Yet he could help her to learn to live more constructively with the hurt. "I'd say it can be."

"It is," Suzie said. "I'm hoping Miss Lucy is right. I don't know if she is or isn't. But Jeremy's four and Lyssie—Alyssa—is two. They're little. Other people can love little kids easier than big kids, and they don't even remember Meriam. She was kind of our mom but she didn't like us calling her that so we called her Meriam. Well, me and Jeremy did. Lyssie was too little to talk when Meriam went to heaven."

Suzie paused for breath, giving Tony time to mentally catch up, then pulled her quilt closer and rubbed her thumb over the appliquéd carnation's petals. "Jeremy and Lyssie are little so they really need a mom. I don't 'cuz I've never really had a mom and I'm nine now, so it doesn't matter to me—as long as she loves them." With a telling shrug, Suzie stared at the ceiling, clearly seeing far beyond the swirls of white plaster. "But if she bakes peanut butter cookies like my friend Missy's mom does, then I wouldn't mind having one, though. Mrs. Wiggins won't let us have cookies. Meriam told her not to—sugar rots your teeth—but Daddy does, sometimes. Mostly when Mrs. Wiggins isn't home. She fusses, and he's too tired to listen to it."

A knot squared in Tony's throat. Suzie wanted a mom more than anything in the world. He hadn't missed that she'd been hurt at having to call her mother by name. Nor had he missed the tremor in her voice on admitting she'd never really had a mom, or her obvious distaste for Mrs. Wiggins, the old battleaxe of a nanny who'd arrived at the inn three days ago with Bryce and the children. Every morning over coffee Bryce read Wiggins's list of Jeremy's previous day's infractions. He was just four, for pity's sake.

Tony bent down beside Suzie's bed then clasped her little hand in his big one. "We'll have to wish really hard for a mom, then—for Jeremy and Lyssie."

Suzie nodded. "How come your fingers are cold?"

He stared at them. What could he say? I have no life. And the absence of life renders the absence of warmth? Would she accept that?

"Tony? You promised never to lie."

He tried, but he couldn't make himself meet her eyes and

maybe see her condemnation of him reflected there. "Being alive makes you warm, Suzie."

"Outside." She touched his jacket over his heart. "But you're warm in here. That's where it's important—Selena said."

To Suzie, Selena obviously was *the* ultimate authority. "She's a wise woman." And with the gift Suzie'd just given him, if he'd ever doubted it, Tony now had seen it proven true: Seascape *was* a magical place. And how he prayed he had the skills to bring Suzie a gift she'd treasure as much as he did her acknowledgment that he had heart: a new mom.

He and Hattie certainly would do everything possible, and they'd pray hard—more than hard, if he knew his beloved, and he certainly did—that the special guests did their part.

"Tony."

"Hmm?"

"I lied to you." Suzie blinked furiously then forced her gaze up to his. Guilt radiated from her in pulsing waves. "I really do want a mom."

"I know." Understanding what that admission had cost her, he swallowed down a hard lump from his throat and stroked her sleep-tangled hair. "Sometimes when something's really important to us, well, we all tell ourselves it isn't important so it won't hurt so much if we don't get it."

"Even you?"

"Even me." He met her big brown eyes, thinking of Hattie. "But I'll share a secret with you. If we wish really hard, you might just get a new mom."

Remorse slithered through him. He shouldn't have told Suzie that. He hadn't meant to, but the longing in her had struck a chord in him, the same chord that reminded him of all those nevers between him and Hattie, and it had just slipped out.

Suzie's eyes sparkled and her mouth dropped open into a big O. "Honest? You're not just telling me that? Grown-ups do that sometimes. I don't like it."

How could he recant after that? "No, I'm not just saying it. It could happen, Suzie, but it could *not* happen, too. That's why we have to wish hard. It all depends on your dad and, er, the lady who's coming."

"She's coming here?" When he nodded, Suzie's eyes stretched even wider. "But what if we don't know it's her? She could go away, and Jeremy and Lyssie—"

"You'll know her. I promise." Tony touched a finger to the flower at his lapel. "She'll be wearing a yellow carnation, just like this one."

"But—"

"Shh, it's time to sleep now. And, remember. No nightmares, not at Seascape." He tucked the thick quilt up under her chin then tapped a fingertip to her nose. "Miss Hattie would pitch a fit."

"Miss Hattie doesn't do that." Suzie giggled, then sobered. "Mrs. Wiggins might, though."

Tony grunted. The battleaxe surely might. "I want you to listen carefully, Suzie. This is very important, okay?"

"Okay."

"We can't interfere with your dad and the lady who's coming here." He dropped his voice to a soft whisper and spoke straight to the child's soul. "But—and this is a promise—if only one has the courage to believe, miracles can happen beside a dreamswept sea."

Suzie looked awestruck, then frowned, clearly worried. "But I don't believe in miracles anymore. I even told Missy and Selena."

The child had grasped the significance of his words to her; no doubt about it. "Then you've got to try to believe in them again. So you'll heal."

For a long moment, the child stared at his jacket buttons and worried her lip with her teeth. Then she looked back at his eyes, her own filled with resolve. "I can't promise, but if you say it's true, then I'll try hard to believe it. I really will, Tony."

Her leap of faith touched him. "Why?"

"Because you promised, and you didn't lie."

Her mother. It had been her broken promises, so many of them, which had taught Suzie skepticism and a fear of believing anyone but her father. Yet Tony couldn't judge Meriam harshly for it; the poor woman had fought her emotional demons, too. How well Tony knew she had from her visit here. She'd, unfortunately, been one of his failures; too far gone before she arrived to trust in herself, to trust in him, and to heal. "Thank you, Suzie." He placed a fatherly kiss to her soft brow, and whispered a silent prayer that he wouldn't fail her as he had her mother. "Sleep peacefully now."

He started to disappear, thought better of it, then walked toward the door.

"Tony?"

Gripping the doorknob, he looked back over his shoulder at her. "Hmm?"

"A yellow carnation. I won't forget."

She wouldn't. She'd be more attentive than Batty Beaulah Favish next door with her goofy binoculars. "Good girl."

"Will it be soon—that my new mom will come?"

The longing in Suzie's voice cut through him like a knife. "Very soon. But, remember now, she won't know she might be your new mom. We don't know for sure, either. We have to let her and your dad figure it out."

"Why can't I just tell them?"

"Won't work, little one." Tony had tried that often enough to know it for fact. "Some things grown-ups have to figure out for themselves. That's how love operates. We can encourage, but they have to decide."

"Shoot."

Tony raised his brows.

"Well, sometimes grown-ups take too long."

He supposed they did. "Then we'll have to be patient." He winked. "And wish hard that they hurry."

Suzie squeezed her eyes shut and clamped her jaw, putting her heart into it. Tony grinned. If wishes alone could do the trick, this case already would be a done deal.

But with Bryce and Caline's challenges, their healing enough to maybe find love would take far more than wishes; it'd take a fistful of miracles. And Tony only hoped they'd find them, and that this case would become a done deal. For Suzie, and Jeremy and Lyssie, but also for Bryce and Caline. Their odds weren't the greatest, but then if they were, they wouldn't be here. Both seriously need loving. Desperately needed loving. And just as desperately, they both needed to love.

Tony eased into the hallway. Slumped between wall and floor, Bryce shivered in his sleep. Eons ago, Tony had grown accustomed to his presence cooling temperatures, though, truthfully, it still rankled. He visualized Hattie's crocheted afghan, draped it over Bryce, then stepped back to study him. If the man held his head at that weird angle long, he'd awaken with a heck of a crick in his neck. "Well, why not?" Tony thought. "In for an ounce, in for a gallon." He visualized a pillow, too.

After situating it under Bryce's head, Tony straightened up, then walked down the hallway. There was a consolation to him chilling rooms. As soon as Suzie spilled tonight's events to Miss Hattie—which would most likely be at the crack of dawn—Tony figured his beloved would be glaring at the ceiling and railing, heating up his own ears plenty.

A smile curved his lips. Heading up the stairs to his attic bedroom, he rubbed his hands together, hardly able to wait. Few things held the appeal of a righteously indignant Hattie Stillman. Even if, in this instance, she had every right to be furious. He never should've told Suzie that "new mom" bit. Never should've interceded into her dream without first knowing the costs. Yet he'd had no other choice. None he could live with anyway. And again he wondered. What would be the penalty for interceding?

And who will be penalized? Sunshine asked in a phantom whisper.

Fear trickled down his spine. Tony came to a dead halt, clutched the banister in a death grip. Why hadn't he considered that his actions *could* affect someone else? Could affect Hattie?

Chapter 3

"I'm tendering formal notice of my resignation, Mr. Richards."

The fire in the fireplace crackled and the image of Meriam sitting beside it, curled up on the rocker's red and white checked cushion and smiling at him, disappeared.

"Mr. Richards? Did you hear me?" Mrs. Wiggins pulled out a chair. Its legs scraped over the tile floor. "I'm resigning."

Irritated, Bryce looked across the round oak kitchen table to the sour-expressioned woman now seated opposite him. Pushing sixty, her hair slicked back into a tight bun that tugged at the skin at her temples, she clamped her square jaw shut and swiped smooth the sleeve of the gray dress she reserved for wearing only on her official resignation days. He rubbed at his neck. She did look about as resolute as he'd ever seen her. Well, hell. "Again?"

She rolled her gaze toward the light oak cabinets and lacy white curtains, clearly not amused. Seeking patience, most likely. He'd opt for a little divine intervention himself. He'd only swallowed half a cup of coffee, had been thoroughly enjoying his now shattered early morning fantasy, and his bones still ached from their night on a chilly hardwood floor, especially his old football-injured knee.

"Yes, again." Staring at the basket of porcelain bisque, yellow daffodils on the table, she steepled her fingers atop two stacked sheets of paper. "But this time I really mean it."

She'd said and meant it at least once a week for three years. Bryce paused, rubbing at his tender kneecap, then held out a reconciled hand for her daily list of infractions. "What did Jeremy do this time?"

Miss Hattie stood at the island stove, stirring a pot of oatmeal and pretending hard to be stone deaf. If it weren't for that disapproving twist to her lips, Bryce might have believed she'd managed it. But did she disapprove of Mrs. Wiggins's resignation, or of Bryce's reaction to it?

Probably the resignation. Though he couldn't deny that his beloved moppets were ill-behaved brats, Miss Hattie, with her kind and gentle ways, had been very patient and nurturing, spoiling them and Bryce rotten. T.J. had said she was in her early seventies, but from her gentle green eyes and blue-veined hands to her generous spirit, she seemed aged and ageless, almost touched by magic.

Sniffing, Mrs. Wiggins passed her list. "What the boy hasn't done would be easier to tell you."

Bryce took the paper, still looking at Miss Hattie. Blue floral dress. Soiled apron and pearls. She looked like the perfect grandmother, not like the type to join her best friend, Miss Millie, for weekly games of penny-ante poker. But, according to T.J. and Maggie, that was one of Miss Hattie's favorite hobbies. Bryce liked that about her. To the bone, the woman seemed approachable.

The steam from the pot had tiny tendrils of snow-white hair coming free from her loose bun and it had turned her cheeks rosy. Why couldn't Meriam have hired Miss Hattie to care for the kids? In three days, they'd come to adore her sunny smiles and tender ways. So had Bryce. Instead—he glanced back to Mrs. Wiggins, then winced at the stark contrast between the women—Meriam had opted for the battleaxe and, because she had, God spare them all, Bryce couldn't fire the woman.

Mrs. Wiggins scraped her cup against its saucer. "After specific instructions not to go into Miss Hattie's greenhouse, the boy not only went inside, but created havoc."

Havoc could be anything from getting a blade of grass on the floor to destroying the place. Awaiting further explanation of this particular "havoc," Bryce settled in and watched

Miss Hattie fill a canister with flour. Little specks floated in the sunshine streaming in through the window above the sink.

She dusted her hands on her apron, pushed the flour back into the line of canisters on the white-tile countertop, then turned to him, looking torn. "Honestly, it was just a minor accident."

"Don't protect him, Hattie. The boy rebels against discipline as it is." Mrs. Wiggins frowned at Bryce. "He ruined several pots of soil and clippings from Hattie's most prized Peace roses."

Weary though the day had only just begun, Bryce looked at Miss Hattie. "I'm terribly sorry. Of course, I'll replace them."

"You can't replace them." Mrs. Wiggins frowned down her nose at him, her arms akimbo.

His coffee mug reflected in the lens of her glasses, and the refrigerator's ice-maker plopped cubes into the empty bin. Bryce's stomach plunged with the hollow sound. "I can't?"

"They're truly not Peace roses, but a new hybrid I'm toying with." Miss Hattie tapped a metal stirring spoon against the edge of the pot. "It's not important, dear."

Geez, a new hybrid. Months, if not years, of work. And it wasn't important? "Of course it's important."

She walked over to the big antique radio behind the rocker, near the fireplace. "I wouldn't presume to intrude, Bryce, but Jeremy was only doing what he'd seen me do."

A new hybrid. Bryce's spirits sank even lower. He was a lousy parent. That's all there was to it. He tried, and tried, but he was no good at it. Love just wasn't . . . enough. "But if he's damaged something irreplaceable—"

"Bosh." Adjusting the wooden knob on the round dial, she cocked an ear. Static gave way to big-band-era music. "Jeremy damaged his fingers more than anything else."

"Excuse me?" Now Bryce was totally confused.

"Thorns," she explained, her eyes twinkling. Walking back to the stove, she held up her hand, signaling. "Three Band-Aids' worth."

"Ouch." Bryce bit a smile from his lips and lowered his

gaze to the salt and pepper shakers atop the table. The angel had given him a way out of this situation. One that would satisfy the battleaxe.

He sipped from his burgundy marble coffee mug, then conjured up his best convince-the-jury voice. "Surely, Mrs. Wiggins, the pain and suffering in three Band-Aid bandages' worth of thorn injuries is adequate punishment. Jeremy was trying to help—wasn't he, Miss Hattie?"

"Oh my, of course, dear." The coffee carafe in hand, she nodded firmly, then refilled Bryce's mug with steaming coffee that smelled like a pint of heaven. "And he was only doing what he'd seen me do."

"There you have it." Bryce lifted his cup, and imagined Meriam winking at him from the rocker. The cushion string had come untied and swept the floor on her forward rock. Irked that she would find this amusing, he blinked her fantasy image away. "I'd say we can consider the matter settled and forget about your resignation, Mrs. Wiggins. Don't you agree?"

Her frown deepened, then faded. "Well, with three Band-Aids' worth of injuries, I suppose I could reconsider. But just this once."

Ah, finally. Peace in sight. "Thank you."

She wadded up the remaining sheet of paper, obviously her resignation. The crunching sound eased the tension in him.

"Though I warn you, Mr. Richards, Jeremy is too willful to do himself a bit of good." Her stiff collar jabbed into her neck. "I realize you feel I'm too strict with the children, but I would remind you that I'm only following Mrs. Richards's—may she rest in peace—explicit instructions."

How could he forget it? While crossing herself, the woman reminded him of that detail with every weekly resignation. But, the knots in his stomach subsided, she had withdrawn it—again—and thankful for that, he straightened his tie. His gold cuff link caught the light from the overhead fixture and winked over his starched cuff. "I've never once believed you've had anything but the children's best interests at heart, Mrs. Wiggins. Nor would my wife."

"Bosh."

Bryce reeled his gaze to Miss Hattie. She looked more surprised by her outburst than he felt. "Excuse me?"

"I, er, dropped the spoon." She glanced at the ceiling, as if looking at someone else, shrugged lamely, then pasted on a bright smile. "Breakfast is ready."

"I'll get the children." Mrs. Wiggins pushed back from the table. Her chair legs again scraped the floor, and grated at Bryce's already raw nerves.

Someone knocked at the mud room door.

He glanced over. A wiry, bald man around Miss Hattie's age, dressed in a postal uniform, stood there, nose pressed to the glass and waving. Vic Sampson. Sea Haven Village's mail carrier, who should have retired, and should have confessed his love for Miss Hattie, years ago. He hadn't done either and Bryce wondered why, just as he wondered why Miss Hattie didn't seem to notice Vic's obvious feelings for her.

"Ah, Vic's early. They must have canceled the Grange dance last night." Miss Hattie raised her voice. "Come on in."

Mrs. Wiggins returned with the kids, and Bryce situated Lyssie in the old wooden high chair Miss Hattie's friend Jimmy had brought down from the attic. "Where's Jeremy?"

"He'll be right along." Miss Hattie pointed through the windows overlooking the garden. "He had an errand to run."

Vic dropped his worn mailbag to the floor near the mud room door. "Morning," he said, wiping his feet on the throw rug. "The new owners of Fisherman's Co-op arrived, Miss Hattie. They're already getting mail."

"Really?" She hiked up her eyebrows.

"Yep." Vic moved to the cabinet, grabbed a cup then, filling it with coffee from the carafe, he looked at Bryce. "Former owners moved back to California to be with the wife's family. Her dad got ill and her mother needed help caring for him."

"I'm sorry to hear that. Maggie and T.J. spoke highly of the entire family." Bryce inwardly cringed. If he got ill, who'd be there to care for his children?

Miss Hattie sighed. "They'll be sorely missed in the village."

"No doubt about it." Vic nodded his agreement.

Bryce adjusted the high chair's tray. It clicked into place. Lyssie grabbed his finger. He tweaked her nose.

"Fine family," Vic agreed. "The new owners have a daughter about Suzie's age. Name's Francine but she calls herself Frankie. Bit of a tomboy, I'd say. She's already been to the lighthouse, visiting with Hatch, and now she's helping Jimmy Goodson work on Pastor Brown's car. From all I'm hearing, Frankie's mother's pretty riled up about that." Vic grinned at Hattie. "Reminds me of Lucy Baker, back when she was a kid. Her mama wanted her to be a perfect little lady, too."

"I remember." Miss Hattie smiled. "Lucy turned out fine, and I'm sure little Frankie will, too."

"I don't know, Miss Hattie. She's something else."

"And the perfect age to be a friend for Suzie."

Vic nodded. "Yep, I reckon she is." He looked at Suzie. "You'll meet her at the festival."

Suzie set a fork down beside each plate. "Is that how come there's a tent in the church parking lot? 'Cuz there's going to be a festival?"

"Yep. We're celebrating the warm weather."

"It's usually colder here in November, Suzie," Bryce explained.

"Sure is." Vic leaned back against the counter. "We ain't had a November like this since 'sixty-three."

"Hmm," Miss Hattie mused, taking more strips of crisp bacon from the frying pan and placing them on a layer of paper towels to drain. "I think 'sixty-three was wet and cold, Vic. Maybe it was 'sixty-four. And you might also recall we're celebrating the founding of the village." Hattie passed Suzie a fistful of spoons. "Would you put these out too, dear?"

"Might have been 'sixty-four." Vic grunted, ignoring Miss Hattie's reminder, then cocked an ear to the radio's bagpipe music and looked to Suzie. "Do you dance the Highland fling?"

Suzie placed a spoon beside Mrs. Wiggins's plate, then gave Vic a solemn, negative nod. "I don't know how."

"Well, now." He set down his cup then hitched up his

pants. "We can't have a festival without your knowing how to do the fling. I'm in serious need of a decent partner." He guided Suzie by the shoulder to the gap between the cabinets and the center island stove. "Scoot over, Miss Hattie, or join in."

With those innocent remarks, the cheerful kitchen—where Bryce had enjoyed in peace but half a cup of coffee and half a fantasy that habitually got him through long, lonely days—erupted into chaos.

Vic instructed Suzie on the dance steps, then began singing along with the radio. Waving her metal spoon, Miss Hattie joined in, charmingly off-key. Mrs. Wiggins ate her oatmeal, crisp bacon, and homemade blueberry muffins in silence. With each sip of orange juice, she gave a little sniff, letting Bryce know she didn't approve the variance from the children's normal routine. He honestly couldn't fault her for that. The racket was a little on the loud side for so early in the morning, but Bryce didn't have the heart to complain. Last night, Suzie had slept peacefully, and this morning, she looked so . . . so happy.

"Bite!" Lyssie smacked her hand down on the tray of the high chair. The bowl rattled and her spoon clanked.

Bryce grinned at his demanding two-year-old. "Okay, munchkin." He filled the spoon, blew on it to cool the oatmeal, then lifted it to Lyssie's mouth.

Suzie giggled.

Unable to resist, Bryce let his gaze drift her way. She and Vic moved fairly rhythmically—more accurately, bounced semirhythmically—but her eyes shone brightly, her hair flounced at her shoulders, and she smiled. Bryce's heart swelled, feeling too big for his chest. Oh, God, how rare was Suzie's smile. . . .

"Mrs. Wiggins!" Jeremy plowed through the mud room door into the kitchen, wearing more mud than a wheelbarrow would hold. "Mrs. Wiggins, I broughted you a present!"

Grimacing at his blond son being more recognizable by voice and the whites of his eyes than by sight, Bryce gave Lyssie another spoonful of oatmeal. She promptly spit it out, and a glob plopped onto her red corduroy jumper. "Geez, Lyssie." Bryce grabbed a napkin.

"I'm sorry I maded you mad." Jeremy crossed the kitchen, his shoes making sucking sounds on the tile.

"Good heavens!" Mrs. Wiggins shrieked, scrambling from the table and knocking her chair over. It thudded dully against the floor.

Bryce jerked around. A muddy frog hopped onto the kitchen table. "Jeremy!" Bryce dropped the spoon into the bowl of oatmeal, grabbed for the frog—and missed it. "Damn!"

"Damn," Lyssie repeated, her mouthful of oatmeal spraying on the floor.

Cursing. The battleaxe would love that. She'd resign again; he just knew it. Bryce paused from chasing the frog, bent low toward his youngest daughter, then wagged a warning finger at her. "No, Lyssie. Animal crackers."

The things a man did for his kids. Swearing off swearing for goofy terms like "animal crackers" was but one of them. Bryce didn't mind looking like a fool for his kids' benefit any more than any other parent, though, like all other parents, he'd prefer to choose his moments.

"Frog."

Bryce followed Lyssie's pointing finger to the table's porcelain centerpiece. Spotting the frog on a yellow daffodil petal, Bryce lunged for it.

His knee banged against the chair seat.

The toe of his shoe snagged the table leg.

To the ominous sounds of rattling dishes, he skidded in oatmeal. A sharp tear wrenched his knee. Pain shot through the bone, straight up into his thigh and down into his ankle. His football knee folded, and he collapsed to the floor in a cold sweat, landing flat on his rump.

And he'd missed the damn frog.

At least everyone was in such an uproar, they wouldn't hear him groaning. Maybe by the time they settled down, he'd be able to get up.

A loud whistle split through the racket.

Silence fell.

Bryce looked toward the sound, to the doorway leading to the gallery and the front entry beyond it. A woman about his own age, thirty-six, stood there in a crumpled cream cashmere sweater and matching long skirt with a floppy felt hat and boots the same shade as her forest-green eyes. A long silk scarf circled her neck. Coffee or cola stained it. Unusual. A willowy image on someone so petite. She couldn't be more than five feet six, if she was that tall. From what he could see beneath her hat, she had honey-blond hair and great bone structure and, thoroughly disheveled, it was obvious she didn't give two hoots about her appearance. He kind of liked that. She was beautiful—and impressive. For a wisp of a woman, she'd belted out a respectable whistle.

Surveying the fallout she'd happened into, she glanced from disaster to disaster. Bryce followed her gaze, more than a little embarrassed. What oatmeal Lyssie hadn't slung onto the floor she had clumped in her blond curls. Jeremy, muddy from head to heels, looked a scant step from tears, and Miss Hattie's once spotless tile floor now bore tracks from him and his frog. Mrs. Wiggins, stone-faced and rigid-backed, huffed like a steam engine on a sharp incline. She'd sure as hell resign again. Suzie and Vic seemingly had frozen, left hands raised, left legs crooked. And Miss Hattie's spoon had stilled midair, as if she were a conductor waiting for someone to turn the page and present the next score of musical notes.

"A yellow carnation!" Suzie gasped. "Just like Tony said."

Tony? Puzzled, Bryce looked from her to the woman in the doorway. Pinned center-front, holding the hat's brim back from her face, was a yellow carnation. But why did Suzie find that significant? And who in heaven was Tony?

"I'm sorry to interrupt," the woman said, obviously trying to stifle a smile. "I called out but no one, um, seemed to hear me."

Bryce gave her credit for diplomacy. They were a rowdy, rambunctious bunch this morning and they'd probably not have heard cannons, much less her soft, smoky voice. He'd didn't much like rowdy, and he liked even less the indignity of meeting a beautiful woman while smeared with oatmeal and landed on his ass on the floor.

The frog jumped right into his lap. Bryce caught it.

The woman laughed.

Bryce's heart caught in his throat, and he looked up at her.

She wasn't just beautiful. She was magnificent. Lovely skin, delicate bones, full mouth, and the sound of her laughter grabbed him right around the heart. He couldn't not smile at her any more than he could not breathe.

"Excellent work, Bryce." Miss Hattie stepped to the counter and set the spoon onto its spoon rest. "Jeremy, would you take the frog back to the garden, dear? I don't think he much likes the kitchen." She turned toward the newcomer, not seeming a bit upset by the uproar or by the mess. "Hello, I'm Hattie Stillman, the innkeeper."

Jeremy took the frog. Bryce slid his son a frown, and heard the woman say, "I thought so. You look exactly as Lucy Baker described you."

"You know Lucy?"

"I had breakfast at her cafe earlier."

Recognition lit in Miss Hattie's eyes. "Oh my, in all the excitement, I'd forgotten Lucy had phoned about you. Do forgive me, dear, and welcome to Seascape Inn."

"Thank you." She looked around the kitchen again, visually paused at Suzie and Vic, who were talking in low, hushed voices, then looked on to Bryce. A mischievous glint flickered in her eyes—until she saw him holding his knee. Then the glint faded and her expression turned compassionate. "I'm sorry to interrupt."

"Interrupt?" Miss Hattie tsked, dabbing at her brow with her hankie. "Bosh, of course not, Caline. We were just—er, um—having breakfast."

Caline grinned, her eyes twinkling. "So I see."

Unusual name, Caline. Bryce only had heard it once before. Gregory Tate's ex-wife's name. If they were at home in New Orleans, he'd wonder if this woman could possibly be her. But Gregory's Caline couldn't be in Maine. What would she be doing up here?

Thankfully, that case was behind Bryce now, and though the man remained a client, their contact had become brief and infrequent.

Suzie bent low to Bryce's ear. "It's her, Daddy."

"Who, honey?" His knee still throbbing, he rubbed at it and looked from the woman to Suzie.

She blinked hard, then slid him a wondrous smile. "Our new mom—maybe."

Surprise shafted straight up his back. "Our *what*?"

"Mr. Richards." Mrs. Wiggins's voice held that stern I'm-going-to-resign-again tone.

When even Caline and Miss Hattie paused conversing to look at Wiggins, Bryce barely withheld a groan. Two resignations inside an hour, on half a cup of coffee, was more than he could stomach.

"I insist the boy be harshly reprimanded for this." She slapped at the mud spatter on the lap of her dress.

Bryce never doubted she would insist. He looked at Jeremy, now back inside, thankfully, without the frog. From his glassy eyes, he was still a step from tears. Nearly caving in from the pitiful sight, and knowing caving in wasn't the best thing for Jeremy, Bryce glanced down at the oatmeal clinging to his once-crisp white shirt, then at Lyssie's hair, smudged roots to end with food, and now—God help him—with orange juice. The kid definitely had a thing for shampoo.

"Jeremy," Caline interrupted. "Miss Hattie is busy right now and I can't carry all my things up to my room. Would you wipe your feet on the rug out in the mud room and then help me?"

Bryce frowned. Caline clearly meant to intercede. And how was he supposed to feel about that? Jeremy looked majorly relieved, and her caring for a stranger's child enough to play rescuer pleased Bryce. Yet what was he? Chopped liver. He was the boy's father, and that she felt the need to protect Jeremy when his father stood—well, sat—right in the room irked Bryce. And it pricked at his pride.

Worse, it reminded him—as if he needed yet another reminder—just how desperately his children needed the gentle hand of a blow-softening mother.

Caline stretched out her hand.

Jeremy clasped it and, half hiding in the soft folds of her long skirt, he mumbled an "I'm sorry" in Mrs. Wiggins's general direction.

"I'll help, too." Suzie brushed past Vic, then slowed

down to tiptoe through the oatmeal and to dodge the mud tracks.

Suzie? Approaching a stranger? Bryce gaped. After three months in school, the child barely spoke to her teacher. He hauled himself to his feet. His knee gave out and, grimacing, he grabbed hold of a chair.

"Are you okay, Daddy?" Suzie frowned, an unreasonable fear in her eyes.

Knowing she was afraid he'd die and leave her like her mother had, Bryce forced the corners of his mouth to curve in what he hoped would pass for some semblance of a smile. His damn knee was on fire. "I'm fine, honey. Just fine."

"Oh my, your poor knee's gone out." Miss Hattie glanced at Suzie. "Don't you worry. We'll fix him right up." She turned to Vic. "Be a dear and get Collin's cane from the Carriage House, hmm?"

Vic nodded, then headed toward the mud room door. Miss Hattie wiped her hands on a fresh dishcloth. "Collin carved the ivory handle on his cane, so you'll have to be particularly careful with it, Bryce. He and his wife, Cecelia, built Seascape, you know. That's their portraits on the stairwell wall. Collin was a fine carver. My, but he did lovely work. Just lovely."

Bryce could've kissed the woman. By talking about normal things and not his injury, she'd reassured Suzie he was okay in ways him saying he was okay never could have reassured her. He gave the angel a grateful smile.

Sliding him a conspirator's wink, she set the cloth back onto the counter, near a bowl of apples, bananas, and oranges. "Jonathan Nelson, the current owner of Seascape Inn, is Collin and Cecelia's grandson. Did you know that, Suzie?" She nodded she didn't, and Miss Hattie went on. "Oh my, yes. He's a judge in Atlanta now, but his heart is always at Seascape. Why, he'd never part with anything from here—which is why your dad must be especially careful with Collin's cane."

"Daddy will, won't you?"

"Yes, I will," Bryce said. Miss Hattie sounded pleased about Jonathan's feelings about Seascape and everything in it, and Bryce supposed it natural she would be. According to Maggie and T.J., Miss Hattie had worked at and lived in the old inn most of her life. ''The cane will help me maneuver until this knee gets better.'' True, even if the idea of Caline's seeing him limping did grate a little at his male ego. But vanity didn't hold a candle to comfort in keeping up with three active kids.

''Of course it will, dear.'' Miss Hattie wiped at a splash of water on the countertop.

''Mr. Richards, dismissing Jeremy hardly qualifies as punishment—''

''I understand your position, Mrs. Wiggins,'' Bryce gritted out from between his teeth, watching the woman right her toppled chair.

''Mr. Richards?'' Caline still stood in the doorway, clasping one each of two of his children's hands. ''I hate to interrupt yet again, but I really do need to get my things out of Miss Hattie's entryway. They're blocking the door.'' She nodded toward Suzie, then Jeremy. ''Do you mind if we go on up now?''

''Not at all.'' Bryce fingered his knee. It was swelling already.

''You can't mean to let the boy get away with this, too!'' Mrs. Wiggins snarled, muttered, then girded her verbal loins and cut loose with her rhetoric. ''Mrs. Richards, may she rest in peace''—the battleaxe crossed herself—''was extremely explicit in her instructions regarding discipline. Jeremy *must* be punished for this.''

''And he will be. Just not right now.'' Bryce raked a weary hand through his hair. ''Right now, he's going to assist Caline with her luggage.''

Caline flashed him a quick smile that set his heart to thumping, then hurried Suzie and Jeremy through the gallery at a good clip, heading toward the stairs as if she half feared Bryce would change his mind and call them back to punish Jeremy now, anyway.

Bryce didn't much like that, either. But he admired it. The grandfather clock ticked loudly, then chimed once. He did not, however, admire his physical reaction to the woman. And in the things he didn't like regarding her, this reaction he liked least of all.

Mrs. Wiggins frowned. "I'd be remiss in my duties if I didn't oppose."

"Your opposition is noted." Bryce reached for the dishcloth, resting on the tile countertop. "Now, you'd best see to Lyssie."

They'd have the devil's own time getting all the food out of the child's hair. Did orange juice stain as badly as chlorine?

Poor Lyssie'd had green hair most of the summer. It'd finally gotten back to normal around Halloween—right *after* picture day at her day care center. His knee aching, he swiped at the high chair's tray. With his luck, she'd have orange hair for Thanksgiving. His parents would get a real kick out of that. And he'd again feel like a Class A failure of a parent. He blew out a sigh reeking of frustration. "Animal crackers."

Muttering her feelings on that substitution, Mrs. Wiggins lifted Lyssie from the high chair and then took her upstairs. From the set of her shoulders, he fully expected another resignation before noon.

Miss Hattie jiggled her reading glasses until they settled inside her apron's pocket. "Animal crackers?"

"Lyssie repeats everything. Jeremy, too," Bryce explained. "I'm sorry for all this mess, Miss Hattie. I'm not sure what I can do about your rose clippings, but if you'll toss me that sponge, I'll get busy cleaning up here."

"Don't worry, dear. This will only a take a minute to fix." She dropped her gaze to his leg, and her smile faded. "But if that swelling is any gauge, your knee'll take a lot longer."

Bryce looked down at his gray wool slacks. The fabric stretched tight across his knee. Wrecked for a week. Maybe two. "You're likely right."

"Does it hurt, dear?"

"Like the devil's pinching it."

Vic returned with Collin's ivory-handled cane. "Here you go, Bryce."

"Thanks." Bryce took the cane. A dolphin had been carved in the ivory. Impressed with the craftsmanship and intricate detail, he lifted his brows, rubbed his thumb over its chiseled surface. "Beautiful work."

"My, but you look debonair." Her eyes twinkling, Miss Hattie patted at her apron. "As debonair as Collin himself—and he was a handsome thing."

Bryce looked down at his crumpled slacks, his oatmeal-infested shirt, and his limp red and gray silk tie. "I don't think handsome or debonair is quite the impression I made on your new guest." Caline probably thought he was a flake and was afraid to leave his own kids with him.

"I'm sure as certain you made a fine impression. The package is a little worse for the wear, my dear, but the goods inside are intact and as interesting as ever." Miss Hattie gave Bryce's freshly trimmed beard a friendly pat. "Speaking of our new guest, would you mind terribly helping her, too? I hate to ask you to deal with the stairs, but I need to get this chicken and cheese casserole in the oven now or we'll be late for lunch." Miss Hattie twisted her lips. "Mrs. Wiggins is rigorously attached to her schedules, and I'd rather not upset the dear woman any more today. Still, Jimmy's busy with Pastor's car and Vic has to get back to delivering the mail, and Miss Tate has so much—"

"Miss *Tate*?" The grin curving Bryce's mouth faded and his stomach dropped to his knees. His client Gregory Tate's ex-wife? The mysterious Mrs. Tate? The stranger Suzie had just referred to as her new mom—maybe? She couldn't be here. How, *why*, would she be here? *"Caline Tate?"*

Miss Hattie nodded, a knowing gleam in her eye.

Chapter 4

Cally loved the Great White Room on sight. Tall paneled walls stretched up to its high ceiling and the plank-oak flooring, scattered with braided rugs woven in soft blue and warm peach, invited a person in, welcomed them the way the entire house did, seemingly opening its arms to shelter any who stepped inside. But the little turret room that opened to the bedroom, she more than loved. Sheer white curtains hung at its windows above fluffy-cushioned window seats, and an oval rug matching the others lay in the octagon-shaped crook before the windows. Obviously the room got first light in the morning. And just the thought of sitting there, staring out on the ocean and breathing in its salty fresh scent had little ripples of pleasure spreading through her insides. Seacape Inn seemed a perfect place to gather perspective and make decisions. And maybe, just maybe, she'd be lucky enough while here to also find a snippet of courage.

Was that why she'd felt drawn to come here?

She'd certainly had no intention of going anywhere except to the cabin in Nova Scotia. But when she'd seen the sign for Sea Haven Village, she'd felt the strongest urge to turn. It was the strangest thing, almost a spiritual promise of peace and serenity. Considering her situation, that temptation had been too potent to ignore. And despite the breakfast fiasco she'd interrupted—God, but Bryce had looked mortified, and every bit as adorable as his muddy son, sitting on the floor covered in oatmeal and mud, hurt and trying hard to pretend he wasn't—she felt at ease here. Not at peace, but somehow comforted. She liked it.

It'd been a long time since she'd felt comforted, or able to deal with her circumstance. It'd been even longer since she'd been able to get a grip on her emotions. And, pitiful to admit, but until she'd seen Bryce catch that silly frog, she couldn't recall the last time she'd laughed. That too felt good. She toed her cosmetic case away from the blue bed comforter near the floor, noting a new scratch near the handle. These days, feeling good was nothing short of a miracle for her. And miracles she fully intended to appreciate.

She looked over to the dresser at the French phone. Maybe here she could find courage and, if Seacape had yet another spare miracle within its walls, those pieces of herself Gregory had slowly stolen from her.

"Here's your purse, Cally." The muddy Jeremy passed her handbag.

It was a little worse for the wear; dirt-streaked on the backside. "Thanks." Caline smiled. Where the endearing-sounding Cally had come from, she didn't know. But she liked it, too. Grandma Freemont used to call her Cally. She'd died too long ago for Caline to remember that firsthand, but finding the reminder of someone who had loved her unconditionally pleasant, Caline Tate decided that here at Seascape she'd do her best to become Cally again. To find Cally's dreams.

A flood of warmth flowed through her. Nice. Very nice, but odd. The room was a little on the chilly side. "Thanks for helping me, Jeremy."

"You're welcome." He stuffed his hands in his jeans pockets and rocked the toe of his sneaker against the rug. His shoelace dragged on the floor.

Suzie, doelike with her large brown eyes, just stared at Cally, to the point that she was half tempted to check the mirror, as much as she hated mirrors, to see if something spotted her face. She studied Suzie's eyes. No, she wasn't staring at Cally's face, but at her carnation. Wasn't she?

To be certain, Cally took off her hat and unpinned the flower. "Would you like to have this, Suzie?"

"No! Please don't take it off. Please."

Why was the child so upset? What had Cally done wrong? "Okay, I won't," she hurriedly added. She couldn't keep her hat on forever, but this seemed important to Suzie and, having wanted a child of her own for so long, Cally wanted to see the girl's eyes shining with happiness again, as they had been downstairs when she'd been dancing with the postman. Not as they were now, clouded with worry. "Where should I put the flower, do you think?"

"On your shirt." Suzie pointed to Cally's lapel.

"Blouse, sweetheart." Cally dumped her purse on the floor beside the bed, and caught a whiff of her narcissus-scented perfume and Jeremy's little-boy, earthy scent. It was a pleasing blend. "Guys wear shirts, girls wear blouses."

Suzie nodded. "Blouse, then."

Caline glanced at the bed. The blue coverlet looked plush and comfortable. The whole house reeked of comfort. She was going to like it here. And she had the eeriest feeling that something important, something special, would happen to her in this house.

Probably stemmed from all that nonsense Lucy Baker had babbled about the legend of Collin and Cecelia Freeport's love being so strong it had defied death and still lingered within Seascape's walls. According to Lucy, Cecelia had been a healer, and Cally admitted that she did feel different here. But how could the love of a couple who'd died shower those here now with the blessings of love and peace as Lucy had claimed? Maybe she was just a romantic at heart. It couldn't happen, of course. But wouldn't it be wonderful if even a part of that were true?

Jeremy shrugged. "Put the flower in your pocket, Cally."

She grinned. "I think we'd be safer with Suzie's suggestion this time, Jeremy." The flower in one hand, the pin in the other, Cally frowned down at her blouse. "I always stick myself doing this."

Bryce hobbled into the room, then deposited her case on the floor near the closet door. "Let me help."

Cally's heart took a little dip. He'd changed into a fresh white shirt, navy slacks, and a different but still ultraconservative silk tie that made him look like a guy fresh off the pages of *GQ*. With luck, she'd stop hoping he'd look less appealing in jeans. Imagining denim clinging to his thighs, she felt a warm rush of heat and nixed the thought. Unfortunately, he'd appeal in anything he wore.

"Daddy's gonna help Cally." Suzie tugged at Jeremy, looking awfully pleased. "Come on, we can go now."

"No, I wanna stay here." Jeremy pulled away. "Mrs. Wiggins is still mad at me."

Suzie rolled her gaze and gave Jeremy another solid tug. "She's gonna be mad forever anyway, so what's the difference? Come on, we've gotta get the dirt off you."

Jeremy frowned down at his mud-crusted jeans. "How come?"

"Because, dimwit." Suzie gave him a firm yank, then smiled sweetly at Cally and her father. "If only we have the courage to believe, miracles can happen beside a dreamswept sea."

A shudder rippled up Cally's back. Her instincts rioted, flashed a warning: *Listen. Take the message's meaning into your heart.*

The feeling burned so strong it nearly buckled her knees. Suzie *had* said something vitally important. Cally couldn't explain exactly what, but she'd understood the importance at gut level, and she swore she'd listen to it—as soon as she deciphered it. She lacked courage, but if she had it and believed—in what, she had no idea—then miracles—what kind of miracles, she again had no idea—could happen.

Swiping at his nose, Jeremy frowned at Suzie. "Huh?"

Bryce held that same baffled expression, and yet some odd light shone in the depths of his hazel eyes. As if he too felt something significant had just been disclosed and his instincts also had gone haywire.

"Will you just come on?" Suzie let out a sigh of sheer frustration. "If we don't get out of here, she's never gonna figure out she could be our new mom."

"Our mom?" Jeremy gaped.

Suzie slapped her hand over her mouth. She'd clearly just let the proverbial cat out of the bag and regretted it. Cally's face burned red-hot.

Bryce's turned purple. "Jeremy, go with your sister. Now."

The door shut behind them and, after a long moment, Bryce lifted his gaze. "I'm sorry, Cally. I'm Bryce Richards, widower and sole parent of the mischievous moppets, Suzie, Jeremy, and Alyssa, aka Lyssie. If you don't believe I'm certifiably looney—I wouldn't bet either way this morning myself—and you'll give me that pin, I'll do the honors and spare you a stick."

Looney, no. But definitely haunted. The dark shadows staining the skin beneath his eyes evidenced he was weary, but the look in them told her far more about troubled Bryce Richards. His trouble ran soul-deep. And, while she hated seeing anyone troubled, it did give her a good feeling to have a kindred spirit. Maybe they could help each other in some way. "Spare me a stick?" she asked, though what she really wanted was an explanation of Suzie's "new mom" remark.

"You said you always stick yourself." Dipping his chin in a mock nod toward her carnation, he smiled.

Breathless. Cally couldn't think of anything coherent to say, so she remained silent. Why did he have this odd, settling and yet unsettling effect on her? Okay, he was attractive, and that look in his eyes made him even more appealing. Being around a man without troubles would just make her feel worse about her own situation. But he was too refined and stuffy for her tastes. Maybe it was the cane, or her sensing he was hurt emotionally and physically. Whatever it was, it made no sense. She'd been through too much with Gregory to be affected like this, to be drawn to a stranger with the same intensity she had been drawn to this house.

Lust, she decided. Even with the beard. She was human and not immune to lust. That had to be it.

Well, if she was bent on lusting, at least she'd chosen herself a dynamite candidate and not a jerk. If he was a jerk, then his kids wouldn't act toward him as they did. There was some consolation in that. She swallowed hard and passed him the pin and flower.

"Thanks for the vote of confidence."

Puzzled, she frowned. He had a soothing voice, the kind a woman craved to hear whispering secrets. She wished she hadn't noticed that, or wondered to whom he whispered his secrets. "Confidence?"

"You obviously don't think I'm looney." He lifted the pin between his forefinger and thumb. "Of course, the day is still young. Who knows what the M and Ms have in store for me between now and dusk."

"M and Ms?"

"Mischievous Moppets."

She laughed, and his smile touched his eyes. Her stomach furled.

He brushed aside the long silk scarf that circled her neck and draped down the front of her blouse to her hips. "I guess I should apologize for Suzie's 'new mom' remark. I'd love to explain it; unfortunately I don't have any idea what she's talking about." He smiled again, but this one didn't touch his eyes. "More unfortunately, when conversing with my kids, my being clueless is not uncommon."

That clearly bothered him. Cally liked that about him. She breathed in his woodsy cologne and her stomach went weak. In fact, she liked a lot about him. But she didn't like liking anything about him. Not at all.

She *never* reacted to men this way. So why to him? What made him different? The lust? Doubtful. Lust didn't have that kind of power. Maybe recognizing him as a kindred spirit? In his way, she was sure he was as wounded as she. That could be it. But it felt stronger. Like . . . more.

She looked up at him. At his coal-black hair that had just the tiniest strands of silver threading through it at his temples, and into his deep hazel eyes that looked a little amused and a lot embarrassed—no doubt due to the M & M's antics. His square-cut jaw seemed suited to his face and that neatly trimmed beard suited his personality. Very conservative—a tie and pristine white shirt while on vacation, for pity's sake?—and distinguished. But, she'd give him his due, he had been just as appealing doused with oatmeal. A grin teased her lips and a potent urge to kiss him blindsided her. Swallowing hard, she looked away.

Bending down, he held the carnation against her blouse. "That looks about right." He slipped his fingers beneath the material. His knuckles brushed against her bare skin, and skimmed over the medal and gold angel she always wore pinned to her bra strap.

"Sorry." He lowered his gaze back to the flower. "What is all that?"

The air between them grew thick and heavy. Tense. Her face flamed hot, and she sucked in a little breath. "Just trinkets."

His eyes danced, silver flecks in wide hazel irises. "Trinkets?"

"A guardian angel." How utterly humiliating. Why on earth hadn't she just ignored his question? He wouldn't have pushed. Instinctively she knew he was too much of a gentleman to push.

"Ah, I see." He held his gaze fixed on the flower, then straightened her collar. "And the one dangling from the safety pin?"

"Saint Christopher." She looked at the line of Bryce's jaw, at his beard. She'd never before liked beards on men, but his struck her as surprisingly attractive. "I mean, it's a Saint Christopher medal." What in the world was wrong with her? Saint Christopher likely rolled over in his grave at her saying he was pinned to her bra.

Pressing the pin into the fabric, Bryce paused. "Are you Catholic, then?"

"Baptist. But he's the protector." She hiked a shoulder. "I figured it couldn't hurt." Actually, she figured she needed all the help she could get.

Bryce chuckled, warm and hearty, and eased out his fingertips from the neck of her blouse. "Angels and saints. Covering all bases. I like your philosophy."

Gregory had ridiculed her for indulging in "superstitious nonsense." It obviously wasn't nonsense to her or she wouldn't do it. But that hadn't occurred to him. Acceptance by Bryce felt . . . refreshing. Even welcome. She smiled back at him. "I like your kids."

Bryce grunted, letting his gaze roam over her face. "They are entertaining."

Here it came, she thought. Now he'd ask if *she* had kids and she'd have to say no. Lord, but she hoped her voice didn't tremble or sound pitiful when she admitted it. Why hadn't she anticipated his reaction and avoided it?

"Sometimes they're also crippling." He motioned toward his swollen knee with the tip of the cane. "But they're worth it."

"I'm sure they are." An empty little ache rippled through Cally's chest, and a tree-size splinter of envy. He was the sunshine of his home. "Does the knee hurt much?"

"Like the dickens." He slid her a sheepish look. "On the improvement front, I guess your first impression of me isn't getting much of an assist from my second one. Not very macho to admit pain, is it?"

"Oh, I don't know." Gregory never had admitted to any shortcoming. To any failing. In pointing out flaws, he'd focused on Cally's. "I think it makes you kind of human."

"Human. Hmm, I'll take it. Human is a start—especially after a rough morning. I'll work on improving it."

He cared what kind of impression he'd made? He was interested in her? Impossible. Never happen. "Thanks for pinning on the flower and sparing me the stick. It, um, seemed important to Suzie that I wear it." More than a little curious, Cally added, "I'm not sure why."

"With Suzie, one can never be sure of much of anything." Something akin to pain flashed through his eyes. "She's going through a few . . . challenges."

"A shame. She's a beautiful child." She should be happy and having fun, enjoying her youth. God knew she'd face a woman's problems soon enough. "I'm sorry, Bryce."

"Yeah, me, too." He studied Cally in much the way she had him, and the look in his eyes warmed.

After years of Gregory looking through her, it felt odd to be looked at as a woman by a man again. Feeling exposed and vulnerable terrified her, but that look also ribboned a length of feminine prowess through her that was sheer pleasure. A ribbon she didn't trust, or think she was ready to feel.

He touched the stem. "Does it look straight to you?" Clasping her shoulders, he turned her to face the cheval mirror.

Cally squeezed her eyes shut, unable and unwilling to look at herself in the oval glass, then turned back toward him.

''It's fine.'' She tried to smile, but even to her it felt more like a grimace. ''Thank you.''

A flicker of surprise passed through Bryce's eyes, then faded to confusion. He'd noticed her avoiding her reflection in the mirror, damn it, and the unasked question of why lurked in his eyes. She ignored it. No way was she going to explain. How could a woman explain hating mirrors because of what she'd been shown in them? Caline Tate. A failure. A woman thirty-two with everything she'd never wanted.

''While I'm groveling,'' Bryce said, ''I want to thank you for the rescue, too.''

Bryce Richards grovel? Highly unlikely. She cocked her head. ''Ah, Jeremy and—Mrs. Wiggins, was it?''

''It was.'' Bryce flicked at a strand of hair clinging to Cally's cheek. She flushed beneath his touch, and he seemed a little bemused by it. ''She's already quit once this morning. If you hadn't stepped in, I'm afraid the frog chase would have earned us a second resignation.''

Cally grinned. She didn't want to, but she couldn't help herself. ''Glad to be of service.'' If it was a service. She had to admit, at least to herself, she wasn't sure. Mrs. Wiggins didn't exactly strike Cally as a warm and loving woman who much liked kids.

And yet she had Bryce's three, while Cally, who adored them, had none.

''Did I say something wrong?'' Bryce sounded worried.

Cally blinked, forced a smile to her lips, then met his somber gaze. ''No. Not at all.''

''That curl is most persistent.'' Leaning on his cane, he reached again to her face.

So did she. His hand topped hers, and his palm against her knuckles felt warm. Safe and strong and warm.

Their gazes locked. He took in a healthy breath, then let it out slowly. ''You're very pretty, Cally.''

She swallowed hard, stretching for sense amid rioting emotions. Problem was, he looked and smelled so good, and he sounded so sincere. He couldn't be sincere, of course, but he sure sounded it and, to her hungry ears, that was sweet nourishment that fed her fasting soul. ''I like your eyes.''

''You do?''

"Yeah." Brilliant. Why had she said that? God, what a conversationalist she was these days. She not only sounded stunned, but like an idiot. He probably thought she was a love-starved fool.

Maybe she was. That, or crazy. Maybe both. She was here to find courage—well, the peace she'd felt on making that turn in Bangor. What she wasn't here for was to find a lover. But from the heated looks passing between her and Bryce Richards, she was definitely going to land in trouble if she didn't keep her hormones straitjacketed.

Freeing her hand from beneath his, she let it drop, then hang at her side. "Thanks again."

He looked torn. About what, Cally had no idea, but it was as if he stood at some mental crossroad. After a long moment, his expression softened. Had he reached some conclusion?

"Welcome to Seascape, Cally." He dipped his chin then brushed her lips with his.

Before she could think, much less move, the fleeting moment had passed. He'd backed away and was limping out of the Great White Room, into the hallway. Her fingertips at her lips, Cally watched him go.

Why had he kissed her? And why did she wish he'd go on kissing her—doing the job right? And why in the world did he seem so familiar? They'd never met; a corpse couldn't forget a man who looked like him. And from the quickening pace of her heartbeat and the number of times she'd foolishly blushed in the past few minutes, Cally Tate knew for fact she was certainly no corpse.

She traced her lips with her fingertips. After what happened with Gregory, she'd never expected to feel like a desirable woman again. But in the simple act of pinning a yellow carnation to her blouse, Bryce Richards had made her feel desirable—and more. And, though she'd longed for that feeling many times, it'd been a while since she'd dared to admit it to herself. Didn't it just figure that she'd admit it now, when she wasn't sure she had the courage to risk feeling anything for any man?

Desirable? Her?

"You are a love-starved fool." Cally clenched her fists at

her sides. How could she do this? Let herself forget so quickly, so easily, the lessons she'd spent fourteen years learning? Forgetting was dangerous. It invited pain.

She jerked the end of her scarf. Tugged it loose from her neck, then shook it out. More pain she did *not* need.

Chapter 5

Bryce sat on the hallway floor, between the Cove and Shell Rooms. Moonlight spilled across the white Berber rug, leaving much of the hall in shadows. It'd been an eventful, chaotic three days since the oatmeal/frog fiasco at breakfast on Cally's first day at the inn, but they'd made it through them without Mrs. Wiggins resigning again, and for that he was grateful. Now—he looked at the Shell Room's door behind which his oldest daughter slept—if Suzie could just get through another night without dreaming, he'd end this day too a happy man.

The bathroom door creaked open. Cally came out, reached back and removed the little Occupied sign from the nail in the center of the door, then put it back in the bath. Beautiful woman, even in a blue flannel robe that covered her, neck to toes. And no idea she was beautiful. When he'd pinned on her carnation, why had she avoided looking in the mirror? He'd noticed since then too that she avoided *all* reflective surfaces: at the pond, fishing; on the boat ride, whale-watching; in the kitchen's toaster. . . .

Maybe one day, Bryce would have the courage, or the right, to ask her. But not today. Today, she didn't know he'd represented her sorry husband in divorcing her.

And, God forgive him, Bryce didn't want to tell her.

They'd spent a lot of time together on Miss Hattie-arranged outings with the kids. A trip to the Blue Moon Cafe for ice cream. To the beach to build castles in the sand. Walking through the woods. Miss Hattie was matchmaking, no doubt about it, but he didn't mind. He liked Cally's company, appreciated her warm sense of humor, admired how calm she was with the kids—like when Jeremy had found that beehive. The woman should have been a mother. She was a nurturer down to her toenails—naturally. God, how he envied her that. Very caring, too. She listened to each of the kids' little worries with her full attention, offered sensible advice, then showered them with tender touches that honesty forced him to admit he envied, too—and felt like a heel and a jerk for envying. She should have had a dozen kids.

So why hadn't she had any? Maybe she liked kids in small doses, but lacked interest in a steady diet of them. Or maybe she couldn't have any. One day, maybe Bryce would have the right to ask her about that, too.

Cally stepped back out into the hallway, then gasped. "Bryce? Is that you?"

"Shh, the kids are sleeping." He whispered loudly enough for her to hear, but hopefully not so loudly that he awakened the kids. His knee still ached like the devil, and he just didn't know if he could go another round of chasing them before resting it.

"Sorry." Cally walked toward him, then stopped near where his cane leaned against the wall. "What are you doing out here?"

"Hmm." He looked up at her. "Well, I could say I just enjoy sitting on hardwood floors in the middle of the night, but I somehow doubt you'd believe that."

"Would you?"

"No."

She propped a shoulder against the wall, then crossed her arms over her chest. "Well?"

"I'm listening for Suzie."

Cally's hair swung forward. She pushed it back from her cheek and a wrinkle creased the skin between her brows. Clearly worried. "Is she sick?"

"No." In a sense she was sick, but not in the way Cally meant, and he couldn't let her worry without some explanation. Bryce tilted his head until the shadow falling across his jaw shielded his eyes. "She has bad dreams, Cally."

His tone begged for company; he knew it and still couldn't

stop himself from revealing it to her. It wasn't pity he wanted, but company and compassion. Someone to share his troubles with, someone to just . . . listen.

John Mystic had been right. Bryce inwardly sighed. He needed a wife.

A pang of guilt shot through his chest. Disloyalty to Meriam. For the children, he told himself. Meriam was gone and she wasn't coming back. He needed a wife to help him with the children.

Cally grunted. "I have bad dreams, too, but these days mine happen when I'm awake."

Should he ask her to share her troubles with him? Probably not. They were nearly strangers. Well, he knew more about her than she did about him, and he had kissed her. Though he still had no idea why he'd done that. It'd just seemed right. At least, it had at the time. He'd have to tell her he was Gregory's attorney soon. Not telling her reeked of being dishonest and, in her marriage to Gregory Tate, God knew the woman had had a bellyful of lies. She deserved better. More. But Bryce really did need to talk, and she might not find that need at all appealing once he told her about Gregory. Would waiting a little longer do any more damage? What could talking hurt? They'd just be two adults commiserating over their troubles. And, after a comment like her last one, it appeared she needed someone to talk with, too. "I'm sorry." He patted the floor beside him. "Pull up a plank and let's swap war stories."

Smelling the perfume he was coming to love, he watched her sit down beside him, then fold her long legs up underneath her, nearly brushing their shoulders. "You really don't want to hear it," she said. "Besides, I'm sick of hearing myself moan and groan. I'd rather you explain why you're out here in the hall instead of curled up in the chair in Suzie's room."

"I told her she wouldn't dream here. If I sleep in her room—"

"Ah, mixed signals. Telling her she'll be fine, but showing her she won't be."

"Right." He nodded. "But I need to be close, just in case."

"And if she should call out and you're in your room, you're scared you won't hear her."

"Exactly." The woman was quick; he'd give her that.

"What are Suzie's bad dreams about?"

Effective shift of topic. Now he couldn't ask without seeming intrusive—which he felt sure had been Cally's intention. "She's drowning," he admitted. "It's the same dream all the time. Every night—except last night—for two years."

Cally frowned and smoothed a delicate hand over her robe-clad thigh. "That's a long time to suffer through the same nightmare."

"Yes, it is." He sighed, letting her see his frustration. "I've tried everything, Cally. Her mother died two years ago—that's when the dream started."

"Maybe she needs professional help. Grief is so hard on kids."

"She's getting it. Has been for eons. Hell, Cally, I've tried everything I know to do, but . . ." A knot swelled in his throat, and he fell silent.

"Nothing seems to work." Cally slumped against the wall and lifted her chin, then shut her eyes. "Kid or adult, losing someone you love hurts—in ways you understand, and in ones you don't."

She hadn't wanted the divorce. The truth slammed into Bryce, and for some totally ridiculous reason, he suffered a twinge of jealousy. That it was directed at Dr. Gregory Tate didn't do Bryce's ego any good. It made him kind of sick. But the mysterious Mrs. Tate didn't seem so mysterious now. Just lonely. And hurting. And hauntingly beautiful.

He turned his head against the wall and looked at her, getting a whiff of her subtle perfume. An unusual floral. He couldn't peg it, though he liked it. "Yes, it does. When my wife, Meriam, died, I thought I'd die, too. I really believe the only reason I didn't was because of the kids."

"You're lucky to have them."

She was alone. How much harder that must have made the divorce for her. But maybe she hadn't wanted kids of her own. "Yes, I am." Might as well get the air cleared now. This dishonesty rankled. She'd gotten plenty of that from

Gregory Tate, and Bryce would rather be damned than be jealous of a liar and cheat *and* emulate one. "You weren't so lucky."

"No." She looked away. "No, I wasn't."

Bryce covered her hand with his on her lap. "Cally, I'm sorry about the divorce. And I'm sorry about Gregory marrying Joleen the day after it." Good God, of course. Gregory and another woman. Cally avoiding mirrors. The bastard had destroyed her self-esteem.

She looked stunned. "How did you know about Joleen?"

Now she'd hate him. The first woman he'd felt so much as a flicker of interest in since Meriam, and she'd hate his guts. "I was Gregory's attorney, Cally."

For a long moment, she just stared at him. When the shock left her eyes and the truth settled on her shoulders, she seemed to relax. "I should have known your name, but I . . . avoided anything to do with the divorce." She dropped her gaze to his sleeve. "Thanks for telling me."

"I should have told you earlier." He lowered his gaze, unable to hold hers. "But I was enjoying your company."

"I understand." From her tone, she really did. "It's odd that we both wound up here, isn't it?"

"Yes, it is." Did she realize his hand still covered hers? He should move it, but feeling a woman's skin again helped to ease a bit of the aloneness from him. It'd been so long; he wasn't ready to give that up. Not yet. "From what I hear about Seascape Inn, though, a lot of odd things happen here."

"Really?" She stiffened her fingers, bent them backward, interlacing them with his.

His heart rate sped. Evidently she too needed the reassurance of another human being's touch. He nodded. "My friends T.J. and Maggie MacGregor met here last winter—around this same time. He was, um, landlocked here."

"Landlocked?" Her eyes stretched wide.

"Shhh! The kids." Bryce reminded her to drop her voice. "Every time T.J. tried to leave Seascape lands, he blacked out."

"Good grief. Why?"

"I don't know, and he won't say. All I know is that he stayed here over nine months."

"Well, what happened so he could leave?"

Bryce grinned. "Maggie Wright came."

"And?"

"T.J. married her. They're expecting their first baby soon—right around Thanksgiving."

"Goodness." Cally smiled. "But there had to be another reason he couldn't leave here, don't you think?"

Bryce shrugged. "What I think isn't as important as what T.J. and Maggie think."

"Which is?"

"That he couldn't leave until Maggie arrived. Meeting was their destiny."

"Ah." Cally stretched her legs out in front of her and crossed them at her ankles. "The romantic version."

Clearly, the romantic version didn't impress Cally. "The truth as they see it," Bryce corrected her. "There are other cases, too."

She let out a groan. "Surely you're not swallowing all that stuff."

"It's true, Cally." He leaned toward her and whispered low. "John Mystic, a client of mine—well, he's a friend, too—came up here. He and his wife, Bess, were getting a divorce. Everyone had given up on them reconciling—even Selena, John's sister, and she's more tenacious than a pit bull. They'd been separated for a long time, but they came to Seascape and found it again."

"It?" Cally too whispered, and lifted a questioning brow.

"The magic."

"What magic?"

"The magic of Seascape Inn." When she blinked her confusion, he added, "Love, Cally. They found love."

"Oh, Bryce. That's absurd. How can a house, for crying out loud, hold the magic of love?"

"I didn't say it wasn't absurd, or that it was logical or reasonable. Only that it was true." He straightened his tie, knotted at his throat. "Honest, Cally, John and Bess were a final decree from divorce. I was his lawyer, and I know that for fact. They came up here separately and—*bam*—they fell in love all over again. If you knew them, you'd say it was magic, all right."

"Maybe they finally spent some time together. Or maybe they'd never stopped loving each other. Whatever it was, it had to be more than just the house. If that's all it took, this place would be stacked to the rafters with couples."

"Probably," Bryce agreed. "But maybe it's the house—and more."

"What do you mean?"

"I don't know exactly." He didn't. But something was there, niggling at the door of his conscience. Sooner or later he'd be able to answer the knock and find out. "There's something special here. I can't describe it, but I feel it. I have since I first saw the house."

"Me, too."

He looked at her. "I like it."

"I'm debating." Looking down the hallway, she seemingly forced her gaze back to his. "I want to thank you, Bryce."

A shot of pure pleasure arrowed through his chest. "I figured once you found out about my representing Gregory, you'd hate me." Bryce dropped his gaze to her clasped hands. "That's why I, er, postponed telling you." His seventeenth impression wasn't getting a lick of an assist from his first sixteen. He barely withheld a grimace.

"It was a surprise, true, but nothing personal against you."

"Why the thanks, then?"

"Because of the alimony. Someone had to insist Gregory pay it or he wouldn't have given me a dime. I'm figuring that someone was you."

"You deserved that money and, I think, probably more."

"Two thousand five hundred sixty-three dollars and eighty-nine cents per month for five years is a lot more than I ever figured I'd see. He shifted all our assets to an account in the Cayman Islands."

Bastard. Bryce grimaced. "He denied it, but I suspected he'd pulled something like that."

"Which is why you insisted he pay the alimony."

"Only in part," Bryce confessed. "It's embarrassing to

admit, Cally, but because you never showed up at any of the client/attorney meets with your counsel, I had a friend do a little checking up on you.''

''Your friend John Mystic. Mystic Investigations, right?''

''Yes.'' Bryce had the grace to blush; the heat scorched his face. ''I wasn't trying to invade your privacy so much as to figure out why you were staying away. I thought it likely you either had something to hide, or Gregory was intimidating you into keeping a low profile.''

She paused for a long minute, then looked Bryce straight in the eye. ''And your friend discovered Gregory had intimidated me long before the divorce proceedings. Years before.''

''Yes.'' Bryce lowered his gaze to his knees.

She sighed. ''Well, what can I say? It's true. He was very good at manipulating things to suit him, including me. And he wasn't particular about how he did it. Intimidation was but one of his means.''

And yet she'd loved him. And she'd grown to hate herself for loving him. After getting to know Cally, that truth seemed crystal clear. Bryce rubbed at his temple, sympathetic, then gazed at her hand. It had felt so small and fragile, linked with his. Now, it trembled. ''I'm sorry for what he did to you.''

''Me, too.'' She gave him a resigned look. ''But, as they say, what doesn't kill you makes you stronger.''

Footsteps sounded on the stairs. They grew louder, then Miss Hattie stepped into view. ''Ah,'' she said from the landing. ''Now, why am I not surprised to find you two out here?''

''We were just talking.'' Cally stiffened, looking as guilty as a high school teen caught lingering at the lockers after the tardy bell.

Miss Hattie smiled, then slid her gaze to Bryce. ''And you're holding up the wall, right?''

''Yes, actually, I am.'' He smiled.

''Bosh. You're listening for Suzie because you fear you won't hear her from inside the Cove Room, dear heart, and don't you be trying to fool this old woman to keep her from worrying about you or the child.''

"I'm sorry," he said, and genuinely meant it. There was something very special about Miss Hattie Stillman that made a body not want to hurt or disappoint her. All those strays who entered her home, she tucked under her wing, and took into her care. It felt good to be cared for, and so . . . alien. "Forgive me."

"Of course, dear heart." She fussed with her skirt. "Now, I expect your knee's getting a mite stiff, so I'm here to relieve you. Maybe since Cally's still awake, she'll take a short walk on the cliffs with you to exercise that knee." Miss Hattie let out a totally false sigh. "Truly, Cally dear, he has been extremely uncooperative in doing that, though I'm sure as certain I've explained it'll work some of the stiffness from the joint."

"Well, we have to respect our joints. We only get one set." Cally stood up then held out a hand to Bryce. "Ready?"

"But the cliffs are slick, and it's dark."

"Which is why you need Cally's steady arm to hold on to while you're walking over them."

Cally added her two cents. "There's a full moon, too."

Bryce sent Miss Hattie a speculative look. He'd heard all about her matchmaking attempts with T.J. But Bryce didn't need a love interest, he needed a woman to mother his children. Fortunately, he strongly sensed Cally didn't need a love interest, either.

Cally wiggled her fingers. "Move it, Richards, before that knee fossilizes and you've only yourself to blame."

"I'm not that old." He hauled himself to his feet and, stretching his leg straight, barely managed not to grimace. "Is 'fossilizes' a word?"

"Of course it is." Cally snorted. "And if you don't come on, you won't live to get that old, either. Didn't you see the determination in Miss Hattie's eyes?"

He had. The angelic sweetheart had a will of iron, a heart of gold, and she was Maine stubborn. She intended that he and Cally walk. Period. "You'd better get a sweater. It's warm, but it's still chilly at night."

"I'll throw on some clothes." She motioned to her robe. "I expected it'd be much colder here in November."

"We're having a warm spell," Miss Hattie said. "But Maine weather is nothing if not changeable, dear heart. Best be prepared with that sweater."

"Be right back." Cally headed toward her room.

Bryce watched her go.

So did Miss Hattie. "She's a lovely woman, our Cally Tate. Isn't she lovely, Bryce?" Fingering her gold locket, Miss Hattie sighed wistfully. "Just lovely."

"Lovely," he agreed. "And the ex-wife of my client."

"Former client, I thought."

"Not officially."

"But their divorce is final."

"Oh, yes. But Tate has other . . . concerns." Ones Cally likely didn't know existed.

"Well." Miss Hattie pushed at a pin coming loose from her bun. "I guess you'd best see to that, then."

He crooked his neck, cast her a sidelong look. "Now why would I do anything about Tate? The only reason to withdraw as his counsel would be due to a relationship with Cally—which I don't have."

"Mmm, I'm sure you know best, dear."

Bryce went still. Not for a second did he buy her acquiescence. "When John was here, I know you heard us on the phone."

"I did?"

"Yes. You heard him tell me to go to Macy's and order myself a wife. In fact, I mentioned it to you later myself. But Macy's doesn't stock wives, Miss Hattie, and Seascape Inn doesn't, either. So stop looking at me like you expect me to just pick out a woman here, go up to her and say, 'Hey, wanna marry me and mother my kids?' I can't do that."

She cast him an innocent look, her green eyes soft and questioning. "Why not?"

"Because." Exasperated, he groaned. "God, Miss Hattie. If I said something like that, Cally would think I was crazy."

"She would?"

"Of course she would. What woman wouldn't? And I'd agree with her. We're practically strangers."

"I see." Miss Hattie smacked her lips. "Well, I'm sure you do indeed know best."

He hated it when she said that. Hated it. Mostly because he suspected she meant he didn't know anything at all. And because he feared she was right.

She patted her bun. "Far be it from me to tell you your own mind on the matter, dear heart—I don't believe in interfering—but it is worth noting I never once mentioned you asking Cally Tate."

She hadn't. And that, he supposed, was her point. He'd denied having any feelings for the woman, then turned right around and mentioned her and marriage in the same breath. T.J. and John had warned Bryce, but evidently not enough for it to get through his thick skull. They'd said Miss Hattie had a way of twisting things on a man until the absurd sounded logical and the impossible, plausible. He clamped his jaw. "Cally would think I was crazy. I'd think I was crazy, too."

Miss Hattie pulled a lacy white hankie from her pocket then dabbed at her temple. "So you've said."

There she went again. Agitated, he tugged his gray sweater closed, then buttoned the third button. "Well, don't you agree?"

"When nip comes to tuck, whether or not I agree doesn't matter, hmm? It's what you and Cally think that is of consequence." Miss Hattie pulled a loose thread from his sweater sleeve. "But it's clear as a cloudless day she adores your children. And after marriage to that beast, trusting a man again could take her a spell. But the children . . . Well now, they're a different kettle of fish, I'd say."

Essentially the same words he'd said to Cally earlier about Seascape Inn and its magic, and it only mattering what John and Bess thought. But to pull the stunt with Cally that Miss Hattie was suggesting, a man would have to be totally without pride. Bryce would do a lot for his kids—he really would—but would it be asking too much to find them a good mother who'd also at least trust him? He didn't expect love. Didn't want it, either. But trust, well, that seemed essential in any relationship.

Cally walked out of her bedroom wearing a feminine version of Bryce's same sweater. ''Oh, look,'' Miss Hattie said, sounding more than pleased with herself. ''You match.''

''Miss Hattie.'' He barely stifled a groan.

''What?''

The picture of innocence. He wasn't buying that bit of business for a second, either. Nor was he willing to let himself even think about her nonsuggestion suggestion of him marrying Cally Tate. He didn't really know the woman. And yet what he'd seen in the past three days he'd liked, and he had the strangest feeling that she might need the kids as much as they needed her. They interacted as if they'd known and loved each other for years. ''Nothing, Miss Hattie.'' He let out a resigned sigh. ''Nothing at all.''

Cally waited for him at the top of the stairs.

''Have a care not to put too much weight on your knee, Bryce. And don't you worry, I'll keep a sharp watch on our Suzie.''

''Thanks, Miss Hattie.''

''My pleasure.'' She nodded, then stared at the ceiling as if talking with someone else. ''She won't have that dream.''

He didn't know why, but Bryce had the strongest feeling Miss Hattie was right. Pacified, he joined Cally on the stairs.

She looked at his sweater, then at her own. ''Hey, we match.''

An inevitable harrumph skidded up his throat. ''Yeah, I guess maybe we do.''

The wind coming off the Atlantic chilled her skin, but Cally wasn't cold. Her arm linked with Bryce's, they walked side by side, and every third or fourth step, because of his limp and leaning on the cane, their sides brushed. They hadn't talked. Just soaked in the calming night sounds of the ocean's waves splashing against the granite cliffs. And that comfortable silence suited her just fine.

She reveled in the feel of the crisp wind ruffling through her hair, teasing her eyelids; in the feel of Bryce curling his arm around her shoulder in a way that using her as support didn't require. He *wanted* to touch her. God, but it'd been so long since she'd known a man wanted to touch her. And not knowing what to do with all the feelings that knowing conjured, she buried them.

To the sounds of the ocean and birds chirping, they walked south on Main Street to the village. The Blue Moon Cafe was still busy, though it was after nine P.M.

"Want to stop for a snack?" Bryce asked. "I hear Lucy Baker makes a mean blueberry pie."

"No, thanks—unless you need to rest your knee."

"It's fine. The stiffness is working out—but don't tell Miss Hattie she was right. There'll be no living with the woman."

A smile tugged at Cally's lips. "She seems to have an amazing knack for knowing what a person needs."

"Mmm, I hadn't thought about it, but you're right. She does." A glint of mischief flickered in his eye. "Maybe that's the Seascape magic."

"Maybe so." Cally refused to rise to the bait, but she saw now where his children got their mischievous streaks. She liked that about Bryce, too. And she didn't like liking it any better than the rest of things she liked about him.

On the stony path beside the road, they walked on past the pristine church with its stained-glass window and high steeple, then turned back toward the inn. When they neared the gravel drive, Cally held her breath, sure Bryce would turn in and their walk would be over. But he didn't. Instead, they walked on, toward the lighthouse which sat on a jutted point its keeper, Hatch, had called Land's End. A shame the Coast Guard had automated the lighthouses and his wasn't operating anymore. Chiseled against the midnight sky, its dark silhouette looked lonely. Cally knew exactly how it felt. And she sensed Bryce did, too. Amazing how different their situations were and yet how much they had in common.

"Cally." He broke their pleasant silence. "May I ask you something?"

The last thing she wanted was to answer questions. Especially ones from Bryce when he sounded more like an attorney than a father or a man. The father, the man, she enjoyed, but she'd had about all of attorneys she could handle. She glanced over to tell him so, but the moonlight shining softly on his face conspired with his earnest look, and her reluctance withered. "Sure."

"Why didn't you want the divorce?" Bryce semigrimaced, pausing at a clump of chickweed next to a mighty oak on the edge of the sand-dusted asphalt where the street met the path to the lighthouse. "I mean, knowing Gregory was seeing Joleen—"

Cally looked away, out to the ocean, and inwardly groaned. Salt-tinged air breezed over her skin and the sounds of the waves crashing against the shore pounded in her ears. If she told the truth, she would look like the fool she'd been. She really didn't want to look like a fool—not to Bryce. But she couldn't lie to him, either. Not without again becoming Caline, and she was quickly growing more peaceful as Cally. Cally was desirable, at least a little, and she was looked at with warmth and tenderness, with smiles that touched the eyes. Caline wasn't. "I didn't know he was seeing Joleen." Cally fixed her gaze on the lighthouse tower. "I had no idea."

"I'm sorry. I didn't mean to upset you." Leaning on her, he walked on. "I shouldn't have brought it up."

"It's okay." She shrugged, and sidestepped an unruly juniper intruding onto the path.

Midway on the upward slope, Bryce stopped near a clump of bayberry. The wind whistled through its winter-barren branches, and a bird cooed. Sounded like a barn owl, though he couldn't spot it in the trees. "Upsetting you isn't okay. Not with me."

So conservative. So reserved. And yet so much passion in his eyes and in his voice. Meriam had been a lucky woman. "I didn't want the divorce because, fool that I was, I loved the man."

Bryce moved to face her, then stopped under an ancient oak. The tip of his cane sank into the pebbly sand and grains sprayed over the toe of his loafer, tapping against the leather. "I don't think loving a man is foolish. Especially not when that man is your husband."

Bitterness? Is that what she'd heard in his voice? Why would Bryce sound bitter? "When that man's Gregory Tate, loving him is worse than foolish. It's a recipe for self-destruction.''

Bryce touched her face, his fingers cool, his eyes tender. ''There had to be some good in him. If there wasn't, you'd never have fallen in love with him.''

''You don't understand.'' She didn't understand herself. No. No, that wasn't true. She understood. She only wished she didn't.

Bryce rubbed his thumb along her cheek. ''Explain it to me then, so I do understand.''

She couldn't meet his eyes. She wanted to, tried to, but she just couldn't do it. Instead, she focused on his tie. ''I loved Gregory from the moment I saw him. His parents said it was lust, but it wasn't. I truly fell in love with him at first sight. He was so . . . perfect. Everything I wanted in a man. And, as hard as it is to believe now, then he loved me, too.''

''I'm sure he did.''

Bryce's of-course tone had her smiling. He had a way of making her feel lovable. Not that she was, or ever could be again. But the fleeting feeling was nice. ''Gregory was a med student then. We couldn't wait to get married, to be together.''

''His family opposed.''

''Boy, did they.'' She shrugged off a memory of the ugly scene. The accusations of her using pregnancy to trap their son. She'd explained she wasn't pregnant, but it hadn't mattered. Only time had proven her truthful on the issue. Considering the way things had turned out, with them unable to have a child, divorced, Gregory remarried, it all seemed rather unimportant anymore. Yet it still hurt. So much . . . still hurt.

''But you married anyway. And you were happy.''

''For a while.'' She let out a humorless laugh. ''I guess I should be grateful it lasted as long as it did.''

''But you're not.''

Too perceptive! ''No. No, I'm not.''

''What happened to you two?'' Bryce shifted his weight and winced.

His knee clearly was aching. He hadn't wanted their walk to end either and, pleased by that, Cally clasped his arm, then sat down on the dew-damp ground. Even in his knife-creased dress slacks, he sank to the earth beside her, and she smiled again. "Everything was great. Gregory's parents cut him off financially because he'd defied them and married me, so I quit college and worked designing window displays for a couple of department stores. Money was tight, but we got by."

"So you put him through med school."

"And his residency. And helped him repay school loans and set up his office. At times I thought we'd be in debt forever." She plucked at a blade of brown, dead grass, then threaded it between her forefinger and thumb. It crackled. "I'm one of those unfashionable women who never wanted a career, Bryce. I only wanted a family." *To be the sunshine of my home.* "So we postponed my dream to get Gregory's. When he went into practice, then it was to be my turn." She let out a self-deprecating laugh. "We were going to have lots of babies and a comfortable home, and live happily ever after."

Bryce's expression turned serious. "But you never got your dream."

"We had to pay off the school loans, then the office setup loans, then save a nest egg. Et cetera, et cetera, et cetera. But I finally got part of my dream—the home part." She lifted a pointed finger. "The trouble started when I mentioned the babies part." The wind caught a wisp of her hair, tangled it. She pushed it away from her face. "I wanted them then, and Gregory didn't. He'd worked so hard for so long, he wanted some free time first."

"So your dream had to wait—again."

She nodded. "At first he just put me off. Then he got irritated if I brought up the subject. For a long time, I avoided talking about kids because I couldn't take the upset it caused. Then *I* got irritated and, finally, I insisted." A shaft of pain arrowed through her chest, and her voice softened. "That's when we found out Gregory couldn't have kids."

"Did you still love him, then?"

What an odd question. "Of course." A racoon scampered across the path then ducked under a clump of bayberry. Cally grunted. "It was hard to accept that we'd remain childless, and I'd be lying if I denied it. But I worked through it, Bryce. I really did. And I accepted that part of my dream just wasn't meant to be."

He sandwiched her hand in his, his fingers strong, yet gentle. "What about adoption?"

"Gregory refused to discuss any alternatives." Alternatives would occur to Bryce. Her chest went tight. But they hadn't occurred to Gregory. How long had he stayed at the hospital the first time she mentioned adoption? Three days, or four?

Did it matter now? She looked up through a spruce's wind-ruffled branches. "He wanted our children, or no children. When I pushed and insisted my wants should count, too, I became the 'lousy, demanding, and ungrateful wife.' "

"I can't imagine that," Bryce said.

"Bless you for sounding as if you mean that."

"I do mean it. You thanked me and asked for help with your luggage. That rules out demanding and ungrateful."

"Ah, but I excelled at lousy." She tossed down the grass blade, lifted a stone, then rubbed it between her forefinger and thumb. The grit of sand clinging to it felt good. Soothing.

"'Fraid not. Lousy women don't protect. And you protected Jeremy from the battleaxe."

"The battleaxe?" A little laugh escaped her throat. "Ah, the estimable Mrs. Wiggins."

He bumped his cane with his knee; steadied it against the rough bark of the tree. "You don't like her."

"Truthfully?" Clouds scudded across the sky and the moonlight softened, then again grew bright.

He nodded. "Always."

Cally liked the sound of that—and added honesty to the list of things she didn't like liking about him. "The battleaxe grates at my nerves."

"Mine, too."

"Then why don't you fire her?"

"I can't make myself do it. Meriam hired her. We both worked long, weird hours—I still do. Mrs. Wiggins isn't the greatest nanny in the world, but she is the only constant in my kids' lives."

Again putting the children's needs above his own desires. And Meriam's wishes, too. Another of his traits went on her list, and a stream of jealousy so fierce she feared she'd drown in it rushed through Cally's chest. Even though she'd been dead for two years, Meriam's wishes were given more consideration by Bryce than Gregory had given Cally's wishes with her alive. And if that didn't prove she'd been a lousy wife, she didn't know what would.

"Besides," Bryce went on, "I'm not a very good parent, Cally."

"You're a wonderful parent."

"No I'm not. I swear I try, but I just screw up left and right." He grunted and stared into the night sky. "Once, Jeremy spilled milk on the kitchen floor and used the garden hose to clean it up."

She smiled. "Very creative."

"He flooded the kitchen." Bryce laced his fingers with hers. "I put him in the corner, then cleaned up the mess. Afterward, I took a phone call, checked my e-mail, puttered in the yard. Suzie comes outside—it'd been a good hour—and says, 'Daddy, aren't you ever going to let Jeremy out of the corner?' " Bryce's expression twisted. "I forgot him, Cally. I actually forgot him there."

"And I'm sure you felt awful about it."

"Of course I did, but that's not the point. I forgot my son. That's the point."

"Hmm, how did Jeremy react?"

"I went inside and said, if he could behave, then he could get out of the corner. He looks up at me with these big eyes and tells me, 'I think I'd better just stay here a while.' "

She laughed from the heart out, pressed her forehead against Bryce's shoulder.

He tensed, unsure if it was at the intimacy of feeling her breasts brush against his arm or at her laughing. The latter more comfortable than the former, he frowned at her. "How can you find this funny?"

"It's hilarious." She reared, lifted her gaze to his, her eyes twinkling. "The angel knew he'd get into trouble again, so figured he might as well just stay put." She patted at his sleeve, then smoothed her hand down it, elbow to wrist, her laughter lingering in her eyes. "Oh, he's special, Bryce. Really special."

"He is. But you're missing my point."

"Am I?" She cupped his chin in her hand. "You got preoccupied and forgot. Do you honestly think you're the only parent in the world to do that, Bryce Richards? If so, you're not only a stuffed shirt, but very arrogant."

"Parents aren't allowed arrogance. Or pride." God, but he loved the feel of her hand on his beard. He'd confess the darkest secrets in his soul for a moment more of feeling her touch. He'd even let her get away with calling him a stuffed shirt, which he wasn't, of course.

"You'll need more evidence to convince me, Counselor. So far, all I see is a single father doing the best he can and stumbling now and then, as all humans do."

"Evidence?" He swallowed hard. "No problem. How does getting caught red-handed at setting the stove timer back five minutes by a three-year-old suit you?"

"I'm not sure. Why is it significant?"

"We have quiet time. Thirty minutes of silence. Bliss. Every afternoon from three until three-thirty. It'd been a really rough day, and at three twenty-eight I just wasn't ready for another round. I eased back the timer five minutes."

"And Jeremy caught you?"

"Yes." Bryce dipped his forehead to hers. "Suzie had been teaching him numbers and he knew eight was bigger than three. I felt like a jerk."

"I think needing that five minutes was pretty human, too." She shrugged. "Why didn't you just tell the kids you needed another five minutes?"

He blinked, then blinked again. "I never thought of it."

"After getting caught, I bet you will next time."

"No doubt about it." He grunted. "But you can see, I'm not the greatest parent. The kids need Mrs. Wiggins. She's stable and—"

"As flexible as a brick wall. Honestly, Bryce, you love the kids and they love you. That's what matters. Mistakes happen."

"But my mistakes have Suzie on an analyst's couch once

a week and having nightmares every night. There are consequences.''

''Your pride really is strutting its stuff here, Counselor. Why are you so sure it's your mistakes that are causing this with Suzie?''

''What else could it be?''

''Grief. Loneliness. Longing for a mother. It could be a million things that have nothing to do with you.''

''I appreciate your support, Cally, but I know in my gut I'm responsible. Whatever the reason, seeing to it that my daughter is emotionally healthy is my job. I'm flunking on a grand scale, and she's paying the price.''

Cally hugged him, pressed her body against his, then held him for the longest time. His heart thumped against hers, and she rested her cheek on his shoulder. ''Be gentle with you, Bryce,'' she whispered, then backed away.

Tears shimmered in her eyes. Tears for him. Bryce swallowed hard. ''You should have had a lot of kids.''

How she wished that she could've. ''Gregory never came around, or I would have.'' She smiled but there was no humor in it. ''The only thing my mentioning adoption ever got me was more time alone.'' Had that been when Gregory had started his affair with Joleen?

''Why do women so often talk in riddles?''

''Sorry.'' She tucked her hair behind her shoulder. ''If I brought the subject of adoption up, then Gregory would punish me by staying at the hospital overnight. Near the time we formally separated, it was unusual for him to spend more than a night a week at home.''

Bryce looked stricken, and maybe a little angry, too. ''I'm sorry, Cally.''

She loved him for that anger. ''I should've left him long before I did. Things weren't right. I knew it. Then they got worse. But by then I believed I didn't deserve better. And I was so afraid of failing out on my own.''

''And maybe concerned at what your family would think, and your friends.''

Her pride had been stomped to death a long time ago. She let out a self-deprecating laugh. ''For the last couple years, the only pride I've had has come out of a perfume bottle.

I'm into symbols. There's a flower that symbolizes pride, so I wear perfume made from it." She shrugged. "I figure everyone ought to have a little, and we get what we need where we find it."

"I wish I knew what to say." He wished he hadn't understood what she'd meant.

"You don't have to say anything." She tossed down the stone then swiped her hand against her thigh, brushing off the grains of sand. They pattered on the spill of leaves blanketing the ground, and the memory of that final heated argument with Gregory nagged at her. It'd been wicked.

She went quiet, buried the memory and the anger of it, too. When she thought she had her emotions under control, she added, "I accepted his sterility, Bryce. I truly didn't hold it against him, or stop loving him because of it. I can feel good about me for that."

His hand on her cheek, he tilted her face to look at her, eye to eye. "You can feel good about you for a lot of reasons."

Her eyes burned. It was the wind. Definitely the wind, and not Bryce's words or the tender look in his eyes. Her chin trembled. "You're a very kind man."

"Not really. Really I'm ruthless—unless. . . ."

"Unless?"

He gave her a charming smile, let his fingertips steal over her lower lip. "Unless you only kiss admittedly ruthless but kind men." He dropped his voice to just above a whisper. "Do you?"

She wanted to. Oh, how she wanted to. "I don't know. The situation's never come up."

"It has now." He let his thumb slide over her cheek, follow the rim of her jaw from chin to ear. "Could you check?"

Oh, God. "I, um, guess it would depend on why this admittedly ruthless but kind man wanted to kiss me."

His voice went husky. "What if he said he hasn't really kissed a woman since his wife died, and he's curious to see if kissing is like riding a bike?"

"Sounds awfully experimental and one-sided to me."

"Or he could say you have the most tempting mouth he's

seen in a long time, and if he doesn't kiss it soon, he thinks he might die."

"Serious stuff." He wasn't smiling anymore, and neither was she. "But I'm afraid I've sworn off serious stuff. Bad for a body's emotional health."

"Or he could say he's lonely, Cally." Bryce clasped her upper arms, curled his fingertips in the sleeves of her sweater. "He's so . . . damn lonely. And just for a minute he'd like not to feel lonely anymore."

An echoing chord thrummed deep inside her. She knew loneliness. God, but did she know it. Hate it. Resent it. Fear it.

If only one has the courage to believe, miracles can happen beside a dreamswept sea.

Suzie's words, her message, flitted through Cally's mind. But why now? Courage to believe? A potential miracle? Cally squeezed her eyes shut, trembling with more fear than she'd felt the day Gregory announced he was divorcing her. She'd given him everything, ended up with nothing. What more did she have to lose?

The spark. *She was the sunshine of our home.* That flicker of a spark.

Courage. Courage. Miracles.

She opened her eyes, looked straight into Bryce's. "Under those conditions, I'd have to say he'd better kiss me, then. I wouldn't want a kind man's missing a momentary respite from loneliness on my conscience—whether or not he's admittedly ruthless. And especially not a man responsible for three beautiful kids."

Had she lost her mind? *Recant! Recant!*

She wanted to, but couldn't. Her insides had gone molten, yet her pride insisted she *do* something. "But I'd also have to say that he could kiss me only once."

"Only once?" He released her left arm, cupped her nape under the fall of her hair.

She nodded, trembling inside. Grateful she was already sitting for fear her legs wouldn't support her. "I loved one man totally and completely. He broke my heart."

"And you don't want your heart broken again." Bryce

dragged his thumb from the soft hollow behind her ear, down her nape.

She shivered in response. "No, I don't. Not now. Not ever again."

"Ruthless but kind loved a woman, too, Cally. Totally and completely, with all his heart."

"And she died."

"Yes." He swallowed hard. "She died."

"I'm sorry." Simple words, but ones carrying a wealth of feeling. He'd loved Meriam deeply; as much as Cally once had loved Gregory. At least Meriam had loved Bryce back. And yet, both he and Cally had ended up alone.

Now both of them were lonely.

Sharing this pain, Cally lifted her hands, then wrapped them around his neck.

He scooted through the grass and sand, closer. "If we're only going to do this once, I want to do it right." Circling her back with his left hand, he rested his right one on her sweater at her ribs.

The warmth from his palm seeped through her clothes and heated her skin. Her heart thumped a staccato beat, pounding out waves of uncertainty. Gregory had stopped making love to her. Had stopped finding her physically attractive long before their final separation. She'd grown repugnant to him. And, even for a respite from loneliness, she didn't think she could bear to see that indifference then distaste for her in the eyes of a gentle man like Bryce Richards. "Wait!"

"I can't, Cally." He dipped his chin. "I would if I could, but I . . . can't." He pressed his lips to hers.

Cally stiffened. She couldn't do it. She wanted to, but she couldn't. He'd turn away, and she'd feel as vulnerable and undesirable and as ugly as she'd felt before. God, but she hated feeling ugly. She hated feeling any of those things. She hated . . . feeling. Feeling brought pain. And responsibility for pain. That responsibility had to be denied or accepted, and either choice brought more pain. Agony. Despair.

"Kiss me, Cally," Bryce whispered against her lips. He pulled her closer into the warmth of his arms. "Please."

The longing in his voice conspired with the longing inside her and she pressed her mouth to his. Lips parting, he gently invaded her mouth, brushing their tongues. Her breath caught, his heart beat hard against her breasts and, certain she'd later regret this, she couldn't resist the lure of being held by a man who wanted nothing more than to hold her, to touch her, to share with her a tender moment and a gentle kiss. She couldn't resist him any more than she'd been able to resist making that turn onto Sea Haven Highway. Letting the sensations come, she welcomed the joy in the moment. Felt it seep past her fears, deep inside, and she prayed that, if only for this moment, that joy would rinse the hurt from her heart.

Hattie looked through the mullioned windows at the end of the hallway, out onto the cliffs. Cally and Bryce had walked first toward the village, then back toward the inn. When they'd walked past the driveway leading up to the inn, she'd smiled. Now, looking at Bryce holding Cally in his arms, kissing her, Hattie felt her heart ready to burst. "Oh, Tony." She snagged her lace-edged hankie from her pocket, then dabbed at her eyes. "Isn't it just the most wonderful thing? They've chosen our tree. Of all the places . . . our tree."

A sourceless breeze whisked over her skin.

"I know, darling," Hattie said, then delicately sniffed. "Our dear hearts have a long way to go. But all their outings with the children, their sitting in the hallway talking in the dark, and now this lovely gentle kiss at our special place . . . Well, you must agree, those are fine bits of progress." She let her gaze drift from the ceiling back out the window.

Hand in hand, Bryce and Cally were returning to the house, and Hattie's memories drifted back to the days when she and her beloved Tony had walked that same way on those same cliffs. They had so enjoyed their quiet walks. Her chest went tight. "Oh, how I miss you, love."

Lyssie cried.

Hattie sniffed and gave her eyes a final swipe with her lacy hankie, then stuffed it back into her dress pocket. "I know, I know. We're needed and fulfilled in helping others. But, God forgive me, just once in a blue moon, I can't help but wish we could help us."

The phantom breeze formed a distinct sentence. "Me, too."

Hattie came to a dead halt. "Tony?" Outside the Great White Room, she frowned at the ceiling, then up the stairwell leading to the attic, toward Tony's old room. In all their years in this house, she'd intuitively known he was close. He'd given her sign upon sign. But never before had she actually heard him. Not aloud. Not directly. And never with words.

Never, until now.

It had to be a warning. Gooseflesh peppered her arms. Something about these special guests was different from any of the others who'd come here in the past five decades. Something that mattered to them *and* to her and Tony. Something that could affect them continuing to be together at Seascape Inn.

She could lose him.

He could not be here with her anymore.

The gravity of the truth pulsed through her, weighed down on her like a ton of granite, and frightened in a way she'd never before been frightened, she glared up the stairs. "I won't have it. I just won't have it. You made a vow to me, Anthony Freeport," she reminded him, her heart thundering inside her head. "I've dreamed it a thousand times, and I *know* it happened. When you were dying on that battlefield, you promised me we'd never be apart. Don't you dare tell me fifty years later you're going to break your word to me. Don't you dare!"

The wind didn't answer.

Neither did Tony.

Chapter 6

Bryce had suspected it.

He'd hoped he'd been wrong, prayed he'd been wrong, but feared he'd been right. Now he knew he had been, and he resented the hell out of it.

Gregory Tate had abused Cally. Maybe he hadn't physically hurt her, but he had severely damaged her tender heart and the woman she was inside. Emotional abuse was still abuse, and that the bastard had done it to such a gentle, loving soul as Cally infuriated Bryce. That Tate had done it, Bryce suspected, to assuage his own guilt at having an affair with Joleen, deepened Bryce's fury to a cold rage. It made him sick. And, because it was a commonality between him and Gregory Tate, it made Bryce ashamed to be a man.

He and Cally had returned to the house shortly after that powerhouse of a kiss. More than the coming together for a moment's respite, that fusion and connection of spirits had rocked him down to his toes. Miss Hattie, looking weary in a way he'd never seen her, vowed she wasn't sick, was never sick, and had gone up to bed. Now the kids slept peacefully, the battleaxe, whose nights were her own, had retired to her room in the Carriage House, and Bryce and Cally stood outside her bedroom door.

She plucked a blade of dead grass off his sleeve. "Are you going to listen for Suzie?"

He nodded. "I'm hoping she won't dream." Hoping? Masterful understatement. Praying. Pleading. Begging. "When she does, it really rattles her. I need to be there."

Understanding passed through Cally's eyes. "I could keep you company for a while, if you like."

She wanted to be with him? His heart skipped a little beat. "I'd like that a lot."

"Let me grab a pillow." She smiled. "The floor's hard."

Didn't he know it. He'd been stiff for an hour again this morning.

She ducked into her room, then came back with two pillows, a hairbrush, and an afghan—the one he'd awakened and found covering him a few mornings ago. If she'd been at the inn then, he would've thought maybe she'd covered him. But she hadn't been. And she'd ditched her sweater that matched his, and her shoes. He smiled at her bare feet.

She wiggled her toes. "I figured we might as well be comfortable."

"Good thinking." He moved aside, so she could pass him in the hallway. She skirted around, and he again caught a whiff of her perfume. It wasn't sickly sweet like so many perfumes. Cally's Pride in a Bottle smelled fresh and clean, subtle yet quietly erotic. Did they make a masculine version? Sell it in gallons?

She stopped midway between his room and Suzie's, then sat down on the floor. "You have me at a disadvantage." She braced a pillow behind her back.

He leaned Collin's cane against the wall, then dropped down beside her. "What disadvantage?"

Tugging at his sweater sleeve, she pulled him forward, then tucked the second pillow behind his back. His stomach warmed. The heat spread through his chest, then fanned out to his limbs and up his neck. It'd been a long time since anyone had bothered with small matters like his comfort. It felt good. He was ashamed to admit just how good.

"Because of all the stuff with Gregory, you know a lot more about me than I know about you." She grabbed the ends of the afghan and shook its folds loose.

It fluttered over their legs and she tugged it up to his waist, then to her own. He could get used to this. "What do you want to know?"

Cally's expression went serious. "Everything."

God, but she was beautiful. "That could take a while." A

week, a month—he thought of Miss Hattie's inference about marriage—maybe a lifetime.

Cally hiked her shoulder. "Time, I've got, Counselor. It's pride, courage, and dreams that I lack."

"Don't we all?"

"Do we?"

She wasn't kidding. And he innately knew his answer was far more important than her inquiring tone would lead him to believe. "Yeah, we do." He turned more toward her, resting his shoulder against the wall. Their knees touched. He liked the feel. "Know what I think?"

"What?"

"I think you're confused right now. You loved Gregory and he was supposed to love you back and he didn't."

"I don't want to talk about me anymore." She looked at Bryce's tie and frowned. "I want to talk about you."

"We are." He checked the knot. Maybe the tie was crooked or something and that's why she kept staring at it. "I think you're feeling as if you gave Gregory everything, but everything wasn't enough."

"That's about how I see it."

No, it was straight. So why was she fixated on it—and still frowning? Maybe she was thinking he was a stuffed shirt again. "I loved Meriam, too."

Cally lifted her gaze to meet his eyes. "And?"

"It wasn't enough, either."

"You weren't happy?"

"No, I was." Confused himself, he closed his eyes for a second and let his thoughts settle. "I adored Meriam. She was everything I wasn't." His voice dropped a notch. "Adventuresome. Free-spirited. She did exactly as she pleased and told the world to like it or kiss her—"

"Animal crackers?"

He smiled. "Yeah."

Cally reached up and unknotted his tie. Pulled it, dragging it from his neck, then worked loose the top button on his shirt. "We're relaxing," she explained.

"Oh." His throat went thick, as dry as dust.

"Oh?"

"Mmm." He wanted to kiss her again. So much he could taste it.

She folded the tie then set it down beside her. "I take it you're not so adventuresome, then. That's why the trait appealed so much in Meriam."

Cally was clever, and quick. It'd taken him years to figure that out. "I was raised in an ultraconservative family. Very loving, very normal—no major dysfunctions, or anything even close. We were happy, Cally. And I didn't realize what a blessing that was until I met Meriam."

"She wasn't raised in a happy home." The hallway cooled suddenly. Chilled, Cally pulled up the afghan and scooted closer to Bryce.

"No, she wasn't. Would you like my sweater?"

Cally gave him a negative nod. "What was her life like?"

"A series of foster homes. So many she couldn't recall them all. Mrs. Wiggins was one of her foster mothers. The only one, according to Meriam, who wasn't out to make her a slave."

"Ah, so that's why you can't fire her."

He nodded. "You'd have loved Meriam, Cally. She was strong and beautiful—looked a lot like Suzie—and she did exactly as she pleased."

"And what was that?"

"Excuse me?"

"What exactly did she please to do?" Cally sent him a questioning look. "I mean, Mrs. Wiggins took care of the kids, right? So what did Meriam do?"

"She was a photojournalist for *Conservation Today*."

"Mmm, sounds like a job with a lot of travel."

"It was." He rubbed at his neck. "Actually, she was pretty much always away on assignment."

"Sounds lonely—if you're the one left behind."

He blinked, then blinked again. Looked at her through somber eyes. "Maybe. Sometimes. But when she was there, the whole house felt energized."

"That would make up for it." Cally lifted the hairbrush then began sweeping it down the lengths of her hair. "How'd the kids take her absences?"

"They were normal." Bryce watched the brush slide

down. "Meriam never stopped working. She went back on assignment weeks after the kids' births, so they were used to her not being around."

He then had been the primary parent and Meriam a woman who flitted through their lives on occasion. Sounded pretty one-sided. But then maybe Cally didn't yet have the full picture of their actual lives.

She paused brushing near her ear. "How did she die, Bryce? Was she ill?"

"No." He stared at her hand. "She was on assignment down in South America. She contracted a virus and, before the crew could get her to a hospital, she died." His hand shook. "She'd been dead three days before her magazine contacted us."

Cally looked back at him. "You're kidding."

"No, I'm not."

That truth hurt him; Cally could see that it did in his eyes. "Why?"

Bryce didn't want to answer her. God, but he didn't want to answer her. That radiated bitterly from him. "Meriam had left her editor as the person to notify in case of an emergency. A lot of people at the magazine didn't know she was married."

Cally's jaw went slack. "But she had you and three kids."

"It's harder for a woman with kids in her job, Cally. It wasn't that she didn't want anyone to know about us, it's that she didn't want to not be considered for plum assignments."

"I see." And boy did she. From the sounds of things, Meriam had had her cake and had eaten it, too. Her career had come first. Well, considering her foster-home experiences, Cally could understand that. Meriam felt she had only Meriam to depend on. And she couldn't risk even depending on the man she'd made her husband. Looking at what Gregory had done when Cally had put her own dreams on hold, entrusting her future to him, maybe Meriam'd had the right idea.

"The kids adored her. So did I." Bryce let his gaze drift up to the ceiling. Shadows danced on it.

Could he really mean that? He sounded as if he did, but

how could he? She'd given him so little. But evidently she'd given him just what he'd wanted or needed.

"Sometimes I still can't believe she's dead. I think it's just a long assignment and one day she'll just come home."

An insight flashed through Cally's mind. "But then you remember Suzie's dreams and you can't quite convince yourself that's true."

Cally glanced over at Bryce. He looked stricken. Under the afghan, she scooted around to face him, bunching the knitted fabric between them. Unsteady herself, she touched the back of his hand. It meant nothing. Not really. Only one human being understanding another's pain and reaching out to touch him because of it. "I'm sorry, Bryce."

Sadness cloaked him like a shroud, and she hated it. Hated seeing the pain etch his face, fill his eyes. She gave his fingers a reassuring squeeze, then pressed his hand against her cheek and, because there were no words that could comfort, she just held it there.

Bryce swallowed hard, and his heart thundered against her arm. Tears shimmered in her eyes, distorting her vision. Tears for him and for herself, because she knew how much loving had cost them both, and she resented knowing.

"Me, too, Cally." His voice gruff and raw, he closed his arms around her. "Me, too."

Not wanting to, feeling too vulnerable, knowing he felt the same way, she couldn't seem to help herself any more than he could help himself, and she hugged him tightly, rested her cheek against his shoulder. It felt solid, strong, able to hold up under life's trials. It felt good. "It's sad, isn't it?"

"What?"

"Love. It's supposed to be so joyful and yet it causes so much pain." She nuzzled at his neck with the tip of her nose, inhaling his cologne, the more pleasant scent of his skin. Men were such jerks. Why did they have to smell so good? "Does it ever work out for anyone—where they're happy, I mean?"

His cheek against her crown, he grunted. "Bad question to ask a divorce attorney."

She sighed. "Yeah, I guess it is." The warmth of his arms

was a haven she had no right to, no desire for, and she'd best remember that and avoid this hormone trap. She pulled back, then settled against her pillow. "I guess it's a fact. Like death and taxes."

"You're doing it again," he said. "Talking in riddles."

"Love." She picked up the brush from between their thighs then set it aside, next to his neatly folded tie. "It just doesn't work out."

"Once in a while it does." He bent his good knee, draped a hand over it, then stared at the thin band of white skin where he'd worn Meriam's ring.

"With who?" She guffawed, shivering at the hall's suddenly cooling again. What was wrong with the heat around here? And he'd been widowed two years. Why was the skin on his finger still white? Stupid question. He still loved her. And only recently had he taken off her ring. "I loved a man to distraction and ended up alone. You loved a woman to distraction and ended up alone. Marriage sure didn't work for either of us."

"I was happy. Content, too. Meriam didn't want to die. She just . . . died."

Cally frowned. Meriam had taken exactly what she wanted but, from the sounds of it, she'd not given back to the children, to Bryce, or to their relationship. Surely he saw that. And seeing it, how could he have been content?

He wasn't. He just hasn't realized it yet. Give him time, Cally. He will. Then you'll both understand.

The man's voice sounded clear, but Cally hadn't heard it—at least not with her ears. She'd heard it . . . internally.

Cold fear streaked up her spine. Her heart rate soared as if propelled by rocket fuel, and she instinctively scooted closer to Bryce.

"What's wrong?"

"Nothing," Cally croaked out. Good grief, what was happening here? Now she was hearing voices?

"I know when something is wrong, Cally, and something is wrong. You're shaking like a leaf. What's upset you?" Bryce scowled, clearly more at himself than at her. "Is it me talking about Meriam?"

"Of course not. I asked you to talk about her." Cally

looked down the hall, then up it. Shadowy, yet light enough to see that it was empty. But of course it would be, wouldn't it? She'd heard the voice internally. What in the name of heaven did that mean?

"What is it, then?"

He sounded wary and uncertain, and hating it that she'd made him feel either, much less both, she stroked his hand. "Nothing. Really." How could she explain hearing a man talking inside her head? She didn't understand it herself. She wasn't psychotic. Weren't they the only ones who heard voices inside their heads? No, she wasn't one of them. Oh hell, maybe she was one of them, because as much as she'd like to deny it, she couldn't't; she *had* heard the man.

Criminy. You're not psychotic, Cally. No, please. Don't scream. And don't be afraid. I swear I'm here to help you.

She shivered again, harder. *I didn't ask for your help. Who are you? What are you? Never mind. I don't want to know—and I don't want any help. Just—just go away.*

She waited a long minute, then another. But heard no more. The hall seemed to warm up suddenly. Or was it just her? Lord knew she had a ton of adrenaline shoving through her veins. The fight-or-flight urge held her in a death grip. Had the man gone, then? Had he really been here? What was he?

"Cally?"

Worry. Doubt. Fear. Hearing all that and more in Bryce's voice, she looked at him, confused, not sure what to think, and shaking to her toes, afraid to think at all. "Hmm?"

"You're not psychotic." He laced his hand with hers, his solemn gaze steady, his fingers stiff.

She tensed and barely stifled a gasp, certain she'd misunderstood him. "What?"

"You're not psychotic."

Oh, God. The truth thrummed through her veins. "You heard him, too?"

"Only that he was here to help you."

Her heart pounded hard, knocking against her ribs, threatening to beat out of her chest. "Who do you think he is? How did he do that? Talk to me internally? And how did you hear it?"

"I'm not sure." Bryce dropped his voice to a whisper. "But T.J., a friend of mine in New Orleans, mentioned a—" No, Bryce couldn't tell her that. She'd think he was nuts. He couldn't believe he was even considering it true. But he was. And, well, what else could it be? T.J. had sworn he hadn't been goofing around, but Bryce hadn't believed him—then. Now, he didn't know what to believe. Could there be another explanation? One easier to accept?

"A *what*?" Cally pushed, squeezing his hand in a death grip.

He couldn't hold her gaze, and let his drop to the pulse throbbing at her throat. "I'd rather not say."

"I'm sure you would. But I want to know."

"Do you?" Bryce looked her straight in the eye. "Are you sure?"

Uncertainty crept through her. Was she? It had to be something weird. Something abnormal. Did she want to know? Gooseflesh prickled her arms. Cally rubbed at it, though her palms were damp. "Not really."

"Until you do, why don't we forget this?"

"Good idea." She set her jaw. "Cowardly, but I'll curse myself later for it. Right now, shameful as it is, I need comforting. With everything else, I just don't need to deal with something weird, too. I just . . . don't."

He stroked her jaw, sent her a look laced with compassion. She thought she might just love him for that.

His stomach in knots, his armpits damp with sweat, Bryce talked on, softly, about the kids, about mundane things that had she not been upset likely would have bored Cally glassy-eyed. A good fifteen minutes crept by before she seemed to calm down. "Better?"

"Yes." She nodded. "I'm far from okay with this, but I'm definitely better."

"Good." He gave her fingertips a reassuring squeeze, for some reason feeling uncharacteristically happy because she'd told him her feelings. She hadn't hedged or denied or withheld from him, and that openness couldn't have been easy for her. Trusting a man even that much had to be sheer hell. Yet she'd done it, and she'd trusted not just any man, but him. Satisfaction warmed his chest and tightened his throat.

He pecked a tender kiss of gratitude to her temple. "Can you answer a question for me?"

"I've been answering questions for you most of the last three days," Cally groused. "Damn. When you look at me like that, how can I refuse? How can any woman?"

He smiled. He didn't want to, but couldn't help himself. Maybe he was improving on the impression front after all. "Will you answer one more?"

Cally sighed. Boyish charm. The man had truckloads of it. Sophisticated and refined, but it was there nonetheless, and oh, so powerful. "Maybe. If you ask me nicely."

"Excuse me?"

He looked confused, and she suspected it likely that he was confused. But the listing of things she liked about him was growing steadily, and it would be better for them both if he understood something very basic about her now. The sooner the better. "I don't need sweet lies and romantic gestures from any man. In fact, I don't want them." She straightened her shoulders and pulled at the handle of her brush. "But when a man—any man—asks me for something, I do want courtesy and to be treated with respect. I will have that, Bryce. So if you want something, anything at all from me, then you have to ask me nicely."

"I'll do my best." He raised the edge of the afghan then tucked it down at her side. "Would you mind telling me why you avoid mirrors?"

That she hadn't expected. Her face went hot and her palms damp. "Why would I do that?"

"I don't know." Bryce dropped his voice to just above a whisper and looked at her from under his lashes, lowered to half-mast. "But I'd like to know, Cally."

She didn't answer. Couldn't bring herself to answer. He looked at her like a woman wants a man to look at her. If he knew the truth, he wouldn't. Oh, she wasn't deluding herself. He was still in love with his dead wife. Or—Cally remembered the man's whisper—Bryce thought he was. But even if it was just a man/woman thing without the emotional entanglement—which she certainly didn't want any part of anyway—she liked those looks. They made her feel less ugly. Less marred. Less like a failure. When a body's self-esteem is down in a ditch it's hard to find courage. And when a woman's starting over at thirty-two with everything she never wanted, her self-esteem has to hike up to be down in a ditch.

"Cally?" Bryce cupped her chin with his fingertips then lifted, urging her to look at him. "I noticed. So have the kids."

He knew. Her mouth went dry as dust. Damn it, he knew. She couldn't think of anything to say. Nothing to redeem herself in his eyes.

His fingertips tightened on her chin. "I know you do it. What I don't understand is, *why?*"

"Do you want the truth?" Her insides quivering like molded gelatin, she tossed his words back at him. "Are you sure?"

"Yeah, I do."

"Why?" So he too could ridicule her?

"I don't know," he said honestly. "We have a lot in common. I think you got a raw deal with Gregory and I hate what he's done to you. I like you, Cally. Aren't those reasons enough?"

He liked her? *Liked her?* "You don't even know me."

"Oh, but I do." His expression softened and his gaze warmed, setting his irises afire with sparkles of silver flecks. "I know a lot about you, Cally."

"You don't."

"Sweetheart, I do." Bryce gentled his tone. "I know you didn't know so much as Jeremy's name yet you jumped to his defense. I know you didn't get upset at Suzie's remark about your maybe being her new mom. And"—he braced himself to feel the brunt of her anger—"I know you visit a stranger's grave in Biloxi every Sunday and bring her a yellow carnation because you don't want her to ever feel forgotten."

Cally gasped. "How did you know that?"

"About Mary Beth Ladner?"

"Yes!" That was private. Something she'd only shared with her family. Her parents, and . . . "Gregory." She clenched her hand into a fist against her thigh. "That sorry son of—"

"An animal cracker," Bryce interrupted.

"I can't believe he told you about Mary Beth." Cally's eyes glittered with anger.

"Honey, calm down." Bryce cupped her arms firmly, then loosened his fingers, easing his hold. "I love that about you. About Mary Beth, I mean."

She went perfectly still. Her expression went lax and the rage drained right out of her. He loved it? How could he love anything about her?

"Don't you see how special you are?"

She looked at him as if he'd lost his mind.

If it weren't so heartbreaking it'd be funny. She didn't see. Not at all. But then Cally was a giver, not a taker. She likely never would see how special this would be perceived to be by others. "Honey, it's a rare thing for a woman—hell, for anyone—to give and keep on giving when they get nothing in return. How long have you been going to Mary Beth Ladner's grave? Since you were a kid, right?"

"You're wrong."

"You haven't been going there since you were a kid?"

"Not about that." Cally slumped back against the cool wall, too weary to fight. The first rays of dawn crept through the window and slid over the floor. "About Mary Beth. She gives back. She always has. Maybe not directly, but indirectly."

"The woman is dead. You never met her. How can she give back?"

"I'm tired, Bryce." She swiped a trembling hand over her face. "I don't want to talk about this anymore."

Bryce stared at her for a long moment, debating on whether or not to push this right now. Her lids were puffy and faint shadows tinged the skin under her eyes. She *was* tired, and upset. A reprieve was in order. "Okay. Okay." He leaned back against the wall, then urged her to him with a hand to her shoulder. She snuggled down then rested her cheek against his chest. God, but she felt good beside him. What did he do with his hand? It wanted to follow naturally, to circle around to her back and rest against her warm skin, but . . . Why shouldn't it? He buried yet another disloyal-to-

Meriam pang of guilt and let it happen—then tensed, awaiting Cally's reaction.

She let out a soft sigh and settled against his side, her arm flat against his ribs, her hand dangling and fingertips brushing his side. "Bryce?"

She expected him to talk? Now? When feeling so much? Sounds. Sounds would be infinitely easier to form than words. "Hmm?"

"I like you, too."

His heart swelled. "I know, Cally."

"Even if you are a little on the stuffy side."

He gave her a solid frown. "Am I really that stuffy?"

She cocked a brow at him, let her gaze slide down to his crisp shirt and knife-creased slacks.

"Hell, I guess I am." He curled her closer, let out a mock sigh of frustration, then smiled above her head. Her hair felt soft against his bearded jaw. Silky. "I think I'm flunking on this impression bit in a bad way. But at least I'm honest."

"I like that, too," she said softly. "A lot."

Yeah, after Gregory, Bryce guessed she would rate honesty even more important.

"I don't like liking anything about you, though."

He could take that to the bank; no doubt about it. And why that had him grinning like a fool instead of miffed at her didn't seem wise to ponder. "I know that, too."

"Do you dislike liking me as much as I dislike liking you?"

This conversation sounded ridiculous. But it wasn't. It cut close to the bone. For both of them. Meriam would have laughed at him for that. She'd have said or done exactly as she pleased and given him her in-your-face "So there." One thing about her, she never failed to back up her words with her attitude. He'd liked that about her. And yet Cally's softer, more vulnerable response affected him on a deeper level. Gut deep. Maybe because Meriam never had needed him and, if only for the moment, Cally did. He liked the way being needed made him feel. Necessary. Important. Valued. "Yeah, I do," he confessed. "I dislike liking you every bit as much as you dislike liking me. Maybe even more." She hadn't been content in her marriage. But he had been—hadn't he?

As if relieved to hear his grumpy response, Cally sighed deeper, then toyed with the third button on his shirt, scraping it with her nail. "Being lonely royally sucks."

"Yeah." Staring at the baseboard, he felt his chest go tight. "It really does."

They fell quiet, and Bryce slid into memories of living alone. BM: before Meriam memories. AM: after Meriam memories. Some were pleasant. Many were not.

Had she ever needed him? Really needed him? Valued him and thought him necessary? He'd mattered to her; of course, he had. But had he been essential, or merely convenient?

Uneasy, he forced himself to open his mind and remember, though what he found hardly comforted him. A dull ache throbbed in his chest. He shut down the memories. Later, he'd think about them. When he wasn't feeling soothed by holding Cally in his arms.

After a while, they talked in spurts. Bryce loved the feel of that. The comfortable silences. The whispered sharing of everything, and all kinds of little nothings. Talking freely about their troubles, his fears about Suzie and the other kids, and even daring to share an occasional secret or dream; things he'd not dared to think about, much less to talk about, ever before.

Cally lifted her head from his shoulder. "If you could have anything in the world—anything at all—what would it be?"

He looked deeply into her eyes and spoke straight from his heart. "Peace."

She frowned.

"You don't like liking that, either."

"No." She lay back against his shoulder, sounding as grouchy as Wiggins when flaunting her infractions list. "I surely don't."

He cocked his head, rested his cheek against her hair. It smelled of coconut shampoo. Lyssie would love it. So did he. "Why?"

"Because that's my dream. I want peace. More than anything, I want peace."

"And courage." He smoothed a wrinkle from the shoulder

of her robe. The fabric felt soft, touchable, like Cally herself.

"Yeah." She sighed. "That, too."

"You'll get them, Cally. Both of them. I know you will."

"Thank you."

"Why do I have the feeling that 'thank you' isn't because you believe me, or because you appreciate the support."

"Because it wasn't, I didn't, and I don't."

More riddles. "Then why are you thanking me?"

"Because being condescending and offering me platitudes gives me something to hate about you. For that, I am grateful."

"Ah, the not liking, liking list again." He loosened his limbs; now that he had a grasp on this, he could relax. Finally, he was getting a fix on how her mind worked. Not an easy task since Gregory had effectively tossed in a few wicked twists. "You're welcome, then."

"You're smiling." She frowned up at him. "You shouldn't smile when someone says they hate something about you, Counselor. Didn't they teach you that in Law 101 or wherever they teach you how not to tick off clients?"

"I cut class that day." He rubbed their noses, then sat back against the wall and closed his eyes.

"But? Go ahead. I hear it lurking, so you might as well say it."

She'd be riled for the rest of the night. Still, he couldn't resist the urge to tease her a little. "But that someone has to look to find something to hate about you is darn nice."

"It's not nice." She grunted. "It's godawful."

"Whatever you say."

"I say, it's godawful." She snatched at the quilt and tugged it up under her chin. "And it is." Sliding closer, she fitted herself snugly against his side, laid her cheek against his upper arm, then curled her fingers around his sleeve, just above his elbow. "Terribly godawful. And don't you dare dispute me on that."

"I wouldn't dare." He tried his best to sound serious, but he couldn't wipe the smile from his lips. He wanted to kiss the upset right out of her but he couldn't. She'd given him that one-kiss rule and he had to turn things around so she was the one who broke it. So instead, he closed his eyes and let his head loll back against the wall. Her stewing might do her some good. Especially if he taunted her a little to coerce her to change her mind and kiss him again. That was a pleasant thought that conjured patience. And her having to look for something to hate about him was wonderful, worth savoring, and that was that.

The morning settled over them, and a gentle awareness warmed inside him. It baffled him at first, then he finally identified it. The lack of dread. With Cally in his arms, he didn't dread the morning, or the night.

That was a first, and he both blessed and cursed it. Grateful and guilty didn't mix well in a man's emotions or rest easy on his soul. Since Meriam had died, he'd gotten through the days—working, taking care of the kids, keeping up with the house, the office, and Mrs. Wiggins's resignations—but the nights had been difficult. They'd been hell, pure and simple. Meriam hadn't been home many nights, yet he'd known she'd be coming home eventually, and that had made them different. After her death, the nights just seemed to stretch and yawn before him. Endless. Empty. He'd hated each of them a little more than he'd hated the night before it. Until tonight.

Until Cally.

"Bryce?" She whispered against his chest, sounding as if she half hoped he was asleep and wouldn't answer.

"Hmm?"

"I swore I wasn't going to tell you this but . . . well, what does it matter? You already know most of my flaws from Gregory, so what's one more?"

Bryce started to interrupt. Gregory was the one flawed. Not Cally.

She plowed on, as though if Bryce stopped her, she wouldn't be able to start again, to say what she wanted said. "I do avoid mirrors."

He couldn't believe she'd admitted it. Humbled, he forced himself not to react emotionally and unnerve her. "Why?"

She stared fixedly at his shirt button. "Because when I look in them, I don't like what I see. Gregory used to . . . make me look, and he'd say . . . awful things. I learned to hate them."

Gregory had done even more damage than suspected. Swallowing his anger at that, Bryce managed to keep his tone soft and nonthreatening. "If you don't like what you see, then you have to change it, honey. Not avoid it."

"I—I want to change it. That's why I came up here. Well, actually not here, but it's how I wound up here instead of in Nova Scotia." She let out a sigh reeking of frustration. "I wanted to change. That's what counts. I wanted to, and I've been determined to try. But now, well, I don't think I can do it."

She sounded so fragile. Helpless. Hopeless. "Honey, why?"

Rocking back, she looked up at him. Sadness and tears that dwelled soul-deep glimmered in her eyes. "Because the me I loved . . . died."

She had to mean her feminine side, her spirit and sensuality. Damn Gregory Tate for doing this to her. Just damn him.

Problem was, how did Bryce fix the problem?

You can't just tell her. She won't believe you.

The man's voice. Bryce swallowed hard, slid his gaze to Cally. She hadn't stiffened or reacted.

She can't hear me.

Oh, great. Bryce cringed. *Now I'm psychotic.*

No such luck. The man harrumphed. *You don't get to slip into insanity. You're doomed to toughing out life sane.*

Why that response eased Bryce's mind when he should be scared stiff, he didn't know. Maybe because T.J. had warned him. Maybe because Bryce sensed the man really had come to help. Or maybe because Bryce knew he needed help . . . desperately.

He glanced down at Cally. Her eyes were closed and her breathing steady. Clearly, she was sound asleep and not hearing any of this. How had she dozed off so quickly?

I, er, assisted her a wee bit.

You didn't hurt her.

Of course not.

Though he couldn't see the man, Bryce blinked, then blinked again. *You've got to be Miss Hattie's soldier.*

Ah, T.J. was thorough in briefing you on me. Ordinarily, I'd oppose, but—

He thought I had enough worries. I didn't need to add to them, trying to figure out you're a ghost, friendly, and I'm not crazy.

I'm inclined to agree.

I'm grateful. The temperature had dropped substantially. Cally still slept; her chest lifted and fell in a smooth rhythm. Bryce tugged at the afghan and tucked in her shoulder. *You're sure she's okay?*

Positive. How about you?

How was he? Bryce was afraid to really think about it. Talking with a ghost, for God's sake. *I'm okay.*

And you accept what I am?

I suppose I have to accept it. Unless you're of a mind to change.

I wish I could, but I'm afraid I can't.

Genuine regret. Boy, did Bryce recognize the sound. Empathetic, he lowered his gaze to the floor. *I'm sorry, for both you and Miss Hattie.*

Me, too. But fate has its own design and we just have to accept it.

I guess we do. That, or let it drive us crazy.

I'm rather partial to sanity. It has its down side, like everything else, but it beats the socks off its alternative.

I agree.

I am Miss Hattie's soldier, but for ease, you can call me Tony.

Tony? Suzie's Tony? Surprise zipped up Bryce's backbone, shot through his limbs.

Guilty.

How did she react to hearing you? The kid must have been scared witless.

She was fine about it. She heard and saw me. Tony chuckled. *Children are wonderful. Everything is strange to them so they don't often get upset at seeing someone they can see through, so to speak. Don't worry, Bryce. Suzie was totally accepting, and I have to admit I was more than grateful for that. Sometimes acceptance is elusive, if you know what I mean.*

I'm glad she was okay about it. She's suffering through some challenges and she really doesn't need to be upset.

She's not upset. You have my word on it. If she had been, I'd have pulled a cease and desist immediately. I'm not into scaring kids. Or anyone else, for that matter.

I'm glad to hear it. With Suzie it's hard to tell, but she hasn't seemed rattled. Actually, she's seemed happy, and kind of secretive. She's mentioned you—

A million times in the past three days. Yes, I know.

Are you responsible for her not dreaming?

She is dreaming, Bryce.

But—

She's dreaming, but she's not alone. That's the difference.

You've been there with her.

Yes, I have.

Bryce's eyes stung and tight bands of gratitude cinched down around his chest, making it hard to pull in breaths. *Thank you.*

You're welcome. Tony cleared his throat. *Now, we've got a dilemma to resolve with your Cally Tate.*

My Cally Tate? She's not my— Bryce halted mid-sentence. The woman lay sleeping in his arms. It sounded ridiculous even to him to deny that at the moment she was his. And, as guilty as he felt in admitting it, there was a tiny flicker inside him that kind of liked the idea.

He squelched it. There was no place in his life for a love interest. He'd been there and done that. What he needed wasn't a love interest, but a mother—for the kids.

Yet he couldn't not care about Cally or her plight. What kind of man could?

One like Gregory Tate.

Bryce squeezed his eyes shut. *Can you hear my every thought, Tony?*

I'm afraid so. And before you get on a high horse and think it's rough on you, let me tell you that it's no picnic for me, either. If a body is inside this house, then I hear every whisper, word, or thought.

You can't turn it off?

No. And typically, that's okay. But there are times—like with the battleaxe and her views on discipline, and with Batty

Beaulah Favish, the nosy woman next door—I'd give my eye teeth for the ability to shut down.

Acceptance, right?

Right. Beats insanity. Now, about Cally.

Do you know how to fix the problem?

Maybe. Maybe not. Women are tough to figure.

Hell, I was hoping I could look forward to that getting easier.

Tony chuckled. *Sorry to shatter your dreams, but not understanding women is universal.*

The worst of it with Cally is that she is desirable. But I agree with you that I can't just tell her.

She wouldn't believe you, or any man. Not about that.

Why should she? For fourteen years, Gregory Tate's pounded it into her head and heart that she's not desirable—or lovable.

True. True.

So what do I do, then?

Do you really want to help her?

Bryce looked down into her sleeping face, resting against his chest. Her lips parted, her cheek red from pressing against his shoulder. Protective feelings surged from deep inside him to the surface. Like the kids, she was fragile, vulnerable. Unlike the kids, she was a beautiful woman who rallied memories in him that he was more than a father. He owed her for that. And more. *Yeah, I really want to help her.*

To get her to believe it, you're going to have to show her.

Vulnerable. *Oh, God. Wait a minute. I know you're not talking an affair here.*

No, I'm not.

Then what exactly are you asking me to do?

Let her see how she affects you. Tear down your internal guard rails and just let her see. Women have this sense of knowing things. Cally needs to see your reactions and run her sincerity check on them. When she does and she sees you're sincere, then she'll know she's lovable because you'll have shown her.

You're asking me to love her? Crazy. Impossible.

I'm asking you to let her see the truth, whatever it is.

I can't. I would, I want to help her, but I can't do that, Tony. I just can't.

Don't panic. You can handle it. If you couldn't you wouldn't be here.

It's not handling it that worries me.

What is it, then?

It's liking handling it.

Meriam's gone, Bryce. She's content. And she wants you and the children to be content, too.

She's content? With—without us?

Acceptance.

Bryce let that truth settle in, not sure what he was supposed to be feeling, but sure as hell certain anger wasn't it. Yet he was angry. He missed her, envisioned her to get through his days, relived their lives together to get through his nights. And she was content without him? Without any of them?

How was your life together? Really?

Bryce's mind whirled, slipped back to a celebration dinner years ago. One with Meriam and the kids at the Court of Two Sisters, Meriam's favorite restaurant, down in the French Quarter.

Suzie nicked her glass and splashed milk onto Meriam's cuff. Her face mottled red. Suzie's bleached white. "I'm sorry, Meriam," she'd said, her voice trembling, her eyes wide with fear.

Bryce hated seeing and hearing both, and interceded. "It was an accident, sweetheart. Meriam knows that." He looked over, silently prodded her to give their daughter a soothing word.

She didn't. Meriam blotted at the spot, then tossed her napkin onto the table. "I've got to go."

She always had to go. Whenever anything was less than perfect, whenever there was the slightest ruffle. She'd just . . . leave.

Bending, she gathered her purse. "I'll be back in a couple weeks," she told Bryce, then swung her gaze to Suzie. "Try to improve your table manners while I'm gone."

And she'd walked out of the restaurant without a backward

glance, leaving them sitting there, without farewell kisses or hugs or even a token "I'll miss you."

What had Bryce felt? Really?

Relief. Anger at her demanding perfection in them, but even more so, he'd felt relief that she was gone and they could all breathe easier again.

It was always that way, Bryce realized. He missed her, honestly. But he was always relieved by the immediate drop in tension in him and the M & M's when Meriam left.

Tony claimed Bryce's attention. *That was a more accurate assessment of your marriage, Bryce, and of how life with Meriam was for the family.*

She was never really a part of us. That hurt. Deeply. Yet it had a cleansing effect, too. As long as Bryce lived, he'd never forget the fear in Suzie's eyes that day. Or his own anger that Meriam didn't see it and do something to reassure Suzie and put an end to her fear. But she hadn't. Maybe she couldn't. Maybe that was asking too much from her, after the life she'd been forced to live. Still, Suzie was an innocent, and yet she'd paid the price for Meriam's not resolving the problem. And Bryce was every bit as guilty. He'd run interference, but not insisted on a resolution. He'd understood, and suffered, too.

Yes, Counselor. You all suffered. But now it's time to let go of that and of your fantasies of a marriage that honestly never existed. Which, incidentally, brings us back to Miss Tate. Are you going to show her?

Reeling, Bryce forced himself to make the mental shift to Cally. He owed her. *Yeah. Yeah, I'm going to show her.*

You've got to be sincere, Bryce. She'll know, if you're not sincere. Women have radar on that.

If I couldn't be sincere, then I wouldn't do it. Hell, Tony, look at her. Who couldn't be sincere?

Valid point. But I had to be sure. I don't want her hurt anymore.

Neither did Bryce. *Tony?*

Hmm?

Thanks for the assist. I'm a little out of practice at taking cold, hard looks. It's been a while since I've been close to a woman, too.

Tony sighed. *Relax, Bryce. The heart never forgets.*

The heart has nothing to do with this.

Ah, I see. Justice, eh?

Yeah, justice.

After Tate, I agree, she's due a little.

Yes, she is. Pride, too. And not from a bottle.

I'll leave her in your capable hands, then.

Tony had gone. Bryce sensed it, and the heat flooding the hallway confirmed it. Talking with a ghost was odd, but it didn't seem odd when it was happening. Only afterward, when thinking about it. Maybe it'd be healthiest to just not think about it. To just be grateful T.J.'s friend was helping Suzie and, through Bryce, Cally.

Cally opened her eyes, stared up at Bryce, then pressed her hand flat against his chest. "What's wrong?"

He shouldn't tell her. He knew he shouldn't, but inside him the dam broke. "Meriam's content without us."

"What?"

"She's content without us."

Cally frowned. "He told you that, didn't he?"

Knowing she meant Tony, Bryce nodded.

"I'm sorry." She feathered a hand over Bryce's jaw. His beard crackled against her palm. "I'm so sorry."

"I should be happy she's at peace. I know I should, but—"

"But you're still angry with her for leaving you. Angry because you've got to deal with Suzie and her dreams and the kids not having a mom, and everything else."

"I guess so."

"Bryce?"

Thoughtful, mulling over all she'd said, he answered with a "Hmm?"

"What did she do for you and the kids?"

Bryce opened his mouth to answer, then realized he had no idea what to say.

After a day of sunshine and a trip with the kids to Boothbay Harbor and the train museum, Bryce felt comfortably tired. He got the kids ready for bed, settled in, and Miss Hattie had gone up to bed a half hour ago, still looking disturbed and swearing she was fine. Maybe Vic would know what was wrong with her. In the morning, if she didn't seem better, Bryce would talk with Vic about it. Or maybe with Tony. He'd know. He said he knew everything here. More at ease about Miss Hattie now that he had a plan, Bryce took up his seat on the hallway floor.

Cally joined him. He schooled the pleasure of her being there from his voice and expression, then looked up at her. "This is becoming a nightly ritual."

She dropped her pillow and the afghan onto the floor. "Guess so. Why waste all your worrying time alone when you can have company, I always say."

The opportunity to begin his campaign to prove to Cally she was a desirable and lovable woman had come. "We could do something other than worry."

She grunted. "Is that a hormone call?"

"Well, it wasn't, though the idea holds merit."

"Don't start."

A bubble of pleasure tickled his stomach. "Actually, it was a suggestion that rather than just worry, we can worry and see what we can fix."

"Ah, solutions." She sat down beside him, flipped the pillow behind her back, then fingered closed the gap in her robe at her breasts. "I always did like solution-oriented men."

"And you didn't like liking them, right?"

"Right." She grinned. "I brought us a snack." She dug under the afghan for a bag of potato chips. "You guys are killing me with all this healthy food."

"Your junk food low-level light is on, eh?"

"Yeah." Her eyes twinkled. She crunched down on a chip.

His breath caught in his throat. "You're so pretty."

"Knock it off, Bryce."

"Seriously."

"Would you stop?" She munched down on another crunchy chip, then dipped her hand back into the bag. It crinkled. "You know I hate that."

"Yes, but you love having things to hate, and I am trying to elevate my impression rating."

"Stop that, too." She twisted the bag, tied it closed with a twistee, then set it aside. "I'm serious." Brushing her hands together, she flicked off clinging grains of salt.

Not this time. He tossed back the edge of the afghan, grabbed his cane, then hauled himself to his feet. He held out a hand to Cally. "Come with me."

"Where?"

He held her gaze, his own unwavering. "To your room."

"Bryce, I'm not going to make love with—"

"No, Cally." He grasped her hand and urged her to her feet. "Just come on. Trust me."

Trust me.

Gregory's voice, his image, flooded her mind. On their wedding day, then later, long after he'd become a doctor and it had become Cally's turn to have her dream. And in her mind, she was there, in their bedroom, standing naked before the mirrored closet door with Gregory behind her, his hand twisted in her hair, his face red and contorted by anger.

"Trust me," he spat at her. "You're not the woman I married anymore. Look at you. Damn you, look at yourself." He jerked her hair, forced her to look into the mirror. "You've let yourself go, Caline. Just the sight of you repulses me."

And she'd looked, seen herself through his eyes, and his damnation seeped into her pores as sterling truth. *Ugly. Ugly. Ugly.*

He shoved her against the mirror, his fist at her back. The glass felt cold against her face and her breath fogged it, obscuring the reflection of her fearful eyes, and she prayed so hard she'd slip through its slick surface and cease to exist. Cease to be condemned by Gregory. Cease to see herself as the pitiful shadow of a woman she'd become.

"Cally?" Bryce whispered.

Trust me. Cally gulped in a deep breath. Two little words. Seven little letters. But boy, they inspired fear like no others. She'd given trust. And she'd seen it ripped to shreds. Violated. Discarded as worthless. All that done by a man who supposedly loved her. Why on earth would she risk trusting a man she knew damn well didn't love her?

An image of Suzie threaded through Cally's mind. Her

tiny chin lifted, her trusting gaze lifted to her father's. Her cupping her hand at his ear, whispering her secrets to him in the kitchen, knowing he was angry about chasing the frog and sliding in the oatmeal. And Jeremy. Jeremy not fearful, but remorseful, about the frog, about the bees. Knowing he'd done wrong, but not afraid of his father's reaction. And even little Lyssie. Mimicking her dad's "Damn" when she clearly knew it was wrong to curse. And Bryce's bending low to face his daughter in that high chair, finger pointed and voice firm, telling her, "No. Animal crackers."

His children trusted him. And though neither a child nor able to trust her own judgment, Cally could trust theirs. The kids had a far better track record than she did in the love and trust departments.

Her insides rattling like the marbles Jeremy stuffed in his pockets, Cally stared at Bryce for a long moment. Expectant, but not threatening. Patient, but eyes shining with hope. Caring, not carnal. Unable to resist, she prayed she wouldn't regret this, gave her hands a final salt-ridding swipe, rose to her feet, then placed her hand in his.

Moonlight streamed into the Great White Room through the turret windows. The disheveled bed looked inviting and, though Bryce had been without a woman for two years and was for the first time since Meriam's death entertaining thoughts of making love with a woman again with only the tiniest twinges of guilt nipping at desire's heels, he knew the woman had to be special—someone like Cally. And for Cally, this wasn't the right time.

He walked past the bench at the end of the bed, over near the desk to the cheval mirror.

As soon as Cally realized his intent, she went floor-plank stiff, slowed her steps, then began dragging her feet. "Bryce, I don't want to look into that mirror."

"I know you don't." He urged her on. "But you need to, Cally. You came to Seascape to find the you Gregory Tate stole. Looking at who you are is the first step."

"I'm not ready." She squared her jaw.

God, but she was beautiful. All rumpled from her stint on the floor, she looked tangled and sleep-tossed, though he knew as well as she that she'd not slept a wink. "You won't ever be ready. It's too big a leap. You've got to just take one step at a time. Think of little victories."

"More like big defeats." She stood fast. Resolute.

"Beats standing still. Winning or losing, you're living. Standing still, you're just taking up space."

"Are you recommending I check out, Counselor?"

"Not hardly, sweetheart. I'm recommending you check in." He moved to stand directly in front of her, between her and the mirror, then clasped her arms and looked down into her eyes. "I don't want to hurt you. I don't want you to hurt. I just want you to see all the good in you I see. There's a beautiful woman inside here"—he touched a fingertip to her chest—"and she's screaming to be let out. You hear her calling. If you didn't, you wouldn't be here. But you have to answer her call. You have to choose."

A tear rolled down Cally's cheek. The glaring moonlight caught it and it sparkled. "I can't."

"You can."

Her voice cracked. "I don't have the courage. He was so . . . vicious. I—I can't forget."

Gregory. Something inside Bryce shattered. He walked his fingers up her arms, circled her back, then pulled her to him. "Cally," he breathed deeply into her hair. "What has he done to you? What have you let him do to you?"

"Let him? You don't *let* someone take you apart, Bryce. They're stronger and sharper—sneakier. They snip away at you, bit by bit, until one day you wake up and find out there's nothing left. Everything good in you is just . . . gone."

"You died." Now, he understood what she'd meant.

"Yes." A shudder quaked through her. "I died."

Rage roared through Bryce. A rage like he'd suffered only twice before. On Meriam's death. On Suzie's first dream. In both he'd felt helpless, frustrated, out of control. But not this time. This time, he wasn't powerless to *do* something. This time he could act.

He cupped Cally's face in his big hands. She looked up at him, so much pain in her eyes he feared he'd fall down under the burden of it. The need to kiss her overwhelmed him. He didn't stop to wonder why, or to remind himself of his stance on her one-kiss rule—that she be the one to break it—just lowered his lips to hers and kissed her thoroughly, letting her feel the riot of emotions raging through him, showing her with lips and tongue and the grazing of teeth, with fingertips gone from gentle to rough to gentle again, kneading and needing, reaffirming that the flesh they touched was not that of a courageless corpse but that of a living, breathing woman with a lot to offer a man with the vision to see beneath her pain.

He tasted her surprise, felt her tense even more under his hands, and he felt her fury. Her own outrage at feeling all she felt, at suffering her own riot of emotions, and of her not knowing exactly what to do with those feelings now that they had been aroused and unleashed.

He separated their fused mouths, softened his touch. His hand trembled on her back. He let it glide over her robe, amazed at how rough the soft fabric now felt against his fingertips, followed the contour of her body from beneath her breasts to her sides, then down her ribs to the swell of her hips. "Cally, you're beautiful," he whispered against her mouth. "To me, you are so beautiful."

"Don't lie to me, Bryce. Please."

"I'm not." He touched their lips, exhaled, feeling their mingling breaths fan over his face. "I swear, I'm not."

The fury in them faded, and the baser awareness of scents and sounds and textures, of man and woman and sensual instincts, surfaced. He wanted to hold her, to be held by her, to feel her against him, to be inside her. He wanted the demons robbing them both of peace to wither and die. For Cally to know she was very much alive. For her to know that, with her, he felt very much alive.

Not like a lonely widower.

Not like a father.

Like a man.

It'd been a long time since he'd thought of himself that way. And just now it seemed too long. "Cally, I—" His heart too full, he couldn't find the words.

She didn't need them. She eased up onto her toes and curled her arms around his neck. Her eyes wide and luminous, reflected in the moonlight all the fear he felt. ''Being lonely royally sucks,'' she whispered, then kissed his lips.

Loneliness had nothing to do with it. Desire, yes. But not loneliness. Yet maybe they both needed the lie. His mind reeling, the taste of her lingering on his lips, he let out a shuddery breath and fused their hips, silently cursing zipper and placket, her soft flowing robe that separated their skins, keeping distant those parts of them this awakening had yearning to join. He relinquished control of the kiss, let himself spiral down into the alluring web of the sensual, and gloried in her coming with him. And she had come with him. Her breathing had grown rapid, ragged, lifting her breasts against his chest. Her hands explored him, learning his feel and clearly liking it. And her lips had grown eager, inviting and eager.

When she parted their mouths, she met his gaze, her eyes as turbulent as his insides. And from somewhere soul-deep, the words he needed came. ''You're alive, Cally.''

''Yes,'' she whispered gratingly. ''God help me, I'm alive.''

He'd expected her to run from the truth. She hadn't. He'd like to think that the reason she hadn't run had something to do with her kissing him specifically, but it didn't. It was the awakening. Maybe not just any man could have aroused the feminine spirit in Cally Tate, but Bryce wasn't arrogant enough to believe he could be the only man to arouse it. For some reason, though, he'd been the chosen one. And that reason could be no more than proximity. Whatever it was, he was grateful for it. Because while he'd been the means through which Cally Tate had awakened—his gift to her—she'd also awakened and given a gift to him. She'd reminded him that he was more than a father. And if a twinge of guilt, of feeling he was betraying Meriam by holding and kissing and caring about Cally Tate, made fuzzy the edges of his own awakening, then he'd willingly suffer them, knowing Meriam was content. He'd gratefully suffer them. Because at that moment, Bryce Richards, father and man, realized that, while Cally Tate thought she lacked courage, in truth, she didn't. In truth, he held in his arms the bravest woman he'd ever known.

Chapter 7

Spineless.

Cally stood in the bathroom, a thick white towel in her hands, her gaze darting from the antique brass shell-shape soap dish to the tan marble countertop that the light had tinged pink. She had to be the most spineless woman in the world.

The mirror was there. Waiting. It ran wall to wall above the vanity. She wanted to lift her gaze and look right into it, right into her own eyes, but she just couldn't do it. Bryce had been right about her never being ready—and he'd been wrong. She might one day muster the courage to look, but she'd never again feel strong enough or secure enough with who she'd become to look at herself and like what she saw.

Think of little victories.

"No, Bryce," she whispered aloud. Shaking all over, she broke into a cold sweat. Her chest went tight, as if held in a vise, and she clutched the towel to it then squeezed her eyes shut. "Big defeats."

If only one has the courage to believe, miracles can happen beside a dreamswept sea.

Suzie's words. Cally covered her ears. Why did they haunt her? They were Suzie's dreams, not Cally's. Suzie's. "Not for me," she told herself. "For me, miracles don't happen, and dreams become nightmares." She'd learned that the hard way, hadn't she?

Suzie hadn't. Though tortured every night with the same

nightmare for two years, Suzie hadn't learned that, nor had she stopped believing in miracles.

Cally forked her fingers through her hair. Maybe children were more resilient. Maybe Suzie was stronger. Cally didn't know the reason, but whatever it was, it hadn't gotten Suzie through anything unscathed. The dreams continued. And the child in her *had* died.

The woman in Cally who dared to dream had died, too. Like Meriam, that woman hadn't wanted to, she'd just died.

For Cally, there'd be no little victories. No miracles. Only defeats and nightmares. She had to accept that.

And Bryce's kiss? Had that too been a nightmare?

The memory of it warmed her all over. She loved and hated it and its memory. Bryce's kiss was the worst kind of nightmare because it made promises that would be broken. It whispered to her soul, said, "I'm here, Cally Tate. I'm an attractive and loving man and I think you're beautiful. I'm with you."

But that wasn't true. Time would prove those promises lies. Lies no more real than reflections in a mirror. Bryce was lonely, for God's sake. *Any* woman would seem beautiful to a lonely man who'd been celibate for two years. Even a woman as unworthy of being loved as Cally. Even one as . . . ugly.

Bitterness rose in her throat and she slapped the towel on the bar, pinning it between the wall and the medicine cabinet. "I won't do it. I won't think of little victories and wake up in another nightmare. I can't go through that again. I just can't. I won't."

Shaking hard, Cally spun away from the mirror. Stalked up the step into the bath, jerked at the tub's drain to close it, then cranked open the water faucets, full blast.

In the gushing water, she heard Bryce's voice. *Cally, you're beautiful. To me, you are so beautiful.*

His words repeated in her mind, again and again. Deep inside she knew they were lies, but she wanted to believe them anyway. Oh, how she wanted to believe them anyway.

Her eyes burned, tears welled, stung the back of her nose, threateningly close. She gripped the tub ledge and gave herself a serious lecture. What was she doing here? She didn't dare to indulge in fantasies of Bryce Richards. Couldn't afford to believe him. Yes, he seemed honest. Yes, he seemed sincere. And Cally felt sure he was sincere—at the moment. But, as Grandma Tate used to say, a stiff penis has no conscience. Crude, maybe, but there was a lot of truth in the remark. A sexually satiated Bryce would find Cally falling far short of beautiful, and that was the sorry truth. And—she banged a hip against the counter until it stung, making herself look at the reality of her situation—come on, she knew who she was, and what she was. Cally Tate. Lousy wife. Ugly woman. Thirty-two with everything she *never* wanted.

She was not and never would be beautiful.

Jerking off her blue sweater, she ordered herself to get these crazy thoughts out of her mind. Courage. She should focus on courage. That was her purpose. Not fantasies of Bryce Richards, or destructive self-talk. Courage.

She flung the sweater onto the floor, toed off her sneakers, then unzipped her jeans. After shimmying out of them, she dumped them onto the pile, then tossed her underwear onto the top of the heap. Was he thinking of her, too?

Grimacing at herself, she acknowledged the unwelcome visions of Bryce filling her head. Him smiling, tender, gently touching her face with hands far too big to feel so gentle. Why—oh, why—couldn't he be a jerk?

She dropped the washcloth into the water, watched it soak through, then sink. Why did he have to be an adorable stuffed shirt? So charming and refined, wearing crisp white shirts, knife-creased slacks, and various conservative ties while on vacation. Collin's cane seemed to suit the man perfectly. As if it fit him somehow. In her mind's eye, she could almost see Bryce standing on the rocky cliffs, surrounded by tendrils of mist, leaning on that cane, his dark brows knitted, his square jaw angled and his chin dipped, his hazel eyes focusing on an old-fashioned pocket watch. Mysterious. Alluring. Sexy. He didn't resemble Collin. At least, not from the portrait hanging in the stairwell. But both men had a look about them. Actually, Bryce had it when he wasn't thinking of Meriam and he was with his kids.

Drawing in a sizzling breath, Cally lowered herself into

the steamy garden tub. She toed away the washcloth, stretched out, resting against the sloped back edge, and let the hot water warm her chilled skin and relax her tense muscles. Bryce's look wasn't hard to peg. Cally recognized and envied it. She also craved it.

Contentment.

Just like Collin's.

From all Miss Hattie and Lucy Baker had said about Collin, he and Cecelia had been wildly in love. They must have been, to have survived the loss of their son in the war and to have kept their marriage strong. Their son had been engaged, too. He was Miss Hattie's soldier, bless her heart.

Now *she* had courage. Tons of it. She'd built herself a fine life alone. It showed in her twinkling eyes, her peaceful manner. Cally lifted the soap. Well, Miss Hattie had looked peaceful until after Bryce and Cally had returned from their walk on the cliffs a few nights ago. Since then, Cally had to admit, Miss Hattie had seemed troubled. Trying hard to hide it, but troubled. Cally and Bryce had discussed it, and had approached Miss Hattie about it, but she'd insisted she wasn't ill and that nothing was wrong.

Like Bryce, Cally knew when something was wrong, and something was wrong with Miss Hattie. Vic had told Bryce that Miss Hattie was a bit preoccupied because Thanksgiving was getting close and her and her soldier had become engaged on Thanksgiving. That could be it, Cally agreed. But for some reason she sensed it was more. That whatever was troubling Miss Hattie ran deeper. Much deeper. And it carried a scent Cally recognized too well: fear.

Miss Hattie had denied that too, and Cally and Bryce were at a loss as to what they could do to help her. Bryce had said he'd talk to Suzie's Tony. Cally shivered and rubbed at her arms. Talking to a ghost didn't sit well on her shoulders, but Bryce vowed Tony was friendly and he'd loved Miss Hattie for over fifty years. Who was Cally to argue with that kind of motivator? If anyone could help the angelic woman, surely it'd be the man who'd loved her so well for so long.

Still, he was a ghost. Before coming to Seascape, Cally wouldn't have believed he could exist. But now, well, she had no choice. She'd heard him. Bryce had heard him. And Suzie had seen *and* heard him. He was real.

Suzie, imparting her friend Selena's sage advice on Tony, suggested that they all just accept his existence. That the older we get, the more we realize how very little of our world and lives we truly understand. Selena was right about that. And while Cally waffled on whether to find that truth comforting or distressing, she surely wasn't ditzy enough to dismiss it as truth, or to deny its validity.

The warm water rippled over Cally's tummy and breasts. Lord, but it felt good to just crank back and relax. Maybe she'd just have to take a walk over to Miss Millie's Antique Shoppe and see if she had any idea what was wrong with Miss Hattie. They were best friends, so it was likely Miss Millie would know.

A saddening thought struck Cally. One that left her feeling adrift and out of sorts. If Miss Hattie couldn't find contentment alone, as angelic and iron-willed and Maine-stubborn as she was, then Cally didn't stand a chance.

She dunked the washcloth, then let the water from it drizzle over her face. "Like I said, Counselor. Big defeats."

Tony watched Hattie. Saw the very second she became aware of his presence in her bedroom. Saw her shiver against the sudden chill. And suffered the immediate shot of resentment that burned in his stomach at having caused it.

Her hair hanging loose around her shoulders like a soft cloud, she darted her gaze wall to wall, then crossed her chest with her arms, bunching her white satin nightgown under her ribs. "Tony?"

It hurt to look at her. He swung his gaze to the desk, to the little gold frame that held their photographs. Standing together, their arms twined around each other's waists. Smiling. Happy. So much in love.

Feeling all the emotions now that he did then, he couldn't resist the temptation to lift the frame, hold it midair and study the two of them together, as they had been. As they should have been. As they should be now, but never would be again.

"I'm scared, Tony. I'm so scared. What's happening here? Why do I have such a strong feeling I'm about to lose you?"

Hattie's voice trembled and shook. "I—I can't lose you."

Tony stayed near the desk. Every fiber in his being insisted he go to Hattie, hold her, tell her everything would be all right. But he couldn't. And even if he could, he wouldn't. It wrenched his heart to see her upset but never, not once in sixty years, had he lied to her. He couldn't, wouldn't start now.

At the north window, he pushed back the soft curtains and looked outside. It was dark. Thin moonlight slanted between the clouds, dappled the stretch of firs and the stony ground. He glimpsed the edge of the Fisherman's Co-op, and wondered about the new owners. A brisk breeze sliced through the trees, tunneled between the leaves on the ground and those still clinging to branches, making crackling sounds. He'd broken the rules. He'd interceded in Suzie's dreams. Repeatedly. And he'd continue to do so until he could find a way to stop them, to alter what would become her history.

Before the first intercession into Suzie's dream, he hadn't thought of what could happen to Hattie, of what his interceding could cost her. Or of how it could affect her. He should have thought about it, should have considered her, but he hadn't. He regretted that. Just as he regretted that, now knowing the consequences and the effect on her, he still couldn't alter his decision and not intercede. Nothing had changed. He'd trespassed into the forbidden to save Suzie's life. To spare her father more heartache. And regardless of the costs to Tony, or to his beloved, to spare Suzie he had to do so again. And again.

Those in his care had to come first. Their needs had to supersede the needs of anyone and everyone else. Even—God help him, and give him strength—his beloved Hattie's.

Never in his fifty years of service had he resented his responsibilities more.

"I love you, Tony." Hattie stood up beside her bed, her gown whisking around her ankles. "I want you to know, no matter what happens, that will never change." Her voice dropped husky soft and she blinked furiously fast. "It's near Thanksgiving. You always get testy around Thanksgiving. So do I. But no matter what else happens, our anniversary will come. I will remember you, and I will love you before and after it. Forever, Tony.'' Her voice cracked. ''I'll love you forever.''

His heart ached, felt sure to shatter. He looked from the woman to the photo, recalling a time when he could have taken her into his arms and loved her, something he could no longer do outside of his memories. He stared at the picture of her in her yellow floral dress. The dress she'd worn the night he'd asked her to marry him. The night he'd developed a deep fondness for yellow carnations. Joy. They meant joy. Hattie had been his joy then, and she was now. She always would be. And in his mind, he again heard her agree to be his wife. ''Of course, love.''

Of course, love. But they'd been cheated out of their marriage, out of their lifetime together. War and destiny had denied them what they'd both wanted most. And now, his own moral choice to help Suzie could separate them forever. In his heart he knew fate wouldn't prove any kinder than destiny. He and Hattie would be separated for good. He ran his fingertip over the smooth glass, awash in regret, in a flood of resentment at having been forced to choose.

But there was nothing he could do.

Powerless.

He stiffened at the memory of himself in Suzie's dream. Summoned his resolve. His hand shaking, he set the photo back onto the desk, hopeless of finding a way out of this situation that wouldn't leave Hattie brokenhearted. His own heart would be broken, too, but he'd chosen for them both. He deserved the pain. Hattie didn't. He could cope better with this if only there were some way to spare her.

The photo frame fell, facedown.

The glass cracked.

Sunshine's message was clear. There was no solution. And there would be no reprieve. Not for his beloved Hattie, nor for him.

God help them to endure the pain.

A light knock sounded at the bathroom door. Cally sat up in the tub, swished away a thick clump of bubbles. ''Yes?''

''Cally,'' Suzie called out from the door between the tub and dressing room. ''Where's my blue sweater?'' She dropped her voice, clearly speaking to someone else. "Cally knows everything. Well, almost everything. She's still figuring out that she might be my new—you know."

"Uh-huh. What doesn't she know?" A second little girl's voice seeped through the closed door, sounding far too old to be Lyssie.

"That she's gonna be my new mom. Maybe."

"So why don't ya tell her?"

"Tony says that doesn't work. She and Daddy have to figure it out themselves. It's a grown-up thing."

Cally groaned, resisted the urge to just slide down the tub and duck her head beneath the water. Everyone in the village would hear this tidbit before dusk. And she and Bryce would be added onto that blasted bulletin board they'd seen down at the Blue Moon Cafe which held shopping lists and the villagers' bets on whether or not the guests at Seascape Inn would become lovers. Miss Hattie insisted it was harmless, so it surely was, yet Cally didn't care to be their target. Most likely, thanks to Gregory, she was just hypersensitive about being anyone's target for anything right now. She needed to work on that, too.

"Suzie." Cally grabbed the bar of soap, gave it a firm squeeze to help her keep her voice calm. "Who are you talking to out there?"

The door swung open and two girls stood there, side by side. Suzie, dark hair, pristine clean in her jeans and shamrock sweatshirt, and a misshapen tomboy with red hair and a fair sprinkling of freckles. At least she appeared to be a tomboy, judging by her jeans, baseball cap, and once-white T-shirt that now had oil smears and fingerprints swiped across the front of it.

"It's me and Frankie, Cally." Suzie pointed to her friend.

The daughter of the new owner of Fisherman's Co-op that Vic had mentioned. Cally slid down under the bubbles, until they threatened her chin. "Hi, Frankie."

"Hi." She tugged at her cap then glanced at Suzie. "She looks like a mom, all right. Even nekkid."

"Excuse me?" Cally stiffened.

"It's nothing," Suzie said quickly, flashing Cally that smile that said it was everything.

"Sweetheart, I like meeting your friends, but when I'm in the bath isn't the right time."

Frankie leaned against the door jamb. "She's ticked off 'cuz she's nekkid."

Darn right she was. Cally frowned. "Frankie, would you quit saying that?"

"Why?" Suzie cocked her head. "We're all girls."

A valid point. Cally swallowed a groan. "I know. But, well, I'd just prefer to meet people when I'm dressed. Okay?"

"Okay." Suzie shrugged. "So do you know where my sweater is?"

"Down in the mud room. It's on a peg right under the Welcome Friends sign."

Suzie grinned at Frankie. "See? She knows everything."

"Not hardly." Cally smiled. "But I'm happy to report that all the blueberry stains came out of your sweater."

Frankie frowned down at her chest. "Ya got anything for grease? Jimmy's working on the pastor's car, and I was watching. I'm building my own for the soapbox derby next summer, and Jimmy's good with cars—even if he does look all dopey-eyed at Nolene Baker. Hatch said Jimmy's waiting for her to grow up. Goofy, huh?" Frankie plucked at her T-shirt. "When my mom sees this, she's gonna pop a cork."

Suzie slid Frankie an empathetic nod. "Mrs. Wiggins doesn't like dirt, either."

"Sometimes you can't help getting a little dirty, you know? 'Specially when you're working on cars." Frankie grunted. "My mom wants me to be a lady. I promised her I would and everything, when I get around to it. Right now, I just wanna be a kid."

Cally barely withheld a smile. There was a lot of wisdom in insisting you get to live out your childhood. A shame Suzie hadn't been gifted with that. Hmm, maybe she had, but she hadn't been gifted with anyone to fight for her to make sure she got it. Some kids—heck, some adults, too—need an advocate. Frankie clearly didn't, though, and Cally bet the girl gave her mother fits. Innocent ones, but definitely an abundance of them. She was adorable, this little tomboy. And so earnest. A perfect friend for Suzie.

"I'm glad the stains came out of my sweater." Suzie grinned at Cally. "You saved me. Mrs. Wiggins would've hit the roof."

"Thank Miss Hattie." Cally rinsed the washcloth, then soaped it again. "She gave me some special cleaner."

Suzie perked up. "Do you think it'd work on Lyssie's hair?"

Cally inwardly groaned. "The stains didn't come out of her hair?"

Suzie shook her head. "But they cover up the orange."

Ouch. Some silver lining. Poor Bryce was probably tearing himself up over that, too, considering himself a rotten parent. "Is Mrs. Wiggins resigning again?"

"Uh-huh." Suzie grinned. "But don't worry. Daddy'll talk her out of it. He always does."

Suzie and Frankie turned to go. "Suzie," Cally called after her. "Lock that inner door for me, will you?"

"Sure. But the lock's broken."

"Wonderful." Now why hadn't anyone bothered to pass along that tidbit of information to her?

"It's okay. The sign's out on the nail."

"Sure is," Frankie yelled. "Occupied. Says so right here."

Great. They could both read—and ignore. And poor Bryce was feeling like a failure because Lyssie's hair, while no longer green from chlorine nor orange from juice, was now tinged blue from berry stains. Only God knew how many more colors it'd be before they convinced the child that everything smelling good wasn't shampoo. And the battleaxe was resigning again.

Cally half wished the woman would stop threatening and really quit. And that Bryce would let her. But even if she did, he wouldn't. Mrs. Wiggins was a tie to Meriam, and those ties he would hold on to for dear life. Forever.

And why that fact made Cally jealous and angrier than hell, when she should find him being steadfast admirable, she hadn't a clue. But it did. Jealous. And angry.

She liked both, and definitely didn't like liking either. They made her feel petty and small, even if they were feelings attached to the battleaxe.

* * *

Tony stood in the hallway, watching the two girls walk out of the bath, a smile curling his lip. Frankie was exactly what Suzie needed. She couldn't recapture her childhood, but if she could get these dreams out of her way, Frankie would give Suzie a run on another one.

"Frankie, what are you doing with that sign?" Suzie moved to take it out of Frankie's hand.

She snatched it back. "I'm taking it off the door, is what."

"Why? No one will know Cally's in there."

"Shh. She'll hear us." Frankie hiked a thumb toward Cally. "That's why I'm moving it. So nobody'll know she's in there." Frankie gave her head a shake, then propped the sign against the wall on the floor, a fair distance from the door. "She's nekkid, remember?"

"She's taking a bath."

"I know." Frankie grinned, ear to ear.

Suzie shrugged. "Don't you take a bath without your clothes?"

"Yeah, but this ain't about her taking a bath." Frankie clicked her tongue to the roof of her mouth. "Look, you want her to be your mom, right?"

Suzie nodded.

"Well, you can't just tell her, so we've gotta help her out a little."

"By taking the sign off the bathroom door? How does that help?"

Frankie's expression went lax, then closed. "I ain't saying. If you gotta ask, you're too little to know."

"I'm as big as you are."

"You ain't as old. I'm nine and seven months. You're only nine and two months. I'm older, and that's that."

"Tell me."

"I can't. My mom'd skin me alive."

Suzie gasped, paled.

"Geez, Suzie. I meant she'd be ticked off at me."

Suzie gulped, lifted her chin. "I knew that."

"Did not."

"Did, too."

Frankie grabbed Suzie's arm. "Come on." She headed

toward the stairs. "Let's go follow Batty Beaulah."

"Who's she?"

"The old lady next door. She wears these goofy hats and has legs like a bird."

"Where's she going?" Suzie stepped down the first of the stairs.

"Ghost-hunting."

"Huh?"

Frankie's eyes sparkled. "She's got binoculars and everything."

Suzie stopped at the crook in the landing. "I don't want to hunt any ghosts."

Frankie halted beside her, looked up at the two portraits hanging on the wall. Cecelia and Collin Freeport. "Hey, I know about her. She was a doctor."

"No she wasn't. She was a healer. Lucy Baker over at the Blue Moon told me all about her. She's why miracles can happen here. Because she loved everybody so much and love doesn't die. It stays forever and forever, and it fixes broken stuff."

"Honest?"

"Selena said." Suzie nodded. "I asked her on the phone."

"Who's Selena?"

"My grown-up friend at home. She says love lingers forever. That's how I'm supposed to know Meriam still loves me and she always will."

Frankie stuffed her hand in her pocket and leaned against the banister. "Who's Meriam?"

Suzie started down the stairs. "She was my mom . . . sort of."

The third stair from the bottom creaked. Liking the sound, Frankie paused to jump on it three times. "How can you have a sort of mom?"

Suzie jumped off the steps and stopped beside the grandfather clock in the gallery, then pressed her ear close to the glass to listen to its ticks. "Be born to Meriam."

Tony grimaced. The kid definitely needed a mother. Definitely.

* * *

"Okay, Tony. I confess." Bryce tossed up his hand and paced the length of the bedroom, his cane thumping dully on the carpet. "I'm having a little trouble dealing with knowing Meriam is content."

Tony debated. He could nix this with Bryce, but it'd be better to let the guy work through it so he could get it out of his system. Tony leaned back against the window, avoiding the mirror in the washstand tucked into the corner. He hated mirrors. Not seeing his own solid reflection but his essence, he empathized with Cally, knowing how cruel those innocuous bits of glass really could be.

At least he'd always had a fondness for this room. His mother, Cecelia, had named it the Cove Room because looking out the window, past the stand of trees and the hint of rooftops in the village, you could glimpse the cove. As it had then, now it still bore all the markings of being a man's room. Deep-stained cherrywood furniture, a king-size bed covered with a forest-green comforter and brown and green print pillows. None of the frills or lace of the Great White Room.

He let his gaze drift over to the armoire on the west wall. It settled on the small crystal bowl atop it, filled with Sea Spray-scented potpourri. Then he looked to the desk in front of the windows, homed in on the stubby brass vase that held a single yellow rose. Hattie's touches were everywhere. Even in the terra-cotta berry box beside the crystal bowl. Bess Mystic had bought it for Hattie. And she'd bought a second one for John, to show her estranged husband she'd welcomed him back into her life and her heart. A precious moment, that.

After a lengthy monologue, Bryce circled back to his opening statement. "I guess I'm having more than a little trouble dealing with knowing Meriam's content without us."

Tony lowered his gaze from the cathedral ceiling to Bryce. He looked like he always did: crisp white shirt, perfectly creased slacks, a navy and gray silk tie. Provided things worked out here—and realizing that, right now, that outcome looked rather grim—Cally had her wifely work cut out for her, getting Bryce to chill out a little. For Tony, the time had come to cut in. *Doesn't it ease your mind to know Meriam's content?*

"Of course it does." Bryce forked a hand through his hair, paced an angry path between the louvered closet doors and the bed. "It's just that—"

You do want her at peace, right? I mean, you couldn't be content knowing she was miserable and unsettled, could you?

"No, I couldn't." Bryce dropped his hand to his side. "But I—I—" Frustration twisted his expression. "Hell, Tony, I don't know what I want. I'm mad. So damn mad. I know it's wrong, but there it is."

Would you mind if I materialize? I'm getting dizzy, trying to keep pace here.

Near the foot of the bed, Bryce halted. "Materialize?"

So you can see me and so, when you're talking to me, I won't have to run you down to see your face. That really does get tiresome, Bryce. When talking or listening to someone, a person always looks at their eyes. It's a lifelong habit that doesn't break just because you die. It just gets more challenging because the person can't see you, you know?

"Um, go ahead, then."

Bryce sounded anything but enthused, and his knuckles went white, gripping the head of the cane, yet Tony sensed the man was sympathetic to his special challenges.

He watched Bryce's expression carefully. Some thought they were ready to see a ghost, but when they actually did, they passed out cold. At least if Bryce fell, he'd fall on the bed and spare his knee any more trauma. Hattie would appreciate that, and Tony had heard quite enough of her ear-blistering for the time being. She'd railed for hours about his telling Suzie the "new mom" bit of business.

Bryce's throat went thick. Tony stood before him, looking as solid as Bryce himself, wearing an old Army uniform with shiny brass buttons—Class A's, Bryce suspected—and a yellow carnation pinned to his lapel. "So that's why Suzie was so knocked out by Cally's carnation."

Tony smiled, clearly pleased about something. What, Bryce had no idea, but the man had a friendly face and, next to Miss Hattie's, the kindliest eyes Bryce ever had seen.

"We need to resolve these feelings of yours about Meriam, Bryce. They're keeping you chained to her, and her chained to a life that doesn't belong to her anymore.'' Tony ruffled a hand through his hair. Brown, but touched by the light, it streaked gold. ''You both need to move on.''

''I'm trying.'' Bryce was, wasn't he? He was here.

''I know you are.'' Tony hiked a hip and sat on the edge of the desk.

''What's it like for her? Being on the other side?''

''She's at peace. And she's content. Isn't that enough to know?''

''I guess not.'' Passing the armoire, Bryce picked up the little terra-cotta berry box, ran his fingers over its rough surface. ''I want her content, but I'm angry because she is. And I feel guilty because I'm angry. It's not logical or rational, Tony. It's garbage, and I don't know where to dump it.''

''I think you're relieved. And I think you feel guilty not because of anger but because you're falling in love with Cally.''

''I'm not.'' Bryce looked up from the vine cut into the top of the box to Tony. ''We're friends. That's all. And I'm trying to help Cally realize she's a wonderful, desirable woman—which she is—remember?''

Tony crossed his arms over his chest. ''Oh, I haven't forgotten.'' He stood up and slid a hand into his pocket. ''Sit down.''

''What?''

''Sit down.'' Tony nodded to the edge of the bed.

Bryce sat, then looked up at Tony.

''Now forgive me if I'm a little out of step with the times. I would remind you that I've been dead fifty-one years. But I think as men we have a responsibility to remember something vital in our relationships with women.''

''We have tons of responsibilities, I agree. You can cut out the sarcasm, and cut to the chase.''

''No problem, Counselor. What you're saying is normal and fine, except for one thing.'' Tony stopped directly in front of Bryce, then looked down at him. ''Friends don't kiss friends like you kissed Cally Tate.''

''Typically, no, they don't. But that wasn't about passion.''

"Looked pretty passionate to me."

"It wasn't," Bryce insisted. "It was about loneliness."

"Ah, well, that explains it, then. Raging hormones and good old-fashioned lust had nothing to do with it. The very basic human need to touch and be touched had nothing to do with it, either. In fact, what you're telling me is that, when you get down to brass tacks, Cally had nothing to do with it. Is that right, Counselor? Is that what you're saying here? That it wouldn't have mattered who the woman was, so long as she was in your arms?"

Bryce lied through his teeth. "Right."

"Animal crackers." Tony backed up to the desk, perched on the edge, then stretched out his legs and crossed his ankles. "You were supposed to be showing her she's desirable. I left her in your capable hands."

"So they're not so capable. That shouldn't surprise you. You know about Meriam, Suzie, Wiggins. Hell, Tony, what did you expect?"

"I expected honesty." Tony snorted, tapped a pen from the desk against his palm. "Sometimes you people really irk me. You've got everything I want right at your fingertips and you lie to yourselves and turn away from it. Well, I know that's comfortable for you. I know it eases your fears of putting your heart on the line again. But it does present us with a little dilemma."

Bryce stood up. "What dilemma?"

Tony rubbed at his neck. "Seascape is a healing house. But you know that already, don't you? You've felt the effects of it, and Suzie's told you and Cally all about it, hasn't she? You just haven't wanted to listen because you'd rather play ostrich and tell Cally how she needs to be looking in the mirror. I strongly suggest, Counselor, that you stop pointing fingers long enough to take a look at yourself."

"I'm trying to help her. Have you forgotten that?"

"You're hiding behind a desire to help her, using it like a shield—and we both know it." Tony gritted his teeth, curled his hands into fists, then forced his tone civil. "I crave—not want, damn it, but crave—everything you've got, and you're not only refusing to appreciate it, you're refusing to even see that it's there."

"You mentioned a dilemma." Bryce clenched his jaw to keep his temper under control. "Will you be getting to it anywhere in our future?"

"Very well." Tony twisted his lips, relaxed his fingers. "It's my job to make sure you have every opportunity to heal in this house, Counselor. That's why I'm here. If you lack the courage to do your part, well, that makes me doing my part more complicated. I don't like complications. And, while I'm empathetic with your situation and the troubles that have kept you straddling the fence and seeking comfort here, I'm going to have to insist you leap to one side or the other. In other words, from now on, every time you lie to yourself I'm going to be in your face telling you that you're lying to yourself. Now, whether or not you elect to be honest with me doesn't really matter. You're damn well going to be honest with you."

Bryce glared at him. "You're nothing like T.J. said you were."

"It's nearly Thanksgiving." Tony shrugged. "I'm a reasonable man, but I get a little impatient with men who run scared, especially at Thanksgiving."

"Why?"

"Because that's when I proposed to Hattie and she accepted."

"But before you could marry her, you died."

"Yes." Tony clenched his jaw. "I died."

Letting all this soak in, Bryce put the box back atop the armoire. "First, I'm sorry for your loss, but to be frank here, I've got my own baggage weighing me down and I damn sure don't need any more. Secondly, I don't need or want you in my face. I am honest with myself and I'm attracted to Cally because what happened to her is tragic, and she's far too special to have been dealt the dirt she's been shoveled by that bastard Tate. And thirdly, I *am* lonely. Sometimes I'm so damn lonely I think if it were lethal, I'd be dead. But I'm lonely for Meriam. My wife, who is content without me. And I'm angry that she's content—even though I know I should feel better for knowing it. I'm angry because I'm so damn miserable without her."

Tony dipped his chin. "You were always without her."

He stuffed his hands into his pockets. "I know that's hard for you to accept. I tried to help her, but I failed."

"I wasn't without her."

"You were." Tony frowned, and compassion clouded his eyes. "She wasn't there for you, Bryce. She was never there for you or for the kids. Take a look at how things really were between you. Forget the fantasies. Look at your lives the way they really were."

"I know how things really were. Don't you tell me how things really were between us. She loved me, damn it!" Bryce slammed a fist down on the desk. The impact sent shock waves racing up to his elbow. His hand stung. He gripped the desk ledge, and his temper. "She loved me."

"Meriam couldn't love you." Tony stared at Bryce, softened his voice. "I'm sorry, but that's the truth. What happened to her didn't leave her the luxury of loving anyone. Think about it and you'll know I'm right. Think about yourself. About the kids. And think about Cally."

"What about Cally? Hell, the last thing she wants is to love again."

"True. In her head. But what about in her heart? You know all about Mary Beth Ladner. Cally's a lot like Hattie, Counselor. She's a giver. A nurturer. And she's got nobody to nurture."

Tony mumbled under his breath, then let out a sigh that would power windmills and talked to the ceiling. "Here we've got a guy who needs nurturing, with three beautiful kids who *sorely* need nurturing, and a woman who is a nurturer with not a soul in her life to nurture. Now, life hasn't been extremely kind to any of these folks, but the man and woman clearly are attracted and care about each other, though they hide from it behind words like 'loneliness' and 'friends.' They kiss. They talk. They go on outings with the kids, and they laugh. Really laugh. Yet both this man and woman are so busy protecting their tattered pride and swearing that they won't let themselves love again that they're failing to see—"

"None of us need more heartache." Bryce interrupted, his voice stone-cold. "Not Cally, not my kids, and not me."

"Ah, true. But you do have what each of you needs. There

are a lot of kinds of love, Bryce. We both know it. So maybe between you and Cally romantic love isn't it. Maybe it's something deeper. That's a distinct possibility, wouldn't you say? Maybe between you there's a chance for a steady and sure love based on trust and caring. A special love that will help to heal the wounds inside you and Cally, and inside your kids. And maybe, if either you or Cally has the strength and courage to venture beyond your pride to find it, you'll recognize that kind of love for the treasure it is.'' Tony stared deeply into Bryce's eyes. ''Do you have that much strength and courage, Counselor?''

His expression bleak, Bryce admitted the truth. ''I don't know.''

Chapter 8

Cally rinsed the scented soap from her shoulder, muttering under her breath.

So far, she'd been interrupted in the bath by Suzie and Frankie; by Miss Hattie, bringing in fresh towels; and by Mrs. Wiggins, washing glue off Lyssie's hands. Thank God the child hadn't thought it smelled good and doused her hair with it or Bryce would be virtually slitting his throat. If one more person knocked on that door, Cally was going to pitch a fit that would make Mrs. Wiggins's resignation tirades look like play time at kindergarten.

Cally grabbed the bar of soap then roughly rubbed it inside the washcloth, turning the bar over and over in her hand. Did mothers routinely go through this? Live day to day where not even a single twenty-minute stint in the tub was considered sacred time of her own that shouldn't be interrupted?

"Cally?" Jeremy's knock on the inner door followed.

Well, hell. Cally's stomach churned. She wanted to be irritated, but she couldn't be too upset. It was Jeremy. He hadn't ignored the sign, he was too young to read it. "Yes, sweetheart."

He cracked the door open, then cocked his head. "How come lizards don't fly?"

Good grief. The bubbles were nearly gone, but she ducked under what was left of them, and draped the wet washcloth over her breasts. "Because lizards don't have hollow bones and feathers. Or wings. They're too heavy to fly."

"Jeremy," a man said from behind him.

He sounded like Jimmy Goodson, the orphaned mechanic Miss Hattie more or less had adopted, who often helped her out around here. Oh geez, another one? Cally's face went red-hot.

"Hi, Jimmy," Jeremy said, grinning. "I was just talking to Cally."

"Jeremy, could you please close the door? I'm in the bathtub, for crying out loud."

Jimmy appeared at the door. His bib-brown eyes stretched wide and his face went bing-cherry purple. "Um, excuse us, Miss Tate."

"That's it." Cally lost it, and thrust a pointed finger toward the outer door. "Everyone out. And I mean now!"

Board stiff, Jimmy muttered an "I'm sorry, Miss Tate," then turned and left. Probably hiding a smirk, though looking at his back, she couldn't be sure.

"But I gotta pee." Jeremy did a dance, cupped himself with his hand, and nearly tripped over his muddy shoestrings.

Cally groaned. What the hell? He was only four—and he didn't look as if he'd make it to the downstairs bath. "All right. Go ahead, Jeremy."

The washcloth clung to her breasts like a second skin. She loosened it, so it wouldn't so clearly outline her contour, and slid deeper into the straggling clumps of bubbles, then stared at the bar of soap in her hand. She'd gripped it so hard it bore indentions from her fingers.

"Jeremy?"

Bryce. Oh, God. Not him, too. She sank deeper, up to her chin. *Please, not him, too.*

"I'm in here, Daddy."

"Jeremy, no!" Cally whispered a shout.

The startled child jumped. Knocked the bar of soap from Cally's hand; it flew across the room. Tripped over his shoelace, fell, then cracked his chin on the floor and wailed louder than a body being tortured to death.

"Oh, mercy." Her heart in her throat, Cally scrambled to her feet inside the tub, splashing water onto the floor. She scooped Jeremy up, into her arms, tried to get a look at his chin. "Let me see, sweetie." No blood. Thank heaven, no blood. "Are you hurt?"

Bryce rushed into the bath. Saw Cally just as his foot hit the bar of soap and his feet slid out from under him. He glided in the water across the tile floor and crashed into the side of the tub. His breath swooshed out. So did a healthy grunt.

"Bryce!" Cally sat down, Jeremy fully clothed in her arms. Water gushed over the side of the tub, soaking Bryce.

Water dripping from his hair, streaming down his face, and soaking his white shirt, he stared up at her, clearly searching for just the right curse word.

Not at all sure the one she had in mind would do, she winced down at him. "Animal crackers?"

Frankie and Suzie stood at the outer door, exchanging a high five. "That should do it," Frankie said. "He's seen her nekkid."

Bryce slung a killer look at his daughter and her friend.

Comforting the wailing Jeremy, Cally reached over the edge of the tub then stroked Bryce's jaw. A bruise was already forming on it. "Are you okay?"

"Do I look okay?" He swung an angry gaze to her. "My knee's reinjured, my elbow's throbbing, and my jaw feels like it's been on the receiving end of a heavyweight champ's left hook."

Jeremy cried even louder. "Shh, Daddy's fine, sweetheart." She smiled at the child burrowing into her chest. "And he's not angry at you. Men just do that."

"Men do what?"

"Roar. When they're irritated at themselves for upsetting their children, men roar. Loudly." Cally slid him a frown and held it so he wouldn't miss it, then nodded down to Jeremy, brushing his hair with the tip of her chin.

Bryce looked at his son, nuzzled to Cally's chest. With a sharp pang of envy for that nuzzle, he saw Jeremy's face twist into a mixture of fear and worry that ripped Bryce's insides to shreds. Animal crackers. "No." He forced his voice calm. "I'm not angry, tiger."

Cally gave him her best smile.

Why the hell was he smiling back at her? His knee burned like a five-alarm fire, and he'd have a goose egg the size of a cantaloupe where he'd banged his head in the fall. Damn if he wasn't seeing stars. He rubbed at a spot behind his left ear and felt a knot. Swelling already. And as tender as a baby's backside. He hauled himself to his feet, wincing and trying to focus.

"Are you okay?"

"I'm fine, Cally." His vision righted itself, and he reached for Jeremy.

"Thanks for helping." He took the boy, who'd finally stopped wailing and now only sniffled, then settled him on his hip.

"Your coloring doesn't look so hot, Counselor. It's kind of pasty."

"I'm okay." He hurt like hell. "Thanks again." He glanced at her and nearly fell again. Her bare skin flushed rosy, creamy smooth, and the washcloth she clutched to her chest did nothing but enhance the shape of her full breasts.

"Bryce," she said softly, then repeated more firmly. "Bryce?"

He heard her, recognized the reprimand in her tone, and forced himself to lift his gaze back to her face. Her neck and cheeks scalded bright red. Not from the bath, from embarrassment. "I'm, um, sorry for the, um, interruption." Damn, he sounded like a stumbling kid who'd just noticed the difference between boys and girls.

"You need to get some ice on that knee. It's swelling up again."

It hadn't been unswollen since the frog-in-the-kitchen fiasco. But she was right. He'd done fresh damage. "Yeah, I'll see to that just as soon as I get Jeremy dried off." Bryce snagged a towel from the rack, then headed toward the door.

At the outer door, he glanced up. The nail was bare, and he grimaced. Women. He called back to her. "Cally, didn't anyone tell you to put the little Occupied sign out when you're in the bath?"

"I did put it out."

"Well, it's not here—Suzie, hold it right there. You too Frankie."

Terrific. He'd caught them red-handed. Cally grabbed for a towel and whisked it over her torso. She had ten seconds—

fifteen max—to get out there in time to prevent a marathon lecture.

"Mr. Richards." Mrs. Wiggins's voice carried through the door into the dressing room. "I hardly think Mrs. Richards would approve of the children visiting Miss Tate while she's bathing."

Cally made an ugly face the battleaxe wouldn't see and rolled her gaze heavenward. What mother would approve? Geez, the woman was a royal pain in the tush.

"I'm sure Miss Tate wasn't crazy about the idea, either, Mrs. Wiggins," Bryce said. "Jeremy, to your room. Change clothes, bring the wet ones down to the laundry room, then find me. Suzie, Frankie—downstairs. In the parlor. Right now."

"And the hard knocks just keep on coming," Cally mumbled, tugging on black slacks, slinging her bra out of the way, then tossing on a gray silk blouse that stuck to her still-damp skin. She grabbed the doorknob, making a vow. If the stuffed shirt made Jeremy start crying again, she'd just blast his ears. And if Mrs. Wiggins gave the child a hard time, or Suzie one, Cally would just desperately need them to do *something* vitally important right away. What something? She had no idea. Whatever it took to get them out of the clutches of the stuffed shirt and the battleaxe.

The hallway was empty.

Praying she wasn't too late, Cally took the steps two at a time downstairs, her heart beating hard against her ribs, pounding inside her head.

She rounded the corner then stopped at the doorway. A pin dropping would sound like a foghorn in the silent parlor. A bad sign, if ever there was one. She held off a grimace by the skin of her teeth.

Bryce stood facing the sofa, his back to Cally. At least his clothes were only wet. Not spackled with oatmeal, berry juice, or mud. There was solace in that. Jeremy had wrapped himself in a towel and sat on the eggshell carpet at Suzie's feet. He looked as if he were awaiting execution, which totally frosted Cally's cookies. He was only four, for pity's sake. And Suzie and Frankie sat like wooden soldiers on the soft green and eggshell tapestry sofa. The darling's eyes were as round as quarters, and her fingers were laced together in her lap so tightly her knuckles had bleached white. The child was under enough stress with those damn dreams; she didn't need more.

The battleaxe sat in a wing chair beneath a gold leaf branch hanging on the wall, holding a fidgeting Lyssie, whose hair, bless her heart, really was tinged blue. If the woman's expression got any more stern her face would crack, and that was that. Poor Bryce. Another resignation appeared imminent.

"Does your arm hurt much, Daddy?" Suzie asked.

He'd hurt his arm, too? Cally glanced at his soggy sleeve, and saw him cupping his elbow. *Animal crackers.*

"Not nearly so much as my jaw," he said. "But that's not important. What I want to know is why in the world you guys interrupted Cally's bath."

"I couldn't find my sweater."

"I needed to know how come lizards don't fly."

"She wasn't mad at us," Suzie said. Frankie nodded to support the claim.

"She will be," Bryce insisted. "When she finds out you two scamps took the sign off the door, she'll be more than mad—as well she should be."

"We didn't want no trouble." Frankie gave him an earnest look, reeking of sincerity. "We only wanted you to see her nekkid."

"You *what*?" Bryce went purple and the veins in his neck bulged.

"Suzie wants Cally to be her new mom," Frankie added, as if that explained it all.

Cally's heart skipped. Suzie had said that once. But to tell her new friend, she must really mean it. She wanted Cally for her mother. *Her mother.* Protective urges, rampant feelings of caring and loving, overwhelmed Cally, and her heart suddenly felt too big for her chest.

Bryce faltered, then regrouped. "What you two did was invade Cally's privacy—and that's against the law."

Frankie's fair skin blanched white. "Is she gonna call Sheriff Cobb?"

Bryce stared down at the child, clearly flustered. "She'd be within her rights to do exactly that."

Frankie groaned, covered her face with her hands. "My mom's gonna kill me dead."

"She's not really, Daddy," Suzie quickly assured him. "Frankie just means her mom's going to be mad at her."

"I'm not going to call the sheriff." Cally stepped forward, then stopped at Bryce's side. "But I do want to have a chat with all of you."

She looked to Bryce for permission. When he nodded, she looked back at Suzie and Frankie. "What you two did was wrong."

"We know, but—" Suzie interrupted.

"No, buts. It was wrong, Suzie, and that's that." Cally sighed. "Sweetheart, you've mentioned this about me being your new mom before. We should've talked about it then, but we didn't. Now I realize we should've because your thinking isn't quite right on this. Your daddy seeing me without my clothes won't make me your mom. What moms and dads feel for each other is a different kind of love than they feel for kids—Frankie's right about that. But a mom loving her children no matter what is what makes her a mom. It really doesn't have anything to do with dads. So no more of these tricks, okay? I want your promise—yours too, Frankie."

"Okay."

"Okay."

Cally stared at Suzie. She'd slipped her hand behind her back, as had Frankie. "Good." She slid Bryce an I-know-what-they're-up-to-look, linked her arms over her chest, then stared back at the girls. "Now uncross everything crossed, and promise again."

Suzie slumped. "I promise."

"Me, too." Frankie grimaced and shut her eyes.

Cally bit back a smile. "Now, that's done." She wheeled her gaze to Jeremy.

"I never didn't touched that sign, Cally." He stared up at her from the floor.

"I know. I just want to talk with you for a second. Is that okay?"

Looking majorly relieved, he nodded.

"I'm happy to answer your questions, but not while I'm in the bathtub. And if you need to use the restroom, then you go right away. Don't wait until you can't make it to the one downstairs—just in case someone is in the one upstairs, okay?"

"Uh-huh." He gave her an enthusiastic nod.

"Now, all three of you apologize for the distress you've caused Mrs. Wiggins." Cally waited until they were done paying homage to the battleaxe. "And now to your dad." She looked at his swollen knee, his elbow, and his bruised jaw. At least the beard would hide most of it. "Say you're sorry he was hurt."

"We're sorry, Daddy." Suzie blinked hard and fast. "Honest."

"Yeah." Jeremy said.

"It's okay." The upset drained right out of Bryce and his eyes turned tender. "You didn't mean to hurt me. But no more underhanded stunts like hiding the sign. And I mean it."

Cally touched his wet sleeve, dropped her voice. "They promised, Bryce."

He met her gaze and, to keep him from working himself into a lather again, she gave him her brightest smile.

Staring at her lips, he swallowed hard. His expression softened, and he smiled back. "So they did."

"Mr. Richards," Mrs. Wiggins said. "I would be remiss in my duties if I didn't object. Mrs. Richards—God rest her soul—was very explicit in her orders regarding disciplining the children, and I don't believe that she—"

Bryce held up a staying hand. "She's content, Mrs. Wiggins, and she'd have no objection whatsoever. The matter is closed." He looked at Suzie and Jeremy. "You two go clean up the mess in the bathroom. Jeremy, first you put on some dry clothes."

The matter was closed. Cally's smile grew by a hundred watts. "Hmm, I think we should maybe put some ice on that jaw."

"Is it swelling, too?"

"I'm afraid so."

"Damn."

Cally pressed a fingertip over his lips. "Animal crackers, darling."

"Darling?" His eyes danced, and the most enchanting silver flecks set his irises to twinkling.

"Slip of tongue." She wanted to look away, but didn't.

"Right." He crooked his arm, tucked hers through it, and they walked out of the parlor, leaving Mrs. Wiggins grumbling in the wing chair and Lyssie muttering, "Damn."

Miss Hattie passed the Ziploc bag filled with ice to Cally, then glanced over her shoulder to the kitchen chair where Bryce sat slumped. "I think he needs that arm in a sling, too, Cally."

"I think you're right." Cally double-checked, then flinched. "It's swollen the size of my kneecap already." She took the bag of ice and gently pressed it against Bryce's jaw.

"Ouch."

She hissed in a breath. "Sorry."

"I wish you two would quit fussing over me, and talking about me like I'm not even in the room."

"He's testy, Miss Hattie." Cally grunted. "Men are the worst patients, aren't they?"

"Absolutely." Miss Hattie fingered through a wooden medicine chest propped open on the white countertop. "I know there's a sling in here somewhere. Hatch—Did I mention that he runs the lighthouse? Well, he lives there. He ran it though, back when it was a lighthouse. Before the Coast Guard took over the ones operating. Anyway, I know we had an arm sling from back in 'seventy-two. Or maybe it was 'seventy-three. Wicked winter, whenever it was. Ice everywhere until June. April's usually our mud month—from the melting snow, you know—but not that year. Poor Hatch slipped on ice out on the rocks. Hurt his pride more than his arm, but I insisted he wear the sling to keep it immobile. The crusty cuss gave me the dickens for it, too, as I recall."

Cally tapped Bryce's shoulder. "Don't get any ideas, Atlas. I don't take the dickens from any man."

"I have to be nice. I remember." He gave her a lopsided grin. "Atlas?"

She adjusted the bag, and avoided his eyes. ''Carrying the world on your shoulders.''

''Sounds better than 'counselor.' ''

''I prefer 'counselor.' Thoughts of you carrying around so much weight brings pain to mind. Cricks in your neck. Muscle strain. Backaches. Naw, I don't think so.'' His shoulders were far too nice to have to sag under all that tonnage. ''Besides, you love being a lawyer.''

''Yeah, I do. But sometimes I like just being a man.'' He let his gaze drift down her. ''Of course, sometimes when you call me counselor, and your voice is as smooth as a shot of good whiskey, I feel very, er, manly.''

Heat rushed to her belly and little flutters filled her stomach. Fighting them, she couldn't think of a snappy comeback. ''Hmm, I'll remember that.''

''There it is.'' Miss Hattie pulled out the sling, then passed it to Cally. ''Have a care not to bump his knee, dear.''

''I will.'' Cally took the sling, wondering why some enterprising soul hadn't created one for a broken heart.

''I'm going to spend a little time in my greenhouse.'' Miss Hattie slid her apron off, over her head, then patted her green flowered dress over her tummy. ''Tell Jeremy and Suzie they're welcome to join me, hmm?''

''Thanks, Miss Hattie.'' Bryce shifted on the chair.

''My pleasure, dear. I do so enjoy your children. They're lovely. Just lovely. Don't you agree, Cally?''

More matchmaking. The kids and now Miss Hattie. At least Cally could answer honestly. ''Positively adorable. All of them.'' She put the bag of ice on the table, knocking the cracking cubes together, then picked up the sling.

Miss Hattie paused at the mud room door. ''I suggest you get out of that wet shirt, Bryce, before putting that sling on. We're having a warm spell, but you could catch cold. Especially once you're away from the fire.'' Then she went out, and softly closed the door.

''Need some help with your buttons?'' Cally's eyes twinkled mischievously. ''Or are you going to go macho on me and insist on struggling with them yourself?''

''I'm too weary to struggle.'' He looked from the fire blazing gold and blue in the grate up at her, his eyes serious.

"Ouch. You're fighting the I'm-a-rotten-parent demon again." The fire popped, crackled, and hissed. Moisture seeping from the logs. "Ease up on you, Counselor." Cally reached for his shirt placket, her heart in her throat. Her hands were shaking. Why were her damn hands shaking? It wasn't as if she'd never touched a man before.

But she'd never touched or undressed *this* man. She forced a little strength into her voice, feeling as weak as water. "The kids are fine. You got a little banged up, but everything worked out okay. And the battleaxe didn't resign again."

"There is that."

"Right." Cally chided herself. She wasn't undressing him, just helping him out of his shirt. Big difference. The first button worked loose from the hole and the front of his shirt gaped at his throat, revealing a strip of dark, springy hair that looked too enticing to touch for her comfort. Now, not only were her hands shaking, she was shaking all over. And her blasted legs were about as stable as wilting flower stems.

"Thanks for helping me out with the kids, and for taking care of me." He sat back, giving her easier access to his buttons. "I'm about maxed out, Cally, and I'm sick of screwing up with them."

"I know. But you do more right than wrong, Bryce. Really." She opened the second button, then the third. Heaven help her, his chest was even more gorgeous than she'd thought. "Um, can you stand up?"

"What?"

Their gazes locked. The breath flew out of her. "I, um, can't pull the tail of your shirt free from your slacks with you sitting down." God, but the man smelled good. And looked good, even with a hint of a bruise peeking out from the top of his beard.

He rose to his feet, his chest brushing against her breasts, then stared down at her. No way could she look into his eyes. Not now. Not when she was feeling so attracted to him and so overwhelmed by him. She looked down at his chest, found that expanse of hair-sprinkled skin only marginally less enticing than his eyes, tugged his shirt free of his slacks, then finished undoing his buttons. By the time she was done, her heart felt ready to burst right out of her chest. Being this close to this much man had her hormones on full alert, and every instinct in her woman's soul wanting to caress and hold.

Clinical, she warned herself. *Think clinical.* She eased the shirt off his left shoulder, then his right. And failed getting even close to a clinical thought. The hormone alert grew to a riot. She skimmed the fabric down his arms. Her hands grazing over his warm skin tingled and, breathless, she brushed along his hard muscles, past his elbows, to his corded forearms, dusted with a sprinkling of fine, soft hair. The fabric bunched at his wrists, refused to slide over his hands and off his fingertips. "It's, um, stuck."

"The cuffs," he whispered thickly.

She glanced up, into his eyes.

Desire glazed them. "You've got to unbutton the cuffs."

"Oh." She couldn't look away. She wanted to, tried to, but stood transfixed, mesmerized. Could the desire burning so deeply in them be real? For her?

His lowered his lids, turned his hot gaze to her lips. His own parted, and he let out a little puff of breath that smelled of mint and warmed her face. "Cally?"

She couldn't talk past the knot in her throat. She moved her hands furiously, but they only became tangled in the folds of his shirt.

"Cally."

She ceased moving, again heard Suzie's haunting words ramble through her mind. Words about courage and believing and miracles. Digging deep, so very deep inside her, she willed her gaze to lift and meet his, damning herself as forty kinds of fool for letting herself get into this position. For wanting to be in this position.

He touched his fingertips to her cheek, rubbed soft circles under her chin with the pad of his thumb. "Look at me, honey," he whispered. "Please."

Oh, God. Her mouth desert-dry, she swallowed hard, let her gaze drift past the bunch of wadded shirt between them, up his middle, following the dark vee of hair on his chest between his male nipples to his throat. His pulse there throbbed against his skin, beating as fiercely as her own. With the aid of sheer grit, she managed to look higher, to his beard, up the slope of his patrician nose, then finally—dear God, finally—to his eyes.

They were solemn, serious, and intent. The thick air between them grew solid, dense. As thick as that morning's fog, blocking out sights and sounds and smells of everything except the two of them. Fabric rustled, then his shirt fell onto the floor, atop their feet. Neither of them looked down, nor reached to move it. He eased a hand to her shoulder, let it glide over her clavicle, down to her shoulder blade to circle her back, then lured her closer. Nose to nose, he whispered on a soft sigh. "Kiss me, Cally."

"That's not a good idea."

"Don't think about it. Don't weigh the right or wrong, or the good or bad in it. Forget that one-kiss rule—"

"We've already broken it."

"I broke it. I kissed you. But I'm asking you to break it now, Cally. I'm asking you to kiss me, because you want to kiss me. Because you ache to kiss me as much as I ache to kiss you. Please."

Lonely. Cally understood all he was feeling because she felt it, too. The togetherness with the kids, the intimacy of her icing his sore jaw. Their teaming up to stifle the battleaxe. Talking softly through the nights on the hallway floor. All of those things they'd faced together vividly reminded him of the many times he'd faced similar situations alone. And those memories had him realizing just how lonely he'd become. How much he missed having a partner. Cally's heartstrings suffered a mighty tug. Her beautiful Atlas was cracking under the weight of his world.

She tiptoed, tilted her face, then touched her lips to his, prepared for the avalanche of lust and desire and yearning to make love with him that would rip through her on contact.

The feelings didn't come. This kiss was unlike their others. This kiss was gentle and tender, less lusty and more loving. A gentle fusing of mouths and sweet caresses that rocked through to her core in ways the others only hinted at and promised. Where the others planted the seeds of desire and tilled it, this one was the harvest. It gathered the physical longing and the emotional yearning and churned them together, concocting a unique, vintage bliss she'd never before known. A whimper rushed out from the back of her throat. She untangled her sleeve from his belt buckle, lifted her hand and let her fingers search, then splay across his bare skin; slide up his forearm, his biceps, to his shoulder, his skin arousing images in her mind of sun-warmed satin over granite. God help her, he felt as wonderful as he looked. Even more wonderful than he smelled, and tenfold more wonderful than she'd imagined him.

He bent his knees, backed down into the chair, pulling her with him. Hooking the back of her thigh with his good arm, he spread her legs and nudged her until she straddled his thighs, urging her closer, then closer still. She sat astride him, her arms curled around his neck, her fingers threaded through his hair, breasts to chest, thighs to thighs, lips to lips, and settled into the kiss.

He separated their mouths, leaving her wanting more, and cupped her face in his trembling hands. His face tensed, a beautiful study of sharp angles and planes, and his words tumbled out on breaths as ragged as her own. "I want you, Cally."

Her hungry ears rejoiced. He wanted her. Her. Cally Tate. Lousy wife. Ugly, undesirable woman. Her. Unlovable her.

Or did he?

A thin film of sweat sheened his skin. Genuine desire glazed his eyes. His chest swelled and hollowed arhythmically, and the hard bulk of him pressed against placket and skirt, firmly nestled against her thighs. "What exactly do you want from me?"

"Everything you're willing to give." He opened his mouth to tell her more, but no words came out. He pressed a chaste kiss to her eyelid, to her cheek, her chin. "I'll give you everything I have to give, Cally. I want—"

"Shh, don't." She pressed a fingertip against his lips, unable to bear seeing him struggle. She never wanted to put him in the position of feeling he had to lie to her. "Something special happens when we touch. It's wonderful, magical. But I think it's all we've got to give each other. We've been through too much, you know? And we're fighting too many demons. Loneliness is just one of them." She hugged him close, buried her face at the cay in his neck, let her fingers fork through the silky hair at his nape. ''I want you, too,'' she confessed in a whisper, her nose brushing the shell of his ear. ''But I don't want to want you, or to need you, or to—'' What had been about to come out of her mouth stunned her silent.

His arms tightened around her. ''What?''

She shook her head; refused to answer, too amazed to believe herself what she'd been about to say to even think it, much less repeat it. Sliding off his lap, she eased the sling onto his arm then positioned his elbow and forearm inside it. When she was done, she looked at him, pain flashing through her chest like an SOS beacon.

He clasped her arm, curled his fingers around her and gave her a gentle squeeze. ''I didn't mean to hurt you, honey. If I said anything wrong, I'm sorry.''

Wrong? He'd said everything right. But she didn't trust right. Couldn't afford to trust right. ''You didn't.'' She looked away, took the bag of melting ice from the table and pressed it to his cheek. He was frowning, and so was she.

''You care about me, Cally. You don't want to, you know you shouldn't, and yet you do.'' He twisted the bag away from his face then looked up at her. ''That's it, isn't it? You care. That's what you had been about to say, wasn't it?''

''No.'' She lied with a good heart and a clean conscience. Bryce still loved Meriam. He didn't need Cally's care any more than she needed to give it.

''Liar.'' He stared at her.

She stared back, and said nothing.

''You'll never love me, Cally. And I'll never love you. We've had our shot at that. But we can care. We already trust each other, and I don't think caring would break any friendship rules.''

Her heart warbled in her chest. How could he make the illogical, the unreasonable, the impossible, sound so damn feasible? Their hormones were in overdrive. They kissed as if half-starved. And yet they called themselves friends? ''I'll think about it.''

Jeremy and Suzie came into the kitchen. Frankie walked straight through to the mud room door.

''Wait,'' Cally called out, grateful for the reprieve. She

needed to get her emotions under control. To bury some of this lust and caring and get back into some semblance of emotional balance. "Miss Hattie gave me some cleaner for your shirt."

"Blouse," Suzie corrected her.

"Right." Cally grinned.

Frankie's eyes lit up from the bottom. "Yeah?"

"Yeah."

"What's this all about?" Bryce asked.

Cally winked at him. "We're trying to keep Frankie's mom from skinning her alive."

"I don't want to get busted—that means put on restriction, Suzie. Not really busted," Frankie chimed in. "The festival is tomorrow, and I wanna go."

"Tomorrow?" Suzie spun toward Bryce, happy and excited. "Daddy, can we go?"

Seeing Suzie excited ranked about as rare as seeing her smile. She looked like a . . . a little girl, Cally thought. Joy bubbled in her heart. God, but was it good to see that.

"Maybe." Bryce's voice sounded thick, as if he'd noticed the change in Suzie, too. "If Cally will come with us. I'm wounded, and I can't keep up with all three of you." He dropped his voice so only Cally could hear. "Zero survival odds."

"Will you come, Cally?" Suzie asked. "Please. We'll be good and stay out of trouble. Even Jeremy."

"Wouldn't miss it." She whispered to Bryce. "I'll bail you out, for Suzie. Just because she looks so happy. But this isn't a date, Counselor. Hold that thought."

"Of course it's not." His eyes glittered, contradicting him, of course.

Not that Cally had expected they wouldn't. "I mean it."

"Okay."

"Okay." She couldn't resist hassling the stuffed shirt and bringing him down a peg or two. He looked altogether too pleased with himself. "One rule."

Bryce lifted a brow in her direction. "Why do I have the feeling I'm in serious trouble here?"

"No trouble," Cally assured him. "The rule is, no neckties are allowed."

Suzie beamed.

"If you insist." Bryce grimaced—but he didn't disagree.

"I do."

He squinted up at her. "I don't suppose it'd do me any good to appeal."

"None whatsoever."

"Okay, then." He sighed. "No tie."

Cally turned to Frankie to cover her smile. "Let's get that shirt cleaned up."

"Blouse," Frankie corrected her. "Suzie has a fit every time I call a blouse a shirt. Even if it's a T-shirt. Her mom told her that shirts are for guys. Girls wear blouses."

Meriam hadn't said that. Cally had. She glanced at Suzie, who looked beet-red and mortified. Touched that Suzie thought enough of what she'd told her to take it into her heart, Cally's chest felt full. "Well, she's positively right about that," she said, carefully avoiding looking at Suzie. "So let's get that stain out of your blouse, so you get to keep your skin and not get busted."

Bryce glanced at the oil smears on Frankie's shirt. "Sounds like a plan."

He was a good man. A great dad, and a good man. A shame they hadn't met earlier. Before Meriam and Gregory and heartache. Back when they'd both had courage.

The strongest urge ever to go to the cemetery and talk with Mary Beth Ladner waylaid Cally. More than to breathe, she needed to pour out her regret that things couldn't be different with Bryce.

But Mary Beth was a long way away. And the past had been lived, struggled through, and survived. It was done. The changes in them because of it were done, too. They couldn't go back and start over. Or undo. She could wish it, but the effort would be a waste of energy. Things couldn't be different for her or Bryce.

For them, no miracles could happen. Not even beside a dreamswept sea.

Chapter 9

For once, the Blue Moon Cafe wasn't the hub of the village.

The church parking lot filled and overflowed onto Main Street with laughing, smiling people, sipping old-fashioned sarsaparilla and Moxie, that distinctly New England soft drink. Beneath the flapping overhang of a blue and white tent, others ate hot dogs, steamed clams, piping hot chunks of lobster, and funnel cakes dusted with powdered sugar. Near the far corner of the lot, a crowd gathered to watch some serious taste-testing and voting on whose blueberry jam entry in the annual contest rated sweetest. Word on the wind predicted Miss Hattie would win hands down—again.

Cally loved the festive air, the sounds and smells and feelings of being surrounded by people who knew each other well and liked each other anyway.

With Lyssie in his arms, Bryce dipped close and whispered in Cally's ear. ''Lydia Johnson sure has her eye on that blue ribbon.''

She did. Holding her back ramrod straight, her chin high enough to be considered snobbish without benefit of any other waspy indicator, she discreetly chastised a young man about seventeen for spending too much time with Nolene Baker but, all the while, she held that ribbon steadfast in her gaze.

On sight, Cally disliked the woman. She wasn't sure why. Maybe it was the tilt of her chin, or the haughty air in her actions. Like a snob, but one who lacked the panache to successfully pull it off. Most likely the reason for the dislike had to do with Lydia's lecturing a boy who looked enough like her to be her son. That dredged up too many memories of Gregory and his mother's opposition to his marrying Cally. An opposition that hadn't weakened one iota during the successive fourteen years of their marriage. Biting into a funnel cake, Cally chewed slowly and wondered if her ex-mother-in-law treated Gregory's new wife, Joleen, with that same disdain and thinly veiled scorn.

"Poor guy's getting an earful." Bryce polished off his fourth funnel cake and looked down at his powdered hand as if not sure what to do with it.

Cally dusted it off with her napkin, and grunted her agreement about the boy. In all their ventures through the village, she'd never before seen the woman, and the only thing she'd heard about her was that Miss Millie, Miss Hattie's best friend, had refused to welcome Lydia to the Historical Society meetings, which grated at her something awful. "Who exactly is Lydia?"

Bryce dropped his voice. "Lydia Johnson, the mayor's wife. They own The Store over there. No, honey. There, next door to Jimmy's garage." Bryce grabbed Lyssie's hand just before it clenched closed around a wad of Vic's cotton candy.

"Nice save." Cally smiled at him.

Bryce smiled back, then wiggled his brows. "Can you keep a secret?"

Teasing her? Her stomach fluttered. It'd been a long time since she'd been teased, and longer still since she'd liked it. With what Bryce's teasing was doing to her insides, she just knew she couldn't like liking it, either. "Depends."

"On what?" His eyes twinkled, as mischievous as Jeremy's.

"How juicy it is." She batted her lashes, then gave him an innocent smile.

"Fair enough. This isn't juicy enough to get me into trouble."

"Darn." She saved some boy's corn dog from Lyssie's reach.

"Darn," the angel mimicked her.

"No, darling." Cally tapped the edge of the baby's nose. "Animal crackers."

The skin crinkled near Bryce's eyes and he whispered so only she could hear. "You're wicked, Cally Tate."

"Nope, 'fraid not. Just lousy—and a lover of juicy tidbits."

He dipped his chin, as if he were looking at her over glasses, and a lock of thick black hair fell over his forehead. "You're not, nor have you ever been, lousy. You've been warned not to willfully perjure yourself, Miss Tate. One more slip and I'm afraid I'm going to have to petition the court for a restraining order against you."

"Gonna save me from myself, huh, Counselor?" So serious. So darling.

He nodded and let out a mock sigh. "It's a tough job, but somebody's got to do it."

"And here I thought chivalry was dead."

"Honey, it's not even napping."

Little bubbles of pleasure popped in her stomach, and she inhaled deeply, catching a whiff of his cologne on the breeze. Subtle and sexy. Almost as enticing as the smell of his skin. "So what's this not-so-juicy, juicy tidbit that has you threatening me with legal repercussions?"

He cocked his head toward Lydia. "Her real name is Lily."

"No." Cally feigned a gasp.

"It's true."

"Under oath?"

"Under oath."

"Well, now, Counselor." She narrowed her brows and dropped her voice to a conspiratorial whisper. "Since you're an officer of the court, I'd say we've got an ethical duty to unravel this mystery. Just what kind of nefarious acts would make a woman with a lovely name like Lily grab herself an alias?"

"Sorry, darling. I know how much you love a good mystery, but this one's already been solved."

She primed her mouth for another "darn," saw Lyssie

watching her closely, and opted for a substitute. "Animal crackers."

"Disappointing, I know. But don't worry." Bryce's lips twitched. "I have it on good authority that small towns and villages are full of mysteries. T.J. and Maggie say it's like living your life in a goldfish bowl. And, from what I've seen, I'm inclined to agree."

Cally couldn't disagree. While stouthearted and anything but malicious, people here did seem to know everything about everyone in the village. And if they didn't know something, it was because they didn't want to know it, not because someone had successfully buried their skeletons in the proverbial closet. The bulletin board at the Blue Moon held shopping lists, bets, and all manner of news. "So why did Lily take on an alias?"

"I'm afraid the story appears rather mundane." Bryce wiped cookie crumbs from Lyssie's mouth with a paper napkin, then wadded it up and again looked baffled at what to do with it.

Cally wadded it up then stuffed it into his slacks pocket. "And?"

"She thought Lydia sounded more regal."

"Hmm, more sophisticated, would be my guess."

"Probably." He lowered his voice to just above a whisper, glanced around to assure no one else could hear them. "But I'm very observant, Miss Tate, and I've got my doubts about the woman. Just look at those beady eyes."

Cally nearly laughed aloud. "Hmm, valid point, Counselor. Sharp tongue, too."

"Sinfully." He stiffened his spine and tugged his soggy cuff out of Lyssie's mouth. "Teething, you know."

"I suspected as much." A board would have noticed the baby drooling, for pity's sake. Cally inwardly grinned. "Who's the young man on the receiving end of that sinfully sharp tongue?"

"Andrew Carnegie. Not *the* Andrew Carnegie, of course. Lydia and Horace's son. He's going to be a lawyer."

Cally's stomach muscles clenched. From Bryce's tone, she innately knew the boy had little or no choice in the matter of selecting his profession. If she were lucky enough to have a son, she'd just pray that whatever he chose to do, he'd be happy doing it. "Hmm, sounds as if Lydia cornered you for advice on the legal profession."

"She did. The best schools. The type of people we encounter in practicing. Salaries."

"That smirk of yours is telling me you filled her ear with a lot of nonsense, Bryce Richards. Did you deliberately mislead the woman?"

"Yes, Miss Tate, I did," he said, as stone-faced as Judge Branson had been when he'd ordered her to appear in court. "But don't bother asking for remorse, because I don't have any, and I won't retract so much as one word."

Atypical behavior from the Bryce Richards she'd come to know. "Ah, Andrew doesn't want to become a lawyer."

"Very astute, Miss Tate." Bryce's eyes lit up from the bottoms.

His compliment warmed her. She liked this playful Bryce—and added that to her list of her dislikes. "Did Andrew tell you that—about him not wanting to practice law?"

"Pastor Brown did. But that's strictly confidential information."

"Got it." She tipped a fingertip to her forehead in mock salute.

"Pastor Brown is very progressive. Gets him into hot water around here on occasion, but because he's got a soft spot for Andrew Carnegie, the mayor helps him out."

Men. They twisted things something godawful. "Why doesn't the mayor help out his son?"

Bryce slid her a devil's smile. "Because he's a man of wisdom, Miss Tate. He knows that to oppose his wife on a matter in which she's issued a verdict means not only no appeal, but no parole, and certainly no peace."

That sure wasn't the way it'd worked around her house. The wind caught the hem of her jacket and spread it like a sail, right over Lyssie's face. "Sorry, munchkin." She tugged it down and held it clasped, dropped a kiss to the baby's nose, then looked back at Bryce. "Is that how it was with you and Meriam?"

Bryce sobered. The teasing light shining in his eyes faded abruptly, then snuffed out.

Great. She'd done it again. "Never mind. I shouldn't have asked."

"It's okay. Seriously. It just hit me that—"

When he didn't continue, Cally gave him a nudge. "What?"

Surprise flickered through his eyes. "I haven't even thought of her today."

"Darling, you don't have to feel guilty about not thinking about her. She's content, remember?"

"Yeah." A frown creased his brow. "Yeah, she's content."

A gusty breeze tugged at Cally's hair, whipping it across her face. She pushed it back from her eyes, and saw a young woman wearing a red sweatband across her forehead place a blue ribbon in front of a pie plate on a long table covered with a white cloth. "Look." Cally squeezed Bryce's arm. "Miss Hattie's pie won."

"Hatch and Vic said it would."

"So did Lucy Baker and Sheriff Cobb."

Bryce adjusted Collin's cane, affixing his grip. "Let's see what Miss Millie is up to with all the kids over there." He hiked his chin toward a huge oak near the little fence that surrounded the cemetery.

Cally had heard all about Miss Hattie's best friend. And she'd met her on a secret visit to see if Miss Millie knew what was wrong with Miss Hattie. According to Miss Millie, the two women had been friends all their lives and, since Miss Millie had been widowed, they'd grown even closer, attending church services together, co-chairing the Sea Haven Village Historical Society, and playing penny-ante poker every Thursday night. Their poker games too were confidential information to not be mentioned to Pastor Brown. It was said that he had a penchant for long-winded lectures against gambling, drinking, and sexy girlie calendars, like the swimsuit issue that hung in Jimmy Goodson's garage.

After losing their men, both women had made a fulfilling life for themselves. And, despite whatever had Miss Hattie fretting now, they'd both been successful at carving out their own niches. Seeing their successes deepened Cally's own resolve to find her niche, to rediscover her dreams. Miss

Hattie and Miss Millie had proven it could be done. Now Cally just had to figure out *how* they'd done it, then summon the courage to take those same steps in her own life.

"Have you been to Miss Millie's Antique Shoppe?" Bryce asked, rubbing noses with Lyssie.

The baby gurgled a laugh. "Once." Cally recalled the shelves in the back of the store that held jar upon jar of different scents of potpourri, together with the bolts of lace from which Miss Millie crafted the most darling sachets. "She has some lovely things."

Miss Millie, wearing a blue dress that made her silver hair look even more violet-tinged, had the children sitting in a semicircle on the ground. She passed out her drop-dead chocolate chip cookies from a lace doily-lined tray, warned the village hound, Walter, Jr., to eat his own and not mooch from the kids, then gave them all a little lecture on village history.

Cally paused to listen. Miss Millie was a natural-born teacher, relaying events in an interesting, almost captivating, manner. A shipbuilder had started the village, and after he'd died and his relatives had shut down the shipyard, the villagers had turned to the sea to provide for them.

"They're loving this," Bryce whispered.

The kids did look enraptured. Was it the cookies, or the storytelling? She listened closely. Heard how Cecelia and Collin Freeport had built Seascape Inn and had lived there all their married lives. How they'd helped all the villagers at some time; Collin with his wood-carving and woodworking skills, and Cecelia with her healing. And heard they were so beloved that on the night Cecelia had died, all the villagers had held a candlelight vigil on Seascape's front lawn. Lobstermen aboard their boats far out in the ocean reported seeing the lights.

Cally felt empty inside. If it'd been her dying, the lawn would have been empty. There would have been no vigil, no candles, no lights.

Hatch cupped his mouth with his hands. "Tell 'em about Little Island, Miss Millie."

Miss Millie set the empty tray down on the ground then straightened up, seemingly fretting. "Did I forget that?"

The kids let her know that she had.

Hatch never let his gaze drift from Miss Millie. Cally wondered if the woman knew she'd captured a heart. Miss Millie and Hatch, Miss Hattie and Vic. It seemed the women of the village had a tendency toward that. And toward not noticing. Maybe they had some special something women from away just didn't have. Of course, the reason for Miss Hattie's oblivion waxed clear. Tony. Dead or alive, the man still held her heart. And she still held his.

Cally rocked onto the balls of her sneaker-clad feet. What would it be like to know that a man loved you so much he refused to let even death separate you?

She couldn't imagine.

"That bit of business from Hatch about Little Island," Bryce said, twitching his nose. "Choreographed, I suspect, Miss Tate."

"Noted, Counselor." Cally smiled at Bryce.

He smiled back, and her stomach furled. She didn't like it a bit, but looped her hands around his bent arm, anyway.

"Well," Miss Millie said. "Once my family owned all the land around here for miles and miles. It owned Little Island, too. And eventually I inherited it." She paced a short path before the kids. "We older locals have watched Sea Haven Village change a lot in our lifetimes. And, while we appreciate tourists and depend on them, a few years ago, it occurred to some of us that our village was getting too *touristical.*"

Bryce whispered, "Too many tourists, Miss Tate?"

"I expect so, Counselor."

"We became afraid that our young people wouldn't have the opportunity to see the beauty here that we'd been fortunate enough to see." Miss Millie paused to sip water from a yellow paper cup. "Villagers, young and old, deserved the chance to know the Maine we had known. We believed, you see, that if they had a special place where only they could go, then they'd nurture it, and respect it, and they'd come to love that place. And they have. That place is Little Island."

Miss Millie let her gaze drift over the kids' faces. "You children are villagers, too. Did you know that you and your parents now own Little Island? Well, you do. And your parents and all the rest of the villagers are depending on you to take care of it."

She looked over at Vic, who pointedly tapped his watch crystal. "Oh my, it's time for the three-legged races. Scoot and find your parents now."

Cally sighed wistfully. "What a beautiful way to teach kids respect for the environment. By loving the land."

Bryce nodded, met Cally's gaze. "There's a lot of good in this village. A lot of care, and even more love."

The sunlight caught on the pristine church's stained-glass window. Reflected color splashed blue, yellow, and green onto the white clapboard. "I think when I settle down again it'll be in a small town. I like the way it feels."

"How did you end up in New Orleans?" Bryce asked.

"Born to it."

"Me, too."

Suzie was holding a very serious conversation with Hatch, the crusty old lighthouse keeper, and he appeared to be hanging on to her every word. He was an interesting character, Cally thought. A face lined and weathered from long exposure to sea salt and sun, a yellow bandana tied at his throat, a rumpled T-shirt and blue slacks that sagged at his knees, and an unlit corncob pipe perched in the corner of his mouth. A lot of people, she supposed, mistook him as a man having little to say worth hearing, but Cally knew better. Looking into his eyes, she saw wisdom. Hatch was special. Gifted in ways she couldn't begin to fathom. Suzie had chosen well, having her serious discussion with him.

Frankie came running, then skidded to a stop beside Hatch and Suzie. Her dirty sneaker gained traction, lifting a little cloud of sand and dust. Hatch grinned at her.

"Hmm," Bryce whispered. "Definitely a conspiracy brewing there, Miss Tate."

"My thoughts exactly, Counselor."

The three of them—Suzie and Frankie, flanking Hatch—linked hands, then walked toward Cally and Bryce.

Suzie had cookie crumbs at the corner of her mouth. On seeing that evidence of the little girl in her, Cally felt her heart was light enough to float.

"Fine day for a festival, ain't it?" Hatch lifted his stubbly gray chin to the warm sun.

"Yes, it is." Bryce shifted Lyssie, crooked in his good arm, then nodded at Hatch. "Good to see you again. We really enjoyed the lighthouse tour."

"We did," Cally added. "Suzie's talked about it for days."

"And complained about the Coast Guard automating all the lighthouses." Bryce nodded. "She's written a letter of complaint to the President."

"Glad to hear it." Hatch slid Suzie a gap-toothed grin. "I'm officially wintercating, but the tour was a pleasure. Amazing what a man will do for some of Miss Hattie's muffins."

"Wintercating?" Cally asked.

"Gearing up to watch the snow fall," Suzie explained, her expression dead serious.

"Ah." Adorable.

"I like Miss Hattie's apple muffins," Suzie said.

Hatch grunted. "Don't be thinking this old man would snub his nose at 'em, but Miss Hattie's got a heavy hand with cinnamon in her apple. Blueberry's my pick."

"Her banana's the best. They've got nuts. I love nuts." Frankie jerked at her skirt, clearly unhappy at wearing a dress, and looked at Suzie. "Better get that cookie off your face before my mom sees it. She can spot a speck at fifty yards and she's determined we look and act like ladies today."

Wanting to giggle, Cally shook out the paper napkin from her funnel cake, knocking the powdered sugar loose, then passed it to Suzie. "This might help."

Suzie gave her lips a swipe. The crumbs tumbled in the sunlight down to the ground.

Biting back a grin, Hatch made a production of clearing his throat then stuffing his unlit pipe into his shirt pocket. "Me and these two upstarts have been talking."

"I'll tell him, Hatch." Suzie looked from the man to Bryce. "I wanna see my island, Daddy."

Bryce smiled at Suzie. "Honey, you're not a villager. Little Island belongs to the villagers."

"Miss Millie was talking to me, too."

Hatch interrupted. "I'm of a mind to take her, Bryce, provided we've got your permission. What I mean is, I'm inviting all of you to come. Frankie's folks, Sam and Edith Green—"

"They own Fisherman's Co-op, Daddy."

"Yes, Suzie, I know."

Hatch went on. "The Greens have a boat, of course. They're from away, but good folks planning on putting down roots here."

"They're planning on making me a lady, too, Mr. Richards," Frankie explained further.

"I believe I've heard you mention that, Frankie." Bryce nodded thoughtfully.

"She's mentioned her mom, Daddy, but her dad wants it, too," Suzie said.

"Listen up, half-pints." Hatch squinted at the two girls. "If you're wantin' me to talk your folks into this, then you've got to let me get out more than two words between your interruptions so I can see the job done. Zip it."

Suzie and Frankie both made motions of zipping their lips shut.

Bryce didn't correct Hatch at the reference to Cally being the other half of Suzie's folks. Cally didn't, either. And she didn't like it that she hadn't. She especially didn't like it that the idea of Suzie being her daughter felt sensational and appealed so much it left her heart feeling like mush.

"Now." Hatch hiked up his pants. "I'm of a mind to build myself a sand castle or two, and these two upstarts have agreed to help me build a double-decker. If it's okay with you two."

"Please, Cally." Suzie covered her mouth with her hand. "Sorry, Hatch. I forgot."

He gave her shoulder a pat. "It's okay, munchkin."

Munchkin. The same endearment Bryce himself often used. Cally felt torn. Suzie wanted to do this; she fairly radiated anticipation, and Cally hated to disappoint her, but she couldn't not disappoint her. "As much as I'd like to go, I'm going to have to pass, Hatch."

"Aw, Cally." Suzie let out a groan worthy of an Oscar. "Please."

"Shoot." Frankie stubbed the toe of her shoe in the sand.

Bryce looked perplexed. "Too many funnel cakes?"

She'd had three. She could lie. But not while looking into his gorgeous eyes and seeing his concern. "I don't like boats." A half-truth was better than a lie.

"Ah, geez, Cally." Frankie motioned. "Hatch got his limp falling down a ladder on a boat, and he still likes 'em. And Suzie has bad dreams about 'em, and she still wants to go."

"Now, now." Hatch put his pipe back into his mouth and squinted against the sun. "Don't be badgering Cally. If she's scared of boats, she's scared of boats, and that's that, in my estimation. Ain't no crime, is it, Counselor?"

"No, it isn't," Bryce agreed.

From his expression, Bryce knew she'd not been totally honest. But he was being a gentleman, not calling her down on it. For that kindness she was grateful. And she positively hated liking that.

Hatch ruffled his stubbly whiskers with the back of his hand. "Though I have to say, we ain't planning on taking no dip in the drink, Cally. Only on riding over to the island and building—"

"A few sand castles—a double-decker," Cally finished for Hatch, embarrassed and not wanting to admit the real reason she didn't want to go had nothing to do with the boat but with the water it was in. Hatch, somehow, had known that. She'd been right about him. Wise. With special gifts she couldn't begin to fathom.

"Lyssie, please stop squirming." Bryce shifted his weight, then cringed.

"The knee tiring out?"

"I'm afraid so." He nodded. "Suzie, I think the ride is a little rough for Jeremy, and it's about time for Lyssie's nap."

Cally took the wiggling baby from him, then settled her against her shoulder. "Are your folks going, Frankie?"

She nodded.

"Hatch, would it be too hard on you to keep an eye on Suzie without Bryce and me there?"

"'Course not." He winked at Suzie. "Me and the up-start'll challenge the Greens and Frankie to a castle-building contest. Maybe even a triple-decker."

Suzie beamed up a smile at the old man and squeezed his gnarled hand until his fingertips went white, then lifted her brows expectantly at Cally.

"Well." Cally smiled. "That's settled, then."

"Yippee!"

"Aw right!"

Hatch faked a grumble. "My ears'll ring for a week."

"Is it settled?" Bryce frowned at Cally.

"Isn't it?" She hiked a shoulder. Oh, boy. She'd stepped over the line.

He stared at her for a long moment, then sighed. "I guess it is."

Suzie let out a whoop. Lyssie bounced in her arms and squealed right into Cally's left ear. Her groan was genuine.

"Kids." Hatch harrumphed. "Ya gotta love 'em." He linked his hands with Suzie's and Frankie's. "Don't you two worry now. We'll be back in time for Suzie to do the Highland Fling with Vic. She promised." He winked at Cally. "I get a waltz."

Hatch looked at Bryce, then back to Cally. "Wander along, if you're of a mind to. Miss Millie and me will see to it Suzie gets home safe and sound."

"Oh, will Miss Millie be going to the island, too?"

"Absolutely," Hatch said. "Goes every festival, sure as dawn. Renews her spirit, she says. Likes the quiet, in my estimation."

The three of them wound through the crowded parking lot to Main Street, then crossed the asphalt and walked on down to the pier behind the Co-op.

Bryce adjusted the sling around his neck, then slipped his free arm around Cally's waist. "It's a conspiracy, Miss Tate."

She pivoted her head to look at him, and nearly brushed their noses. "What is, Counselor?"

He pretended to make sure they were out of earshot. Impossible considering the crowd. "I have it on good authority that the entire village is conspiring to get us alone together."

They were. And had been since the day Cally had arrived. "Really? I hadn't noticed."

Bryce sent her a skeptical look. "The penalties for perjury are steep. Are you sure you wouldn't like to reconsider your testimony?"

The challenge in his eyes didn't tempt her half so much as the dare in his tone. Her voice dropped to husky. "Bad question to ask a courageless woman, Counselor."

He cupped her chin in his big hand and his eyes went serious. "A woman who willingly spends the better part of her days and nights with a widower and his three small children isn't courageless, Miss Tate. She's golden-hearted and brave."

"She's lonely." Cally spoke before she thought.

Surprise flickered in his eyes, though she'd not said anything she'd not openly admitted before. But, by unspoken agreement, they only had talked of their feelings under the cover of darkness, out in the hallway outside Suzie's bedroom door.

Until now.

His breath fanned over her face. "I hope she's less lonely with us than she is without us."

Warmth oozed through Cally's stomach. She met his gaze, so solemn, so intense. Could she do it? Tell him, openly? "She likes the racket, and the snacks, when they're not straight health food."

"Is that a yes?"

He needed, not wanted but needed, to know. "That's a yes."

"I'm glad."

"I'm debating."

"You're making a big difference in our lives." The sun kissed his hair, sheening the black strands glossy.

"Not really."

"Really," he insisted. "Especially with Suzie. She's becoming a little girl again, Cally. Not nearly so serious or worried. Do you realize how much that means to me?"

"Yes, I do." After their heart-to-heart talks, how could she not understand? "And I'm glad to see it. But Selena is Suzie's ultimate authority. Her and Tony. Not me."

Bryce cocked his head. ''She quotes them both a thousand times a day, that's true. But it's worth noting that she's never once turned to Selena for permission. Or to Mrs. Wiggins, for that matter.''

''What?'' What was he talking about?

''Just now. Suzie didn't ask me if she could go. She asked you. That's a first. She's always come to me.''

Boy, had she stepped over the line. Lyssie had dozed off, drooling against Cally's neck. ''Did it bother you—for Suzie to ask me?''

''Should it?''

''I don't know.'' What did he want from her? Did he think she was manipulating, insinuating herself into their lives? ''I guess that depends on what you mean.''

He dug the tip of his cane into the sand-swept ground. ''I don't know what I mean.''

He truly didn't. And if he didn't know, then how the heck could she? ''I see.'' The steady breeze off the ocean had her lips dry. She licked at them. ''I didn't mean to offend you, Bryce, or to usurp your authority. Honestly, I just responded without thinking. I didn't mean to step over the line. If that's the problem, I'm sorry.''

He looked away.

Maybe he felt Suzie had slighted him. Or that he'd let her down. More likely the latter. ''We've been spending a lot of time together with the kids, and I guess Suzie was just doing what felt natural to her.''

''Yeah, I guess she was.'' He studied Cally's face, blinked then blinked again. ''Guess it felt natural to both of you. You responded without thinking.''

Cally inwardly groaned. Now she'd made him realize again what his children were missing in not having a mother. And, damn it, he was right. She *had* done what had come naturally in answering Suzie.

Great. Just great. He'd been teasing, for the first time looking halfway relaxed, and she drags him and herself down emotionally. More proof, as if she needed it. *Lousy.*

''There you are.'' Mrs. Wiggins joined them, swatting at her neck. ''Aren't these black flies just awful?''

''What black flies?'' Bryce asked.

Cally hadn't noticed any, either. It wasn't even the right time of year for black flies.

Lyssie made a soft sucking sound and Cally rubbed tiny circles on her back, inhaling her sweet baby scent. Ah, there were no flies. Mrs. Wiggins was filing another protest. Though this one was a bit more subtle than her usual. She'd tired of the festivities and wanted an excuse to return to her stringent daily schedule.

She reached for Lyssie. "I'll take her. I'm going back to the inn. Jeremy is bobbing for apples with Vic and Hattie, Mr. Richards. She's says she'll bring him home with her after they ride someone named Sobey's pony."

"All right." Bryce gave Lyssie's back a gentle pat.

The tenderness in his expression brushed over Cally's heart. Watching Mrs. Wiggins and Lyssie go, Cally imagined Jeremy's excitement. "Riding a pony. He'll love it."

"Most kids would."

The man hadn't a clue. "Bryce, Jeremy talks nonstop about horses."

"He does?" The sling's band had a red mark circling Bryce's neck.

Cally adjusted it so it stopped cutting into his skin. "Nonstop."

"I hadn't picked up on that."

Oh, boy. She lowered her hands to her sides. She'd done it again. Telling Bryce something he hadn't noticed about the kids did raise the man's hackles. She hated seeing him chewing himself up inside, telling himself he was a rotten parent. Maybe the festivities would—nope. There it was. That self-deprecating snarl. Well, hell.

"Don't be surprised." She squeezed his forearm. "Kids' interests change daily. Sometimes even quicker."

"I didn't know that, either."

"True, Counselor," she said, deliberately forcing her tone light. "No way can a mere mortal keep track."

"That's comforting." He stroked at his temple. "But these observations make me feel like I'm far out of the loop."

"Don't be ridiculous."

"I'm serious." He lifted a stone, then tossed it to the ground.

"Look, Counselor. I'm the queen of lousy, so I know rotten when I see it and, when I look at you, it just ain't there."

"I would remind you, Miss Tate, that you're under oath."

"I haven't forgotten." Seeing doubt in his eyes bugged her. She wanted that teasing light in them again. She hated loving that teasing light. "I think you're a wonderful parent, Bryce. I mean that sincerely." Looping her arm through the crook in his, she gave his forearm a second, reassuring squeeze. "Miss Tate petitions for a brief recess, if counsel has no objections."

"Counsel reserves the right to know the reason for the recess prior to issuing an opinion."

Cally slid him a look filled with longing. "A few minutes of peace and quiet. A short walk on the cliffs should do it. If counsel's knee isn't too sore."

Bryce sank his teeth into his lower lip but failed to bite back a smile. "Counsel has no objection whatsoever, Miss Tate."

They made their way through the maze of people, crossed the street to the shore, then walked down the asphalt street a short way. "Take care, Bryce. The sand makes the road slick."

"I noticed." He circled her waist with his arm, tucked her close to his side.

She was about as transparent as Saran Wrap film, but the ploy had worked. He was holding her. She eased her arm around his waist, knowing she should be angry with herself. And she would be . . . later. Right now, she just felt too darn good.

The sounds of the festival faded to those of the ocean. A slatted bench facing the sea looked inviting, and Bryce truly did seem to be having a hard time walking on the slippery sand, leaning more heavily than he had been on both Cally and Collin's cane.

"Let's sit for a while," she suggested. When he nodded, she let go of his arm, sat down, then patted the bench seat for him to join her.

He settled at her side, brushing their thighs, and let out a relieved sigh that proved his knee was giving him fits. Taking his weight off the cane had grains of sand scattering his shoes and faintly pattering. ''You earned kudos today, Counselor.''

''What for?'' He propped the cane against the end of the bench then leaned back and scanned the frothy ocean.

Cally touched a fingertip to his bare throat. ''No tie.''

He looked down at his blue polo shirt, khaki slacks, and casual loafers. ''Didn't have one to match.''

''Ah.'' She smacked her lips. He'd be gorgeous in an inflated space suit, or anything else, but in casual clothes, the man fairly robbed her of breath. ''And here I was thinking I'd won a little victory.''

He held his gaze on the horizon, and his lips didn't curve, but the skin near his eyes crinkled in a smile. ''Victory acknowledged. You insisted, remember?''

''Yes, I do. But I didn't think for a second you'd accommodate me.''

''Why not? It was a small request.''

A small request. Oh, how special this man truly was. How very, very special. A little shot of sheer pleasure laced with yearning then darted through her chest. ''You do look more comfortable.''

''I am.'' He leaned close and dropped his voice to a secretive whisper. ''Confidentially, Miss Tate, I hate ties.''

''Honest?''

''Always, darling.''

She hated loving that response. ''Then why wear them when you don't have to?''

''Old habit.'' He swung his gaze to her and she sensed that habit had started with pleasing Meriam and just hadn't faded. ''Incidentally, I've been wondering. Do you like the way I look?''

''Don't start, Counselor. We agreed there'd be no more of this proving to me that I'm a desirable woman business.''

He stretched out an arm over the back of the bench and let his fingers draw circles on her shoulder. ''For the record, I like the way you look. Very much. And I admit my memory could be faulty, but I don't recall—''

''Oh, no you don't. We agreed. Two nights ago, in the hallway. Somewhere around three A.M., I'd say.'' She narrowed her eyes. ''That was you, wasn't it, Counselor?''

"It was." He slid her a frown and held it so she wouldn't miss it. "You didn't let me finish."

"Sorry," she said, feeling anything but.

"I recall our conversation and agreement, Miss Tate, but I don't recall its terms including me lying to you. In fact, I'm sure as certain it didn't. We have a contract, promising honesty, and lying would be in direct conflict—"

"Excuse me?" And he complained about women talking in riddles?

"I agreed I'd not attempt to prove anything to you. I didn't agree to lie to you about my genuine feelings, or about the way I react to you—i.e., your looks."

Her heart nearly stopped. Then the fool thing raced like a runaway train. She looked away, out onto the sun-spangled water, and ordered herself to calm down. To not make too much of what he was saying. Then lifted her chin to the cool breeze. "For the record, I don't like liking this about you, either."

"Noted." He rubbed a strand of her hair between his forefinger and thumb.

Gulls circled overhead and waves splashed against the rocky shore. Mist from the sea rose and gathered on her face, cooling it. She wouldn't think about his remark, she decided. He hadn't meant anything by it. Not really. Certainly nothing that should have her hormones sliding into overdrive. And even if he had, the man couldn't know his own mind. He was still celibate, far from satiated, so how could he?

"Darn shame you lost kudos today, Miss Tate."

She glanced over at him. Her hair whipped over her face. She smoothed it back and cocked her head so the wind would keep the loose strands out of her eyes. "How did I do that?"

He clicked his tongue, cast her a look loaded with disappointment. "You committed perjury."

"I did?" Had she? Lying ranked atypical, but not impossible. These days, if something cut close to the bone, she'd succumb to a white lie in self-defense. "About what?"

"The boat."

That she hadn't expected. More relieved than upset, and even more confused, she hiked her brows in question. "Excuse me?"

"The boat. You said you didn't want to go to Little Island because you didn't like boats."

"I don't like boats."

He stared deeply into her eyes. "But that's not why you didn't want to go."

"It wasn't a lie."

"Was it the whole truth and nothing but the truth, so help you?"

"Geez, Counselor. Isn't there a law against cross-examination during a peace-and-quiet recess?"

"Can you tell me the truth?"

"Is it important?" Something had changed. This wasn't just playful banter, he was serious. But why?

"It's important." The laughter lingering in his eyes faded. "A man needs to know he can trust a woman's word, just as a woman needs to know she can trust a man's. Justice—that it works both ways, don't you think?"

Her face flamed hot. Well, hell. Even a white lie would seem sinister after a lecture like that one. "It wasn't the boat. I don't know how to swim and I'm scared to death of water, okay?"

"Okay." He smiled at her then pressed a chaste kiss to her cheek. "Thank you."

She wanted to be angry with him for insisting she answer, but he hadn't insisted, merely encouraged. And how could she be ticked off at a guy who looked as if he stepped off the pages of *GQ*, had an arm in a sling, a bruise peeking out from his beard, and a busted knee? Discarding, of course, his hinting at finding her desirable. Definitely, inadmissable evidence. She knew it was faked due to special circumstances. It had to be.

How could it not be?

Because she fleetingly wished it weren't, sadness seeped into her heart, then burrowed down into the secret place inside her that harbored her dreams. For some reason, she thought of Mary Beth Ladner, of the woman who had been the sunshine of her home, and that flicker of a spark ignited inside her, burned brighter. And the desire to be the sunshine of her own home grew stronger, to a yearning that touched her soul-deep.

* * *

Cally glanced expectantly at Bryce. "You're sure you don't think it macabre?"

"Not at all." He stepped to her side. "Walking through a cemetery might not be a typical thing to do on a date, but—"

"This isn't a date, Counselor. We agreed."

"Right." He stroked his beard. "As I was saying, walking through a cemetery might not be a typical thing to do on a nondate date, but it certainly isn't bizarre." He cocked his head. "Now, Tony. His presence at Seascape—that's bizarre."

"It is."

"But you know what, Cally?"

"What?"

"It's comforting, too. Knowing he's with Suzie, and she's dreaming but not terrified because she isn't alone, well, that's very comforting to me. And I'm sure it is to Suzie."

"Bryce?"

Cally's tone set his teeth on edge, his senses on alert. And she'd stopped. Standing stiffly, she stared down at a headstone. "What is it, honey?"

"Look at her name."

Baffled, Bryce looked down to the gray marble, to the chiseled lettering. "Mary Elizabeth Freeport Nelson." Not making any connection, he glanced back at Cally. "Collin and Cecelia's daughter maybe?"

"Yes." Cally unpinned the yellow carnation from her lapel and placed it on the ground where the headstone and earth met.

"I don't get it."

"Mary Elizabeth. Mary Beth." Cally looked up at him. "Same birth and death dates. Isn't that strange?"

"Cally, they're not the same woman."

"I know." She shrugged, dusted the dirt from her fingertips, then stood up. "But they have a lot in common, and their names are close, and I'm—"

"Missing Mary Beth?" He curled an arm around Cally's waist.

She nodded.

"Ah, I think I'm seeing some friendly encouraging of the Tony variety here."

"What do you mean?" Under the shadow of an evergreen, she looked up at him.

"I think he's led you to Mary Elizabeth so you could keep her company while you're here. Kind of a hot line to Mary Beth."

Cally looked at him as if he'd lost his mind. "Bryce, do you realize how ridiculous that sounds?"

"Not at all, Miss Tate. It's perfectly logical. You always talk over your troubles with Mary Beth, right?"

"Right."

"So to be comfortable here you need to talk, but Mary Beth isn't here. And you haven't exactly been welcoming to Tony. But Mary Elizabeth, a trusted sister, is here. It makes perfect—"

"Trusted sister? Whose sister?"

"Tony's."

Cally's face went white. "Tony can't manipulate people like that, can he?"

"Yes, Miss Tate. He can." Bryce answered softly, and without flourish. "Remember when you were driving to Nova Scotia? That almost irresistible urge to come here?"

"Oh, God." Cally slumped against Bryce.

"Are you going to faint?"

"No."

"I think you're going to faint. I've seen women who were about to faint before, and you really look like you're about to faint."

"I'm not going to faint."

"Why don't we go into the church and sit down, just in case. I'd feel a lot—"

"I'm not going to faint, Bryce." Cally dragged in a breath and demanded her heart to slow its beating. Her temples fairly throbbed, and she wasn't at all sure she wasn't going to kiss the dirt in a dead faint. "He's manipulating us."

Bryce cupped her face in his hand. "He's helping Suzie. He intercedes in her dreams, so she's not alone. Hatch says Tony's not supposed to do that—intercede—but he's doing it anyway. For Suzie and for me."

"Hatch knows about him, too?"

Bryce nodded. "Tony protects her, Cally. I don't give a tinker's damn if he's a ghost, or an alien from Planet Funnel Cake. He's helping my daughter."

Her mouth stone-dry, Cally stared up at him. Bryce meant it. Every word. He didn't care. With Tony helping Suzie, Cally understood that. But how well did she understand? Was she grateful enough to set aside the fear of the oddity that he existed? Question was, Did she care?

He was helping Suzie. Suzie who'd wanted a mother and deserved a childhood. Suzie whose eyes shined love whenever her gaze fell on her father, her brother or sister, on Cally. Precious, tormented Suzie. Cally owed Tony for what he was doing with her. And she owed him for his treatment of her as well. He'd reached out to help her, too, talked to her internally, until she'd become frightened. Then he'd respectfully backed away. She'd suspected the truth about him, true. She'd been told it. But knowing it deep in her heart and soul, having it confirmed by Bryce, a man she trusted . . . It still felt . . . shocking.

So did she care? No. She didn't. Not at all. Tony's being a ghost and being here was weird. Bizarre. Different. It defied social acceptability, theories that death is final, the belief that life exists in a single dimension. It shook to the roots a myriad of basic societal foundations, and a hell of a lot of philosophies. But so what? It was good.

He was helping Suzie.

Thanks, Miss Tate.

The man's voice. An arrow of shock shot up her spine, set her nerve endings to tingling. *Tony?*

A warm rush whisked through her, head to toe. *At your service.*

She opened her mouth, then did what any sane woman would do when she'd mentally accepted a ghost had come into her life. She fainted.

Cally joined Bryce in Suzie's room. It'd become a ritual, tucking in the kids together. Most girls nine didn't want that kind of attention, according to Frankie, but Cally figured Suzie hadn't had it earlier, so she needed it now. And only to herself did Cally admit how much she loved hating the good feelings the ceremony gave her. How much she looked forward to them all being together, sharing their lives.

But as much as she loved hating those things, she hated knowing how much she was going to miss them when their vacation was over and they went home without her. She'd again be alone. Even more empty than before because, with them, she'd been given a taste of what her life as a mother would have been like.

From under the quilts, Suzie looked up at Bryce and Cally, standing side by side near the edge of the spool bed. "On Little Island, there are two graves behind this little fence. Hatch said one was Dixie Dupree—that lady Uncle John used to look for, Daddy."

"John Mystic," Bryce reminded Cally.

"I remember, Counselor." That John had investigated her for Bryce had her prickly, and knowing he and the children would be leaving Seascape Inn without her already had her sad. Prickly heaped onto sad didn't stack up as a peace-inducing mix of emotions to lug around.

She buried the feelings and tucked the quilt up under Suzie's chin. Suzie had said there were two graves on the island. That piqued Cally's interest. "Who's in the other grave?"

"Hatch said it's a lost soul. It couldn't find its way home because it refused to believe it could."

An odd sensation crept over Cally. Hit her hard. Something else of importance had been disclosed to her through Suzie. And again Suzie's first message replayed in her mind. *If only one has the courage to believe, miracles can happen beside a dreamswept sea.*

Suzie stared at the ceiling, her eyes unfocused. "I think that makes my island even more special."

Bryce smiled, but didn't remind her again that the island belonged to the children of the village and not tourists from away. "I agree. It's a big responsibility."

She nodded. "I'm nine. I can do it, Daddy."

"I know." He dropped a kiss to her forehead. "Good night, munchkin."

"'Nite." She curled her arms around his neck, hugged him tightly, then held out her arms for Cally.

She stepped into them, her heart in her throat, vowing she wouldn't start counting how many more nightly hugs there'd be on her calendar before they left her and she had only the cherished memories of them in her heart. "'Nite."

Bryce gave her a heavy-lidded look, as if he knew how vulnerable and isolated she was feeling, then clasped her hand.

They walked out into the hallway. Bryce flipped off the light. Cally reached back to close the door, heard Suzie's whisper, and paused.

"Tony?" she said. "Okay, I just wanted to make sure you were here."

I'm here, little one. We're all here. Me, your dad, Cally, and Miss Hattie. You can go to sleep now.

Comforted at hearing Tony's voice, Cally quietly eased the door shut.

"Miss Tate." Bryce turned to face her. "You're confusing the court."

She stood so close to him, he filled her senses, and she felt more than a little confused herself. Attempting to step back, to gain perspective, she backed into the door. "I am?"

Bryce nodded, clasped her arm and inched her over, against the wall. "I had these strange feelings in there. That you were riding an emotional roller coaster. You felt content, then devastated, then scared as hell, and then incredibly sad. Now you look content again."

Moonlight from the mullioned windows bathed them in soft, wispy shadows. Her face went hot, and she blessed the darkness for hiding it from Bryce. But being totally honest, if only under the obscuring cover of the night, had grown comfortable. She could tell him the truth. And she would. That much courage, at least, she'd garnered here. "I felt all that, and more."

He slid a gentle thumb along her chin, stared deeply into her eyes. "Why?"

"A lot of reasons." She dipped her chin to her chest to avoid his eyes.

"Would you think me a stuffed shirt if I said I like you content?"

"No."

"Would you, if I said it makes me feel good to know you're content when you're with me?"

"No, I wouldn't. I like feeling content. It's fleeting, but at least I'm glimpsing it again, and that's a start."

"I'm not content." A fingertip joined his thumb on her face, then trailed a winding path down to the soft hollow behind her ear.

"I'm sorry to hear that." She was. She truly was. He was such a wonderful man. He deserved contentment, and so much more. Loving. He deserved loving. But that he didn't find contentment with her didn't surprise her; she hadn't expected he would. Still, a pang of disappointment rattling around in the region of her heart couldn't be denied.

"I'd be closer to contentment with a little assistance."

What did she do with her hand? She couldn't continue to hold it midair, and to put it behind her back, she'd have to get even closer to the man. From the hum of blood singing through her veins she was plenty close already. "What kind of assistance?"

He laced their fingertips until their palms touched, then bent his elbow and pressed their clasped hands against the small of his back. "A hug would help. A kiss would be even better." He lightened his tone, but his expression stayed serious. "I would remind you, Miss Tate, that I'm a man suffering from a multitude of injuries. When Jeremy scraped his elbow, you kissed it to make it better, but . . ."

Con artist. But what a good one. "You want me to kiss your knee?"

"No."

"Your elbow?" She ran a fingertip along his sling.

"No."

"Your bruised jaw?"

"You're getting warmer." His eyes twinkled and he dipped his chin, touching his mouth to hers.

"Take care with your arm, darling."

"It can fend for itself. Hugs are rare and I intend to indulge myself to the legal limits." He pulled off the sling, curled his arms around her, and let out a satisfied sigh that shot sheer joy through her woman's heart. "God, but that feels good." He pressed a soft kiss to the cay at her shoulder. "It truly is a nuisance, Miss Tate, to want to hold a woman and not be able to do the job properly."

Sober and tense, she cocked her head and looked up at him. "Is this more of your campaign? Because if it is, I'd really rather you kept to our agreement and didn't—"

"No, Miss Tate. No campaign." He pressed a fingertip to her lips, outlined them with flutters of touch, and his eyes glazed. "This is for me."

Her heart swelled into her throat then dropped to her knees. No, she couldn't believe it. Couldn't do this to herself. "Under penalty of perjury, do you swear, Counselor?" Why had she asked that? Why couldn't she have recalled Grandma Tate's crude words of wisdom and not opened herself to this?

"I swear." He kissed her eyelids, her cheeks, then paused, hovering over her lips. "Cally?"

"Hmm?" Oh, God, this was too good. It couldn't be real. She'd have to be crazy to believe even for a second it could be anything close to real.

"Let's dream."

"Dream?" She dragged her fingers through the hair on his nape. Dreaming sounded good.

"Mmm, just for now, let's forget everything that's happened to us. Let's pretend that there's only us, and only now. I—I need to dream, Cally."

Forget. Pretend. Dream. Yes. Yes, she could do that. She could kiss him from the heart out, knowing it was only a dream. "Oh, Bryce. Sometimes you're just so damn perfect."

"I'm not." He cupped her face in his hands, breathed against her lips. "But you make me wish I could be. I want you with me. I want you to want to be with me." He shuddered and his hands trembled on her face. "Dream with me, Cally. Please. Dream with me."

Her fears crumbled, and she settled into the kiss, eager to dream.

* * *

The rocking chair squeaked.

Her hand at her chest, Cally darted her gaze over to the fireside chair. "Miss Hattie. Good grief, but you startled me."

"I'm sorry, dear." She held some sewing in her lap, but her reading glasses sat on the stone ledge of the fireplace. "Can't you sleep?"

The light from above the stove shone on the lenses. Without them, Cally felt sure Miss Hattie had been doing more thinking than stitching. At the fridge, Cally poured herself a glass of milk, then softly closed the door. "Evidently not."

"Bryce?"

"In the hallway, on the floor."

"I thought you two had stopped that, since Suzie hasn't been bothered with that dream."

"We had. We just wanted to talk." Cally inwardly sighed. What they'd wanted was to prolong their dream. God, but it'd been magnificent. It would have been so easy to let it lapse into making love. So easy . . .

"I see."

Cally feared Miss Hattie did see. Too much. Stifling a sigh, she sat down at the kitchen table and took a long drink of milk. The cold going down her throat felt good. "Men."

"Isn't it the truth?" Miss Hattie sighed and tapped the floor with the toe of her slipper to set the chair to rocking. "As Hatch says, 'Ya gotta love 'em.' "

Its squeak sounded comfortable. And comfort felt good. "You know Bryce is making me crazy." No surprise there. Miss Hattie seemed to have the pulse on the feelings of everyone at the inn. "Is Vic what's getting to you?"

"Oh my, no. Vic is one of my dearest friends, but no more than that." Miss Hattie's cheeks went rosy. "I'm just missing my soldier."

And clearly worrying. Did she see and hear Tony, too?

Surely not or she wouldn't be missing him. Should Cally tell her he was here? That he was a ghost? Would that comfort her and give her a measure of peace?

She knows, Cally.

Tony. Her fingers stiffened on the glass, but she was determined not to fall into another faint. He was good. Real and good, and that was a blessing. A miracle even. *If Miss Hattie knows you're here, then why is she missing you? And why is she so worried?*

I can't explain that to you. I know the answers, and I would explain if I could, but I can't. I am doing everything I can, Cally. I swear I am.

Miss Hattie wasn't the only one worrying here. Tony's voice fairly reeked of fear. Whatever this was about, it was bad, bad news for both of them. *I see.*

Not yet. But you're beginning to. Look, I don't want to intrude on your chat with Hattie, but I wanted you to know I'm doing all I can for Hattie and to ask you not to mention me hanging around to her. It upsets her, Cally. Because we can't really be together. Frankly, it upsets me, too.

I'm sure it does. They had that kind of love Lucy Baker and Miss Millie had talked about Cecelia and Collin sharing. That rare and mystical, forever-after kind of love that Cally hadn't so much as glimpsed and doubted she ever would.

I wanted to also tell you that I'm proud of you.

Tony, proud of her? *For what?*

Dreaming with Bryce. No, don't be embarrassed. I didn't play voyeur, Cally. That's a promise. I just waited to see if you'd dare to dream. When you did, I left. That leap took a lot of courage on your part, and you did it. You've beaten yourself half to death for it ever since, though. Because you have and you shouldn't, I figured I'd best point that out to you—that you should be feeling great about your progress. That's what's important, Cally. You took the leap. When next you doubt you have courage, you remember that, okay?

Choked up, Cally swallowed hard. *I'll try.*

And quit telling yourself you're forty kinds of fool for indulging in a little fantasy. Reality is a hell of a taskmaster at times. Dreaming a little is a blessing that can get you through a lot of really rough spots.

It can be a curse and create some rough spots, too—if you're foolish enough to forget you're dreaming.

Talk to Hattie about that, hmm? I've got a few chains to rattle.

She gasped.

Criminy, Cally. I was just kidding.

Miss Hattie claimed Cally's attention. "I don't want to intrude, dear heart, but you seem troubled."

Maybe she should take Tony's suggestion and talk with Miss Hattie. What could it hurt? "I am troubled." Nervous at opening herself up to anyone besides Mary Beth, Cally fidgeted with the daffodil petals on the porcelain bisque centerpiece.

"If I can help, I will. I hope you know that."

An angel if one ever walked the earth. "Thank you, Miss Hattie. I do know it. But I'm afraid there is no easy answer." Cally made herself meet Miss Hattie's gaze. The gentle concern there totally unraveled her. "I've done the most stupid thing I've ever done in my life, Miss Hattie. And there's been a lengthy list of stupid things. But this is the worst. Even worse than marrying Gregory."

"Nothing can be that awful." She dropped her sewing into a black bag with yellow flowers on it, then set the bag to the floor beside her rocker. "You sound devastated."

"I am devastated."

"Whatever it is, we can work through it."

Close to tears, Cally shook her head that they couldn't. "I'm afraid we can't."

She pressed her fingertips over her lips, and a creased formed in the smooth skin between her brows. "Oh, my. You've taken the leap."

The same words Tony had used. "What leap?"

"You've fallen in love with the children." Miss Hattie cast the ceiling a worried glance, then looked back at Cally.

Her heart wrenched. "It's even worse than that."

She stopped cold, mid-rock.

"I've fallen in love with the kids *and,* God help me, with Bryce."

Miss Hattie's mouth rounded. "Oh. Oh, my."

A tear slipped out from the corner of Cally's eye. She swatted at it. "Isn't that just the most stupid thing you've ever heard of? I'm supposed to be getting my life back together. Building a life for myself alone. I just got divorced, for God's sake, and I know that loving a man doesn't do a thing but bring a woman pain."

"Oh, Cally. I understand your upset—honestly I do, dear heart—but that's just not true. Love—"

"It *is* true," Cally interrupted, her emotions exploding. "I lived it, Miss Hattie. I know it's true—and, as stupid as I surely am, I let it happen anyway. Love just isn't enough. It just isn't . . . enough."

"Sometimes it's not," Miss Hattie agreed. "But love isn't always painful, dear. I know it was in your case. I mean, in your case with Gregory."

"It wasn't him, it was me." She dragged her hands through her hair, slicking back the tangles. "I can't believe I let this happen to me again. I just can't believe it."

Miss Hattie gave her a sober look. "Cally dear, you know as well as I do that you don't let love happen. It just happens. If a woman could choose to love, then I'd have chosen to fall in love again and married years ago." She sighed softly. "No, we can't choose. When the heart knows, it knows, and nothing convinces it otherwise. Regardless of what we want to do, what our heads and logical thoughts tell us to do, we love. We just . . . love."

Cally pulled herself stiff. Tears streamed down her face. "We just love, and the men we just love go on without us." Bryce could never love her back. No more than Gregory could have kept on loving her. But at least Bryce hadn't broken promises and sacred vows to her. He'd been honest. He'd told her from the start that he could never love again. For Bryce, there had been and only ever would be one woman: Meriam.

"Yes, sometimes they do." Miss Hattie pulled her lacy hankie from the pocket of her robe then dabbed it against her soft cheek. "Sometimes they just go on without us."

Cally permitted herself a Class A cry. So did Miss Hattie.

When she'd cried herself out, and Miss Hattie's soft sniffles had stopped, Cally grabbed two paper towels, passed one to Miss Hattie, then blew her own nose. "I won't do it, Miss Hattie."

"How can you stop loving him and the babies?"

Cally's chin trembled and, though she felt bone-dry, she

feared a fresh surge of tears would come anyway. ''I don't know.'' She stiffened her shoulders, then tossed the soggy paper towel into the trash bin, in the cabinet under the sink. ''But I'm going to do something. I have to do something.''

Chapter 10

Suzie rapped lightly on the bedroom door, then peeked inside. ''Cally?''

''I'm over here, sweetheart.'' She looked up from the desk and the list of affirmations she'd been constructing, plans on getting her life in some kind of order. Her life alone. Without Gregory. Without the children. And, God help her, without Bryce.

Worrying her lower lip with her teeth, Suzie stopped beside the desk, crushed her red skirt in her hands at her sides. ''Are you mad at us?''

Cally's heart wrenched. She put down her pen. ''Of course not, Suzie.''

''Then how come you don't want to do anything with us anymore.''

She did. Oh, but she did want to, which is exactly why she couldn't. ''It isn't that, Suzie. It's complicated.''

''Selena says just say what you feel. That's not complicated.'' Suzie looked soulfully into Cally's eyes. ''Did Daddy hurt your feelings?''

''No, honey. Honest. All of you are just perfect.''

''Then how come you don't like us anymore?''

''I do like you. All of you.'' She liked them too much. ''It's important to me that you understand this, Suzie. It isn't that I don't like doing things with you, it's that it's not good for us—any of us. See, I came up here to figure out some things. But I haven't been doing that because—''

''We take up too much of your time.'' She let her gaze

slide to the floor. "We did that with Meriam, too. But we don't mean to, Cally. Honest."

"No. No, sweetheart. You're worth *all* my time. But I need to work out some things inside my mind. That's all. And you and your dad came here so that you could spend some time together. Just you kids and him. And you can't do that if I'm always there."

"But we like your being there."

"I'm glad." Suzie inched under her guard, and Cally's resolve took a nosedive. She had to end this conversation before she lost sight of why it was important to handle this situation the way she'd chosen to handle it. Before her emotions could cloud up the reasons until even to her they seemed irrational. "But you need to spend time with each other. Your dad needs you, Suzie. And you need him. So do Jeremy and Lyssie. You're a family, honey, and you need to be close, you know? Without an outsider interfering."

Suzie stared at her for a long moment, then turned away and headed toward the door. Her hand on the knob, she paused and leveled Cally with an accusing look. "You just had to say you don't want us." Her chin trembled, and she fought tears hard. "That's all you had to say."

Cally grabbed the desk's ledge to keep from running to Suzie and locking her in a protective, loving embrace. An empty ache inside her cut so deep, but she had to stay put. To not move and do any of them more damage than she'd already done. She'd suffer—God, but she'd suffer—but she couldn't cause any of them more pain.

Her heart ripping apart in her chest, she pressed her hands over it to help hold in all the hurt. Tears flooding her eyes, she stumbled over the rug to the little turret room, then plopped down onto the window seat. Damn it, why did love have to hurt so badly? *Why?*

She shoved aside the filmy white curtains billowing in the breeze, then stared through the open window out onto the angry, dark blue ocean. Boats rocked on huge swells and whitecaps streaked over the water's surface like jagged lightning tearing through a storm-swollen sky. Being lonely royally sucked. Sometimes life did, too. Sometimes doing the right thing felt so wrong, and it tore you up from your toenails to your earlobes, but you had to be strong enough to do what was right anyway, because it was right, because it was the only thing you could do without hating yourself. And sometimes you had to hurt people you love, people you'd rather die than hurt, because only by hurting them could you help them.

You didn't have to like it. But you had to do it. All of it.

For them.

And for you.

Cally swatted at her tear-soaked cheeks. But who was there to help her? To reassure her that what she was doing *was* the right thing? Who would talk to her, hug her, hold her, and keep the demons of fear and doubt from sinking their razor-sharp talons into her soul and ripping it to shreds? Who would ever be there to help her?

Not Bryce. Never Bryce.

The salt-tinged breeze chilled her skin to ice and dried her angry, hopeless tears almost before they fell to her cheeks. The peace and comfort she'd felt during her stay here eluded her now, when she needed it most. And swearing she was cried out, that she just didn't have another tear left inside her, she propped her elbows on the window ledge, then cupped her chin in her palms, and cried some more.

She'd been a crazy fool to dream—even for a second. And crazier still for letting herself forget even for that short time the truth about who and what she was. It'd snuck up on her, not that there was solace in knowing it. It'd just been so damn easy to let the feminine side of her flourish under Bryce's tender touches and open smiles; to leave herself wide open to his gentle requests spoken straight from his heart that proved him every bit as vulnerable as she herself. No woman with blood in her veins could have staved off the torrential flow of feelings his kisses inspired. They were too powerful and strong. Too fantastic. No woman could have done it. On feeling her touch, he'd trembled with pleasure. On touching her, he'd sighed his satisfaction. On looking at her, genuine desire had glazed his beautiful eyes. What woman could *not* dream on looking into his eyes?

Cally sighed. Certainly not her.

"So the moral of the story is, you just don't gaze." Just

off the shore, a gull dived for a fish. ''You just don't gaze. That's your only way out.''

A burning ache hollowed her insides until she felt empty. She *was* doing the right thing. She *was*. Suzie had looked abandoned, discarded. Cally felt as if she had abandoned them all. The guilt was crushing, but she had no choice. She'd thought about it until she'd dropped, and there wasn't any alternative. Total severance. No contact. That was the only thing she could do. And she had to trust that it would prove the best thing for them and for her.

Oh, Mary Beth. It isn't only loving a man that can kill a woman inside. It's loving anyone. Everyone. Yet life without love, well, what's it worth? It hurts. They hurt. I hurt. Do you know how it's killing me inside, knowing I've hurt them? I've wanted children all my life. I wanted to love and care for them, to nurture them. I lost everything once. Why, damn it, must I lose even more again? Why?

Tony cleared his throat. *Have you considered that maybe you hurt and they hurt because this decision is wrong?*

Tony. Cally thought over his question, though she could have answered right away. ''I've considered it to the point of exhaustion. More than once. It's not wrong, Tony. I wish to God it were, but it's . . . not.'' She let her fingertip glide along the bead of caulk seaming the window ledge and the window. ''When I made this decision two days ago, it wasn't wrong, and it's not wrong now. And tomorrow, when I ask myself it again, it won't be wrong then, either, though I'll foolishly pray it will be. It won't be wrong because it's right.''

Maybe you've figured this all out, but I haven't. Care to enlighten me?

''Not really.''

Do it anyway. I'm testy because of Thanksgiving, so I'm not really as compassionate as usual. And I'm tired of seeing Suzie hurt. Getting her back on track and over these nightmares is my responsibility, and your interjecting what's certain to prove a major setback is destined to cramp my style. So, if disassociating yourself from Bryce and the kids is the right thing to do, how come it hurts all of you so much?

''I can't believe I have to explain this to you. Of all people, you should know the answer, Tony. Hell, after fifty-one years of disassociating but staying near Miss Hattie, you still mourn not talking with her, not holding her. And she still mourns, too. I know you know that. So why don't you tell me? If it's right, then why does it hurt?''

This isn't about me and what I think. It's about you and Bryce and the kids, and I want to understand your situation from your perspective. Enlighten me, Cally.

She smiled, but there was no joy in it, only sadness. ''Because love hurts. It hurt me with Gregory. Bryce with Meriam. You and Miss Hattie. Now, it's hurting me with Bryce and with the kids. It's hurting Bryce and the kids, too.''

Pausing to collect herself, she let her words flow out unchecked. ''I didn't expect to love the kids, Tony. But I do. And that only reinforces the lessons I should've learned already. No matter how good it starts out, or how innocently, in the end, love always hurts. I've hurt all the people I intend to hurt. And I've hurt all I can bear for love, Tony. It's that simple.''

Is it? Aren't you forgetting something important here?

''No.''

You are. He sounded impatient. *You've felt a lot of joy in loving Bryce, and the kids too, Cally. I know you have. I've seen it. Felt it. Sensed it. And I've had a lot of joy in loving Hattie—even without special circumstances. A lot of joy. I'm not going to stand here and let you forget that or deny it.*

''Miss Hattie sure didn't look joyful the other night in the kitchen. She cried her heart out.''

That's different.

''The hell it is. She hasn't seemed joyful since Bryce wrenched his knee.''

I said, that's different. Something else is happening here that you know nothing about.

Cally turned toward his voice, and gasped. Tony stood there, just off the edge of the braided rug. ''Oh, God.''

Don't faint. He held out a hand, as if that'd keep her from it.

''I'm—I'm not. Just—just next time give me a little warning, okay?''

Sorry. I got emotional. He ran a forked finger through his golden-brown hair. The sun set the brass buttons on his Army uniform to winking. "I know Hattie's hurting. This is a rough time for both of us."

Thanksgiving was coming fast. Cally knew from Bryce that Tony had proposed to Miss Hattie on Thanksgiving night, but she didn't mention it now. Tony looked ready to crumble, or explode. He needed to talk, and he lacked having a lot of options on listeners. Knowing how much a friendly ear could help, thanks to Mary Beth and Bryce, Cally couldn't *not* offer to listen. "Care to enlighten me?"

He leaned a shoulder against the wall, crossed his arms over his chest, much as she had, to hold all the hurt inside. "Sometimes I wonder if Hattie would've been better off without me." He shoved away then stuffed a hand down into his pocket. "You know what I mean."

Cally turned, folded a leg up under her, and watched him pace. "No, I'm afraid I don't."

He shrugged, looked over her shoulder out onto the cliffs. "Maybe she would have fallen in love again and married and had children."

"She wouldn't have."

"She might have," he insisted. "Vic's been in love with her for more years than I can count."

"He loved you too, though. He couldn't have married Miss Hattie. Not loving both of you."

"He might have."

"I don't think so." Cally cocked her head. "I've heard about you and him and Hatch being the Three Musketeers of Sea Haven Village. He wouldn't have. Vic's too proud to be a substitute in the heart of a woman he loves."

"Someone else, then. She'd have had all she dreamed of having. A life with a family and children. I'm ashamed to admit this, Cally, but it's only just occurred to me that by vowing to always be with her, and keeping that vow, I've robbed Hattie of a life." Tony's expression twisted. "I shouldn't have done that."

"You love her."

"Yes." His eyes grew glossy. "I always have."

"And you always will." Cally sighed wistfully. "That's the thing about this love business, Tony. It does what it wants, regardless of what we want.'' Miss Hattie's words, the night of their crying jag, came back to Cally. And finally she fully understood them. ''It wouldn't have mattered.''

He slid her a questioning look.

''If you'd stayed or broken your vow and gone away. It wouldn't have mattered,'' Cally said. ''Miss Hattie loves you, Tony. It's that rare kind of love, like Collin and Cecelia had. The one that started the legend of love surpassing death because it's stronger and lives on.'' She paused to collect her thoughts. ''Whether you were here, or somewhere else, it wouldn't have changed anything. She wouldn't have married. She's not the kind to marry without love, and that she couldn't give to anyone else because she's felt it only for you.''

Tony turned his back to Cally and swallowed a knot from his throat. Now, because he had interceded in Suzie's dream, because he continued nightly to intercede in Suzie's dream, it appeared he and Hattie were going to lose what little they did have together—if Sunshine proved right.

He'd broken the rules. Had willfully breached the chain of command. And he had attempted—and still was attempting—to alter what would be Suzie's personal history.

It was wrong. He knew that. And yet to live with himself, he'd had to do it. Just as he had to keep on doing it.

I know you're upset, but remember your duties.

Sunshine. Tony held off a grimace. *I know my duties.*

Well, far be it from me to interfere, but—

Then don't interfere. Who are you, anyway?

It doesn't matter any more now than it did the first time you asked, Tony. Just help Cally muddle through this. That's your job.

I know my job.

Then quit fritzing around and do it.

I hate bossy women about as much as I hate blueberries.

Help Cally, Tony. And consider the costs of what you're doing with Suzie. I know your heart's in the right place, but it's going to land you in big trouble. And it's going to break Hattie's heart. Haven't you hurt her enough?

I never wanted to hurt her at all. Never. But I can't turn my back on Suzie. What kind of man could do that?

But you're no longer a man. That's my point. You're a ghost.

I still feel like a man, damn it. I still love and hate and—

Hurt. Yes, dear, I know you do. I know. . . .

Sunshine left. For where, Tony had no idea. Nor did he care. And he'd croak again before admitting it, but he *was* letting this issue with Hattie sidetrack him from his duties here. But how could he help it?

He looked back at Cally. Slumping on the window seat, her arms folded, her chin resting on her forearms, her eyes unfocused, she looked so . . . sad. A flicker of resolve inside him blazed to a flame. "Cally?"

"Hmm?" She stared out the window.

"I know you've made up your mind that staying away from Bryce and the kids is the right thing to do."

"What choice do I have? They're going home, Tony. They'll have each other. But I'll be here. Left behind with the sand pails and other memories."

"Know what I think?"

No answer.

"I think you're running scared. You're letting the fear of getting hurt keep you from reaching out."

"I've reached out before. I got knocked down."

"I know. But there's something else you're forgetting."

"I remember it all, Tony. Every cutting word, every slur, every pain, and every tear." She smoothed a shaky hand over the soft folds of her skirt.

"I can see that you do." He looked her straight in the eye. "But are you remembering that Gregory isn't Bryce? That *this* man isn't *that* man?"

"I'm not confusing them. They're nothing alike, and I know it." She stood up, then pointed at the cheval mirror. "But the point isn't them, it's me. I still can't look in that glass and like what I see. Until I do, I can't risk anything else. I don't have anything left to lose."

"You're hurting, I know that. But you're also hurting them. All of them."

"I know." She squeezed her eyes shut, her hands into fists at her sides. "But this pain is nothing compared to what it would be if I really let myself love them."

"The heart—"

"Knows the truth," she interrupted. "I know that, too. Don't you think I know that, too? But they can't love me."

"Cally, they do love you. You are lovab—"

"No, don't even say it. It's not true and it won't change," she firmly insisted, lifting her chin. "I know they hurt right now. But they'll get over it soon enough. By Christmas I'll be a fleeting memory and no more."

Those words hurt her throat. She swallowed hard, curled her hands into fists, and lowered her voice. "I understand what you're saying, and I appreciate what you're trying to do. But things are different from your perspective, and in your situation. Hattie loves you every bit as much as you love her, Tony. Bryce doesn't love me. He loves Meriam."

"Does he?" Tony wanted to scream. The woman had seen Bryce's desire for her, seen it with her own eyes, and yet she still didn't trust it. She still felt unlovable. Why wouldn't she see the truth? Why—

The truth hit him with the force of a hundred-pound sledge. That's it. She needs more than to be shown. Because of Gregory, even showing her wouldn't be enough for her to recognize *and* to trust the truth as the truth. There had to be a way to get them together long enough for them to see what they could have with each other.

She guffawed. "How could you doubt he loves Meriam?"

"Call it intuition." Had she forgotten he was privy to the man's thoughts? What would be enough to prove to her—to them both? Tony went quiet. Rubbed at his neck, then at his jaw. The germ of an idea took seed and then rooted. It was a far stretch, unorthodox to be sure, but just far enough out of sync with the norm to maybe keep both of them off balance long enough to stare the naked truth in the face and be forced to accept it.

"Cally, I've been thinking." Tony walked over to the desk, hitched a hip up onto its corner. "Maybe what you and Bryce need isn't love."

"Ah." She slapped at her thigh. "Finally, he sees the light."

Tony slid her a solid frown. She loved Bryce, she loved the kids, and yet she'd stayed away from them for three days, knowing it was tearing them all up inside. "Maybe both of you have been hurt too much by love for it to ever work for you."

"Exactly."

Tony's thoughts reeled. Bryce. Aw hell, of course. Bryce. "Yet I can't see you giving up your dream. Can you?"

The animation left her face and her eyes clouded. "I might not have any choice. Being the sunshine of my home isn't apt to happen without love, is it?"

"It would be challenging," Tony agreed. "But if there were a way, I'm sure you'd consider it."

"Of course I would."

Perfect. The plan blossomed. Now, Tony only had to convince Bryce to bring it to fruition. But from the way things had been going around here lately, that wouldn't be a picnic of a task.

Bryce missed her.

Why she'd suddenly backed off from him and the kids remained a mystery. Maybe she liked kids in small doses. Maybe she liked playing at Mom, but his reaction to Suzie's asking Cally for permission had scared the socks off Cally. Maybe she just wasn't interested in a man with a built-in family.

Or in any man.

With Gregory, Bryce knew that held truth and yet, until three days ago, she'd seemed to love being with him and the kids. And she'd certainly responded to Bryce physically. They'd talked about everything and nothing. Laughed and whispered serious secrets and frivolous ones. They'd just enjoyed each other. So what the hell had happened?

What had he done wrong?

He lay in bed in the Cove Room, his hands tucked behind his head, and stared at the shadows the oak limb outside his window cast on the cathedral ceiling. Rain pattered softly against the window, splotching it and the ceiling with shadows of droplets.

She liked him; he'd have to be dead not to know it. She liked the kids. Actually, she loved the kids, and it showed. Being asked for, and granting, permission with Suzie had come natural. Patching up Jeremy's misadventures and keeping him out of hot water with Mrs. Wiggins had, too. And Cally was always softly nuzzling Lyssie. Criminal how jealous he was of those nuzzles, but he'd be lying to himself if he denied he had been. And knowing how much the kids needed those tender affections made his jealousy even more criminal. But he needed them, too.

And Cally had given them to him. In icing his jaw, in sitting with him during the nights in the hallway outside Suzie's room, she'd nurtured him, too.

Until she'd come along, he hadn't realized that he'd lacked nurturing all of his adult life. Meriam didn't nurture. He'd understood why from the start, and she'd been up front about it. But she hadn't shared. Even in their marriage, with the kids, she just hadn't shared.

And until Cally, he hadn't realized it.

But he recognized the difference now, and he liked feeling special and important to a woman. He liked knowing he mattered. And he was going to do some serious looking back at his relationship with Meriam. Serious and objective looking back. He had to resolve his feelings before moving on, and it was time. Maybe then he could look Suzie straight in the eye and say he hadn't made Cally angry with them.

Boy, she'd been tough on him. The kid hadn't thrown a temper tantrum in her entire life, until then. If he lived forever, he'd never forget her tears, her pain-twisted expression, the anguish in her screaming, "What did you do to her, Daddy? She was going to be our new mom, maybe. Why are you making her stay away? Are you believing, Daddy? It won't work if you're not believing with your whole heart."

If only you believe, miracles can happen beside a dreamswept sea.

Was he believing?

Hell of it was, he couldn't deny he hadn't been, or that he might have done something to hurt Cally. But if he had hurt her, he had no idea exactly how, or what he'd done.

He scrunched up his pillow, then rolled onto his side, facing the window. Wait. Wait, maybe he had every idea of what he'd done. Maybe—a bubble of anticipation burst in his stomach—it was time to move on and both he and Cally realized it and were scared stiff of it.

It *was* time to move on. And he wanted to move on. He wanted to give himself permission to love a woman again. Not just any woman. Cally. He wanted to love Cally. Without guilt. Without reservation. But that wasn't possible.

But she couldn't love him back, anyway. Not after Gregory. She'd never let herself love another man.

I happen to agree.

Bryce nearly jumped out of his skin. "Damn it, Tony. Give a man a little warning, okay?"

Sorry.

"Are you here to ream me out? Because if you are, let me tell you that Suzie already beat you to it. And, for the record, I honestly tried showing Cally she was lovable and all it got me was exiled. She's staying away from me and the kids. I'm not even sure exactly what happened. One minute she's fine, the next—*wham!* She's busy. She's got things to do. She needs some time alone to think."

Maybe she's scared.

"I'd be worried about her if she wasn't. What's happening between us is damn scary. It's happening too fast."

I don't think your heart cares about clocks or calendars, Counselor.

"Yeah, well. Whatever her reason it doesn't much matter anymore, does it? It's over. She wants no part of me or the kids."

You don't have a clue, do you?

Bryce sat up. The bedspread under him crinkled. "What do you mean?"

Think about it, Counselor. You came here looking for a mother, not a wife. Cally came here not to be a wife, but a mother. You two falling in love is just mucking up the works here, don't you think?

"Love? Who said anything about love?" He couldn't love her. And she surely couldn't love him. They cared. That's all. Just cared.

Exactly.

Bryce stared at the little antique washstand. The cream bowl and pitcher. "Ah, I get it. We can't love."

I knew logic would work its way through the maze in your head at some point in time. Now, I trust you'll make the moves to get this settled so everyone can be a little less miserable around here.

He needed a mother for the kids. She needed kids to mother. It was a match made in heaven, literally—so long as love stayed out of it.

"Yeah. Yeah, I'll see what I can do." He really would. Just as soon as he figured out what the hell it could be.

Sunset had been spectacular. Bryce and the kids had watched it from the deck off Suzie's Shell Room. He glanced over at his oldest daughter. Her eyes were still puffy red and swollen from crying about Cally. As if he hadn't felt like a jerk already, before leaving for home, Frankie had laid a glare on him that nearly knocked him to his knees. Cally had been right about her; she was a good friend to Suzie.

Cally had been right about a lot of things.

To the chirping of birds, he looked out into the darkening sky. The house was settling down for the night. Mrs. Wiggins had rented a car and driven over to Boothbay Harbor. What she'd do there, Bryce hadn't a clue, but the house seemed more peaceful somehow without her in it. He should fire her, and he knew it. But he couldn't. She'd been good to Meriam, and he owed the woman for that.

"Okay, guys." Bryce clapped his hands. "Bedtime."

When he had the kids tucked in, he sorely missed Cally standing at his side. It just didn't feel the same without her there, giving their blankets a final tuck, giving them a final peck on the forehead good night. Strange how quickly he'd become used to her being a part of their lives. And how acutely they all felt her absence.

"Daddy." Suzie looked up at him from her pillows. "You don't have to sleep on the hallway floor tonight."

How did she know that he ever had?

"Tony told me," she said, solving the mystery. "I know I'm going to dream, but it's okay. Tony will be there. I'm not scared when Tony's there."

Bryce swallowed a lump from his throat. One with pity for his daughter, of gratitude to Tony, and one of regret that it couldn't be him there, protecting his daughter. "I'm glad you're not scared."

Bryce gave her a hug, then left her room and walked to the Cove Room. Before he'd closed the door, he'd stripped off his tie, leaned Collin's cane against the desk, and wondered what Cally was doing.

Probably sound asleep. Or else sitting in the turret room, staring out on the ocean. She liked to do that. A lot. What would she do if he knocked on her door? If he just knocked on her door, and did his damnedest to kiss the fear right out of them both?

She wouldn't like it. And no kiss held that kind of power. Besides, if the way he'd been feeling for the last three days was any gauge, this caring was dangerous stuff. As dangerous as loving. He flung his shirt over the arm of the desk's chair. It was a stupid idea.

He crawled into bed alone, and resented it. Imagined Cally there with him, and resented that even more. Tony was right. Love *was* mucking up the works. He didn't need a wife, he needed a mother for the kids.

Hell, he needed both. But the woman he wanted didn't want a husband.

A tingling started along his spine, worked its way up to his neck, down to his heels. The truth Tony had obscurely passed along traveled with it. Cally didn't want a husband, but she did want kids. She did want to be the sunshine of her own home. And God knew their home could use a little sunshine.

It seemed perfect. Except for him maybe stretching beyond caring and falling in love with her. But if he nixed that, then the situation would be perfect for both of them.

He tossed back the quilts then crawled out of bed, determined to give the idea a fair hearing with her. It might not be an ideal situation, but it held too much merit for them not to seriously consider it.

Grabbing a fresh shirt from the closet, he then reached for a tie. No. Cally hated ties. He tossed down the shirt, then snatched up a green pullover and a casual pair of slacks, certain she'd like them better. He tugged them on, and bumped his sore knee on the corner of the bed. Wincing, muttering, he snagged Collin's cane and headed for the door. It wasn't until he had a foot in the hallway that he realized he'd been in such a hurry to talk with her that he'd forgotten his damn shoes.

He turned to go back for them, and came to a dead stop. Cally sat there on the hallway floor outside Suzie's room. Alone.

She'd been afraid Suzie would dream.

His heart turned over in his chest. He walked down the dimly lit hallway. A night-light burned in the bath and spilled a soft circle of yellow over the floor. "Cally?"

She looked up at him, and her expression closed. "I thought you were sleeping."

He dropped to sit down beside her. "Couldn't."

"Is your knee hurting?"

"Yes, but that's not why I couldn't sleep."

"Oh?" She pulled the pillow out from behind her back and pressed it over her stomach, as if needing a barrier between them.

Seeing that gave Bryce the confidence he needed. "I was missing you."

Surprise flittered over her face. She masked it. "I'm only doing what I think is best for all of us, Bryce." She looked up at him, let him see the pain in her eyes. "I know it seems cruel, but I don't know what else to do. You and the kids are a family."

"And we'll leave, and you'll miss us?" He didn't dare to hope it. Didn't dare. Not without having confirmation, regardless of what Tony had said.

She stared at him for a long moment, clearly debating lying to him.

"Please." He touched a hand to her bent knee. "Tell me the truth. I need the truth."

"Yes," she whispered on a strained sigh. "I'll miss you."

Relief scudded through him, kicked against his ribs, exploded in his lungs. "What if I made a suggestion that would mean you wouldn't have to miss us, and we wouldn't have to miss you? Would you be willing to at least hear me out?"

"I guess so."

Not enthusiastic, but not without curiosity. Knowing the

woman loved mysteries was coming in handy. And he'd settle for curiosity. "I have three kids who need a mother desperately."

Leave out the love stuff, Bryce. Don't mention it or she'll run so far and so fast you'll choke to death on her dust.

I know, Tony. I know. Now, beat it. This is private.

All right. But don't muck it up.

I'll do my best.

Pacing a short path up and down the hall, Bryce went on. "You've got no kids and, unless I've misread you, you want them."

She pressed her lips together tightly, and a furrow formed between her eyebrows. "You know I want to be the sunshine of my own home, Bryce. We've talked about that many times, sitting right here."

"I know." He stopped beside her, then waited for her to look up at him. "It seems to me I have something you want, and you have something I want. Kids."

"What exactly are you suggesting?"

He swallowed hard. "I'm asking you to marry me, Cally."

"What?" Her mouth rounded then dropped open.

"Shh, you'll wake Suzie." Good grief, she couldn't be that stunned. He studied her wide eyes, her lax jaw. Well, evidently she could. Gregory. How could Bryce have forgotten the effects the man had had on her?

"Well, excuse me, Counselor. I just didn't expect a proposal from a man in love with another woman. This has to be the most asinine thing I've ever heard of in my entire life."

"Why?"

"Why?" She turned a frown on him, then held it. "Are you serious?"

"Yeah, I am."

"Well, for starters, you're in love with your dead wife and I'm never going to love a man again as long as I live. Marriage is kind of intimate, you know? Going into it with love is hard enough, but without it, it'd be hell."

"Would it?" Bryce leaned a shoulder against the wall, and lowered his voice to a serious whisper. "Look, we loved and we got hurt. I've thought about this a lot, Cally. My marriage wasn't great. It wasn't even good. And I wasn't content. But I did love the woman and, as best she was able, she loved me. Like you with Gregory, love just wasn't enough."

"No, it wasn't. And if love, with all its power, didn't make the cut, what in the world would come of a marriage without it?"

"A lot less pain. We both have needs and wants and they're compatible. We both love the kids. We like each other. We can talk. And on the physical side, well, I liked our kisses. I'm sure making love—"

"Sex," she corrected him, her voice hard and snappy. "It'd be sex, Bryce. We don't love each other."

"Okay, then. I'm sure sex would be great between us. You appeal to me, Cally. Do I appeal to you?"

"You know you do." She crushed the pillow to her stomach. "That's not the point."

"What is the point?"

She squeezed her eyes shut. "I'm not sure. I'm confused." She looked up at him, all her misgivings there in her eyes. "But there is a point, Bryce. I know there is. I'm thinking big defeats."

He stroked her cheek, her chin. "Think little victories instead. And don't be upset. Please. I hate your being upset. It makes me sad."

She turned her face into his hand. "It's a marriage of convenience we're talking about here. That's it."

"What's wrong with that? They've been done for centuries."

"And a lot of the people in them were miserable."

"But they weren't typically choosing for themselves. We are. That's a big difference, Cally." She was weakening. The idea was growing on her; the stiffness was leaving her shoulders, her expression. "Think about it, okay? I want to marry you. I know in my heart you'd be a good mother to my kids and a good wife to me. I can't love you—I'll never be able to love you. But I promise I'll be good to you and do all I can to make sure you're content."

She stilled for a long moment, then a soft light glistened in her eyes. "Will you promise me fidelity and honesty?"

Gregory's affair. His getting remarried to Joleen so soon after his divorce from Cally was final. ''I will.''

''And you'll never side against me with the M and M's? Parents putting on a united front makes kids feel secure. I won't have insecure kids, Bryce.''

''I won't side against you.''

''And we forbid the use of that word 'stepparent.' I'm not saying I agree to this, but if I do, I'll never permit that word to be spoken in our home.'' She shrugged. ''That yours-and-mine attitude causes a lot of problems between parents, and a lot of nightmares for kids. I won't have any of that, either.''

''Sounds reasonable. In everyone's best interests.''

''I won't love you either, Bryce. I just don't have that left to give a man now. But I'd be good to you. I care. I really do. But it can't be love. Not even fifty years from now. So you can't ever expect it.''

''I understand. Same here.''

''And you mustn't think you can't talk about Meriam. You can. But I won't have you comparing us, or flaunting her in my face.''

He smiled. ''Cally, that sounded positively courageous.''

She looked surprised, then her mouth settled into a smile. ''Yeah, it did, didn't it?''

He nodded. ''How did it feel?''

She hiked a shoulder. ''Pretty damn good.''

He laughed softly. ''So will you think about it?''

''Yes, I will.'' She cocked her head. ''And you think about it too, because if we do this, it's permanent. I can't go through another divorce. Not even when the kids are grown and you don't need me anymore.''

He'd always need her. Always. And if he'd doubted that before walking into the hall tonight, he'd never doubt it again. But he'd live his life without once telling her. This very conversation forbade him the privilege of ever telling her. ''No divorce. I'll draft it up as a term in our contract.''

''Do we need to put it in writing?''

''I trust you, but I'm a lawyer, honey. Everything gets put in writing.''

''Not everything.'' She stroked his beard. It rustled softly and her voice went husky thick. ''Your proposal didn't.''

Her lips parted, and an intense, low beam of desire whirled in his stomach. "I thought a proposal needed a more personal touch than a formal written agreement."

"I think so, too. Still, you lawyer types do love your agreements official, and we don't have a formal proposal contract."

"What's your point, Miss Tate?" Playful. He rather liked seeing Cally playful, her eyes shining mischief.

"We need some kind of signature on the dotted line to assure you this proposal is getting serious consideration."

He swallowed his surprise, but his heart started a hard, slow beat. So she wouldn't hear its thumps, he ruffled his beard. "Sounds reasonable. What do you suggest?"

Her lids dropped a notch and a sexy little puff of air escaped from between her lips. "A kiss."

With a grunt of pleasure he couldn't hide, he lowered his lips to hers. She'd think about it. For now, that was enough. She needed time to weigh the matter and, unless God was napping, she'd agree. Eventually.

Entice her, man.

Bryce internally grumbled, irritated at the interruption. *Out, Tony. Now.*

I was just trying to help.

Out.

Color me gone.

Smiling at the pout in Tony's voice, Bryce put his heart and soul into the kiss. He couldn't give Cally the words, could never give her the words, but he could let her know that he cared, and show her his love. And he could pray that letting her know and showing her would be enough and she'd be content. It'd worked for Tony and Hattie for years, so it could be done. Bryce dared to believe it could be done again. For them.

And, in their kiss, he dared to dream.

Chapter 11

Dawn.

That special moment of time where the brink of a new day promises rebirth and renewal. A day where anything is possible, plausible, just waiting for its witnesses to decide whether to leap on it and cherish its treasures, or to idly watch its opportunities and possibilities come and go unrealized.

Before coming to Seascape Inn, Cally never would have believed that potential and those opportunities in dawn's promise could include her. Now, today, she permitted herself the luxury of wondering if they might.

She looked down the legs of her jeans to nudge at a pebble with the toe of her sneaker, hunched her shoulders inside her jacket against the early morning chill. Tendrils of mist clung to the sky, ribboning through the clouds and hovering above the granite cliffs like party streamers. The constant ebb and flow of the ocean usually soothed her. But feeling as if dawn's promises might include her had her agitated and unsure, afraid to hope that they might because if she did, and they didn't, then she'd once again set herself up for a major disappointment.

At the tree line, a deer peered out of the thick clump of spruce. It looked frightened to see her there; as frightened as she felt inside. Not wanting to intrude—this was the deer's turf, not hers—she turned away, crossed the dew-slick cliffs to the stone steps, walked down them to Main Street, then headed toward the village, kicking at pebbles, patches of dry, brittle grass, little hills of windswept sand.

Confused and weary of challenges, she wanted dawn's promise. Wanted life to make sense again. It'd been a long time since life just had made sense.

The sun rose above the horizon in a fiery burst of orange, filling the sky with spectacular beams of brilliant pink and lavender. A little breathless, Cally paused to appreciate its beauty and fleetingly wished Bryce was with her. That he wasn't had her off balance again, worrying. She walked on, down the weedy dirt path running parallel to the street, on to the cemetery. Life-altering decisions had to be made. And she had to make them. She needed to weigh them out, explore them. These decisions wouldn't only affect her life, but Bryce's and the precious M & M's. The responsibility of making the right decision rested on her shoulders. It terrified her. And humbled her.

If at home, she'd make a beeline for the oak and talk this over with Mary Beth. But Cally wasn't at home. She was in Sea Haven Village, Maine. A warm and wonderful, sleepy little village, filled with a quaint old inn that had lured her, an angelic innkeeper who pampered and nurtured and cried with her, and a remarkable ghost who was so very loving and special that he devoted himself to protecting Suzie. Cally appreciated all of Seascape's treasures but, right now, her heart yearned for the familiar. For Mary Beth.

Passing the post office, Cally glanced through the window. The glass-front post boxes had to be antiques. Their polished brass locks gleamed. When she reached the fence beside the little cemetery, down a bit from where Miss Millie had lectured the kids on village history, she stopped, remembering Suzie, so earnest and serious, insisting that Little Island belonged to her as well as to the other village children. Despite Bryce's explanations, she still insisted. Cally smiled. After Hatch had taken Suzie to see the island, the oldest M & M had successfully negotiated her father's promise to come back to Seascape at least once a year so she could check and be certain her property received proper care in her absence. "The tourists dump trash in the water, Daddy," she'd said, ''and the tide will sweep it onto my island. I can't let trash get on my island.''

Bryce, God love his heart, hadn't so much as cracked a smile. Nor had he expressed any doubt that his daughter could accomplish the impossible and hold back the tide. ''Of course you can't,'' he'd simply said. ''While we're away, Frankie will keep watch.''

That had set Suzie's mind at ease. Otherwise, Cally suspicioned, Bryce would have a hard time convincing Suzie to ever leave the village.

Would that be such a bad idea?

Bryce had a successful practice in New Orleans. Family and friends. So did Cally. And he also had memories of Meriam. He'd never consider leaving permanently, and maybe they shouldn't. Maybe they needed to remember where they'd been to fully appreciate where they were going.

And where exactly were they going?

Cally slumped against the fence. The yellow carnation in her hand drooped over the top fence rail, its petals teased by the stiff breeze. In her thoughts she already had accepted Bryce's proposal, and that disturbed her. She couldn't do that; she had to be logical, systematic about this decision. It affected too many lives.

In the end, would she accept it? Wishing she knew, she moved over to the foot of Mary Elizabeth Freeport Nelson's grave and heard children laughing. Two boys wearing blue jackets and white helmets riding their bikes hell-bent-for-leather down Main Street, their tires kicking up clouds of dusty sand and loose pebbles. They looked happy. Content.

She took in a deep breath, then bent down and placed the carnation against the headstone. *I hope you don't mind me talking with you, Mary Elizabeth. My own Mary Beth is far away, and Bryce thinks you're a hot line to her. I hope you are, because I really need to talk with her about this proposal of his.*

A sense of warmth veiled her and, feeling welcome there, Cally sat down on the ground, still damp with dew, then smoothed her jeans over her ankles. The moisture soaked through the seat of her jeans. *See, this thing with Bryce really has me stumped. I know I'm not lovable, Mary Elizabeth, but he makes me feel as if I am. I like it.* This wasn't going to work. Not without unvarnished honesty. It was time to strip bare the fluff and get to the substance. *Actually, I love it. And I'm crazy about him and about his kids. That's the problem.*

She looked away from the stone, through the light mist to the fence. Clusters of spiky chickweed hugged the bases of the slats and bent to the breeze. Sunlight streamed between the boards and cast thin streaks of shadows on the ground; cool strips of gray eclipsing brown leaves and wet sand and rock. Feeling as malleable as they looked, she stared at them. *I don't know, Mary Elizabeth. When he first proposed, I thought he'd lost his mind. But the more I think about it, the more sense it makes. I guess that sounds goofy to you, considering your mother and father had that rare love that people like me don't even dare to dream about.*

But since I don't dream of finding that kind of love, I'm thinking maybe Bryce's suggestion is a good alternative. We'd both have what we need. Kids and partners who respect us. There's a lot to be said for respect. I don't think he'd ever make me feel ugly. I hate feeling ugly. I really hate it. Bryce sees beauty in me. I'm not sure why. And I still can't look in the mirror, but he makes me want to look into it. He makes me want to look at myself and see beauty, too. And I believe him about being faithful and honest. He's just that kind of man.

At least, I think he is. My judgment isn't up to snuff, I know. After all, I thought Gregory felt those things, too, and I learned the hard way that he didn't. But I was naive then. It honestly hadn't occurred to me that men wouldn't be faithful and honest with their wives. Now, of course, I know they can be conniving and dishonest, and I think my judgment is probably better for having learned that. Anyway, I trust Bryce. More importantly, the kids trust Bryce, and I trust them.

Actually, I think it'd be a perfect marriage. Care, concern, respect—good foundation blocks. And I'd be lying if I said I wasn't anticipating making love with him. I'm worried about disappointing him, of course. What woman wants to feel lacking or ugly then? But he tempts me, Mary Elizabeth.

Something fierce. Even after Gregory, Bryce can make me melt with just a look, a glance, a smile. It's almost obscene. And, from what I've seen of it, he has a body that just won't quit. I'm not crazy enough to think he finds me as appealing as I do him, but he hates loving our kisses and he likes touching me. Sometimes when we're walking, he puts his hand at the small of my back, and he often touches me when he doesn't have to—deliberately, I mean. God, but I hate loving the way that makes me feel. He's so strong, but when he puts his arms around me, he's gentle. And when he touches my face, he gets this look in his eyes that takes my breath away. I can't describe all it makes me feel, but . . . oh, I really hate loving the way he touches my face.

A bird cawed overhead. Molten and bittersweet, Cally spotted the gull and watched it fly away. *I love him, Mary Elizabeth. God help me, I thought I was smarter than to ever love another man. But Bryce sneaked in on me. While I was sidetracked, falling in love with the M & M's, he slipped right into my heart.*

The problem is that he doesn't want it. And I'd be nuttier than Batty Beaulah Favish if I wanted him to want it. But I do want him. And the kids.

She rocked back and dusted a brittle brown leaf from her shoe. It crackled, tumbled to the ground. *I think with them I could be content. When I came here, I thought I'd never be content again. I didn't see how I could be. But he's promised me all the things I've wanted for most of my life. With him, I could be the sunshine of my home. I know you have no idea how much that means to me, but Mary Beth knows.*

A woman's voice sounded in Cally's mind. *I know exactly what it means to you, Cally. You're thirty-two and starting over with everything you've never wanted. You believed you'd never get what you wanted and suddenly you're offered a new dawn. A chance for all your dreams to become realities. And it's scaring you half to death.*

Cally jerked, looked through the trickles of mist, but saw no one. Internally. The woman had talked to her internally . . . just like Tony. Oh, God. "Who are—" Her voice gave out, and she paused, swallowed, then tried again. "Mary Elizabeth?"

I understand, Cally. My name isn't of consequence, only that I understand your dilemma.

Cally told herself to get a grip on her emotions. She wanted to run, but her legs were about as stable as sand. No way would they hold her. Okay, this was strange. Bizarre. But so was Tony, and he was helping Suzie. Maybe this woman was Mary Elizabeth. She hadn't confirmed or denied her identity, but maybe Tony's sister had come to help Cally. Did it really matter who she was? She was right, she understood Cally's situation, and Cally had promised herself to appreciate miracles here. If this didn't qualify as a miracle, she sure didn't know what would.

Ah, you've stopped shaking. Good. Your blood pressure spike made me uneasy. I'm glad it's nearly down to normal now.

"Me, too."

Talk internally, dear. People are milling around and we wouldn't want them to think you've snapped your crackers.

Cally glanced over. Lydia Johnson stood outside The Store. Her husband, Horace, was filling a half-barrel with ice and beer near the front door. And Jimmy Goodson tinkered under the hood of an old green pickup in the parking lot of his garage.

Back to business. I hear all you've been telling me, Cally, yet I'm sensing a huge obstacle that you've not yet mentioned. Do you know what it is?

She did. *I have the chance to get everything I want. But is it the right thing for Bryce and the kids? That's the obstacle that's driving me insane.*

The children simply need your love. Can you give that to them?

I wouldn't consider this for a second if I didn't love the M & M's.

Well, that resolves that. Now, Bryce. Well, he's a bit more ticklish a situation.

He is. See, I'm okay with what he's proposed. I'll get everything I want. But to do it, I'll have to lie to him. That rankles.

As well it should. If you agree to this, then you'll have promised him honesty.

Exactly.

But I'm a little confused—oh, wait. I've got it now. You'd have to agree to a loveless marriage to Bryce when you really do love him. That's the lie.

Yes. Desolate, Cally watched the sun burn through the last remnants of mist. *I don't think I can do it. I've been lied to, and I hated it. So has Bryce. He deserves better. We both do, and—*

Marriage vows are sacred.

Yes. Yes, they are.

Of course, if you don't lie when stating the vows—which you wouldn't be doing in repeating them because you do love Bryce—then you wouldn't be sacrificing honesty or violating your own code of ethics.

I wouldn't? But Bryce wouldn't know it. Or else he'd know the truth. He surely wouldn't miss me vowing to love, honor, and cherish him, Mary Elizabeth.

It's tradition. And he's a very traditional man. I doubt he'd think twice about it.

That's a really thin line.

Ah, but it is a line, Cally. Remember what Suzie told you, hmm? If only you have the courage to believe—

A hot tingle rippled up Cally's spine. *Miracles can happen beside a dreamswept sea.*

Take the essence of that message into your heart, into those secret places where all your hopes and desires live, and dream. You're far too special to walk away from everything you ever wanted out of fear of tripping over a thin line.

But what if he does think twice about me making the vows? What if he senses I love him? Can I live with the man for the rest of my life, loving him, and he not know it?

I'm not sure.

That's the real obstacle. His knowing I love him could destroy everything. Now, or even years from now. I could lose him and the kids, Mary Elizabeth. Thinking they'd be my family forever, I could lose them all.

You could. I'm sorry to have to agree, but truth is truth. Mmm, I guess that makes the real obstacle a question of whether or not you love him and the M & M's enough to take those risks.

I guess it does.

And your answer?

I wish I knew. I love them, but—

You fear you lack the courage to live out the masquerade.

Cally nodded, staring down at the stony ground.

Bryce awakened in a cold sweat.

His pajamas clinging to his damp skin, he sat straight up in bed, blew out a shuddery breath, and dragged his fingers through his hair. He shook inside, all over.

It'd been a long time since he'd dreamed of Meriam. And never had he dreamed of her as vividly as he had tonight.

The room was dark, and the sweat clinging to his body had him chilled. He grabbed a fresh pair of pajamas, his robe, then headed for the shower.

The hallway was empty. Suzie had sent Cally to bed, too, he imagined. Cally. Pursing his lips, he put the little Occupied sign on the nail centered in the door, then turned on the shower. On the white half-moon rug just outside it, he stripped then stepped under a stream of hot water and let it sluice over his chest.

She hadn't yet accepted his proposal. But she hadn't yet rejected it, either. And after tonight and what he'd dreamed, he only prayed she wouldn't reject it.

Angry all over again, he slapped soap on his body, and visualized her. Laughing, giving him that secretive smile, looking at him and letting him see she was feeling fragile, vulnerable. His hands gentled and, in his mind's eye, he saw not his own but her hands, her long, slender fingers, gliding lazy trails over his bare skin. Heat furled in his groin, and he grew aroused. Merely thinking of her, he'd tripped into hormone hell. Again.

Grimacing, he jabbed the soap into its dish, then flipped the tap over to cold. When the water turned frigid, he jerked, clenched his teeth, muttered a healthy "Animal crackers."

His teeth chattering, he forced himself to stay under the icy spray. Pangs of conscience attacked him, full force. Could he marry Cally, loving her, and denying he did? Promising her he never would? He'd given her the words and, at the time, he'd meant them. But at gut level, he must have known the truth back then. Even if he hadn't, after the dream tonight, he couldn't deny it anymore; not to himself. The question was, Should he tell Cally the truth? Should he keep his vow to be honest with her and tell her he'd done the singularly most stupid and irresponsible thing of his life? Should he tell her he'd fallen head over heels, heart over ass, in love with her?

She'd take off like a jet propelled with rocket fuel.

He'd lose her.

He slumped against the shower wall. How the hell had he gotten caught in this web of deception? He batted at the tap, and the water shut off. Snatching a towel from the bar, he rubbed it briskly over his skin. The kids loved her, needed her, and they'd lose her. The M & M's played an important part in this relationship, but they weren't the bottom line. He would lose her. That was the bottom line. He'd lose her, and he didn't want to lose her.

But to keep her, he'd have to pull a Gregory-type stunt and lie to her. Bryce jammed the damp towel between the bar and the wall, then tugged on his robe. He just couldn't do that to her, or to himself. Tugging at the sides of the robe, he cinched it closed with a belted knot. Pulling a Gregory Tate antic ate at everything decent inside Bryce. He couldn't live with it. Not even for Cally.

He returned to his room with a heavy heart; tried going back to bed, but only tossed and turned. Finally, he just got up. His knee aching like hell, he paced the room to work out the stiffness, and muddled over their mess. How could he resolve it without losing her?

Inside his head, he heard a knock.

He stilled on the corner of the rug and stared at a snow globe paperweight on the desk. "Tony?" he asked, surprise skittering through his voice. It couldn't be anyone else, but why would he be knocking?

You wanted a warning I was coming, so I gave you one. Having a rough night, eh, Counselor?

He'd forgotten. "Yeah, I am."

It's not easy seeing the truth. Sometimes it's not pretty.

Tony knew about the dream and what it had revealed to Bryce about Meriam. "No." His voice went flat. "It's not."

If you talked it over with Cally, you might feel better about this.

"I'm sure I would. But I don't think the woman I've proposed to would feel better at hearing my realizations about my former wife."

Maybe you're right. Women are hard to figure. Hmm, I'm just talking off the top of my head here, but I seem to remember in Relationships 101—you cut that class, too—there was an in-depth discussion on a topic called trust. Probably structured by some wimp—not a real man—but this guy suggested that when a man asks a woman to share the rest of her life with him, he should trust her. Radical concept, isn't it?

"I hate it when you get sarcastic, Tony. Especially right now. In case you haven't noticed, that dream knocked me on my ass."

If I hadn't noticed, I wouldn't be here.

"Then drop the sarcasm."

Okay. Here's the straight skinny. Trust Cally. And talk to her about this.

"I don't want to hurt her."

I don't think you really trust her. I think you tell yourself you do so you can keep your secrets to yourself and not risk losing your pride.

"Pride has nothing to do with this. I have none, and she gets hers from a bottle of perfume, remember?"

Pride has everything to do with this. I warned you I'd be in your face, that you could lie to me, but not to yourself. Pride is the problem, Bryce. Way down deep inside you, in places you don't like to acknowledge even exist, you want Cally Tate. You need her. And you want love. You damn well crave it. But to admit any of that you have to risk your pride, risk having her toss those cravings right back in your face. And that's why you proposed a contract for a marriage of convenience to the woman you love. So you get what you want, but avoid risks. You copped a plea, Counselor. Played it safe. But that won't give you what you crave. Only risks will do that.

"You're finding fault with the proposal? You're the one who said love was mucking things up. Now you're feeding me this garbage about pride and risks being the problem? No way, Tony. Pride isn't the problem. Having been in love before and not being loved back—that's the problem."

Exactly. Tony's voice softened. *Loving and not being loved back. Being afraid it'll happen again. That it can't not happen again.*

Bryce went stock-still. He had said that. And he'd meant it. Meriam hadn't loved him. Ever. He knew that from the dream. He'd loved her, but she'd never loved him. In all of their marriage, all of his adult life, he'd never been loved by a woman. And because he hadn't, he doubted he was lovable.

Just like Cally.

Talk to Cally, hmm? Maybe you can help each other. Maybe not. It takes guts to believe. And to dream for longer than the span of a kiss. To tell you the truth, Bryce, I'm not sure either of you have enough guts to handle it. But I figure your odds together are better than they are apart.

Bryce grimaced and grabbed the snow globe from the desk, then clenched it in his palm. "Sometimes you're a real bastard, Tony."

Yeah, I know. The prognosis is that I'll get worse before I get better. Thanksgiving is only three days away.

The anger fell away from Bryce like a thin layer of sun-warmed ice. "I'm sorry about you and Miss Hattie."

Just talk to Cally and get this worked out, okay? I swear to God I can't take another Thanksgiving around here without things working out right for somebody.

"I'll talk to her. And, if I might make a suggestion . . ."

Why not?

"I think you should talk with Miss Hattie, too. She's really worried about something, and she won't discuss it even with Miss Millie. It has her rattled."

I can't talk to her.

"Why the hell not? You two love each other."

Yes, I love her. I've always loved her. Tony let out a heartfelt sigh. *Imagine this, Counselor. Imagine loving a woman, hearing her talking to you every day, but never being able to converse with her. Imagine seeing her, day in and out, but never—not once—being seen by her. Imagine never being able to touch her, or to hold her, or being touched or held by her. And imagine her loving you with all her heart and never having more than your whispers inside her mind. That's all you can give her. Signs. Cool breezes. Never a word, a smile, a simple kiss good morning. Imagine it, Bryce. For you, and for her. That's the position I'm in with Hattie. Or, more accurately, the position I have been in.*

Bryce struggled to talk around the lump in his throat. "It's pretty grim."

Yes, it's grim. I've been a damn fool, Counselor. That's hard to admit, but it's true. I've been content to be close to Hattie most of the time, but she deserved better. She deserved the best of everything and, because of me, she got nothing.

"Anyone who knows her, knows she only wanted you, Tony."

But if I weren't here, then maybe she'd have gone on with her life. Maybe she would have—

"She did go on with her life."

I meant without me.

"If you think that's possible, you're crazy as hell."

I hope not. Because from what's in the wind, she's soon going to have to do it.

Dread snaked through Bryce. He'd imagined all Tony had said. Living it for a few seconds had been painful, but they'd lived it for fifty-one years. Their circumstances were familiar, and they'd adjusted. Now they were going to have to adjust again? That seemed too much to ask of any couple. "That's why you've been so different from how T.J. described you. And why Miss Hattie's been so worried."

Yes. It's totally my fault. I busted the regs. But we both get to pay the price.

"It'll break her heart." Bryce couldn't imagine Miss Hattie without her soldier.

And mine. Tony let out a shuddery sigh that blew a cool wind across Bryce. *Look, the problem with me and Hattie can't be fixed. Yours can. Go talk to Cally. Please. At least when they force Hattie and me apart, we'll have the satisfaction of knowing you two and the kids are all going to be together and you'll be okay.*

Force them apart? Who? Bryce shut out the question, certain he really didn't want to know. "I'll talk to Cally, but don't you give up on finding a solution for you and Miss Hattie. You're always telling the rest of us miracles are possible here. Maybe you need to believe it, too."

I wish I could. But Seascape's miracles are for special guests, not for Hattie and me. Never for Hattie and me.

Bryce walked into the salon. Cally hadn't been in her room, but following the light seeping from here into the stairwell, he'd come downstairs. She lay sleeping slumped against the sofa, her breathing soft and easy, her full lips slightly parted. A thick, cloth-covered photo album lay open on her lap. Old photos of the Freeport family.

He lifted the book, set it onto the coffee table, then just looked at Cally. At her sweet face, unguarded in sleep in ways she'd never let anyone see when awake. Her hands lay at her sides, her fingertips curled, bunching her teal skirt, and the memory of her touching his face eased into his mind. Desire drugged him like a sucker punch.

He sat down beside her on the brocade sofa, then leaned over and lowered the hemline of her skirt. When he'd lifted the album, she'd shifted, and it'd crept up her thigh. His chest brushed against her forearm, and her lips tempted him. He shouldn't do it, but couldn't resist, and touched a tender kiss to them.

"Bryce." She sighed his name, and her lashes fluttered open.

"Hi." Her eyes were unfocused, dreamy, and he sensed that's exactly how they'd look when she was making love. Desire curled deeper, coiled tighter, filling the crevices of him with longing. They would be loving, he promised himself. But first they needed to talk, to resolve his emotions regarding Meriam. He had to put her to rest. She was content.

And now Bryce wanted contentment, too.

"You fell asleep," he whispered, smoothing a hand down Cally's side, ribs to hip.

Her cheeks turned the warm pink of Miss Hattie's Peace roses. "I guess I did."

"Are you awake enough that we can talk a little?"

"I think so." She stretched out, turned toward him and slid on the cushion, then tucked up one leg. "Just don't expect any brilliant deductions. I'm not comatose, but I'm lingering in dream state. I kind of like it there.''

He'd like to be there with her. ''Dreams are what I want to talk about.'' He lifted her hand and brushed his thumb over her nail. The grating friction felt good. ''I had one a little while ago that was . . . different.''

''Good, or bad, different?''

''It was about Meriam.'' He searched Cally's eyes, let her see his uncertainty. ''Would you mind my talking about it?''

Curiosity fell to compassion. ''It rattled you.''

He nodded. ''In ways I didn't expect.''

''Sounds ominous.'' She laced their fingers, sandwiched his hand between hers, then rubbed her fingertips over the back of his hand. ''I think we'd better talk about this. I don't like seeing you tensed up, Counselor.''

''Thanks.'' Now what did he say? He hadn't thought beyond confronting her with this. They'd surpassed that, so where did he go from here? He wanted to talk it out, but where did he start?

''Don't struggle with it. Just let it come.'' Cally glimpsed their reflection in the television screen. They looked good together. Him, dark-haired and handsome; her, fair and blond. Sensing him at a loss and needing a show of support, she again clasped their hands. When he clamped down on hers, she knew she'd been right. He was floundering.

''Maybe I can help,'' she said. He hadn't been this uptight since he'd proposed, and she felt ninety-nine percent sure she knew what in his dream had brought that tension on. ''You dreamed strange things about Meriam, didn't you?'' He nodded, and she continued. ''Did you dream about things the way they really were, and not the way you remember them being when you're awake?''

He stiffened and looked up at her, stunned. ''How did you know?''

''No great mystery, Counselor.'' She gave him a soft smile. ''I've lived through this, too. An unexpected divorce is a lot like an unexpected death. Both are mourned.''

''Of course.'' He lowered his gaze to their linked hands.

''My guess is that you saw Meriam as independent. A woman who refused to need you or the kids, and who refused to let any of you get close. You understood why, but deep down you resented it. You admired her adventuresome spirit, her thumbing her nose at the role society thought she should play, and her doing what she pleased. You admired those things in her because they were traits you'd tamped in yourself. We've discussed that before. So that tells me you saw something else in this dream. Something you didn't know, not even deep inside. Or maybe you knew it and refused to see it, because seeing the truth hurt too much. Is that what happened?"

"She never loved me, Cally." Pain riddled his voice.

It cut into her heart, and she softened her voice. "I don't think she could, sweetheart."

"I know. And yet I still feel so angry. So . . . So—"

"Unlovable?"

He nodded, avoided her eyes.

"The anger you can deal with. It's the feeling unlovable that doesn't sit well on your shoulders."

"No more easily than it sits on yours."

"You know, darling, in a way that this happened is good. Quit glaring at me, I'm serious. I mean, it hurts like hell, but we truly understand each other's feelings because we've both lived through this. That's bound to be advantageous."

"There should be some redeeming quality."

"Quit pouting."

"It hurts."

"Yes, it does."

"You understand totally. I'm sorry for that." He curled an arm around her shoulder and drew her to his side. "But you're right, Cally. This isn't the kind of thing you can explain to someone who hasn't experienced it."

"Who'd want to?"

"Not me," he said, then went stone-still.

"Bryce?" He looked thunderstruck. What had happened? "What is it?"

"Tony was right."

"What?"

"He was right. This is about pride."

Cally pressed her face against his shoulder, then tilted her chin and looked up into his eyes. "You know, I've been thinking about that. I think it's about time we got to keep a little of ours. What do you think, Counselor?''

''You're talking in riddles again, honey.''

She gave him an apologetic smile. ''Gregory married Joleen within days of divorcing me. Meriam didn't even tell the people at work she had married you. They made us feel unlovable and our pride took a real battering.''

''I told myself those things didn't matter. But deep down they did matter, Cally. I couldn't admit that before, but I have to now. They mattered a lot.''

''Of course they did. They mattered to me, too.'' Tension knotted the muscle at his nape. She rubbed at it. ''I finally figured this out. Those things would have proven to us that we were important to them. But we didn't get them, so we doubted we were important until we felt sure we weren't important. The result: we feel unlovable.'' She grunted. ''Wickedly simple, really.''

''Hmm, but hard to face.'' Bryce understood why perfectly—now. He glanced back from the carpet to Cally. She had the strangest expression on her face. Kind of awed, kind of irked. He didn't know what to make of it. Or what to expect. ''What are you thinking?''

She wheeled her gaze to his. ''I'm thinking fear and doubt are horrible monsters. We let them keep us in our relationships a long time after we should have gotten out.''

He rubbed at the back of his head and debated. Bottom line, he'd promised her honesty. ''I know we disagree on this, but Gregory and Meriam didn't do anything to us that we didn't let them do.''

''For the record, we don't disagree anymore,'' Cally said. ''I always blamed Gregory and wanted back everything he had stolen from me. He did take those things, but he didn't make me an easy victim. I did that, Bryce. I let him steal from me. Let him chisel away at the good in me until I couldn't see any good anymore.''

''Just as I let Meriam take and take from me without once asking her to give.''

''In my humble opinion, Counselor, we screwed up.''

''I hate to have to agree, but it appears we did.''

"But"—Cally jabbed the air with a pointed finger—"by gum, we spared our pride."

"Yeah. And paid dearly for the privilege."

"It left us damn lonely."

"Damn lonely," Bryce agreed. "And unwilling to love again."

"After our experiences? We'd be crazy."

"Idiots."

"And we shouldn't feel bad about it."

"No, we shouldn't." So why did he feel godawful?

"Not everyone can have that rare kind of love Collin and Cecelia, and Miss Hattie and Tony, shared."

"If they could," Bryce commented, "it wouldn't be rare."

"Right." Cally stood up, then tugged Bryce's hand, urging him to his feet. "I'm not agreeing to your proposal yet, but if I did, then we could care, Bryce. We do care. And caring is more honest and lasting than the kind of love we've known. That would fade, but us caring, that would last a lifetime."

He smoothed his hands over her narrow shoulders, his hands warm. "So we're smart not to love."

She let her gaze drift to his chest. "Appears so."

"Cally?" Standing chest to breasts, he stared down at her, the truth in his eyes. "Tell me."

Her fingers at his waist went stiff. She dragged her gaze up to his, then sank her teeth into her lower lip. "You are lovable, Bryce. If I could choose to love any man, I'd love you. I really would."

She would. Too moved for words, he curled his arms around her waist, then kissed her lovingly, longingly. Desire flooding his body, his heart thundering, his hands trembling, he whispered against her cheek on short rasps of breath. "I'd love you too, Cally."

He kissed her again. Then again. And still again.

"Bryce?" She parted their fused mouths, dreamy-eyed. "Make love with me."

Desire increased tenfold, nearly knocking him to his knees. Mentally staggering, he cupped her face in his hands and whispered the only thought he could latch onto. "I'm going to hate it."

She went stiff in his arms. "A simple no would have sufficed, Counselor."

God Almighty, had he lost his mind? "No." He stroked her face. "I'm going to hate loving it, Cally. That's what I meant."

Primed to blister his ears, she said not a word, just stared at him. Something in his expression must have redeemed him, because her expression softened and she said, "Me, too." Expelling a soft sigh that resembled a purr, she curled her arms around his neck. "I can't wait."

Determined that neither of them would have to, he grabbed her hand and headed to the stairs in a near run. At the landing, he turned to her. "Your room, or mine."

"Mine."

A soft rain fell against the Great White Room's windows. Bryce clicked on the tulip lamp beside the bed. A warm rosy glow spilled over the bed, over the floor, over Cally. His heart slid up into his throat. She stood atop the braided rug, her long blond hair mussed, her striped robe gaping open at her breasts. She looked desirable. Beautiful. Lovable. She also looked self-conscious and scared stiff.

He hated knowing she was feeling those things. He wanted her at ease with him, thinking him lovable. Hell, he wanted her eager for him. As eager for him as he was for her. One day she would be, he promised himself. One day she'd look right into that damn mirror and see herself beautiful. See herself as he saw her.

But not tonight.

Tonight she stood woodenly, like a sacrificial virgin. He couldn't make love with her knowing she felt like a sacrificial virgin. Yet if he didn't, she'd feel ugly. She'd think he was like Gregory. That Bryce too found her undesirable.

Asking him to make love with her had to have been one of the hardest things the woman ever had done in her life. Knowing it, and that she'd done it anyway, touched something in him. Something precious and good and deep. The woman had more courage in her fingertips than he had in his entire body. And before they left this room, so help him, she'd know she was lovable so deep in her soul there'd be no denying it. "It's been a long time for both of us," he said, attempting to ease some of the tension. Hers and his own.

"Uh-huh." She clenched and unclenched her hands at her sides.

He tried a smile. "Are you as nervous as I am?"

"If you're terrified, Counselor, then you've got company."

The smile became genuine. "Good. I'd hate to think I was going through this alone."

"Not a chance." She folded her arms over her chest.

Her brush lay on a silver tray, atop the heavy wood dresser. He picked it up then walked around the bench at the foot of the bed to the opposite side of it from Cally. When he motioned, she clasped the blue coverlet near the pillows, and they peeled it and the quilts back, revealing white eyelet-edged sheets that tinged pink in the soft light and smelled of sunshine.

Without a word, Cally reached for the belt of her robe. So did he. They laid them across the foot of the bed; his on the left, hers on the right. The robes looked good there, and knowing it possible he might see them like that the rest of his life started a fire deep in his gut that warmed him, body and heart. Cally *would* accept his proposal. She *would.*

He glanced up at her, and felt he'd been kicked in the chest. She looked like a barefoot princess. Her gauzy white gown clung to her breasts and to the tuck at her waist. Hiking up the hem, she crawled into bed. He slid in beside her, his heart chugging like a train. She scooted down onto the pillow then smoothed her hem down over her ankles. A fold of it creased over his pajama-clad thigh. Navy silk and white gauze. Him and Cally. A perfect match—except for love.

He held up the brush. "I've watched you do this and I'd like to. . . . Would you mind?" Damn, he sounded like a kid who'd just hit puberty. He'd been married for eons, for God's sake. Why was he so nervous?

Unlovable.

"No, I don't mind." She sat up, then turned her back to him.

Nerves were normal. He hadn't been married to her. Hadn't made love with her. She didn't like liking anything about him. And more than he wanted his next breath, he wanted her to ferociously hate liking making love with him. He wanted her to marry him, to spend all her days with him and the M & M's, to spend all of her nights in his arms, and to hate loving being there. He wanted her content and happy, satisfied and satiated, and at peace. Wanting all that and more, how could he not be nervous?

Her back was as gorgeous as the rest of her. Pale, smooth skin, dusky with a film of scented talc that smelled soothing, like the sea. Her gown cut far below her waist, into a tempting deep vee that had him nearly drooling with wanting to kiss the skin over each vertebrae. One by one. To start at her nape and work his way down her spine. His pulse pumped hard in his throat. He lifted the length of her hair into his hands. In the mellow light, it gleamed like spun gold. "I love your hair long."

"That's because you don't have to take care of it."

"I'd like to, though. I'd like to take care of all of you, Cally." He let the brush glide down the lengths of the strands, scalp to ends, and eased his free hand up her side to the curve of her waist, pausing just beneath the fullness of her breasts, over her ribs. "Will you keep it long for me?"

She shivered. "At the risk of ruining the moment, Counselor, I'd like to remind you that we vowed honesty. My hair being long or short can't matter at all to you."

Cranky, scared as hell. She was loving this. And hating loving it. He nearly smiled. "You want honesty?" She didn't. Not really. But he'd give it to her anyway. "Everything about you matters to me, Miss Tate. Every"—he punctuated his words with kisses to her nape—"little . . . thing."

She let out a low, sexy moan on a shiver, and he leaned closer, pressed his chest flush to her back, then buried his face in her hair and inhaled the scent. His throat went thicker still. "Mmm, peaches. Fresh, lush peaches. I like peaches, Miss Tate." He dropped his voice to a growl and confessed.

"Though your coconut shampoo does wicked things to me, too."

"I'll, um, remember that."

"Good." He nuzzled the shell of her ear, growled, low and deep. "Sexy."

She sucked in a quick little breath and her fingers sank into his thigh. "You're forgetting again."

"I'm not forgetting." He pulled the brush down slowly, rhythmically, letting himself drift into fantasies of him and Cally and them making love. Of her touching him, letting out little moans of pleasure that told him she liked what he was doing to her, liked what she was doing to him. The erotic fantasies sent him spiraling, deeper and deeper into desire's web, and he wanted Cally there with him, free of inhibitions; free, and feeling beautiful. He paused brushing, kissed the tempting tender skin at her nape, nosed the cay of her neck, then whispered raggedly, "Cally?"

She laid her palm over his hand at her ribs, and encouraged, he kissed the soft hollow behind her ear. "One day—not today, but one day—I'm going to undress you before that mirror. And I'm going to make love with you until you look at yourself and see all I see." He dropped the brush onto the floor. Heard it land on the rug with a thump. Cupping her breasts in his hands, he felt her chest heave, saw her nipples draw tight. He trailed kisses to her temple, her chin, her shoulder, winding his way down to them. "But for now, I'm just going to adore you."

Through gauzy fabric and shuddered breaths, he captured her breast in his mouth. She locked her hands in his hair, drew his head to her chest, and murmured sweet sounds. When he'd paid homage to both breasts, she lifted his face to hers. Their lips met, melded, eagerly mated. He nudged her shoulder and hip, and she lifted, then straddled his thighs. The contact stunned him, innocently seductive, sensually provocative, mind-drugging. He skimmed her sloping curves, pausing to embrace, to nestle, to caress, clasping bits of her gown, craving the heat of skin. She sighed against his mouth, parted her lips, and welcomed his tongue, then raised a hesitant hand and let it hover at his chest. Darling Cally. So unsure. So fearful of doing something wrong. He held her with one arm and unbuttoned his pajama top with the other, then unsnapped his pants at the waist, his arousal pressing firmly against her thigh. "Touch me, Cally." He looked deeply into her eyes, let her see all he was feeling. "I need your touch."

Cally couldn't breathe. Couldn't move. Couldn't fathom that the hunger in Bryce's eyes was genuine, was for her. He hadn't been with a woman in two years; that had to be spurring the fire in his gaze, the strain etching his face. It'd been a long time. His primal instincts had engaged and any woman would arouse him. That should bother her. Instead it set her emotions free. She just happened to be the lucky one.

With wavering hands and pounding hearts, they eagerly removed each other's clothes, tossed them onto the floor, then hurriedly pressed bare skin to shuddering bare skin. She wanted to touch him everywhere at once, to feel all of him, now. She gazed down his broad chest to his flat stomach, followed the vee of dark springy hair to his groin and saw the evidence of his desire. Her heart skipped a full beat and she had to remind herself to breathe.

"Touch me, Cally." He lifted her hand, pressed it flat on his heaving chest, over his heart, between his male nipples.

They were peaked and taut, and she couldn't resist the temptation to taste them. Both tempted and aching to please him, she splayed her fingertips on his heated skin, then caroused his body, delighting in the ripple of his flesh, the quiver of his muscles reacting to her slightest touch. Thoughts of her being lacking, being ugly, or not satisfying him fled and, celebrating their departure, she let her fingertips drift down and capture his essence.

From the back of his throat quivered a grunt of pure male joy that sang to her woman's heart, and again he claimed her mouth. Heat swirled and rippled, flowed and burned. His arms circling her, he rocked back and then tugged; clasped her hips and positioned her atop him, mouth to mouth, thigh to thigh, heart to heart. His arousal pressed hard against her belly, and the sweet pressure rippled her enchantment into riotous waves, glorious crests, and fulfilling swells. The silken hair sprinkling his chest taunted her breasts, and fingertips suddenly gone sensitive seemed tempted beyond redemption by texture, by design. His hands smoothed down her back, over her buttocks, down to her thighs. Against the back of her knee, he bunched her gown, skimmed his gentle hand to the skin beneath it, murmuring sweet, breathless words, lover's secrets that seeped into her heart.

She broke their kiss and studied his face, his slumberous eyes, heavy-lidded and smoldering with passion, the tense line of his jaw, the straight slope of his nose with nostrils slightly flaring, the perfect arch of his thick brows. His eyes captured, entranced, enthralled. She let herself get lost in them, in the thick haze of heat and hunger swimming in their depths, and the truth arrowed through her like honey-tipped spears. This was real. Not honest with love lies between them, but real. He wasn't thinking of Meriam or of other women with whom he might have made love. He wasn't thinking of proving Cally lovable. He wasn't thinking at all. He was feeling. Yearning. And so was she. But for her pride, she wanted the words. "It's only us here, Bryce," she said, more than asked.

"Only us," he vowed, then reinforced his promise by praising her body with short raspy kisses, with long languorous ones, and adoring all of her with wisps of featherlight touches that seemingly dripped flame, setting her skin and soul on fire. And when they came together, a great shudder rippled through him, inciting sensations of belonging and joy too potent to persevere, too precious to protest. She shimmered over the first crest and plunged into sensation, mindless, boneless, reckless, opening herself totally to him, body and spirit and soul.

He sensed the change in her, stilled, then looked deeply into her eyes. "I was right. I hate loving making love with you, Miss Tate." Sweat sheening his skin, he favored her with a slow, seductive kiss that had her cresting the summit again.

Her heart hammering, taking flight, she knew at that moment her decision on his proposal had been made. "I hate loving you, too, Counselor."

Chapter 12

Cally awakened alone.

Sometime during the night Bryce had returned to his room. In that place deep inside where secrets dwell, she knew he hadn't wanted to leave her, but in the cold morning light she didn't dare admit that, not even to herself. If it proved false, then allowing herself to feel she'd been desired and adored—as lovable as he'd made her feel—would be too far an emotional fall. The struggle it would take to again find some semblance of inner peace just wasn't worth the risk.

Her breasts and thighs, even her limbs, felt heavy and sore, lethargic from a full night of lovemaking. The first time had been a tender coming together, asserting and affirming desire; solely for their hearts. The second time was pure heat. Lusty and fervent, satisfying their too-long-abstinent physical selves. The third time, just hours before dawn, had been different still. A potent sensual implosion that fused heart, body, and soul in a way Cally had never before experienced. Bryce hadn't, either, and they both had admitted to hating loving it.

She tossed back the covers and crawled out of bed, wanting nothing more than to fall right back in and bring Bryce with her. Flushing, she crossed the cool floor, dressed quickly in jeans, a blue blouse, and her parka, then went down the stairs, gliding her hand along the slick banister that smelled faintly of lemon oil. She paused to wink at Cecelia's portrait, to smile at Collin's, at the contentment in his eyes. Last night, when Bryce had been deep inside her, she'd seen that contentment in his eyes; a contentment that until then she'd only seen in them when he was with the M and M's. That look belonging to her did more for her heart than all the sweet words and promises any man could give any woman.

The third stair from the bottom creaked. She cringed, hoping she hadn't awakened anyone, then headed outside. She needed a walk. Needed to get past the glow of lovemaking and back to logical thought. It was early, just after dawn, and the brisk chill in the air guaranteed to clear away any lazy remnants of sleep.

Veering off the stone walkway, she cut through the woods between Miss Hattie's greenhouse and the lean-to where guests parked their cars and the Carriage House that had been remodeled into overflow rooms, where the battleaxe was staying. It had a new roof.

In a copse of trees, she passed a little clearing where a bench nestled beneath overhanging limbs, climbed over the prone trunk of a downed oak, then glanced over at the gazebo. Freshly painted, it looked pretty in the morning mist, sitting as it was at the foot of the pond. A low stone wall separated Seascape lands from the next-door neighbor's. Everyone called that neighbor Batty Beaulah Favish, but Hatch had told Suzie not to say so in front of Miss Hattie. Both Cally and Bryce knew that, of course. At the Blue Moon, Lucy Baker had told them about the woman traipsing through the woods with her binoculars, ghost-hunting. Seeing Tony could prey on a body's mind, and wondering how he came to be as he was could drive a person insane—unless they accepted him unconditionally. Suzie's friend Selena Mystic had been right about that.

Cally sat down on a protruding root, beneath a sprawling oak that had shed its leaves for winter, then gazed out onto the water. Curls of sun-streaked mist rose from it, dreamy, lovely, and a little rowboat hovered just off the opposite shore. Even through the mist she recognized the craggy, bent man aboard it as Hatch.

Wondering about Tony could make a woman crazy. Funny thing was, Batty Beaulah was sane. Everyone just thought she was crazy, except for Miss Hattie, who took serious exception to such remarks. The villagers all deferred to Miss Hattie, and never risked upsetting her. Cally understood why. Who could resist her? A unique blend of guardian angel and magical Mary Poppins with an iron will, a pure-gold heart, and a broad streak of Maine-stubborn that people from away could marvel at but never emulate. And her devotion to her soldier inspired others, proved being loved was possible.

Poor Tony. How it must hurt him to be denied all that love. To know it was there and to not be able to bask in it. Cally moaned, sad for them, amazed at how little store people put in oddities that only others could see.

She picked up a leaf, crunched it between her forefinger and thumb. Wondering what to do about Bryce's proposal could make a woman crazy, too.

The wind nipped at her fingers. She tucked them into her pockets and admitted she wanted to marry Bryce. Last night, while making love with him, she thought she'd made her decision, that she'd be a damn fool if she didn't marry him. He was gorgeous, had three totally adorable kids, a good sense of humor, a body to die for, and he was financially secure in a respected position within a respected profession. Well, respected by those who don't hate all lawyers. He trusted her. He'd made her promises. And for some reason—which she prayed didn't prove she hadn't learned thing one from her experience with Gregory—she truly believed Bryce would keep his promises. He would be faithful to her. And be honest. He cared. She knew he cared.

If only she weren't in love with the man, she'd jump on his proposal with both feet. He'd be perfect. They'd be perfect. And at peace.

Grating sounds of the little boat being dragged up onto the shore snagged her attention. She smiled at Hatch. "Good morning."

"Well, good morning." He dropped the rope and it hit the stony ground with a healthy *thunk*. The water rippled around his rubber waders, and the string at the bottom of his parka dragged a line in the water. "Fine day for fishin', ain't it?"

"It's a beautiful day." She smiled up at him.

"Uh-oh. Man trouble." He squatted down beside her and

pulled his pipe out of his shirt pocket. "I can spot it a mile away."

Did he ever light that pipe? "The troubles are easy to spot." Cally shrugged. "It's the solutions that are as misty as that pond."

"You listen to this old man, girl. You gotta figure out what you want in life."

She'd recognized the wisdom in him before, and now some sixth sense warned her what he was telling her was exactly what she needed to know to do what was right for her, Bryce, and the M and M's. "I know what I want, Hatch. I have since I was a little girl. It's getting it that's been the problem." She tossed down the crumbled leaf. "I thought I'd found it once, but I hadn't."

"Yeah, I heard about your husband running off with that biochemist. Joleen, wasn't it?"

Geez, did everyone in the village know she'd been dumped? "It was." No sense denying it.

Hatch skipped a stone over the water's surface. It bounced three times, then plunked down with a little splash. "Maybe you deserved better than him." Sun-dappled under the oak branches, he squinted over his left shoulder at her. "Ever thought of that?"

She hadn't.

"I didn't think so." He dusted a sprinkling of sand from his hands, then stepped over a gnarled root, coming closer to her. "Point is, little lady, no matter what happens to us in life, it's for our greater good. We gotta make our climbs and take our tumbles believing that deep down in our guts."

"Sometimes it's hard to believe."

"Sure is. But if faith came easy, then there'd be no need in our going through some of the things we do, now would there?"

He sat down in the rocky sand beside her, bent his knees and propped his elbows atop them. "Life's a lot like fishing, in my estimation. If you wade into it rigged to catch bass, you ain't likely to land a cod. But if you go for cod, and you're meant to have it, then you'll get it."

Cally gave him a soft smile. "In other words, know what

you want and why you want it, then go after it with all you've got."

"More or less." He gave her a gap-toothed grin. "If you're going fishing, you might as well rig for the fish you really want. Otherwise, why not just stay home?"

"Ah, love." His meaning dawned on her. "You're talking about love. No, don't deny it, Hatch. I know you are." She let out a spectacular sigh that heaved her shoulders. "That brings us back to solutions. So what if you find love, but it wasn't meant to be found?"

"Impossible."

"It happened."

"Darling, you listen to this old man. I been around the block a time or two in this love business, and I'm telling you that love don't find a soul it ain't supposed to find. It might not be comfortable, or easy, or even wanted, but it ain't never happened by mistake."

"Mmm, greater good, right?"

"That'd be my estimation on the topic."

She stretched out a hand, then shook his. "Thanks, Hatch."

"You're welcome." As they clasped hands, a strange light lit in his eyes. His brows knitted and his leathery skin pulled tight. Looking pensive, he released her fingertips, then stood up. "Cally?"

"Yes?" What had upset him?

"I know you ain't exactly comfortable with folks knowing all about your situation."

"Would you be?"

He scratched at his neck. "No, I can't say I would be, and that's a fact." He lowered his hand to his side, and his eyes went serious. "But the villagers mean you no harm, only good, and you've got my word on that."

The bulletin board bets down at the Blue Moon Cafe. That's what he meant. "I believe you." She did. That he hadn't spoken from the heart never crossed her mind.

He pulled a gold coin out of his pocket that looked like a Mardi Gras doubloon, then cocked an ear, as if listening to someone. Did Tony talk with Hatch, too?

"If you ever need special help," he said, "you come to me at the lighthouse straightaway."

"Special help?" An alarm went off inside her mind. One that had her knees weak, her chest tight. "What do you mean?"

Eyes that she would have sworn could be no more serious became so. "Hatch?"

"You'll know, Cally. Just remember. You come to me. Straightaway." He pointed at her with a gnarled fingertip. "I'll be having your word on that, little lady."

"All right." She didn't know what in the world she'd just promised, but she knew for fact it was important. More than important, if Hatch's tone were any gauge. And deep inside, that sixth sense warned her it was not only a gauge, but an accurate one.

But a gauge for what?

"Miss Hattie?" Bryce looked up from the third stack of pancakes she'd dumped on his plate.

"Yes, dear?" Pausing beside the table, she held the egg turner poised midair.

"You know a lot about flowers." She'd been grafting roses, working with a hybrid. She had to know more than he did.

"A little." She walked back to the stove, ignoring the din of racket the M & M's were making a morning ritual these days. "But Millie is the master gardener."

He poured homemade blueberry syrup over the steaming pancakes. A droplet landed on the table. Without thinking, he dabbed at it with his fingertip, then sucked it off.

Mrs. Wiggins grunted her disapproval.

Suzie giggled.

And Jeremy looked relieved it wasn't he who had gotten caught.

His face hot, Bryce muttered, "Sorry." He had to get a grip on this early morning fantasy of his night with Cally. It'd been three days, for God's sake. Three long, confusing, bewildering days. What had gotten into her?

"Did you have a question about flowers, dear?" Miss Hattie set the griddle back onto the stove. "I'm sure as certain Millie or I can figure it out."

"Yes, I do." He swallowed a succulent bite from his fork, scraping the tines with his teeth, then savored it. "Mmm, good. Very good." Lifting his napkin from his lap, he dabbed at his mouth. "Cally mentioned a flower that means pride, but not the name of it. Do you happen to know what it is?"

"Not right offhand." Her eyes twinkled with obvious pleasure at this development between him and Cally. "Millie has a list, though. Let me give her a call."

"Thanks." Bryce winked at her.

"Where'd Cally go, Daddy?" Jeremy swung his legs and rocked his chair. "I need to tell her about Toby—the horse I rided."

Bryce steadied it, then pressed a hand to his son's knee. "You've already told her about Toby."

"Yeah, but I wanna tell her again." Jeremy dropped his fork. It clanged against his plate, and he cast a worried look at Mrs. Wiggins, scrunched his shoulders, then looked back at Bryce. "She likes Toby."

Cally liked Jeremy. And why had he flinched on looking at Wiggins? Glancing her way, Bryce knew. Her reprimanding expression had her face looking harder than stone. "You can tell Cally later, after she wakes up."

"Honestly, Daddy." Suzie laid a you-should-know-better frown on Bryce. "She's not sleeping."

"She ain't in the bathroom crying," Jeremy said. "I checked."

Suzie held her frown leveled on Bryce. "She's down at the pond talking with Hatch again. He's trying to find out why she doesn't like us anymore."

Mrs. Wiggins grunted her disapproval.

Ignoring it, he gentled his voice. "It's not that she doesn't like us, Suzie. Cally likes us all very much. She's just busy right now."

"Uh-uh." This from Jeremy. "She's mad. I heared—"

"Heard," Bryce corrected.

"I heard her crying in the bathroom." He held up his fingers. "Two times."

''When?'' Suzie moved her glass of milk aside so she could see her brother from across the table.

''When I asked her to marry Daddy yesterday.''

''Jeremy, you asked Cally to marry me?'' Oh, boy. How was he going to convince her he hadn't put the M & M's up to coercing her?

Suzie's glare turned frosty. ''Daddy, you made Cally cry twice?''

''I didn't make her cry at all.'' Why did she assume he'd been at fault?

''Uh-huh, Daddy.'' Jeremy nodded. ''You did. She cried a long time, too.''

Had he? Guilt swam in Bryce's stomach. ''Well, if I did, I didn't mean to.''

''You made her cry a long time—twice?'' Suzie pinched her lips together so hard they turned white. ''I told you miracles could only happen if you believed. Are you believing, Daddy?''

''Yes, Suzie, I am.'' He had no idea what had gone wrong with Cally. The woman had made love with him as if she'd never get enough of him, then had backed off cold and dropped him. She wouldn't talk about it, or about anything else. At first he'd thought what they'd shared in bed had scared the hell out of her. God knew, it sure had him. Who could've been prepared for that kind of emotional explosion? They'd talked about it, and it was new to both of them. But now, he wasn't sure that fear was the problem. And she wasn't talking.

Miss Hattie patted Suzie's shoulder. ''I'm sure as certain your dad is believing, dear.'' She bent low to whisper at Suzie's ear. ''That's what the flower that means pride is for. To show Cally.''

''Oh.'' The anger and hurt and disappointment left Suzie's expression. She looked amazingly serene.

''Remember,'' Miss Hattie said, ''it takes grown-ups a while longer sometimes to figure things out. We have to be patient.''

''Like it's taking me a while to get both oars in the water. We have to be patient, and to wish really hard.''

"Exactly." Miss Hattie nodded, then smiled up at the ceiling. "Let me give Millie that call."

Once again the angel of Seascape Inn had saved his bacon with his kids. How she managed, Bryce had no idea, but none of them looked ready to murder him anymore, and for that he was grateful.

"Shampoo."

"Lyssie!" Suzie shouted.

Bryce spotted the syrup pitcher poised over the baby's head. He grabbed it out of her little hands just in the nick of time, thunked it down on the table, then pointed a finger at the angelic-looking moppet grinning at him. "No, Lyssie."

She twisted her lips. "Animal crackers."

Ah, bliss. He sank back into his chair. Another peaceful, quiet morning with the Richards family. He glanced to the rocker, but Meriam's image wasn't there. Cally's was. And she didn't smile. She crooked a come-hither finger at him. He nearly came unglued.

Miss Hattie hung up the phone, then clasped her pearl earring back to her earlobe. Pancake batter smudged her apron. Why, oh why, hadn't Meriam hired her?

"Millie says the narcissus symbolizes pride, dear."

"Narcissus. Thanks." He polished off the last of his pancakes. "Is there a florist in the village?"

"No, but Millie has some if you're wanting them."

"Great." He scooted back his chair.

Miss Hattie rinsed her hands at the sink, then dried them with a dishcloth. "Bryce?"

"Yes, ma'am?"

"Far be it from me to interfere, dear, but I think this morning would be a good time to give them to her."

The flowers to Cally. "Oh?" Obviously, from the M & M's, Cally was upset. He only hoped it wasn't because she regretted their making love. He could handle a lot of things, would endure nearly anything, but he couldn't handle feeling unlovable again. Not after what they'd shared. Not and ever again be content.

"Jeremy was right about Cally weeping. And Suzie, too," Miss Hattie said. "Cally left the house at the crack of dawn, looking very troubled, bless her heart."

"I see."

"Not yet, dear heart. But I think you're beginning to."

"She's debating."

Miss Hattie nodded, and stepped close so only he could hear. "I think she could use a little more friendly persuasion."

Surprise streaked up his back. "Miss Hattie."

"Bosh, don't give me that stunned look, Bryce Richards. The woman needs a steady dose of loving, and we both know it. For that matter, dear, so do you." Her face bright pink, she put the dishcloth down on the counter, beside the metal batter bowl. "My solider used to say that instinctive reactions are the only ones worth trusting. Hatch agrees. When we start mulling over things, then what's important gets muddy. For what it's worth, Bryce, over the years, I've learned they're both wise men."

"Do you know where she is?"

Miss Hattie nodded. "Down at the pond by the big oak."

"Hurry, Daddy." Suzie beamed a smile at him and nodded so hard he thought she'd snap her neck. "Tell her we love her, too."

"Wish me luck."

Mrs. Wiggins snorted.

"Always, dear heart." Miss Hattie patted his beard, her kind eyes shimmering tears. "Never doubt it."

As he headed to the door, she called out. "The children and I are going to the village. Tuesday's my errand day, and Mrs. Wiggins needs a little respite."

"I'm quite capable of fulfilling my duties, Hattie."

"Of course you are. Truthfully, I was hoping you might drop next door to check on my friend Beaulah. Maybe have a cup of tea with her. Earl Grey is her favorite, too, and she's alone, you know. When Meriam was here, she and Beaulah became very close. I thought maybe talking about her would be helpful to Beaulah—if it wouldn't be asking too much of you. She misses Meriam something fierce."

"My Meriam?" Mrs. Wiggins's eyes lit up and her voice elevated an octave.

"Oh my, yes. Haven't I mentioned that? Meriam and

Beaulah spent hours talking together and traipsing through the woods."

"Of course. I'd be delighted to assist, Hattie."

"Thank you. I confess I've a lengthy list of errands today and I have been fretting on how I'd get everything done in time for our weekly, er, meeting tonight."

"Historical Society?" Mrs. Wiggins asked, scooting back her chair.

"Not exactly." Hattie smiled enigmatically. "We're planning a wedding."

"Who's getting married?" Suzie asked.

Miss Hattie wrinkled her nose. "It's a secret."

"I'll take Lyssie with me," Mrs. Wiggins said. "It'll be easier for you to shop without her grabbing everything in the world and trying to dump it in her hair."

Bryce gave his littlest angel a smile. The blue had faded from her hair. Maybe she'd be blond for Thanksgiving, after all.

"That's fine." Miss Hattie turned off the stove. "Bryce, do run along, dear. Millie's waiting."

"Thanks, Miss Hattie." He kissed each of the kids.

"You forgotted Miss Hattie, Daddy," Jeremy told him.

"Forgot." Bryce grinned, then planted a gentle peck to her soft cheek. "Now who could ever forget Miss Hattie?"

Bryce found Cally sitting on a root at the base of a sprawling oak, her legs stretched out, her back tilted against the rough bark of its trunk, her face lifted to the sun. Beautiful. Inside and out. His hands at his back, he stepped between her and the sun, watched his shadow melt over her, and grew jealous of it. Ridiculous, but he was uneasy and hurt, feeling shut out, and honest enough to admit he hated it. "Hi."

Her cheeks went rosy. "Hi."

She didn't smile. Neither did he. He saw no regret in her eyes. Uncertainty, but no regret. Pleased and relieved and hopeful that maybe this time she'd finally talk with him about what had her upset and staying away from him and the M & M's, he damned logic straight to hell and followed his instincts, bending over and kissing her lightly. "My pride, Miss Tate." He held out the flower.

"Looks like a flower to me, Counselor." She took the white blossom, and inhaled its scent.

"Astute, as always, but this isn't just a flower. It's a narcissus."

She squinted up at him. "Its meaning is pride."

"Indeed it is. Brilliant deduction." God, but she was beautiful. Vulnerable and fragile, and strong and courageous, all wrapped into a delectable package that tempted him beyond belief.

"So." She stood up, dusted at the bits of bark clinging to the seat of her jeans. "Is there a particular reason you're giving me your pride, Counselor, or is this just a general I-thought-you-needed-a-little kind of gift?"

She'd been crying; her eyes were red-rimmed and still glossy. No regret, so Miss Hattie had to have been right. Cally was struggling with her decision on whether or not to marry him. God, how he wished he could make it easy for her. What could he do? What hadn't he done? "What you said the night we were together made a lot of sense—about Meriam and Gregory. And about us. The flower is my way of telling you I realize that. It is time we got to keep a little pride."

"Yet you're giving yours to me. Why?" She let the blossom slide down her cheek.

The time had come for truth. As much as she could accept of it, anyway. He let it shine in his eyes, sound in his voice. "Because you're important to me and I want you to know it. Because your being comfortable with me is important to me, and I want you to know that, too." He clasped her hand, pressed a lingering kiss to her knuckles. "And because I don't want you ever again to have to say to anyone that you have no pride left because a fool of a man coerced you into forfeiting it to him. That won't happen with me, Cally. I swear it. You have your own pride and, if ever you run short, you have a whole new supply to draw from. Mine."

"Yours." A bittersweet expression fluttered over her face and a tear leaked from her eye. "You care."

More than you'll ever know. More than I'll ever have the right to tell you. But I'll show you, Cally. I will show you. What he would give to be able to say all of that to her. But he couldn't. Instead he told her what she would willingly hear. "Very much." He pressed his lips to each of her fingertips. "Enough to want to spend the rest of my life with you."

She dipped her chin, fingered the white petals. "You're a special man, Counselor."

With her, he felt special. Wanted, needed, and lovable. Only she understood how much those things meant to him. "Marry me, Cally."

"I'm weighing the matter." She looked up at him, her eyes serious, solemn. "It's an important decision for us and the kids. I can't afford to screw up."

"Is that why you've avoided all of us for the last couple days?"

"It's been a big factor."

"You won't be screwing up, honey, unless you refuse. You know we need you. And you need us." He cupped her chin in his big hand. It was trembling. She was touched by the flower; he could see it in the way she looked at him, her heart in her eyes, and he remembered what Miss Hattie had said about Hatch and Tony. "What are your instincts telling you to do?"

"To say yes, but—"

"Do you believe in wise men?"

She blinked, then blinked again, adjusting to the abrupt topic shift. "Yes, I do. After my experience with Hatch, how could I not?"

Wonderful. Terrific. Excitement bubbled in Bryce's stomach, flowed to his limbs. "Hatch *and* Tony, according to Miss Hattie, say following your instincts is the only way to get the right answers. You think, you muddy the waters and complicate things that are simple."

"My instincts have been wrong before."

Gregory. Damn the man. "Ah, but before logic wasn't involved. Love was handling the defense."

She hiked her brows, thoughtful. "True."

Bryce stroked the line of her jaw with his thumbs, looked at her intently. "We care, Cally. If there were any doubt before, our night together proved it. Can't we just believe that caring will guide us?"

She exhaled, her warm breath fanned over his fingers on her face, and her eyes clouded with fear. "You're stronger, Bryce. I'm not that brave."

"You say that, but I know better. We made love, Cally. You feared doing it, but you reached out. You trusted us both, and that took a lot of courage."

"Lust is a powerful motivator."

"Lust was there, I agree, but what happened between us was far more than lust. It was magic, honey. Magic."

She rolled her eyes, clearly agreeing and not wanting to agree. "Here we go again with the magic business. We're not Collin and Cecelia."

"How can you deny there was magic between us? I know we both felt it."

"Bryce—"

"Think perjury, Miss Tate." Temper frosted his voice. "And beware. I have indisputable evidence."

She backed away and folded her arms over her chest, affecting a show-me stance.

He gave her his most sincere look, and spoke straight from his heart. "You made me feel lovable."

Her breasts lifted and she drew in a sharp breath, looking as if she'd been struck. She stared at him, silent, still, and then a tear rolled down her cheek. She knew the value of that feeling. Understood his meaning. And she cried. For him. Maybe for both of them.

Tenderness flooded him, and he pulled her into his arms. "I didn't mean—"

"It's a happy tear, Bryce," she said, her voice husky and low. "Making someone feel lovable is magic. I didn't think I could—"

"You did. And in here"—he covered his heart with his hand—"I know you would again." He pressed his forehead to hers, rubbed their noses, and whispered. "Say yes, Cally. I swear I'll be a good husband to you. I swear I will. The kids need you and you need them. If anyone can get Suzie to put and keep both oars in the water, it's you. And . . ." He let his voice trail.

"And?"

He looked her straight in the eye and took one of the

biggest risks of his life. "And I need you, too."

A second tear followed the first, trickling down her cheek. She swallowed hard. "Do you need me enough to consider an additional term to our agreement?"

He didn't hesitate. "Yes."

"After we're married three years, I want to adopt the M & M's."

That he hadn't expected, and frowned his confusion. "Why?"

She shrugged, and stepped out of his embrace. But by the stiff set of her shoulders and jaw, he knew this was important to her. "Because you never know when something might happen. Miss Hattie didn't with Tony, and you didn't with Meriam. I want the kids to be more secure than that. I want them protected, just in case something should happen."

"Valid reasons." Bryce pinched his beard at his chin between his thumb and bent forefinger, thinking this through, and finding no logical reason to oppose and every reason to be pleased. "All right—provided they agree. And I'm certain they will."

Relief skittered over her face and she smiled.

He smiled back.

Walking back toward the inn, Cally stepped over the fallen oak, then sat down on its trunk and patted the bark beside her for Bryce to sit. "Before we formally agree, I want you to know something. Actually, two things."

He sat down, propped the cane against the tree trunk. "Shoot."

She smoothed her hair back over her shoulder. "The night we made love, I felt lovable, too. I can't tell you how much that meant to me."

Feeling tender, he laced their fingertips. "I know, honey."

"Of course you do." Her eyes glistened.

"And the second thing?"

"Marriage is sacred. We have to be certain we can live with our agreement for the rest of our lives."

Had she forgotten he'd agreed to a no-divorce clause? "Honey, if I weren't sure, I wouldn't have proposed."

"You might have. You were in lust."

He slid her a wicked grin. "With you, I think that's going

to be a perpetual state. One I'm looking forward to enduring."

Her cheeks pinkened, but still she asked. "Honest?"

"Always."

Looking more than a little pleased with herself, she stroked his knee. "One thing is niggling at me, Bryce. That's why I'm hesitant."

"What's that?"

"Love." She let out a sigh that lifted her shoulders. "We don't have it. I'm scared that could adversely affect the kids. I couldn't handle that, Bryce. I just couldn't."

"We both love the M and M's, Cally, and we have so much else going for us. Love's an illusion. We both know that." God, but he hated this. Hated seeing doubt in her eyes. Hearing it in his own voice. "What we have is real. It's a strong base for a good, lasting relationship."

She tilted her head in that way he was coming to love. "Are you sure?"

"Yeah." Was he? Yeah. Yeah, he really was. He gave her fingertips a gentle squeeze. "Are you?"

"Most of the time. But my judgment's proven pretty sorry." She stared out into a copse of spruce. "With Gregory, my sense of worth nose-dived to zero. Because of you with the alimony, it elevated to $2,563.89 per month for five years. But his remarrying Joleen so quickly, well, that knocked it right back down to a goose egg nothing. To me that's what love does; lifts you then drops you on your animal crackers. I don't want it."

He feared they both wanted it but were to afraid to admit it. Just like Suzie had told him about her wanting a mom. Tony had told her we all lie to ourselves to protect our feelings so if we don't get what we want, then it doesn't hurt so much. He'd been right. And wise. "What do you want?"

"A lifemate. A partner who respects me." She looked back to Bryce. "I want to feel needed and appreciated and desirable. Totally lovable, even when I'm bitchy as hell. I want to always know you care. I want the dream, Counselor, all of it except love." The look in her eyes turned pleading. "And I don't want a husband who makes me feel like a weirdo because I bring Mary Beth Ladner yellow carnations on Sundays."

Bryce took a moment to digest all that, then clasped their hands. "You know how I feel about the Mary Beth thing. You're special, sweetheart. The gesture is endearing and admirable. Hell, it's a lot more than that, but it's not weird."

More than anything, she wants to be the sunshine of your home.

She already is, Tony. The kids know it. And so do I.

But she doesn't know it.

Cally dug the toe of her sneaker into the sand. "Will you answer a question for me, Bryce?"

"If I can."

Their linked hands rested on his thigh. "You weren't content in your first marriage, Counselor. I can't live with another man knowing he's not content with me."

He couldn't imagine that she would, or that he would himself. "Technically, you didn't ask a question, Miss Tate. But I'll answer the one you didn't ask." He raised their laced hands to his cheek. "I have every confidence that, married to you, I will be very content." How could he not be content? She made him feel lovable. Important to her. Valued. To her, he mattered.

"Because I love the M and M's?"

"Partly."

"Is that why you're settling for so little yourself?"

What did she mean, so little? She offered a lot. More than he dared to expect much less to hope for; certainly far more than he'd ever had. "I don't understand."

"You ask for so little and yet offer so much. You'll care. You'll protect. You'll trust. You'll be honest and faithful and ask me nicely for what you want. Yet you're asking me for so little. Don't you realize that half the women in New Orleans would love to give you more? Everything?"

He had no idea what to say, so he said nothing.

"So why don't you want more? Why are you willing to settle for so little?"

She didn't see the truth, or didn't want to see it. And if he pointed it out to her, there was no way she'd marry him. But he could answer her. "Because knowing my wife loves the M and M's and cares for me, that's not a little, Cally. To me, it's a lot. But even more so, I can't see me married to any one of those women and being content. I can see me being content with you."

"For how long? Will it be enough tomorrow? The day after that? Ten years from now? Twenty?" Agitated, she swiped her hands down the thighs of her jeans. "What about after Lyssie's grown and out on her own and it's just you and me? Will you be content then?"

"The way I see it, we have options."

"So you won't be content then."

"I didn't say that."

"What are you saying, Counselor?"

"That life just doesn't issue guarantees. But with what we've got, we can grow together, and then this scenario of discontent won't be an issue." He tapped the toe of his loafer with the tip of his cane. "I don't think this contentment bit is the real question here, though. I think it's your backdoor way of asking me if I want more kids." He lifted his gaze to hers. "Am I right about that?"

She answered with a question of her own. "Do you?"

"Evidently. We made love three times without protection."

The color drained from her face. "Oh, God. We did."

It hadn't occurred to her, either. "It wasn't deliberate, Cally."

"No. No, it wasn't. We didn't think. I didn't . . . think."

"I didn't, either. It'd been a long time since we'd had to think and we hadn't planned—"

"When did this occur to you?" Her eyes reeked of suspicion.

"This morning at breakfast. That's another reason I sacrificed pride this morning. To apologize. I promised to protect you, and I didn't. But if you did get pregnant, I won't lie and say I'm sorry. I wouldn't be sorry, Cally."

Her jaw fell open. "You want more kids?"

"Only if you do, and only if they'll be treated—"

"Don't even think it." Her voice went rock hard. "If we marry, then I marry you and the M and M's, Bryce. They'll be my kids too and there'll be no difference. If I couldn't swear that to you and to myself, I'd never consider your proposal."

"I know that down deep." She wanted to adopt them. Would forbid the word "stepparent" to be spoken in their home. "Just tag it as a fatherly instinct that insists on being voiced."

Her expression softened. "Rest easy, Counselor. Your Miss Tate loves the M and M's totally and completely." She held up a hand. "But I draw the line at the battleaxe."

"Understandable." He grinned, wanting to kiss her just for that.

"I hoped it would be."

"So, are we agreed? You'll marry me, then?" His heart nearly halted its beats and his armpits went damp.

"I need a little more time. This is a big step and, if I make the wrong decision, then too many innocents get hurt."

How could he fault her for not wanting to hurt him or the kids? He looped his arms over her shoulders, then pecked a kiss to her lips to show her he understood. "Don't make me wait too long, hmm? It's sheer hell."

"I know it is, and I'm sorry. But I want this to be right for all of us, including you. You deserve so much good, Bryce. And I need to know in my head and heart that you'll get it."

He smiled at her. "You're exactly what I need."

She smiled back.

Stunning. A knot swelled in his throat. If he'd been wearing a tie it'd have choked him to death. Talking past it, his voice came out gruff. "Answer me soon."

"Soon," she promised, and accepted his kiss.

Lost in a sensual haze, they walked back to the inn, hand in hand.

In the mud room, Cally hung her jacket on a peg beneath the Welcome Friends sign. Bryce hooked his on the one next to it. She liked the look of that, their sleeves touching. She didn't like liking it, but she liked it. A lot. "You've got mud on your cuff."

He shrugged.

She inwardly smiled. A couple weeks ago her stuffed-shirt counselor would have been miffed about the dirt. Now, it was no big deal. She hated loving that, too. Her list was growing darn lengthy.

He held open the door leading into the kitchen, and she walked through.

Mrs. Wiggins stood in the kitchen, her hand raised to slap Jeremy.

Cally saw red. ''Don't you dare hit him!'' She stormed over, snatched Jeremy up, planted him on her hip, then pivoted so she stood between him and Mrs. Wiggins. He looked scared to death. ''You okay?''

He nodded, on the brink of tears.

Cally cradled his head to her shoulder, rubbed his tiny back, and glared at the battleaxe. ''You will never raise a hand to him, to any of the kids again. Not ever.''

Wiggins went as white as the curtains and her voice chilled to ice. ''Miss Tate, I'll thank you not to interfere. I understand your relationship with Mr. Richards, but my instructions on disciplining the children are explicit—''

''And you can stuff them right up your left nostril. Whatever Jeremy has done, he doesn't deserve to be slapped. I will not stand by and see you do it. Mrs. Richards, God rest her soul, is dead. I hate it for Suzie and Lyssie and Bryce and mostly for Jeremy, because you have so little tolerance for anything he does. And I even hate it for you. But hating it doesn't change the facts. The woman is dead, and your days of hiding behind her instructions to stay on Jeremy's back are over. I'm sick of it. God knows Jeremy's sick of it. And it's going to end right now. You're fired, Mrs. Wiggins.''

''I don't work for you. You can't fire me.'' She glared at Bryce. ''She can't fire me.''

Cally held her breath. So did Miss Hattie, who had come in during Cally's tirade, paused at the back door, and now stood with her eyes squeezed shut, mumbling something at the ceiling. Cally screwed up her courage and then looked at Bryce. He seemed stunned and damned angry. Whether at her or at Wiggins, Cally didn't know. And right now, she didn't give a flying fig. He'd best remember his promise to not challenge her authority with the kids. Of course, if he didn't back her in this, he wouldn't be breaking his promise because it was the battleaxe, not the kids, she was challenging. But if he didn't back her, then God help him. If he tolerated that woman slapping Jeremy, Cally'd never marry him. Never in a million years. And she'd make his life a living hell.

"Well?" Mrs. Wiggins urged Bryce, looking too damn confident for Cally's comfort.

Bryce looked at Jeremy, clinging to Cally's shoulder for dear life. He wasn't crying, though. Not a single tear. At Cally, shooting visual daggers his way, warning him he'd better not cross her on this. At Suzie, who stepped to Cally's side, her jaw tense and her eyes saucer-wide. Cally slipped an arm around her, drew her closer. At Miss Hattie, who looked alert and attentive, not bothering to pretend ignorance this time, but closing her expression to unreadable, keeping her thoughts to herself. And, finally, he looked at Mrs. Wiggins. Her strained expression had her tight skin stretched over her bones. Frosted to the gills. He didn't trust himself to speak.

"Mr. Richards!" Mrs. Wiggins stomped her foot. "I insist you set her straight on this."

"I fully support Cally's decision, Mrs. Wiggins. You're fired." He'd have fired the woman himself, but Cally had beaten him to it. Though it raised a hell of a problem, he felt good about that.

The woman's jaw dropped open. "You can't be serious!"

"I most certainly am serious." He gentled his tone for the kids. They still looked terrified. "If you think past your indignation, you'll realize this is what you've wanted for a long time. You only stayed for Meriam. In fact, I'll bet you've already prepared your Thanksgiving resignation, haven't you?"

Looking guiltier than sin, the woman lowered her gaze.

"You always deliver it immediately following breakfast, so everyone is upset at what should be a festive dinner. You're not a mean woman, Mrs. Wiggins. So why do you think you do that?"

"Because I'm tired of raising children!"

"I know. And I thank you for the sacrifices you've made

for mine. But Cally's right. I can't have you slapping Jeremy. It's time for you to go on with your life."

"Very well."

Miss Hattie, who was the only person in the room who appeared calm and sedate, unclipped her earring. "I'll book your flight, Mrs. Wiggins. Jimmy will take you to the airport."

"Thank you, Hattie." Mrs. Wiggins announced her intention to return to the Carriage House to pack her bags, then left the kitchen, looking more relieved than upset.

Cally smoldered. "I owe you one, Counselor."

"No you don't." He owed her. And he didn't regret his decision—the battleaxe'd had to go—but if Cally refused his proposal now, he'd be in a helluva fix.

Jeremy smothered Cally in a bear hug. Over his shoulder, Cally sent Bryce a look of gratitude, and picked up on his worry. The reason for it hit her right between the eyes.

She'd fired the only constant in the M & M's lives.

"Oh, God, what have I done?"

Chapter 13

Mrs. Wiggins had departed, and Bryce couldn't help but notice that none of the kids had seemed the least bit sad. That truth had guilt tumbling through his stomach, even though Cally pointedly had asked Jeremy if Mrs. Wiggins had hit him a lot, and he'd held up his fingers and specifically said, "Only three times."

Three times. And Bryce hadn't known about any of them. More guilt heaped onto the already sizable hill stuffed into his chest. What kind of father doesn't know things that important about his own son?

A rotten one. *Rotten. Rotten. Rotten.*

Alone in the kitchen, he poured himself a cup of coffee, denied himself a bowl of peach cobbler, recalled vividly the scent of Cally's peach shampoo, then sat down at the table to stew a while. Hell, maybe he'd just sulk, too. Really wallow in it. Sooner or later, he hoped to God, he'd run out of ways to stop failing his kids.

The grandfather clock in the gallery ticked softly, reminding him of what Miss Hattie had said about Bess Mystic calling it the heartbeat of the house. The rhythmic sound did help to soothe his frayed nerves. Jeremy had forgiven Bryce, but it'd take longer for him to forgive himself.

Cally came in, dressed in winter-white slacks and a forest-green baggy top that kissed the tops of her thighs. The same color combination she'd worn the day he'd first seen her. It suited her—the white for her purity of spirit, the deep green for her hidden depths—but the woman would be gorgeous in a flour sack.

"Jeremy and Lyssie are down for their nap." She walked to the fridge, filled a glass with ice, then poured tea in it from the stoneware pitcher Miss Hattie kept on the countertop near the fruit bowl. "Mmm, I'd offer a penny for your thoughts, Counselor, but I don't think they're worth it."

He looked up from his steaming mug.

Before saying anything more, she sat down opposite him. "I can tell by your grim expression you're beating yourself up over this situation with Jeremy."

"He's my son." Anger again roiled in Bryce's stomach. "I'm not supposed to be upset?"

"Upset, yes. But not feeling as you do. You might as well have a sign on your forehead, darling. One that says Rotten Dad. And that you don't deserve."

Suzie came in, took one look at his face, then turned to Cally. "Can I go with Frankie to Miss Millie's? She's gonna show us some pictures of my island from fifty years ago."

Cally glanced at Bryce. He shot her a why-not look.

"Sure, but be back"—she glanced at the clock—"no later than five, okay? And nowhere else, not without first calling home."

"Okay." Suzie dropped a kiss to Cally's cheek, then turned to him. "Daddy, I didn't know about Mrs. Wiggins slapping Jeremy, either. I felt really bad about it until I talked to Tony. He said that we can't know everything, and what's important is that, when we find out, we do something. I think he's right. And I don't think you ought to be mad at yourself. Jeremy's not. He's not mad at me, either. So it's okay now. We fixed it, and she won't hit him anymore."

Tears stinging the backs of his eyes, Bryce hugged Suzie hard. "Thanks, sweetheart. And thank Tony, too. Okay?"

She nodded, then skipped out the back door.

"She's a helluva kid, Counselor. So wise and so beautiful." Cally watched Suzie through the window, running toward Frankie's full-speed down the stone walkway. "Sometimes I look at her and she's so beautiful I could just cry."

Bryce's throat went tight and his heart melted one more

time at the simple complexities that comprised Cally Tate. And in his mind, he smelled the narcissus. It smelled exactly like her perfume. Soft, subtle, sexy. He had to be the luckiest man in the world. "Thanks, Cally."

She looked back at him. "What for?"

"Being you. And for bringing this to light about Jeremy and Mrs. Wiggins."

She came around the table, circled his head with her arms, then drew him to her chest. "Oh, Bryce." Bending down, she pressed a comforting kiss to his crown. "It really is okay."

He burrowed his face between her breasts and hugged her tightly, needing her strength, wanting her comfort.

She held him for a long few minutes then, as if sensing he'd gotten an emotional grip on this, she kissed him again. Longer. Deeper. Giving the father in him a rest, and awakening the man.

"Mmm, nice." He cupped her bottom and pulled her closer. Standing between his thighs, she bumped her knees against the seat of his chair. "I'm hoping your firing the battleaxe was a declaration that you've accepted my proposal." She'd been magnificent. Defending the M & M's like a lioness protecting her cubs. That they were his cubs made him appreciate her protection even more.

She tilted her head in that adorable way. "Well, Counselor, I suppose that since I've fired the only *constant* from the kids' lives, I'll have to accept."

"Really?" A lie, of course. But one she needed. One that was easier to admit than confessing they'd both blown their agreement to hell and back before they'd officially started it. He certainly wasn't going to complain. She might change her mind and, truthfully—he took a long look at his own motives—he too still needed the lie.

"What else can I do?" She shrugged in that teasing, Miss Tate manner, but her eyes were glossy and overly bright.

"You can do whatever you choose." He didn't want her feeling trapped into marrying him.

"Then I choose to be the constant in our kids' lives."

Our kids. Well, that said it all. Nearly giddy, he bit a smile from his lips. ''Can we seal this yes in—er, that was a yes, wasn't it, Miss Tate?''

''It was, Counselor.''

Immensely satisfied, he hiked a brow. ''Can we seal it in our contract with a kiss?''

''Absolutely. I know you lawyers like everything tied up all legal like.'' She raked her fingertips through his beard.

They were cold from touching her glass, yet warmed him far beneath the skin she touched. ''Exactly, Miss Tate. And to be binding, consideration must be exchanged.''

''In this case, a kiss.''

''Actually, two kisses.''

Her eyes sparkled. ''Hmm, interesting.''

''I'm feeling magnanimous, and I don't want a reputation as a miser in these negotiations.''

She looped him with her arms, kissed his eyelid, his brow, then purred against his throat. ''Generosity becomes you, darling.''

He circled her waist, let his hands roam her back, shoulder to thigh. ''Yeah, I like the way it feels.''

''I'll remember that, too.''

He felt certain she would. ''Before you kiss me and I can't think straight—''

She laughed, low and husky. ''I'm definitely going to remember that.''

He nipped at her neck. ''Don't even think about blackmail, Miss Tate.''

''Counselor, would I do that?''

Damn right, she would. ''Let me finish so I can have my kisses.''

''By all means. You go right ahead.'' She dipped her nose to his skin, teased and taunted.

How the hell was he supposed to think straight with her doing that? ''Um, I think we should, um, wait to tell the M and M's the day before the wedding.''

''Excellent, Counselor. About twenty-four hours of 'Is it time yet?' is a reasonable max.'' She nibbled her way down to the soft hollow of his throat, then over to his earlobe.

Bryce nearly came up out of the chair. He groaned and tightened his hold on her. ''When Miss Hattie gets back with the kids, we'll go talk to Pastor Brown. I like the idea of a Thanksgiving wedding. For Tony. Is that okay?''

She scraped his neck with her teeth. ''It won't give our families time to get here.''

God help him, he was going to melt. Or to embarrass himself. ''I know, but they were at the first ones. This one I want special. Just for us without any reminders of the past. I guess that sounds selfish, but—''

''It sounds perfect to me.'' She let out the sexiest growl he'd ever in his life heard and ran her hand down his chest. ''Just us and the kids. Private.''

She understood. He'd known that she would. ''Hmm, Cally?''

''Mmm?''

''I'm thinking you'd best give me three kisses.''

''Three?'' She reared and looked down at him, her eyes smoky. ''That's extortion, Counselor. Reeks of greed.''

He gave her a negative nod. ''Only two are for me.'' They had the house to themselves, and it appeared his Miss Tate wanted more than a kiss to seal their contract. He'd oblige her of course and, with luck, they'd make it upstairs before he obliged her.

''Then why three?''

His eyes sparkled. ''We're lacking an official notary.''

''Ah, I see.'' She lowered her gaze to the hollow at his throat, setting his pulse to leaping. ''Will a mere kiss suffice in lieu of a notary? Seems to me that's a very import—''

''No, Miss Tate. It will not.'' He caught her behind the knees, then stood up, bringing her with him.

She locked her knees around his waist, her arms around his neck. ''Then we'd best do whatever's needed to avoid loopholes, Counselor. Right away.''

''My thoughts exactly.''

Tony smiled down on Cally and Bryce, watched them leave the kitchen in a dead run for the stairs, laughing like children. It did his heart good. They walked the cliffs and kissed under the special oak, and sat on the same kitchen chair and necked, drunk on love—just like Tony and Hattie used to do. Now, they were planning a Thanksgiving wedding.

Of course these two would choke before admitting they were drunk on love, but they both recognized love for what it was. Sooner or later, they'd admit it. If they had Tony's experience—which he'd wish on no man or woman, not even Batty Beaulah or the battleaxe—they'd trip over their tongues to give each other the words. But they didn't. And he couldn't tell them. To fully understand, that experience had to be lived firsthand.

So they're planning a Thanksgiving wedding.

Sunshine. Where had she been hiding? *Yes, they are.*

And what about Suzie?

He withheld a frown by the skin of his teeth. *She's still dreaming.*

I know that. Just as I know you're still interceding so she won't be alone in those dreams. They're not very pleased with you upstairs about that, Tony.

I gave her my word. That means something to me.

Yes, it does. How is Hattie handling the knowing?

That we'll be separated after all?

Yes.

About like you'd expect. She's devastated. Putting up a front for the kids and Bryce and Cally, but she's crying herself to sleep every night, and she's having some wicked dreams.

I'm sorry to hear that. She's a lovely woman.

The best.

I have to say I admire you, Tony. You've handled your situation well. You and Hattie have helped a lot of people who would have been lost without you.

That's our purpose, isn't it? Tony chided himself for letting his less than charming attitude leak out. Sunshine was invading his turf. He still didn't like it, but some sixth sense so deep he didn't want to acknowledge it—because it brought that *powerless* memory to mind—warned him she had to be here. Focusing on that powerless feeling usurped his confidence, so he shunned those thoughts and buried his attitude, determined to be cordial. *It's been fulfilling. I'd be lying if I said it hadn't. But sometimes I wish I had just one more day with Hattie. Just one more night.*

A chance to say all the things you've regretted not saying, mmm?

Her understanding didn't surprise him. And he felt it wise not to think about why it didn't. *Yeah, exactly.*

I'm not supposed to tell you this, but swamping yourself with guilt is sidetracking you something awful. So I'm going to do something I've never done before. I'm going to break protocol—and pray I don't regret it.

Surprise shimmied through Tony's chest. The woman sounded wary. Actually, scared stiff. So why would she be willing to do this for him? He'd been as grouchy as a bear with a thorn in its foot. *What?*

I'm going to tell you the truth, Tony. Even if you'd died on that battlefield and not vowed to never be apart from Hattie, even if you'd gone on and never returned to Seascape Inn, even if she'd never had any idea that you were near, Hattie Stillman never would have married another man. She'd never have given her heart to anyone else.

She might have.

She couldn't, Tony. Think about it. It's so simple really—if you look at it with your heart and not your head. Hattie could never give her heart to anyone else because it was no longer hers to give. She'd already given it to you.

He wanted to believe it. Needed to believe it. And the ferocity with which he needed to believe it shamed him. What about Hattie? What she wanted? Needed? *Maybe with time—*

No, Tony. Never. Not ever. For Hattie there never has been, nor ever could be, anyone but you. Don't you see? You're lifemates.

Lifemates. Cally had told Bryce she wanted him as a lifemate. An antenna rose, sparked a whole new line of thinking. One that shook Tony to the core. *From the start, had Bryce and Cally's relationship been inevitable?*

It's best I don't answer that.

There had to be something valid in the thought. But what? And why didn't he understand the mission? He'd never before been kept in the dark. *Why?*

I have my reasons.

Sunshine had taken a big risk to put his mind at ease. Truth to tell, guilt about what he'd done to Hattie in staying with her had kept him off balance and not focusing fully on the job at hand. He was second-guessing himself, his decisions, fearing her reaction to their being separated. *Thank you for telling me, Sunshine. I suppose I should regret Hattie's devotion and, inside, a part of me does. But there's another, bigger part of me that feels relieved that I haven't ruined her life. I worried making that vow had robbed her of her dreams.*

She's been happy. Very content and happier than most, I'd say.

I'm grateful, Sunshine. So inadequate to express all he was feeling, but innately he knew she understood. That understanding roused questions about her she wouldn't answer. But curiosity got the better of him, so he had to ask. *I'd be even more grateful if I knew who the heck you are, and why you're involved in this.*

I'm just an emissary, Tony. Not important enough to warrant speculation. But I expect you are grateful, considering Thanksgiving is only two days away. For what it's worth, I'm glad you won't have another sad one, Tony. Next to Christmas, when you and Hattie were to wed, that's always been your most challenging day. And yet—

What?

Yet you've managed to perform some wonderful work then. Odd, that. Don't you think?

Not really. We do what we have to do. Suddenly feeling as if he'd been horse-kicked in the gut, he stilled. *Hattie says we teach by experience. That pain brings personal growth. I guess because we're hurting we then pull up that extra something—the magic.*

Astute woman.

The magic. Yes, of course. Lifemates. *Astute and very wise.*

You've gained so much for others and for yourselves. So why is it, I wonder, that you do everything except to believe in miracles for yourselves?

That's a luxury we can't afford.

No, I expect you can't—not right now, anyway.

After the first fifty years, you learn to waive your personal expectations.

That's a lot of years' worth of disappointments. Reminds me of what you told Suzie about the white lies.

He didn't recall. He and Suzie had talked so much about so many things, there was no way he could recall everything.

You told her that when we want something badly, we often tell ourselves we don't want it at all so that if we don't get it, we won't be hurt.

Yes, I did. And I guess it's true. But Hattie and I have endured. What we're doing here is important.

Indeed it is. And you've prospered, too, Tony.

Something in her tone alerted him. Subtle, but a message. And he wasn't getting it. *You sound like a woman with something else on your mind. Go ahead and say it, Sunshine. I'm first to admit that, these days, my receptors are a little clogged.*

I don't want to say it.

But . . . ?

But I've no choice.

The regret in her voice set his hands to trembling. His chest went tight. *A message from on high.*

I'm afraid so.

His heart nearly stopped. *I'm being reassigned.*

Not yet. You're being ordered not to intercede in Suzie's dreams anymore—officially.

Oh, God.

And briefed that the premonition regarding her will come to pass in two days. .

Thanksgiving night?

Yes, I'm sorry, but I'm afraid so. That wasn't to be included in the official message, Tony, but I felt you needed to know . . . to prepare yourself.

Feelings stormed through Tony. Feelings of being hopeless and lost, incredible waves of pain and sadness. Feelings of having failed Suzie as he'd failed her mother. And more sadness. Deep, crushing sadness that tripped over into the abyss of despair, into anger. *I've tried everything I know to try to help her. Everything! I don't know what else to do.* His eyes stung. If he were in her dream, he knew tears would wet his face. In his spirit state, the tears still fell. They were just all inside.

You've got to try harder, Tony. You've got to do something. If that child drowns it's going to kill Bryce and Cally.

I can't let this happen. I just . . . can't.

How are you going to stop it?

I—I don't know. God help me, I don't know.

Chapter 14

Sea Haven Baptist Church looked a lot different without the festival going on in its parking lot. The steeple stretched up into the dark sky, and thin rays of sunlight broke through the heavy clouds, filling the air with the scent of rain, and reflected on the stained-glass window, showering blue, yellow, green, and pink streaks onto the pristine white clapboard building. The light *had* to be a sign that Cally was doing the right thing in marrying Bryce. It had to be.

She linked their arms and smiled at him. "Miss Hattie says Pastor Brown is proud of the stained-glass window. I can see why. It's beautiful, isn't it?"

Looking preoccupied, Bryce clasped her hand. "Beautiful."

They walked up the steps that led to a wide double door.

Bryce reached for it, then hesitated. "Cally, I don't think we should mention to anyone else our attitudes on love and caring and our relationship—for the kids."

His brows had knitted and his jaw looked tense enough to make steel look soft. He was lying to himself, and hating it.

"And for our pride?" she suggested.

"That, too." He rubbed his thumb over her knuckles. "I want the kids to feel secure. We know the truth about love, and I'd like to spare them the illusions, but what if it could be different for them? What if they could have the illusion, but because we told them it was an illusion, they lost their chance? I don't want to do that to them. I don't think we should—if it sits okay with you."

"I see no reason to talk about our private lives to anyone else, including the kids, but I won't lie to a pastor, Bryce." He looked crestfallen, so she quickly went on. "Yet I can't see any reason why he'd feel the need to ask our opinions, considering why we're here."

"What about when he asks us to make the vows?"

What then, indeed? "That presents a little dilemma."

He eased his hand into his slacks pocket. What the man did for clothes should be illegal, but in a dark gray suit that did wonderful things to his eyes, he should come with a warning label. "Maybe we could compromise?"

"I won't lie in a church, Bryce. That'd be like lying to God, and I just can't do it."

"Of course not." He gazed off toward the ocean, then back at her. "Can we make the vows during the ceremony and then after the service, in private, revise them?"

She thought about that for a moment. Smoothed the skirt of her fawn silk suit with a hand that was far from steady. So long as they revised the vows, that should be okay. Of course, loving the man, she'd be lying during those revisions. If Bryce knew that, he'd just die. Actually, he wouldn't. But he wouldn't marry her, either. Their chance would be gone. But maybe she could avoid the revising, and thus the lying. God, why did this have to be so complicated? If only she hadn't agreed to a marriage of convenience then goofed up by falling in love with the man, things would be fine. But she had, and that left her in a dilemma. One that, if she let herself think about it, would give her nightmares. Could she live with him, be intimate and loving with him, and him not guess the truth?

"Cally?"

She buried her doubts, then met his gaze. "We'll work it out privately."

"Good." Looking as relieved as she felt pensive, he opened the right-hand door.

Inside the church, just to the right, Cally saw a small bridal chamber with frilly curtains and a cheval mirror. Her stomach filled with flutters. She avoided the mirror as if it carried plague, and again prayed she was doing the right thing in marrying him. Maybe the counseling with the pastor would put her mind at ease on the matter. Her heart knew, but her head was having a hard time. It was the dishonesty. But the truth would stop this chance dead in its tracks.

They walked deeper into the church; over wooden floors and past empty pews that time and attendance at services had worn smooth. The light streaming through the stained-glass window appeared much stronger inside than she would have believed possible, considering the thunderheads building up outside, and bathed the altar and a huge, rugged cross suspended above it in a rainbow of soft, soothing color.

"Collin carved that cross," Bryce told Cally, his voice low, reverent.

"I know." Miss Hattie had mentioned it when showing Cally Collin's wood carvings in the glass case at the inn. "He helped carve the bar at the Blue Moon Cafe, too."

"He did?"

"Lucy Baker told me. She said it's her husband Fred's pride and joy." Cally nodded, then let her gaze drift around the church. A sense of well-being, of rightness, suffused her. "It feels good in here."

"It does."

The door opened then closed behind them, and a flush-faced Pastor Brown hurried down the aisle, over to them. "Sorry I'm late." He paused to grab a quick breath and offered them a winning smile. "Emergency Planning and Zoning Commission meeting."

"This close to Thanksgiving?"

He nodded. "I'm afraid so. When situations arise, the council pays little attention to calendars or schedules."

It fit. The villagers were Mainers, through and through. Devoted. Disciplined. Dedicated and caring. Regardless of calendars or clocks. Cally found all that touching. But, gauging from his tense expression, the meeting couldn't have gone smoothly. She smiled her sympathy, guessing him near forty. Of medium height, with a well-trimmed beard that, while handsome, didn't affect her at all like Bryce's did. Yet Pastor Brown was handsome. According to Lucy, nearly every marriageable-age woman in the village was after him, though he was a bit progressive-minded to truly suit the majority of them, and a bit too close-minded, constantly trying to get Jimmy to take the "girlie" calendar off the wall of his garage, and to get Horace Johnson—the mayor, no less—to stop icing down a barrel full of beer outside the door at The Store on weekends, which mortified his snooty wife, Lydia. Both men staunchly resisted. The calendar girls, Jimmy said, were clothed in swimsuits and Adam and Eve wore fig leaves, and Horace insisted Jesus drank wine and regular folks too needed to quench their thirst.

Bryce shook the pastor's hand. "I'm sorry you felt rushed. We only just arrived."

Cally extended her own hand. The pastor had a nice firm grip. A woman could tell a lot about a man from his handshake. No limp, wimpy hold here. Firm, but gentle. Yes, with his looks and a handshake like that, she imagined a lot of female hearts had been lost to him.

"Word is all over the village that you want to have the ceremony on Thanksgiving."

"Is there a problem with that?"

"No, Cally. It's fine. I'm usually at Seascape for Thanksgiving dinner, anyway." He grinned. "I love Miss Hattie's pumpkin pie best, but don't tell the others. You'll start a war that'll net me gaining twenty pounds."

Cally crossed her heart with her fingertip. "What time do you suggest?"

"Two in the afternoon?"

Cally looked at Bryce. He hiked a shoulder. "Sounds great to me."

"To me, too."

"Two it is, then." Pastor Brown smiled. "Miss Hattie serves dinner around six, so this should work out perfectly."

Sensing the meeting at an end, Cally again extended her hand. "Thank you."

Bryce seemed uneasy, and surprised. "Hmm, isn't there any type of counseling or anything we have to go through?"

The pastor's eyes twinkled and his lips curved into a semismile. "Do you need it?"

"No." Bryce placed a protective hand at Cally's back.

"I doubted you did, so I thought we'd skip it. In the fourteen years I've been pastor here, I've never heard of one

Seascape couple divorcing.'' He shrugged. ''Hard to beat a hundred-percent success rate.''

''Good point.'' Bryce smiled. ''Can we buy you a cup of coffee at the Blue Moon?''

''I wish I could join you, but the commission meeting is just in recess. I've got to get back to City Hall.'' He rubbed at his chin in the same forefinger-and-thumb way Bryce often did, rustling his whiskers. ''I hope it isn't as spirited as it was this morning. Truth to tell, I'm a wee bit weary.''

''Busy season?''

''No, I just got back from vacation. Skiing.'' He let out a grunt of a laugh. ''Now I need a vacation to recover from my vacation.''

Bryce chuckled. ''I know that feeling.''

''See you on Thanksgiving.''

''We can't wait,'' Cally said, then walked outside with Bryce.

Black clouds sheathed the sky, and the first drops of rain fell, pattering against the walkway. She dipped her chin. ''Very nice man.''

''I'm glad he dispensed with the lectures,'' Bryce said. ''I was scared stiff we'd be put to the test on lying.''

Her hand sliding on the handrail, Cally went down the steps, guilt swimming through her stomach, and deliberately avoiding his gaze. ''We'll work around it.''

In silence, they walked over to the Blue Moon. By the time they reached the huge, rusty anchor outside it, her nerves had settled and her stomach had stopped heaving. She hadn't been forced to expose the truth. Grateful for the reprieve, she warned herself yet again that she could never slip. Never, not even in the heat of passion, could she tell him she loved him. He'd run as far and as fast as he could away from her.

If she had any sense, she'd run herself. Evidently she totally lacked it, because what he offered appealed to her like being a princess appeals to a little girl. Their agreement, Bryce himself, was Cally's brass ring. It held all she wanted—her hopes, her dreams, her wishes—everything except her being unconditionally loved. Still, it was more than she dared to hope to find, and there was no way she was turning her back on it. Or on Bryce Richards.

"Cally, do you have a pen in your purse?"

She reached down to the floor and grabbed her handbag. It was late afternoon, but the Blue Moon Cafe buzzed. Sheriff Cobb had come and gone, so had Beaulah Favish, Miss Hattie's eccentric next-door neighbor, and Jimmy had come in for a quick cup of coffee. He was such a nice kid. Teaching Suzie how to use a shovel without cutting her foot, mowing Miss Hattie's sizable lawn and keeping everything at the inn looking nice. Miss Hattie loved that boy as if he were her own. It was easy to understand why. He had a good heart—and, it appeared, a healthy crush on Nolene, Lucy's teenage daughter.

Cally passed the pen to Bryce, then dropped her purse back onto the floor. "What are you writing?"

"A note to the villagers to come to the wedding." He scrawled, and the pen made a scratching sound.

"On a paper napkin?"

"Why not?" He gave her that mischievous grin Jeremy had perfected. Like father, like son.

"No reason, I guess." Lydia Johnson would have a snit fit at the tackiness of a paper-napkin wedding invitation, but no one much liked Lydia, anyway.

He finished writing, then got up.

"Where are you going?"

"To put this on the bulletin board." He pointed to the wall behind the bar.

Right below a Budweiser beer clock hung a cork bulletin board, covered with colorful pushpins and notes of various sizes and types. Several appeared to be shopping lists.

The old jukebox on the far wall cranked out an Alan Jackson tune that vibrated the walls. Cally hummed along and watched Bryce make his way through the maze of tables with the aid of Collin's cane, shamelessly admiring his backside.

"Fills out a decent pair of slacks, that man."

Recognizing Lucy's voice, and realizing she had been caught bun-gazing, Cally felt her face become hot. She fingered the napkin still spread across her knees.

"Maybe you'd best switch to iced tea, sugar." Lucy cracked her gum. "Dang me if you don't look about to flame."

"Quit teasing me. I've seen how you look at Fred. Positively carnal."

"Yeah, but don't tell him." Lucy grinned. "He might think the honeymoon's over and quit working at it."

"You've been married nearly twenty years. How long do you think he's going to believe a honeymoon lasts?"

"Another twenty." Lucy winked, then pulled out the end of the bar cloth tucked into her back pocket. "If I'm darn lucky."

Cally laughed.

"I ain't supposed to tell you this, but a couple of the villagers are planning some special touches for after the wedding. I figured you'd want to know you ain't gonna get your man to yourself for a while, if you know what I mean."

The heat crept down her neck. "Anything I need to be concerned about?"

"Naw, nothing serious. Just a little friendly torment."

Bryce turned from the bulletin board, thunder in his expression. Now what in the world had him so angry?

He walked back over to her. "Are you ready to go?"

"Sure." Whatever it was, it was bad. She'd never seen him grind his teeth before and, if he held his jaw any tighter, he was apt to crack the bone. "Is something wrong?"

"We'll talk about it on the way back to the inn."

"Okay." She whispered to Lucy. "Maybe you'd better get the villagers to tone down their plans. I have the feeling my beloved's a little . . . upset."

"Hostile, would be my guess. But I'll do it."

"Thanks. See you later."

"Sure thing, sweetie."

Bryce and Cally walked outside and, near the big, rusty anchor, Bryce stopped cold. "Do you know they're taking bets on us getting married?"

"Doesn't everyone know it?"

"I didn't." He went down the steps.

"Obviously." Cally joined him on the sandy parking lot. The sounds of the ocean just over the cliffs grew louder.

Amazing, she feared boats, feared water, but loved the sounds of the roaring surf. Maybe if she'd learned to swim . . .

"Why didn't you tell me?" He shoved his hand into his slacks pocket. "I felt like a fool posting that notice on the board and seeing wagers listed with our names, times, and dates. Do you know that snobby Lydia Johnson bet we wouldn't marry at all?"

"Imagine that." Cally bit back a smile. "Is it any wonder no one likes her very much?"

"Not to me."

"They say she has a nose for romance."

"What's romance got to do with it?"

"In our case, not a lot. But typically . . ."

The fire went out of him. "I'm sorry, honey. That sounded crass. I didn't mean it like it came out."

"No problem." She hoped she sounded as if she meant it, and looped their arms. "Life in a small town is like this. They're not wagering to be mean, they're wagering because it's entertaining and fun."

"I know. I guess I'd be in there right along with them, if we weren't the couple they were gambling on."

She bumped her hip against his. "So who won?"

"Excuse me?"

"Who picked Thanksgiving afternoon at two?"

"Suzie," Bryce grumbled.

"Our Suzie?"

"None other. Probably schemed up between her and Frankie."

Cally laughed out loud. "Odds weigh heavily in that favor, Counselor."

"She bet a dollar."

"A whole week's allowance?" Cally didn't know whether to hug the kid or give her a lecture. She should be appalled, but she was thrilled. At least Suzie had no doubts about this wedding. Not with her wagering a whole week's allowance.

"Seriously, honey." He gave Cally a woeful look. "We've got to get a grip on these M and M's. They'll have us gray before we hit forty."

"We'll survive, darling." She gave his arm a soothing

stroke, forgetting for a moment that she wasn't supposed to love him, that he'd never love her.

A thin film of sand dusted the asphalt road. Normally they'd walk on the dirt path beside it, but with his knee, Bryce needed the stability of a firm surface under his feet.

They passed the driveway leading to Batty Beaulah's house, then walked on, up the sloped drive leading to Seascape Inn. Gravel crunched under their feet. As they rounded the side of the house, Cally slipped into melancholy. Bryce looked at her with love. Touched her with love. Talked to her with love in his voice. And she was doing something very dangerous for them. She was forgetting all too often that he didn't, and never would, love her.

She had to stop that. Before it landed them in serious trouble.

On the front porch, outside the door, he stopped and straightened a little sign that read: Seascape: Established 1918. "Cally, what's wrong?"

She forced a bright smile. "Nothing."

He looked down at her. "You promised me honesty."

"I know." She had. But there was no way she could tell him that what she was feeling was regret. Regret that they couldn't have the illusion. Couldn't have it all.

Regret that they couldn't love.

"Cally!" Jeremy bolted at her, nearly knocking her off her feet. "I broughted you a present."

"Ooh, goodie. I love presents." She squeezed her eyes shut and held out her hands.

Jeremy hesitated.

Cally cracked open one eye, peeked at him, and saw his frown. "Did you lose it?"

He shook his head. "You better look. I don't want you getting mad at me."

She looked and saw a lizard. "Oh, my."

"Do you like him?"

"He's beautiful." *God, please don't make me touch it. Please!* "The best lizard I ever saw."

"His name is Luke. I thought about calling him Fred, but Suzie said Mrs. Baker might get mad 'cuz her husband's name is Fred. I don't know why she'd get mad about that."

"I can't imagine. Luke is a fine lizard, don't you think?"
"Uh-huh."

Bryce smiled. "Jeremy, I think you'd better let Luke play in the garden."

"Good idea." Cally nodded to lend weight to her opinion. "Remember how unhappy the frog was at being cooped up in the kitchen. "I'd hate to think Luke wasn't happy. He's such a special lizard."

"Yeah." Jeremy looked at the wiggling critter. "Okay."

"Wonderful." She pecked a kiss to Jeremy's dirt-streaked face. "Thank you. He's the best lizard I've ever seen."

"Welcome." Jeremy beamed, then ran full-out to put Luke in the garden.

Cally sighed her relief. "I owe you one, Counselor."

"I'll collect." He pulled her into his arms. "That was really nice of you, honey. You didn't even shriek."

"I wanted to."

"But you didn't." Bryce kissed her cheekbone. "Would you have held it?"

"If I'd had to. But, boy, am I glad I didn't have to."

Bryce laughed, then kissed her, and she thought that for one of his kisses and ten seconds of them dreaming and living the illusion, she'd hold a dozen lizards.

"I don't wanna go to sleep, Daddy." Suzie wadded the corner of the little quilt in her hand. "I told you, Tony won't be here. He says he can't."

Bryce slid Cally a worried look, then glanced back to Suzie. Light from the bedside lamp pooled on her bed. "Honey, when we go home, Tony won't be able to be there, either. Are you going to stay up all night forever, then? Never sleep?"

Cally sat down beside Suzie. Her weight on the mattress had Suzie rolling to her side. "Did Tony say why he couldn't come?"

"No. Just that he couldn't." Anger filled her trembling voice. "He promised. I thought he was like Daddy, but he's not. He's like Meriam."

Cally stroked Suzie's wrinkled brow. "I don't understand."

"She broke her promises, too."

Something Tony said came back to Cally. "You know, sometimes it looks like people are breaking their promises but they're really not. Sometimes we just think they are. If Tony promised, then something very important must have happened for him to change his mind."

Bryce fingered his beard. "Tony takes care of a lot of people. Maybe he had to help someone tonight who's in more trouble than you are, Suzie. Maybe he knew Cally and I would be here with you, and maybe someone else was going to have to be alone."

Suzie was thinking it over; Cally could see that in her eyes. She looked at Bryce, silently mouthed, "Let's tell her."

He nodded.

"Suzie," Cally said, her voice thick. "Maybe whoever is keeping Tony away doesn't have a dad, and maybe they aren't getting a new mom."

Suzie gasped, blinked, then blinked again. "Am I getting a new mom?"

Cally nodded. "If you want one."

"You know I do. Really? You're not just telling me that? Grown-ups do that sometimes, but I don't like it. I even told Tony."

Bryce put a hand on Cally's shoulder. "We're not just telling you that. Cally's going to be your new mom."

"Why didn't you tell me?"

Bryce answered. "We were waiting until it was closer to time, sweetheart, so you wouldn't have so long to wait."

"But I was worried." She gave Cally a solemn little look. "Sometimes it takes you guys a long time to figure things out."

Cally chuckled, low and soft. "Yes, I guess it does."

"Daddy, Tony was right." Suzie's eyes sparkled. "He said."

"I remember."

"We both do." Cally tucked the covers under Suzie's chin, then bent to drop a kiss on her brow. "See? Tony kept his promise after all. And sometimes things happen we can't control, Suzie. If Tony can't be here, you can be sure he's got a good reason."

"Yeah." She sighed. "And you and Daddy are here."

"Right." Bryce kissed her on the cheek.

"I'll still be by myself in the dream, though."

The fear in her voice rocked Cally to the core. "I know, sweetheart. And if we could change that for you, we would. But we can't." Cally stood up. "What we can do is to be here for you when you wake up. And that we will do. That's a promise."

"Okay." Suzie snuggled down and curled up her knees.

Bryce lowered his hand to the small of Cally's back and urged her to the door. Just as Cally stepped into the hallway, Suzie called out. "Cally?"

She looked back. "Yes, sweetheart?"

"Do you keep your promises?"

Cally's heart felt squeezed. She'd made vows to Gregory and broken them. She'd promised not to love Bryce, and she loved him with all her heart. She couldn't look into Suzie's trusting face and lie to her; she just couldn't do it. "I try never to make a promise I can't keep, Suzie. Sometimes, I can't help it. But if I can help it, I keep my promises."

"Can we call you mom and everything?"

"I'd love that, Suzie."

"Are you sure? Meriam didn't like us calling her—"

Oh, God. "I'm sure. Everything, Suzie. I promise."

Bryce's voice came out husky. "We'll be right here. If you need us, you just call out and we'll come."

"Okay, Daddy. 'Nite."

Bryce softly closed the door, and his expression crumbled. He clenched his hands into fists.

"Bryce?"

He stared deeply into her eyes, his own flooded with pain. "She's going to dream, Cally. She's going to do it again, and I can't be there to help her."

Because there was nothing she could say, because she felt every bit as helpless and frustrated as he did, Cally opened her arms and just held him tight.

* * *

She's dreaming again, Tony.

Standing beside Suzie's bed, looking down on her, he heard Sunshine's familiar voice. Who was she? Meriam? Mary Beth? Mary Elizabeth? Surely not Mary Elizabeth. Even after fifty-one years, he'd surely recognize his own sister's voice, wouldn't he? *I know. Don't you think I know? I see the signs, just as you do.*

I'm not the enemy, Tony. I know how hard it is for you to stand here and watch and to do nothing. I'm here to help support you through it.

He squeezed his hands into fists, clenched his jaw. *She's going to drown.*

Only in her dream.

Tonight. But what about tomorrow night? What about then?

You know the answer to that as well as I do. We can't do anything more to stop it. We have our instructions.

Damn them.

You don't mean that. In your heart, past the pain of watching this tragic thing with Suzie, you know there's a reason. You know it as well as you know Hattie—

Tony stole inside Suzie's thoughts. She was dreaming. Already in the boat. *You said to try harder. There's got to be something I can do. What is it? Do you know? Help me. Whoever you are, please help me.*

I can't. Sunshine's voice cracked.

Frustration so strong it threatened to buckle his legs attacked Tony. He rebelled against it, locking his knees. *You could intercede.*

I'm forbidden, just as you are.

Fine. He couldn't do it. Even knowing the price he would pay, that his reassignment would be speeded up, that he'd never again see his beloved Hattie or hear her blister his ears, he couldn't do it. He couldn't stand by and watch Bryce's and Cally's lives destroyed by watching Suzie die. He couldn't do it. He *wouldn't* do it.

Don't do this, Tony!

I have to. If I don't, I'll never forgive myself. I won't respect myself and I sure as hell won't be the man Hattie loves and believes me to be. I have to help Suzie. I know the costs, Sunshine, but it's one of those things I just have to do.

He closed his eyes, whispered a message he prayed would linger inside Seascape's walls, would echo and remind Hattie Stillman how deeply she was loved. *In my mind, we'll always be walking on the cliffs together, Hattie, just like we used to. And I'll take the yellow carnation from my lapel and give it to you. It's a symbol for joy, Hattie. You've always been my joy. You always will be. Whether or not we're together ever again, I'll love forever, Hattie Stillman. Eternally. That, too, I vow.*

Sunshine wept.

And Tony stepped into the storm, into Suzie's dream.

He stumbled over the oak, as he did every night, but his foot stinging long since had ceased to surprise him. He knew now that this wasn't an ordinary dream, it was a premonition. Knew now that tomorrow night it would become a reality.

Glimpsing her nightgown, he dove in and retrieved Suzie.

Clinging to him, her lips blue, her teeth chattering, she sputtered. "You weren't supposed to come!"

"I know. But it worked out so that I could."

"Oh, Tony." She latched her arms around his neck, squeezed him tightly. "I love you."

"I love you, too, Suzie." Tears stung his eyes, and he wept.

When they arrived back on the shore, a woman stood there, waiting.

Stunned, Tony paused, the water lapping at his ankles.

"Who is she?" Suzie asked, tensing in his arms.

"I don't know."

"She's pretty."

She was. Her hair was dark brown, flowed in waves down to her shoulders, and she had an ethereal air around her that rippled out vibrations of serenity and calm.

"Hello, Tony. Suzie," the woman said.

It was the same voice he'd recognized hearing so often before. "Sunshine? What are you doing here?"

"I wanted to tell you, face-to-face. I have no choice but to report this, but in my heart, I understand."

His reassignment definitely would be speeded up. "Tonight will be the last time, won't it?"

Sadness filled her face, and shone in her expressive eyes. "I'm afraid so."

"Oh, God." He felt as if the life had been sucked out of him.

"Tony? What's she mean?" Suzie grabbed his chin, looked into his eyes. "What's she mean?"

"My being here with Miss Hattie, munchkin. I'm, um, being put on restriction."

"Un-uh. Grown-ups don't get busted."

"Suzie, honey, I've never lied to you."

"No, but—"

"You have to trust me on this. You don't understand—"

"Yes, I do." She frowned at him. "You said if only you have the courage to believe, then miracles can happen beside a dreamswept sea. You said, Tony. I believed you, and now I'm getting a new mom. And she wore a yellow carnation, too, just like you said."

"But that doesn't have anything to do with this."

"Yes, it does. I know it does. In here." Suzie thumped her chest. "You gotta believe, Tony. Just like me. The lady has a headband on. Did you see it?"

He hadn't noticed. Now, he looked. It was fashioned from flowers. Yellow carnations.

"I'll bet she believes."

How could he tell Suzie that miracles only happened for special guests? How could he tell her that miracles were impossible for him and Hattie? And how could he bear going on, knowing he'd seen his beloved for the last time?

Chapter 15

"I'm not sure why she didn't dream, Bryce." Cally took a healthy bite of peach cobbler, holding steady the white petal bowl. Piping hot, it tasted rich and sweet.

Bryce smoothed partially melted vanilla ice cream into his cobbler. "It doesn't make sense. Why would Tony tell her he can't be there, to warn us to be close by, and then Suzie not have the dream?" His spoon scraped the sides of the bowl. "No, she dreamed. She never stopped. Why would she stop now?"

"She wouldn't." Cally set her spoon into the bowl. The warm sweet fruit turned bitter on her tongue. She swallowed it down. "Something had to have happened for Tony to change his mind. He had to have been there anyway. Unless . . . Did she ever not wake up? Not cry out for you?"

"Until we came to Seascape, not once in two years. That's why I'm convinced something more is going on here. What it is, I don't know. But it's something."

The grandfather clock in the gallery chimed seven times. Another half hour and the kids would be up. "Deep down, I think you're right or maybe . . ." Should she tell him? Did she have any choice? This was about Suzie. Of course Cally had to tell him.

"Maybe what?"

"Maybe Tony didn't come to her. Maybe the woman did."

"What woman?" His spoon stilled midway to his mouth.

"The other morning, I went to the graveyard."

"Mary Elizabeth's grave." He nodded. "I figured that—when I saw you leave with the carnation."

"Right." Well, he didn't sound as if he thought her weird. That was a good start. "Anyway, while I was there, I heard this woman talking to me. Like Tony does."

Bryce stared at Cally for a long moment. A shudder rippled through him. It set his silk robe to shimmering.

"God, Cally. I'm not sure I'm ready to think there's another one like Tony around."

"I know. I felt the same way. But Tony is . . . well, Tony. He's wonderful. And I figure she must be, too, or he wouldn't allow her to be here." There. She'd said it. If he thought she'd lost her mind, so be it.

"Valid point." Bryce leaned back, rubbed at his beard. "With Miss Hattie here, especially."

He'd accepted it. Immensely relieved, Cally opened the door to her feelings. "I think the woman might have helped Suzie. It's the only thing that makes any sense."

"It's possible." Bryce paused, then shook his head as if to clear it. "Do you realize how bizarre this entire conversation would sound to anyone else?"

"Yeah, but they're not here, living it. We are. And that makes a lot of difference."

"It does. But even to me it sounds weird."

"It *is* weird." Cally shrugged. "But that doesn't mean it's not happening."

"No, it's happening." He lifted his spoon and took another bite. "Tony's been really worried about something. Miss Hattie, too."

Cally emptied her bowl and set it aside. It was still warm to her hands. "We know they became engaged on Thanksgiving. It's tomorrow and maybe they're upset—"

"No," Bryce cut in. "It's more. There's a sense of finality in Tony. Something this Thanksgiving is different. Worse." Bryce's eyes glittered with speculation. "What could be worse for Tony and upset Miss Hattie so badly?"

"Being separated." A shiver of dread raced up Cally's backbone. "That's the only thing I can imagine upsetting both of them so much."

"Exactly, Miss Tate." Bryce leaned forward over the table, then laced his hands atop it. "So what exactly could force them to separate after half a century together?"

"I have no idea, Counselor."

"Me, either. But when we find out the answer to that, I'll wager—" He stopped cold and his face went white. "Suzie."

"Suzie?" Cally frowned. "I'm not tracking."

"He promised Suzie he'd be there. Then says he can't be. There's more than one like him. Tony and the woman. So if he can't be there for Suzie, knowing how he is about his promises, maybe it's because he wasn't supposed to be there to start with, and—"

Cally gasped. "And someone insisted he not be there anymore."

"Probable."

"Logical. And maybe the penalty for being there anyway—"

"Miss Hattie."

"Oh, God." Tony separated from Hattie. Suzie could never learn of this. She'd die from the guilt. Suzie! Cally shook so hard she nearly rattled off her chair. "If that's the case, Bryce, then this nightmare of Suzie's isn't an ordinary dream."

"I know." Pain tensed his features gaunt.

"But she drowns in the dream!"

His haunted eyes glossed over. "Yes, Cally. Suzie drowns."

The phone rang.

"It's for you, dear." Miss Hattie waved toward the kitchen table where Bryce and Cally sat, seeming extremely distracted. Mixing up a batch of brownies for Suzie, she looked a blink away from tears.

Cally cast Bryce a worried look, then reached for the phone. "Hello."

"Caline?"

The man sounded oddly familiar, and surprised. How had he known her name? Everyone in the village called her Cally. "Yes?"

"What are you doing there?"

Oh, God. Gregory. She started shaking. "I'm, um, on vacation." Why had he called? What did he want from her now?

"I guess you can afford vacations with what I'm giving you in alimony."

All those old feelings, those old fears and doubts and intimidations, came out of hiding and churned in her stomach. *Ugly. Undesirable. Lousy wife.* Her hand holding the receiver grew damp. "What do you want?"

"I called to speak to my attorney, Bryce Richards. Strange that you'd both end up in the same inn. Or maybe it isn't strange at all. Maybe you've been screwing around with him for a long time. Is that the case, Caline?"

She drew in a sharp breath, grasped her chest hard to keep her heart from exploding.

"Cally?" Bryce covered the mouthpiece of the phone with one hand, then clasped her chin with the other and urged her to look up at him. "What's wrong? Is someone hurt?"

"It's Gregory," she mumbled. "He wants you."

Bryce curled an arm around her and took the phone. He should have known. She had that same stricken look she got every time he so much as mentioned a damn mirror. "Richards." He held Cally gently, making little swirls on her upper arm with his fingertips, wishing he could reach through the phone and pummel Gregory Tate.

"What are you doing there with my wife?"

"Hold on a moment." He looked to Miss Hattie, hoping she'd understand his meaning.

The angel nodded. "Cally, dear, will you come out to the greenhouse and help me with this bag of potting soil? I'm afraid I can't lift it onto the counter."

"Of course."

The women left, Miss Hattie's arm looped through Cally's, patting it comfortingly. Bryce lowered the mouthpiece back to where he could talk into it. "Your wife is Joleen. Is she here?"

"You know I meant Caline."

"Oh, Caline. The woman you abused, slept around on, and then divorced? But she's not your wife, Dr. Tate."

"Look, I called because I want my alimony payments lowered. Joleen and I just had a baby. A boy, Scott, and—''

After all the years he'd denied Cally a child, he's wanting to lower his alimony payments because of one? ''Forget it, Tate. You owe Cally that money, and a lot more. We both know it. Withdraw some money from your stash in the Cayman Islands. Oh, and find yourself another lawyer. I won't represent you anymore, and I'm damn sorry to have to admit I ever did.''

''You're sleeping with her.''

Bryce grimaced. ''I'm marrying her.''

''The hell you are.''

''The subject isn't open for debate, Doctor. I think that concludes this call.''

''Damn right it does. But I'll tell you this, you son of a bitch. You marry her, and you'll regret it. I'll call the bar association and file a complaint—conflict of interest. You insisted on the alimony because you would benefit from it. I'll add misconduct, and I won't stop until I see you disbarred.''

Bryce hung up the phone. ''Damn it! On top of everything else, this I do not need.''

And the worst of it still lay ahead of him. How in the name of God was he going to tell Cally that Gregory had become a father? That he'd given Joleen the child Cally had desired for so long? And how could Bryce do it, and make sure that her feelings didn't revert back to the *lousy wife, the undesirable woman*?

God help him, he didn't have a clue.

Miss Hattie and Miss Millie had taken the kids down to a pumpkin farm to handpick the ones that would become their Thanksgiving pies. All morning villagers had been dropping by the inn with special food-gifts for the wedding feast. There seemed to be a lunchtime lull, and for that, Bryce felt grateful. He had to tell Cally about the baby, and he'd just as soon tell her while everyone else was away and she had a little privacy in which to react.

She was at the kitchen counter, cutting up onions for the bread dressing. The knife clacked rhythmically against the wooden chopping block and, judging by her rapid blinks, her eyes were smarting. Her jeans were streaked dark across her thigh, as if she'd swiped them with wet hands.

He sat at the table and folded his hands over his chest, watching her, debating the wisdom of delivering news such as this to a woman with a knife in her hand.

"The temperature has fallen like a stone. Hatch says there might even be snow." She sniffed, grabbed another onion from the red net bag, then washed it beneath the faucet at the sink. "Did the kids all have their coats?"

"Yes, they did." He should tell her now. The knife was on the cutting block. "Did you get your dress hemmed for tomorrow?"

She smiled back at him. "Miss Hattie did it this morning. It's gorgeous."

"Good." Do it now, Counselor, before she gets back to—damn. Too late.

She arced the knife. "I've been thinking."

"Yes?"

"About Gregory's call." She looked at Bryce from under her lashes.

"I know it upset you." Mildly put.

"It did." She grunted and sliced through the onion hard enough to send half flying across the counter. "Oops."

Good thing he'd waited.

She grabbed the onion, put it back on the board, then returned to her chopping. "You know what really ticks me off?" She glanced at him, her eyes red-rimmed from onion-sting. "I fell right back into that old trap of being intimidated."

She had. Bryce had seen it. She'd tensed up like a client waiting for the jury foreman to read its verdict. "They had a baby, Cally."

She dropped the knife. Stared at him. "What did you say?"

Good God, how could he have just blurted it out like that?

"Bryce?" She walked over to him, stopped beside his chair. "What did you say?"

He craned back his neck to look up at her, swearing he'd give everything he owned not to have to repeat the god-awful words that would break her heart.

"Damn it, Bryce, what did you say?"

"I said, Gregory and Joleen had a baby." He spoke slowly. "A son, Cally. They named him Scott."

"He—he has a son? A son? And he gave the child what was to be my son's name?" She swayed on her feet.

Bryce grabbed her arms, guided her to a chair.

She plopped onto it, her face pasty white, her jaw hanging loose. "I can't believe this. How could he have a son? He can't have a son, Bryce."

"He does, sweetheart." Bryce swallowed a knot of emotion from his throat. This hurt her deeply, too deeply for tears.

"He can't, I'm telling you." She frowned. "Remember? He's sterile."

A shiver rippled up Bryce's back. The hairs on his neck stood on end. Cally had told him that. She'd waited for her dream of a home and a family only to find that, with Gregory, she'd never have kids because he was sterile.

And she'd continued to love him.

And he'd refused to discuss adoption.

"I remember." What the hell was Tate pulling now? "But I'm telling you, honey, the man just told me he and Joleen have had a son."

Cally shoved back her chair, walked straight to the phone, then dialed a long-distance number.

"Who are you calling?"

"Marianne. A friend of mine at Dr. Alexander's office. She'll, by God, know what's going on here."

"Cally, she can't give you that information. It's a breach of the Privacy Act."

Cally glared back at him. "We worked together decorating windows. She put her husband through med school, too."

And he too had left his wife. Cally didn't say it. She didn't have to say it. From her tone and the expression on her face, a dead stump couldn't miss knowing it.

"Marianne, hi. It's me, Cally." Cally turned toward the wall.

Bryce watched her, sure as certain it'd be an additional year before he got her to even glance at a mirror. He'd expected her to be devastated, and she was. But more than anything, she was angry. He never thought he'd be glad to see Cally angry, but angry beat the socks off devastated.

"That sorry son of a—"

Bryce nearly smiled. She was going to come through this fine. Thank God. Thank God.

"Thanks, Marianne. Bye." Cally hung up the phone, then spun around to face Bryce and planted her hands on her hips. "I don't believe that man. I just don't believe him."

"Are you going to keep me in suspense forever?"

She narrowed her gaze on Bryce. "How good a lawyer are you, Counselor?"

"Damn good. Why?"

"Because I'm going to murder that animal cracker, and I want to make sure you can get me off."

"Murder?" Bryce sat up straight. "Cally, it's not your nature to murder anyone."

"I'm making an exception."

"Would you can this and just tell me what the animal cracker did?"

"He had a vasectomy. He wasn't sterile. He had a vasectomy."

"Then the baby couldn't be his."

"Oh, yes, it could." Her voice fairly rattled with outrage.

"How?"

"He had it reversed!" She slapped at her thigh and stared ceilingward as if talking to herself more than to Bryce. "Which explains why he'd refused to make love, of course. Why he stayed at the hospital all the time. That sorry excuse for a man couldn't risk impregnating his wife and his mistress at the same time." She glared at Bryce. "I mourned him. I believed all the garbage he fed me about me being a lousy wife. But I wasn't lousy, Bryce. Honest. I was a damn good wife."

"I'd bet on it." This reaction he'd never suspected. Never in a million years. But, God, was he grateful for it. And he strongly suspected Tony had a hand in it.

Tony?

No answer.

Tony?

Still no answer.

Odd. He'd always come when called before now.

"That's it, Bryce." Cally stomped back to the chopping block and picked up the knife. "That man has caused me the last ounce of misery he's ever going to cause me."

I strongly suggest you tell her about the threat to disbar you, Counselor.

A woman's voice? A shiver crept up Bryce's spine. *Who are you?*

Tony calls me Sunshine. Cally's got enough anger right now to deal with this threat constructively. If you let her cool down and then tell her . . . well, I wouldn't do that.

I'll consider it. Right now she's pretty steamed. Wouldn't a breather between shocks be better for her?

No answer.

"I'm still scared to death of him," Cally said. "I know how he twists things. Boy, can he twist things. But I'm not going to be miserable because of him anymore."

Hey, Sunshine. Did you hear that? She's scared of the guy. How's she going to react when I tell her about the threats? She'll come unglued, is what she'll do.

Still no answer.

I could use a little guidance here. That's what you guys do, right? Do I wait, or tell her now? What the hell am I supposed to do?

He called out twice more, but still with no success. Watching Cally rail, he waffled on what to do and wished Tony or Miss Hattie were around for advice. He loved the woman. He couldn't be objective when it came to her. And he sure didn't want her any more upset than was positively necessary.

One last time, he called out. But Sunshine didn't answer. Neither did Tony.

Remembering Cally's deduction, about Tony and Miss Hattie being separated, sent rivers of dread streaming through Bryce, and sweat beaded on his forehead. The sense of calm and serenity and well-being he'd felt since coming to Seascape had vanished. Had Tony also vanished? He hadn't answered Bryce's call. Sunshine had.

Every muscle in Bryce's body clenched at once.

Where was Tony?

* * *

Hattie walked in the mud room door, pegged her black coat on the wall. It was late, just after ten. The children were tucked in bed, everything had been prepared for dinner and the wedding, and she should be elated. Tomorrow was Thanksgiving, the day Bryce would make Cally his wife. It would be a good Thanksgiving. But it might also be her first Thanksgiving without her beloved soldier.

Fear gripped her hard and its talons clawed deep. A knot of tears rushed up her throat, stung her eyes. At the back door, she reached inside her pocket, pulled out her lacy hankie, then dabbed at her eyes. God help her, she didn't think she had the courage to walk through that door and up those stairs, knowing that Tony might not be there. Knowing he might never be there again.

When she'd seen Bryce and Cally walking on the cliffs that first time, Hattie had suspected Tony wouldn't survive this case. But the feeling had ebbed . . . until this morning. Now, it burned so very strong. She'd tried her best to convince herself she'd been mistaken, but the signs were there. The grandfather clock's ticks, always so rich and resonant, sounded hollow. The attic room, Tony's room, which was cool when he was there, was hot. Not warm, but hot. And she'd been afraid. So afraid.

To prove her fears wrong, she'd pulled up the white dustcovers, draped them over his furniture and bed, over the chest that still held his clothes, and the dresser that still held his photo of her taken the day he proposed all those years ago and the photo of him and Hatch with the prize fish they caught the day they found that silly doubloon. Tony had fussed about her keeping that picture because his beautiful golden-brown hair had been mussed, but she couldn't part with it. She never would. She loved that touchable side of him as much as she loved everything else about him.

Shivering from cold, she forced herself to go inside. The kitchen was empty, the light above the stove on. The fridge motor whirred softly, and she walked on through to the gallery. The clock's ticks echoed into the stairwell, and she gripped the banister then began to climb, not daring to think.

The third stair creaked under her foot and tears blurred

her eyes. She fixed her gaze on the portraits of Cecelia and Collin, and whispered an urgent plea for their help to get her through whatever came. She'd always felt Cecelia's love reach out and embrace her, always felt comforted when the pain of losing Tony became too great to bear. But this time, she felt nothing.

Nothing.

Except fear.

God help me.

Hattie turned at the bend in the stairs, made her way to the upstairs landing, then stared up the polished walls smelling of lemon oil and gleaming softly, her knees threatening to buckle. "No, Hattie," she told herself. "You're not a spiny woman and never have been. No, you'll go on. You'll do what you must because, in you, he's still alive. In your mind and heart, he'll always be alive."

Tears streamed down her face and the fear she would have sworn could grow no stronger doubled. She placed one foot in front of the other, began that last climb up to Tony's room, recalling he'd moved up there to gain that safe independence in his journey from boy to man. And there he had remained until he'd left home for the war. Until he'd died saving the life of one of his men. Her soldier. Her beloved soldier hadn't been spiny. He'd been brave, and she would be brave, too.

She reached the top of the stairs, then turned on the light.

Stark and white, the dustcovers lay still atop the furniture. The temperature remained warm.

Her heart shattered.

Her beloved had gone.

Chapter 16

The TV was on in the salon. Adrien Paul gathered more power on *The Highlander,* then the screen changed to an update on the late-night news. A lamp on a table beside a wing chair near the windows cast a circle of soft light onto the eggshell carpet. Bryce ignored it all and focused intently on Cally.

Sitting on the sofa beside him with a bowl of popcorn on her lap, she popped a kernel into her mouth, then crunched down on it. Butter sheened on her lips, almost more tempting than he could bear, but he had put off talking to her about Gregory and his threats as long as Bryce dared. They'd be getting married tomorrow. She had to know the truth tonight. She deserved honesty; he'd promised her that. And she deserved time to react.

"Cally?"

She licked the salt and butter sheen from her fingertip. "Hmm?"

"Gregory thinks we've been having an affair. That's why I arranged the alimony."

"Well, he's wrong." She dug into the bowl for more popcorn. But her hand wasn't quite steady.

"He says if we marry, he's going to file a complaint against me with the ethics committee. I imagine he'll also file suit for conflict of interest and professional misconduct."

Buried beneath the kernels, her hand went still. "Can he do that?"

"Honey, anyone can sue. We can prove the charges aren't

true, but the court and publicity will be messy. And he's said he won't stop until he has me disbarred."

"Oh, God."

"I didn't tell you this because I want you to panic. Only because you have the right to know what's up ahead."

"He'll do it." She finally wheeled her gaze to Bryce. "Even if he has to lie. He's a manipulative bastard, Bryce, and an accomplished liar." She set the bowl onto the coffee table, then wiped her hands on a napkin. "I'll do what I have to do."

A fissure of fear cracked open inside him. "What does that mean?"

She cupped his face, smoothed her fingertips along his beard, and swallowed hard. "I won't let him hurt you and the children. He can't put all of you through this—it'd affect your ability to provide for the family financially. I can't let that happen."

"I don't like the sounds of this, Cally." Bryce grimaced, fearing he knew what next would come out of her mouth, and honestly hating it.

Her eyes shining overly bright, she whispered, "I can't marry you."

"That's not an option."

"It's the only option I have. You and the kids need calm and security. If I don't call him and put a stop to this, you'll have neither. And I'm telling you, Bryce, I have fourteen years' worth of experience that tells me he'll stop at nothing—at nothing—to get what he wants. Her swallow rippled her throat and her voice went husky thick. "I love the kids, and I care for you. I can't, I won't, let this happen."

She stood up then headed toward the door.

Bryce went after her. At the bookcase near the hall leading to the gallery, he caught her by the shoulder. "Cally, wait."

She kept going.

"Cally, please." Bryce held her more firmly, insisting she stop.

She turned to look at him, her heartbreak clear on her face, in the depths of her tormented eyes. "I have to do this. I wanted to be sunshine to you, Bryce, not storms. I can't live with me, causing all of you pain." Her chin quivered. "I just can't."

He closed his arms around her. "You are sunshine to us. Being with you, even with trouble, is better than being without you, Cally. Don't you see that? Isn't it obvious to you that we all need you? The kids and me?"

A sob escaped her throat and deep shudders wracked her body. She buried her face at the cay in his neck. "Why is he doing this? He's gotten exactly what he wanted. Everything he wanted. Why isn't that enough for him?"

Bryce had his suspicions. After the conversation today, he felt certain Gregory Tate didn't want Cally, he just didn't want anyone else to have her. Bryce couldn't tell her that, of course. Or that he had done the unthinkable and fallen in love with her when they'd agreed that love would have no part in their relationship. Yet without telling her, he had no way to hold her. He needed her. He and the kids needed her. Wanted her. Loved her. And no way was he going to let Gregory Tate take her from them. Not now. Not ever.

When her sobs weakened to sniffles, he kissed the tears from her damp cheeks, letting his thumbs whisk across the ruddy blades of her cheekbones. "Let's think about this overnight, okay? Before we do anything. We're emotional about it, Cally. And we both know what happens when we act on our emotions rather than on logic."

She nodded. "Okay. But I won't let him hurt you or the M and M's, Bryce. I could sleep longer than Rip Van Winkle and that would never change."

Her insistence yanked hard at protective chords inside him, and he gave her a tender smile. "I know you won't, sweetheart."

Just after dawn, Cally awakened in a cold sweat. She sat straight up in bed, her heart pounding in her temples, and waited for the dread and fear from the dream to subside and the cobwebs of sleep to fall clear from her mind.

"It was just a dream." She buried her face in her hands and repeated the litany a few more times, praying it'd take hold in her mind. "It was just a dream. It was just a dream."

But was it?

Suzie's wasn't an ordinary dream. Cally knew that as well as she knew she sat in her bed in the Great White Room. She pulled up her knees, scrunched the quilts at her chin, then tried to put into order the vivid images she'd seen in her mind.

She'd been at Mary Beth's grave at home in Mississippi, with the yellow carnation. She'd put it there at the base of the headstone, just as she always had, but when she'd straightened up and turned around, Hatch had stood there beside her, his corncob pipe propped between his lips. With his wizen eyes, he was staring intently at her. Words he'd said to her before, and those she'd heard others say, tumbled from his lips in a great rush:

Decide what you really want, Cally. Seek your strength in love. Decide what you fear more. Is it Gregory? Or is it loving and losing Bryce and the M & M's?

She did fear Gregory. She knew how low he'd stoop, how far he'd go. With the vasectomy and the reversal of it, how could she not know? But more than she feared him, she loved Bryce. And the M & M's. And, God give her strength, she feared losing them more than she'd feared anything in her life.

You've got to get and keep both oars in the water. Suzie's dream's a premonition, in my estimation. You'll be their new mom, maybe.

The oars. Suzie's grown-up friend Selena's words to Suzie. The premonition. A warning from Hatch? He was the only man she'd ever heard use that "in my estimation" phrase. Cally wasn't sure, but it seemed like a warning, and it felt like a warning. In the dream, Suzie drowned. Was the warning that Cally should watch over Suzie more closely, or that she could drown in real life? And the "new mom" verbiage. Suzie's prophesy—or maybe Tony's prophesy related by Suzie to Cally, on the day Cally arrived at Seascape Inn.

If only you have the courage to believe, miracles can happen beside a dreamswept sea.

Are you believing, Cally? Are you believing?

Cally stilled. Was she believing?

All of this. Hatch's saying down at the pond that if she

ran into special trouble to come to him. The woman's voice at Mary Elizabeth's grave.

Oh, God, this with Suzie tonight hadn't been a dream. It'd been a message to Cally—from the woman. A warning.

Who was she?

Cally stared past the mirror and thought hard. There were two possibilities. Meriam or Mary Elizabeth.

Frankly Cally considered Meriam too self-focused for it to be her. And she was content. Poor Bryce had been terribly upset about that. No, not Meriam. Between the battleaxe and Bryce, Meriam had left them feeling certain of their ability to deal with whatever lay ahead.

That left Mary Elizabeth. Why she'd bother, Cally had no idea. But maybe enough of her mother, Cecelia, was in her daughter that when Cally had gone to Mary Elizabeth's grave she'd felt compelled to somehow warn Cally. Or maybe not.

For some reason, the messenger being Mary Elizabeth fit, and yet it didn't fit. It felt both right and wrong.

Why, Cally would have to sort out later. Right now, she had other things to do. A priority listing. She was going to marry Bryce today. But not until after she confronted a demon that she damn well should have confronted a long time ago.

She tossed back the covers and walked over to the mirror, fury fueling her steps, then stared directly into her own eyes. Gregory Tate had pushed her hard for a long time. But in threatening her now, in threatening Bryce and the kids, the man had pushed her too far. He'd pushed those she loved.

And now she was going to push back.

The ivory and white phone on the dresser beckoned her. Knowing the thing worked more often than not only when it wanted, she was determined that it would work right now.

She lifted the receiver, then put it to her ear. On hearing the dial tone, she smiled. "If only you have the courage to believe . . ."

After dialing the number, she jotted down a note to herself to tell Miss Hattie about the charges, then let her gaze drift out of the windows. Pink and lavender tinged the sky in languid streaks, and the sun sat like a brilliant orange ball out over the ocean on the horizon. It was dawn. About five

A.M. in Mississippi, where Gregory and Joleen now lived. He wouldn't be awake yet—not for another two hours, typically. And it gave Cally a perverse pleasure that she'd disturb him at an inconvenient time. Not very noble, but pleasing nonetheless.

The phone rang for the third time.

Groggy-voiced, he answered. "Tate."

"Gregory, this is Cally. I want to talk to you."

"Caline." He sounded surprised. "I want to talk to you, too." Something rustled in the background as if he were shoving at covers to get out of bed. "Hold on and let me get to another phone."

Obviously, he didn't want to wake his wife. "Fine."

During the wait, she crossed her free hand over her chest, stood bouncing her hip against the side of the dresser.

"Okay." He came back on the line. "Listen, Caline."

"I prefer Cally."

"I see. Well, what I want to say is that I'm sorry I flew off the handle yesterday. The trouble is"—he paused dramatically, as only Gregory could—"I'm not happy."

The sorry animal cracker. The fear inside her dissipated. She'd slipped back into the habit of giving him power over her. But fear wasn't as strong as love. And she loved Bryce. "A guilty conscience can do that to you, Doctor."

"Yes, it can. Would it help if I said I was sorry?"

"It couldn't hurt."

"I am sorry, and I—I—hell, Caline, I want you back."

"Excuse me?" She pulled the phone away from her ear, stared at it as if it'd sprouted horns.

"I'm not happy. Joleen is just like my mother. She has all the time in the world for kids, but none for me. She doesn't do all the things you did for me."

His mother, the pediatrician, and his wife, the biochemist. "No other woman would do all those things for you. And it's damned selfish of you to expect them to. It's even worse for you to compare us. How dare you do that?"

"What's gotten into you?"

Love, she wanted to shout. A huge, unselfish dose of love. "Nothing. You've gotten *out* of me."

"Don't say that, Caline. We had a lot of good years together."

Had they? Had they really? "You had a lot of good years, Gregory. I was just along for the ride, making them better for you."

"You were happy, damn it. Don't tell me you weren't happy."

"At first, yes. But then things changed." Something miraculous was happening inside her. Something so miraculous she couldn't tag it with a name. Yet she understood it completely. For the first time, she saw their relationship exactly as it had been. Exactly. And she felt, honestly felt from the bone out, that she deserved better. She deserved Bryce and the M & M's. "Look, I didn't phone you to rehash our pasts. That's all over now."

"I don't want it to be over. I want you back."

"No. You have a wife and son, and you belong with them."

"Because of the child?"

"Your child needs you, but the simple truth is I don't want you, Gregory. I don't love you."

"Caline!"

"Don't, okay? My love never meant anything to you. If it had, you wouldn't have done what you did. So don't insult us both now by pretending otherwise."

"But—"

"But, nothing." She paused to pull in a breath and prayed a second wind of courage would infuse her. "I called to warn you not to mess with me anymore, Gregory. Or with mine. That includes Bryce and our kids."

"You don't have any kids."

"At two o'clock today, I'll have three—officially. And if you stir up so much as a puff of air to hurt any of them, any of us, I'm going to come at you from places you didn't know you had."

"Don't threaten me, Caline. We both know you're too weak to—"

"Don't bet on it, Gregory. You'll lose. I was weak. I feared you. But I'm *not* weak and I *don't* fear you anymore. I never will again. You mess with me or mine and you're going to find out exactly how strong I've become. It won't be pretty. We were married fourteen years. You swept a lot of dirt under rugs and hid a lot of skeletons in closets. We'll start with the IRS. Maybe wave a few red flags at the insurance commissioner and the attorney general. The point is, you have dirt and skeletons. I have the dustpan holding all your dirt and the keys to your closets. If you do anything, anything at all that even carries a faint scent of harm, I'm going to sneeze and open locks."

His breath rattled through the phone, but he said nothing.

Her palms were soaking wet. The phone slick in her hand. She swiped her palm over her nightgown, grabbed the phone, then swiped her other palm dry. "You know I can do it, Gregory."

"You won't."

"I love them. You know from experience the lengths I'll go to for those I love. How in hell can you doubt it?"

"Damn it."

A burst of triumph exploded in her stomach. "I take it we're agreed then, and you'll be leaving us alone."

"It doesn't appear you've given me any choice."

"No, I haven't."

Smiling, she hung up the phone.

Someone tapped at her door. She looked toward the heavy wood. "Yes?"

"Cally, it's me. Bryce."

"Don't you come in here. It's our wedding day and I can't see you before the ceremony."

"You mean you've decided to go through with it?"

She walked to the door, pressed her palms against the wood, as if she were touching him. Tears of joy stung her eyes. Her sense of worth was restored. "You bet I am, Counselor."

"Cally."

One word. Five little letters, but they held so much meaning she couldn't hold it all in her heart. "I phoned Gregory, Bryce. He won't be bothering us anymore."

"I would have handled him, honey."

"I needed to do it myself." She smiled, her vision blurred. "And now I have."

"I'm proud of you."

"Me, too."

"Tell me about it."

"Later," she sniffed. "I've got a wedding to get ready for." A wedding that would be perfect if only she could tell the wonderful man on the other side of the door that she loved him. With all her heart.

"Okay. But later."

"Okay." She muffled a sniff behind her hand.

"Did I remember to tell you Jimmy's picking up Selena at the airport?"

"Suzie's Selena?"

"Yeah, Selena Mystic. She could only come in for the day because she's on a business trip. Suzie invited her."

"Selena's very important to Suzie. I'm glad she's coming."

"You're something, Cally Tate."

"I keep good company, Counselor." Sensing he was about to leave, she called out. "Bryce?"

"Yes?"

"Tell Suzie to stay away from the water."

"What?"

"Just tell her, okay? The pond *and* the ocean."

"Okay, Cally. Is there a special reason, or is it just a general warning?"

She leaned a shoulder against the door. "It's probably nothing. But it might be important. See, I had this dream . . ."

A gentle knock at the door had Cally and Miss Hattie swiveling their heads to see who had come.

"I do believe the entire village has traipsed through this bedroom this morning, Cally." Miss Hattie tsked, and shuffled to the Great White Room's hallway door.

"Only half," Cally said. "The women."

The door opened, and a beautiful brunette stood there. Petite and classy, dressed in warm autumn colors that made her skin look translucent, she walked in smiling. "Hi, Miss Hattie." She gave the angel a warm hug.

Cally lifted a questioning brow. Over her shoulder, Miss

Hattie gestured she had no idea who the bubbly woman holding her was. She looked to be in her twenties. Very pretty in an offbeat kind of way.

She released Miss Hattie and stepped fully into the room. "My God, there's a lot of love in here. So much it almost knocks you off your feet."

Miss Hattie smiled, clearly liking the woman. "That's because it was Cecelia and Collin's room at one time." She let her gaze drift fondly over everything in the room. "Most of the important things in their life happened in this room."

"You can feel it, can't you?" She closed her eyes, as if sucking in the ambience. "It's so powerful."

"It's soothing," Cally said, more to remind the woman she was there than anything else.

"That, too." She grinned and extended her hand. "Sorry, I was awed. I'm Selena Mystic."

"Oh, dear heaven." Miss Hattie beamed a smile. "John's sister, Cally. You've heard Bryce mention John and Bess Mystic."

"Yes, I have. But I've heard Suzie talk even more about Selena. You're her ultimate authority on everything."

"Don't be jealous, for pity's sake."

"I'm not." Cally lied. In a real sense she was. She wanted to be that important to Suzie.

"You are," Selena assured her.

A fissure of surprise opened up in Cally. "Are you psychic?"

Selena's face went red. "I'm embarrassed. The truth is I'm, er, sensitive. But I'm usually much more restrained. I was so excited to finally meet the woman who'd captured Bryce's heart, I forgot my manners."

Cally smiled, and forced herself not to think that she hadn't captured anything. "Well, I'm really glad to meet you."

"Thanks. Suzie told me all about you and her island."

"Well, it's not exactly hers."

"Now, Cally, dear," Miss Hattie interrupted, fluffing a pillow on the bed. "Suzie was sitting with the children when Millie told them that the island belonged to them, so I expect it is hers, too."

"It belongs to the villagers," Cally explained to Selena.

"Yes, I know." Her eyes gleamed with excited curiosity. "Jimmy mentioned that there were two graves out there."

"Yes, dear." Miss Hattie patted a spot on the bench, inviting Selena to sit down. "Dixie Dupree's and that of another lost soul."

"John nearly destroyed himself looking for Dixie. I'm so glad he's finally at peace on the matter."

"And with Bess." Miss Hattie let out a sigh. "My, but we were worried about them."

Selena nodded that she'd been troubled, too. "They're fine now. They would've come, but T.J. begged them to stay and help him keep Maggie home." Selena looked to Cally then added, "Maggie's due to have her and T.J.'s first baby any day now, and there's no way she'd let John and Bess come to Bryce's wedding without her coming, too."

"She always has been a sassy thing." Miss Hattie smiled.

Clearly sassy was a great compliment. Cally looked to where her dress hung on the outside of the closet door. "I'm looking forward to meeting them. Bryce speaks so highly of all of you."

"They're dying to meet you, too. For the record, we're all immensely relieved. Bryce didn't get a fair shake with Meriam. Even Bess thinks so, and she and Meriam were close. Well, as close as anyone could get to Meriam." Selena tipped her chin and looked deeply into Cally's eyes. "He'll be content with you."

Cally felt as if the woman had looked into her soul. "I hope he will."

"I know he will." Selena smiled, lifted a hand, palm up. "Sensitive, you know."

She stood up. "Don't let me keep you. I just wanted to say hi and to check you out so I can call home and lord it over them that I met you first. They're going to love you as much as Bryce does, Cally. No fears there."

She turned to Miss Hattie. "You did well, Miss Hattie."

What she was talking about, Cally didn't know, but obviously from her moist eyes, Miss Hattie did.

She dabbed at them with her handkerchief. "I know you have to leave right after the wedding, Selena, but I hope you'll come back to Seascape when you can stay for a while."

"I'd love to." She left the room with the same burst of energy in which she'd entered it.

"She's a whirlwind." Cally smiled.

Miss Hattie turned from the door back to Cally. "She's a troubled soul, dear. But she'll be back."

Not for a second did Cally entertain a thought of Miss Hattie's being wrong about Selena. She was troubled, and she would be back.

Surprised at the number of villagers who'd come, Cally walked up the aisle of the little church, her hands trembling around the bridal bouquet of narcissus and yellow carnation blossoms. She resisted the urge to check her tea-length dress one more time. Miss Hattie had pronounced it perfect, and if the angel said the soft cream crepe adorned and trimmed with pearls was perfect, then that was that.

Miss Hattie sat right up front, of course, next to Miss Millie. Vic and Hatch were there, too. Hatch had traded the yellow bandana he wore at his throat for a silk ascot. That he had gone to the trouble for them made Cally smile.

Mayor Horace Johnson and his snooty wife, Lydia, sat on the left with their son, Andrew Carnegie, who kept his gaze glued to Nolene Baker, who sat with Lucy and Fred. Jimmy watched Nolene, too, and Cally fleetingly wondered if Nolene had any idea she held the man's heart. Probably not yet. From all Cally had heard, Jimmy was waiting for Nolene to grow up before claiming her.

Pastor Brown stood at the altar, smiling. And turning to look at her, to watch her walk into their lives permanently, were Bryce and all three of the M & M's. Her heart felt too full. Just too full.

Bryce looked gorgeous in a black tux. He looked gorgeous in anything, and in nothing. And, though she hadn't figured out *how* she was going to avoid revising their vows before leaving this holy place, she held firmly to the belief that somehow she would. Something would happen. She would not lie in God's house, and she would not vow she didn't love Bryce Richards when she loved him with all her heart.

Sunlight broke through the blanket of clouds and streamed in through the stained-glass window, bathing Bryce and the M & M's in an array of pastel colors. He smiled. Suzie beamed. Lyssie looked curious and held Suzie's hand. And Jeremy fidgeted with his tie as if it were choking him to death. For the rest of her life, she'd be wary of checking his pockets before laundering his clothes, and that too she looked forward to with relish. They were waiting there for her, just as she'd asked Bryce. All of them. So the children too knew that when Cally took her vows she was also taking them, not just their dad, into her heart. They would be her family.

Tears stung her eyes; her heart overflowed. Finally. Dear God, finally. Her family.

Bryce offered her his hand. "Welcome, sunshine."

A tear slipped to her cheek.

Jeremy frowned up at his dad. "You're making her cry."

"Shh," Suzie scolded him. "This time it's okay."

"How come?"

Behind them, from the front-row pew, Frankie groaned. "'Cause I said, twerp."

"It's fine, Jeremy," Cally whispered. "These are happy tears."

Pastor Brown smiled down on them. "Are we ready?"

Cally and Bryce nodded. The kids all answered, too.

"Dearly beloved . . ."

Chapter 17

Outside the church, the villagers showered Bryce and Cally with bird seed, then gathered around and wished them well. It was warm, wonderful, as if the whole village had opened their arms and included them as the locals.

Neither Cally's parents nor Bryce's had attended, and that was as they'd wanted it. Not that they didn't want their families as part of their lives, but because of their special circumstances, they didn't want them worrying. Their folks would come to understand that the marriage would work and be a happy one for all of them—with time.

Miss Hattie clasped Cally's and Bryce's hands. "Oh, what a wonderful Thanksgiving this is!" She gave their fingertips a squeeze and her eyes grew moist. "My soldier would have been so very pleased."

A lump of tears settled squarely in Cally's throat.

"We think so, too, Miss Hattie." Bryce wrapped an arm around her shoulder, and pecked a kiss to her cheek. "I want to thank you for everything. You've—"

Lucy Baker grabbed Cally in an enthusiastic hug. "I'm so happy for all of you, sweetie."

"Thanks, Lucy." Cally laughed. "Me, too."

"Best thing in the world. Suzie looks positively over the moon happy."

Cally glanced over at Suzie. She radiated happiness from the heart out, giggling with Frankie—most likely conspiring, too—like children. Suzie acting childlike. What a blessing.

Bryce touched Cally's arm. "Honey, we need to go back inside for a second."

Her heart rate doubled. "Okay." Oh, God, how was she going to get out of this? How was she going to walk back in there and lie? She looked up at the rugged wooden cross Collin had carved—Collin, who had shared that rare and special love with Cecelia, who had inspired the Seascape Legend because he'd loved Cecelia so much that even death couldn't separate them. When Cecelia had died, Collin's ghost had come back for her, had carried her away in his arms—Cally just couldn't do it. She couldn't say she didn't love Bryce. She couldn't—*Oh, God, Tony. Where are you when I need you most? Where's the woman who's come to me before? Please. Somebody, please, help me!*

Tony didn't answer. Neither did the woman. But the urge to talk this over with Mary Beth nearly knocked Cally to her knees. But there was no way to turn to the woman buried in Mississippi with Cally's troubles now. Bryce stood staring expectantly, waiting for her.

Hatch caught Cally's eye, nodded as if he understood her plight. "Bryce, you'd best be grabbing Jeremy. Last I saw the boy, he was beating a path toward Seascape."

Bryce looked torn. Cally slid him a serious look. "We'd better hurry. Lord only knows what he'll dig up next."

He stared at her long and hard. "Are you sure? I know what this—"

She sent Hatch a look of sheer gratitude and, unless she was seriously mistaken, saw a little boy who looked an awful like Jeremy clinging to Miss Hattie's hand near the cemetery fence. "We'd better hurry, Bryce. Remember that dream? If anything happened to the kids, I'd be devastated."

"Okay, honey. You ride as planned. I'll run ahead."

"No." She laced their hands. "We're in this together."

They hurried out of the cluster of people, then down the sand-dusted street toward Seascape. Heavy, dark clouds hung out over the ocean and seemed to be moving closer to shore. A wicked storm was brewing out there.

When they passed the Blue Moon Cafe, Cally clutched at a stitch in her side and stopped. "Bryce, it's okay. Jeremy is back at the church with Miss Hattie."

Bryce stopped, looked at her, clearly waiting for an explanation.

She shrugged, and said nothing, determined not to lie to him.

"I presume there's a reason for our hasty exodus."

"Yes." The wind tossed a lock of his hair over his forehead. She brushed it away from his eyes. "But I'd rather not discuss it at the moment."

"Any particular reason?"

She let her hand drift up his chest, then gave him a sweet smile. "Several."

"In the mood for mystery?"

"A little."

"Ah, a trust-test kind of mystery." The wind tugging at his glossy black hair, he smiled down at her, then pecked a kiss to her lips. "I think I'm going to love being married to you, Miss Tate."

The question was, Would he hate loving being married to her? And that question, she couldn't ask. She wasn't that brave. Not today. "That's Richards, Counselor. Mrs. Richards. Has a nice rhythm to it, don't you think?"

"Yes, by God, it does," he said, sounding more than a little pompous and even more pleased with himself.

Then he kissed her again, sweeping her into a potent moment of desire-laced love. And long before he parted their fused mouths, she was praying hard that, one day, in his heart, he would love being married to her. That, despite their agreement about caring, he would love her.

One day.

The celebration feast ended early because of the severe thunderstorms, and the guests departed. Miss Hattie put the children to bed, and Bryce and Cally stole away to the Great White Room to be alone.

"I've been looking forward to this all day." Bryce removed his tie and slung it onto the bench at the foot of the bed.

"Me, too." Cally stepped out of her shoes. "It was fun though, wasn't it? Especially at the table, when Jeremy yelled down and asked you, 'Daddy, what's sex?' " She laughed hard. "I thought Pastor Brown was going to choke to death."

"Lydia Johnson sputtered stuffing halfway down the table."

"Horace got a kick out of that."

Bryce grinned and growled at Cally's neck. "He did."

She curled her arms around Bryce. "I thought it was very clever of you to answer that it meant whether you're a boy or a girl."

"I heard a lot of relieved sighs."

"Me, too."

Reaching for the buttons on Bryce's shirt, she slipped her fingertips between the first and second buttons. "I wonder where he heard it?"

The button popped free of its hole, and she pressed her fingers against his bare skin.

Bryce shivered in response. "No telling."

She looked up at him, dreamy-eyed. "Your voice sounds husky, Counselor."

"That's because I'm trying hard to think and talk when all I really want to do is to make love with my wife."

She gave him her best "you're lovable" look. "Your wife wants to love you, too."

He glanced at the cheval mirror. So did Cally. Their gazes met in the glass and surprise flickered through his eyes. "Cally?"

"Shh, let's talk later." She lifted onto her toes and kissed him, lovingly, longingly.

Clasping her to him, he walked over to the mirror, set her down, then broke their kiss and looked deeply into her eyes. "I need this, Cally. If you can do it." He ran his hands over her face, then holding her gaze, unzipped her gown, slid it free from her shoulders, and then down, over her hips.

Shivering from the nip of cool air against her skin, she stepped free of the crepe and lace. "I can do it now, Bryce."

His tense jaw and wary eyes reeked of skepticism. "Show me."

She finished undressing, while he stood, watching her hungry-eyed, longing, as if fearing if he so much as drew breath she'd lose her courage. She could promise she wouldn't, promise that with his gentle smiles, tender touches, and loving ways, her sense of worth had reemerged, but all that telling took too many words. And none of them showed her husband that he was lovable. He needed to be shown. And his wife delighted in the showing.

She stood before him naked, her heart leaping at the sight of sheer male pleasure in his looking at her. And, though it was a challenge, she stood still, let him look his fill. When the stiffness eased from his spine, she undressed him, pausing to caress, to nurture, to please.

And then when he stood as naked as she, all flaws and scars exposed, she turned her back to his chest and looked into the mirror.

"See what I see, Cally," he whispered at her nape.

She let her gaze drift down her body, then to Bryce. "I see beauty."

He curled his arm around her waist. "You are beautiful, Cally. To me, you are so . . . beautiful."

She looked at her husband's reflection, and her heart melted. He understood completely, for from the corner of his eye rolled down a poignant tear.

Lightning flashed.

Thunder boomed, its rumble vibrating the walls. Cally awakened in Bryce's arms, tangled in crumpled covers and her nose to his chest, smelling his warm, sweet skin. She pressed her lips to his shoulder, scooted out of bed, then grabbed her robe from the bench at its foot.

"Honey, what's wrong?"

"Nothing," she whispered. "I just woke up with this . . . feeling. I'm going to go check on the kids."

He rolled out of bed, then snatched up his robe. Halfway to the door, he belted it closed. "I'll check Jeremy and Lyssie. You check Suzie."

"I didn't mean to alarm you."

He pecked a kiss to her cheek. "I know. But the sooner we check them, the sooner your mind will be at ease, and the sooner we can get back to bed."

She smiled. "You're incorrigible, Counselor."

"Yeah." He grinned.

Cally's heart was thumping hard by the time she reached the Shell Room. Since she had awakened, her feeling of dread had grown stronger. Now it pounded out lethal warnings that throbbed in her temples, her heart. She cracked open Suzie's bedroom door, looked inside, and saw what she'd most feared.

"Bryce!" Cally screamed out. "Bryce!"

He ran to her, tripping over the edge of the Berber rug. "What is it?"

Cally turned, stark fear throbbing through her veins. "Suzie's gone!"

Miss Hattie looked so worried.

Down in the kitchen, Cally patted the angel's shoulder, though Miss Hattie's worry only worsened Cally's own. "We'll find her."

"I can't believe she'd leave the house." Wrung incessantly, her lacy white handkerchief hung limp in her hand.

"Me, either. But clearly she did. At church, I thought she and Frankie were planning something. I never dreamed it'd be at night, or out in a storm."

"Frankie, of course." Miss Hattie headed toward the mud room door. "The storm has the phone lines down. I'll run over to Fisherman's Co-op and see if Suzie went to visit Frankie."

"No, Miss Hattie." Bryce pulled on a slick yellow jacket. One of its sleeves was turned inside out. "You'll get wet and sick."

"Bosh, I'm never sick."

Cally fixed his sleeve. "We need you here with Lyssie and Jeremy, Miss Hattie. Please."

"All right, dear. I'll keep trying the phone." She cast a wistful look at the ceiling.

Cally knew Miss Hattie was wishing Tony were here. Cally wished it, too. Oh, how she wished it, too.

Bryce grabbed a flashlight from the counter. "I'll check the cliffs."

"Be careful, dear." Miss Hattie clicked her tongue to the roof of her mouth. "They're slick when dry. Treacherous, wet. Hatch looks for the patches of weeds growing out of the sand. Try to step there. It's a little safer."

Bryce nodded.

Hatch. The man flashed then stayed in Cally's mind. Hatch at the pond. *If you need special help, you come to me. I'll have your promise on that, little lady.*

Sensing that same mystical luring she'd felt at making the turn in Bangor onto Sea Haven Highway, Cally didn't question herself, just headed toward the door. If ever she needed special help, now was the time. "I'm going to get Hatch."

"Good idea," Miss Hattie assured her. "Nobody knows every nook and cranny—land or sea—around here like Hatch."

God, but did Cally pray Miss Hattie was right.

Bryce headed toward the stone steps, the cliffs.

Fighting back frustrating and fearful tears, Cally ran full-out up the sandy path to the lighthouse, half sliding, half falling her way to its base. The rain beat down hard, pelting her, stinging her skin, and obscuring her vision.

At the base of the lighthouse, near the little fence, Hatch stood waiting for her in a yellow slicker and hat and black wading boots.

He'd expected her. "Hatch?"

"I know, Cally." He looked both sad and relieved.

She held a stitch in her side that ached from running, dragged in deep breaths. "Help me. Please."

He reached into his pocket, then pulled out a shiny gold doubloon. "You take this, and I'll take you to Suzie. But I need your word that you'll not take this into Seascape Inn. When you don't need it anymore, you give it right back to me, and you never mention it to Miss Hattie. She's had enough heartache. We do our best to save her any more."

Cally took the coin. How it would help her, she didn't know. Little of what Hatch said made sense to her. But not for a second, looking into Hatch's eyes, could she doubt that the doubloon would help her, or that he made perfect sense. Both were just beyond her comprehension.

But she didn't have to comprehend. She only had to find Suzie.

As of two o'clock Thanksgiving afternoon, Cally was thirty-two with nearly everything she wanted. She'd waited so long. So long. She couldn't lose Suzie. Not now. Cally's dreams couldn't shatter so soon. She couldn't bear it.

"Don't even think it, little lady." Wizen-eyed, Hatch clasped her arm, then moved swiftly toward Seascape. When he hooked right at a Y in the path leading away from the house, toward Batty Beaulah's, Cally remembered the dream. "Oh, God, she's in the pond. Suzie's in the pond!"

Near the roots of the gnarled oak, Cally scanned the turbulent water through the rain—and saw Suzie adrift in the little rowboat.

"Suzie! Sit down! You're going to fall in!"

"No, Cally. I can't." She held up a long wooden paddle.

"Oh, God, she's trying to get the oars in the water." Cally spun to tell Hatch but he wasn't there.

Tony was.

And so was a dark-haired woman.

"Tony, thank God." Cally swiped at the rain dripping down her face. "Help her."

He didn't move. And the anguish in his eyes stopped Cally cold. "I can't."

"You have to." What did he mean, he couldn't? "For God's sake, Tony. *Please!*"

"He *can't* do it, Cally." The woman's voice was soft.

Cally darted a frantic glance at Suzie. The boat rocked on a swell, lurched, and Suzie fell over the side, into the water. "Oh, God. Oh, God. He has to!" She grabbed his sleeve. "Tony, for God's sake, please! *Please,* " Cally cried. "You can save her."

"Cally," the woman interrupted again, sounding infuriatingly calm. "He can't. Tony broke the rules. He's restrained to observation only. If you want Suzie saved, then you must save her."

"Me?" Cally stared at the woman. "Damn it, woman, I can't swim!"

Her serene expression didn't alter. "If only you have the courage to believe, miracles can happen beside a dreamswept sea."

Suzie sputtered.

Cally panicked. Squeezed the doubloon in her pocket. Was this why she'd needed it? To swim? That had to be the reason Hatch had given it to her. He'd led her here, hadn't he?

"Save your daughter, Cally," the woman said. "You can do it."

"God help me." Cally ran into the water, spotted Suzie, and inched her way to her, splashing, half drowning herself, praying, begging, pleading—and believing.

When she snagged Suzie's nightgown, she experienced her first taste of sweet success. Tears of relief, of gratitude, streaming down her face, she grabbed her daughter by the neck, hoisted her to her, and latched onto the slick wooden hull of the boat.

"You did it. You came and got me." Her voice a blend of excited squeal and awe, Suzie squeezed Cally so tightly she nearly couldn't breathe. "I told Tony not to worry. I told him you would come."

"Hold on to me and the boat, sweetheart." Shivering from cold, from fear of the frothy water swirling around them, from reaction at what was happening here, Cally held Suzie in a death grip, terrified.

But the boat turned. Now it was floating *toward* the shore. Why? The wind was blowing the boat *away* from it. She didn't understand this, either. But whatever the reason, she was grateful for it. "You've got some explaining to do when we get back to the inn. Did you forget that I can't swim, Suzie? You could've drowned." And I would have died. In my heart, I would have died at losing you because I love you so much.

Suzie grinned up at her. "You did swim. For me. Just for me."

Cally touched bottom and nearly fainted from relief. Suzie's words stopped her cold. She'd never, not once, told the kids she loved them. Not once.

Frigidly cold, Cally stilled, the water splashing at her chest, her feet sinking into the muddy bottom of the pond. "I love you, Suzie."

Eyes shining, lips blue, teeth chattering, Suzie smiled back. "I know. I love you, too, Mom."

Something special passed between them. Something warm and wonderful and good. The test Cally had passed had been divinely inspired and played out. She didn't understand its intricacies any more than she understood a lot of the unusual things that happened at Seascape Inn. But her daughter hadn't drowned. They loved each other. And they'd be there for each other all the rest of their days. That bond was sacred and sweet and cherished. And real. Those things were all that really mattered, and those things Cally understood perfectly. In her mind, her soul, her heart.

Suzie cradled in her arms, Cally stepped onto the shore.

Tony looked elated. "You did it, Cally."

"I told you she would." This from the pretty dark-haired woman, who still looked as serene as she'd been during the crisis, though her eyes glistened.

"Mary Beth did tell you that, Tony," Suzie said, then went to him.

He picked her up in his arms, and tweaked her nose. "She did, little one. Didn't she?"

"Uh-huh."

"Mary Beth?" Surprise streaked through Cally. "*My* Mary Beth?"

The woman nodded. "You've asked me many times since coming here in what you must believe. I think you have your answers now. Believe in yourself, Cally. And always, always, believe in love."

"But—"

"Love gave you the strength to swim and save Suzie. It will always give you the strength to do whatever it is that you must do. But only if you believe in it."

Cally blinked, then blinked again, still dripping onto the cold ground. "That's why I needed Hatch's doubloon. Because I believed it would give me the ability to swim, it did."

Mary Beth Ladner smiled enigmatically. "Did it? Really?"

"No. But I thought it did. Love for Suzie gave me the ability."

"And your belief that you could."

"That, too." Cally gave the woman a watery smile. "I can't believe that after all these years, I'm standing here and talking with you."

"I had to come. For years, you've let me know that I made

a difference. I've never been forgotten. Tonight, I wanted you to know, neither have you."

She mattered. Her skin pimpled from cold, Cally never in her life had felt warmer. "Thank you, Mary Beth. And you, too, Tony." Cally spoke around a lump in her throat. "For everything."

"Cally!" Bryce shouted. "Suzie!"

Cally turned toward the sound and saw him running toward them. "Here, by the pond!"

She looked back, and Suzie stood smiling at her. Mary Beth and Tony had gone.

Bryce swept them both into his arms. "Thank God." He kissed Cally on the temple, then brushed one to Suzie's forehead. "What happened? Are you two okay?"

"Suzie fell into the pond." Cally wrapped her arm around his waist.

"Cally swam out and saved me."

Bryce stared at them. "Cally *swam*?"

"I did."

Hatch came up. On seeing Suzie standing there with Cally, his leathery cheeks split into a smile and he handed them each a blanket to wrap around their shoulders. "I see you ladies went for a midnight swim. In my estimation, the daytime's the best—a lot warmer—but I hear that some nighttime swimming ain't bad, though it ain't exactly a forgiving sport when it's done in a storm."

Cally eased the doubloon into the old man's hand. "Sometimes swimming is a treasure far more precious than gold."

He winked at her. "I might just have to try it myself sometime. Provided I don't catch pneumonia and die from being out in this rain running after you two free spirits."

Bryce hugged his girls. "We'd better get you two home and dried off. Hatch, come with us. Miss Hattie's making hot chocolate."

"Can't do it, though I surely do like Miss Hattie's hot chocolate. Uses those miniature marshmallows, you know. I never did care for hot chocolate with them big fat marshmallows in it."

He couldn't come. He had the doubloon. Cally realized.

"Come as far as the house and I'll bring you a cup to take with you on the walk home."

"Well, now, in my estimation, Cally, that's a fine idea."

Cally grinned at the wise old man. Touched by magic. As much as Miss Hattie and Tony and Seascape Inn itself.

But what about Tony? What had happened to him? "Suzie?" Cally whispered, leaning low so only Suzie could hear her. "Is Tony still here?"

Suzie shrugged. "He's on restriction for breaking the rules. When he's not busted anymore, he might get to come back. If he does, he'll be in his room." She pointed up to the attic of the house.

"How long will he be on restriction?" Miss Hattie would be so lonesome without him.

"I don't know. Mary Beth didn't, either. She said they didn't tell her."

That "they" sent chills racing up Cally's spine. But surely they would let Tony come home. Without him, Miss Hattie would be lost. So would Tony.

"Hey." Bryce cupped Cally's shoulder. "What are you two whispering about?"

"Girl talk." Cally smiled at him.

"Yeah, girl talk." Suzie smiled, too.

"Oh, boy." Bryce looked at Hatch. "There's three of them and only two of us guys. I think we're in trouble, Hatch."

"Yep." He stuck his pipe in his mouth, his eyes twinkling. "Women. Ya gotta love 'em."

"Yes, I guess you do." Bryce's laughing gaze met Cally's. "I guess you do."

Chapter 18

"You look happy." Bryce looked at Cally over the kitchen table.

"I am happy." She shrugged, and her cheeks turned the prettiest shade of rose he'd ever seen.

Suzie was back in bed, snug and warm and safe, and the house was quiet again. "We Richards do add excitement around here." The grandfather clock in the gallery ticked softly. "It'll be good to get home tomorrow, but I'm going to miss Seascape."

Cally smiled wistfully. "Me, too. It's true what they say. All of it." Her gaze drifted to Bryce's. "There's a lot of love in this house."

"There's a lot of love in the woman I'm looking at, too." He shook his head and set his mug back down on the table. "I have to confess something."

"What?"

"I was at the pond. I saw Tony and the woman, wearing the crown of carnations."

"Why didn't you come help Suzie?"

"I couldn't move." Bryce let out a grunt. "It was the weirdest thing, Cally. I swear. It was as if my feet were planted in the ground. I couldn't move so much as an inch—totally powerless. I hated the feeling."

"Tony couldn't move, either." She paused to sip from her cup, then to lick marshmallows from her lips. "I had to do it."

"Do what?"

She cocked her head. "Believe in miracles."

His lips curved in a wondrous smile. "Mary Beth gave back."

Cally nodded.

Mary Beth had chosen her battle to fight for Cally. And when most needed, she'd found a way to help Cally. She hadn't forgotten that she'd been remembered. "It's amazing." Bizarre too, but mostly amazing. Awesome and amazing. And humbling.

"We were wrong, Bryce." Cally didn't quite meet his gaze. "We thought caring was more powerful than love." Cally looked straight into his eyes. "It's not."

It wasn't. Bryce knew it as well as he knew he sat in Seascape Inn's kitchen. Cally had believed, and she'd succeeded. She'd won. And Bryce wanted to win, too. He wanted to win her. He wanted to believe. To dream with her while awake and not pretending. "I know I promised I wouldn't do this, Cally. And I know you're probably going to be upset with me because I have, but—"

"You love me, Counselor."

He stilled and just stared at her.

Her gaze softened and she reached over the table to touch his hand. "I love you, too, Bryce. With all my heart."

Stunned, he let her words—the truth—soak in, then wash through him. Warmth and joy seeped into his soul. "I should have realized at the church—your mysterious trust-test—when we didn't go back and revise our vows. But I didn't."

He went to her, urged her to her feet, then closed his arms around her and hugged her tight. Suzie's words ran through his mind: *If only you have the courage to believe, miracles can happen beside a dreamswept sea.*

Everyone was in the car, waiting to leave. Suzie yelled out. "Wait, Daddy. I forgot my quilt."

"Okay." With a little groan, he opened the door to let her out so she could run inside and get it.

Miss Hattie stood on the front porch. "What's wrong, Suzie?"

"I forgot my quilt. I can't leave my quilt."

She sailed past Miss Hattie, past the L-shaped registration

desk in the gallery, then, at the foot of the stairs, came to a dead halt.

"Forget something, little one?" Tony leaned against the wall and smiled down at her.

She gasped, and her eyes sparkled pure delight. "Tony, you're home!"

"Yep."

"Are you off restriction for good?"

"I hope so." Never again did he want to come this close to losing Hattie. He tossed the quilt down to Suzie. "Catch."

She hugged the little quilt to her chest. "I love you, Tony. And I love my new mom. You picked me the best mom ever."

Tony smiled, crossed his chest with his arms. "I didn't pick her, though I couldn't have chosen better. We can thank Mary Beth for that."

"Will you?"

"Yes, I will." Sunshine had returned home, but he'd get Suzie's message to her.

"I have to go." She waved behind her. "They're waiting in the car."

"I know."

"I'll miss you."

"I'll miss you, too, Suzie." He walked down the steps, scooped her up and hugged her tightly, then set her back onto the floor.

She wadded the quilt at her chest. "Did you like my grown-up friend, Selena?"

"She seems like a nice woman." What was the munchkin up to now? She had that look in her eye. . . .

"She doesn't have a mom or dad."

"I'm sorry to hear that." Matchmaking? The child had spent too much time with Hattie.

"She doesn't have someone special, either. Like Daddy has Cally, and Uncle T.J. has Maggie, and Uncle John has Aunt Bess."

"I get your point, Suzie." Tony held off a smile by the skin of his teeth, then gave in to a wink. "I'll see what I can do."

"Thank you." Suzie turned.

"Wait." He plucked two petals from his yellow carnation. "You keep one for you, so you don't forget me—"

"I'll never ever forget you."

"Then keep it just because," he said. "And give this one to Miss Hattie." His throat went tight. "She'll know what it means."

Her eyes glossy with sweet tears, Suzie looked up at him. "I believed, Tony."

"Yes, you did."

"Did you?"

The force of her words hit him like a thunderbolt.

"Suzie," Miss Hattie yelled from the front door. "Your dad says to hurry, dear, or they're going to catch the commuter traffic in Bangor."

"Bye, Tony."

"Bye." He waved and watched her go, then cast a suspicious glance at the portraits of Cecelia and Collin hanging in the stairwell. *Had he believed?*

Hattie had rocked in her rocker until she thought the quiet house would drive her insane. When Suzie had given her the carnation petal, she'd thought Tony was back. But she'd climbed the stairs to the attic and his room was still warm. The white dustcovers were still draped over all the furnishings.

And inside she'd died just a little more. Her beloved hadn't come back to her.

Now, she turned over in her bed and dabbed at her cheeks one more time. If he were here, he'd blister her ears for being spiny about this. Yet how could she not feel lost and frightened? For the first time ever she was alone.

She closed her eyes and whispered a prayer for him to come back to her. Just once more. Just . . . once more.

Tony waited patiently for his beloved to drift off to sleep, to drift into a dream. It hadn't been until Suzie had asked him on the stairs if he'd believed, that he'd truly understood what had happened here with these special guests.

He wasn't needed.

Mary Beth had come to help Cally.

He'd breached the rules and not been punished, though if

Cally had lost faith, he'd have had to watch Suzie die, and that would have been so painful he couldn't imagine it.

He'd felt the physical. In a dream, he'd felt the physical. He'd assumed because he'd broken the rules by interceding in Suzie's dream, he'd be punished. He wasn't. But only when Suzie had asked him if he'd believed had he realized he was being rewarded.

The first time he'd interceded into Suzie's dream, he hadn't realized the potential personal sacrifice. That he and Hattie could be separated forever. Which is why he'd had to be tested again.

And he was. Two nights before Thanksgiving. When Mary Beth had come and officially warned him not to intercede, warned him that the repercussions would cost him everything. Would cost him Hattie.

Yet he had known himself, and his beloved. Had known that if he'd refused to help Suzie, he would forfeit his self-respect, and Hattie's respect. And so he'd willingly sacrificed all for the child. In doing so, he'd earned a reward—or so he'd thought.

As he watched his beloved sleep, the truth of the matter settled onto him. These special guests were here to heal, but they were also here to help Tony and Hattie heal. Being separated from each other grew harder each Thanksgiving, more painful for both of them. But because they did what they could for others, reaching out as best they were able, they were being rewarded. Sunshine, Mary Beth Ladner, had come to show Tony a way that he and his beloved Hattie could touch, could hold, could—at least, for a time—be together.

Words he'd once said to Suzie came tumbling back through his mind. *Sometimes when we want something a lot, we tell ourselves we don't want it, so then if we don't get it, it doesn't hurt so much.*

He'd believed in miracles for Suzie, but not for himself. And certainly not for him and Hattie. Because he hadn't believed miracles possible for them, he'd misread the signs.

Now, he understood.

Hattie lay dreaming. In the dream, she stood out on the inn's front lawn, her hand cupped over her eyes, blocking out the brilliant sunlight, looking up toward the attic room. Toward his room.

He fingered the petals on the yellow carnation, loosened it from his lapel, then held it in his hand. His heart rocking against his ribs, he stepped into his beloved's dream.

He came up from behind her. Heard and felt the gravel on the drive crunch under his heels. All sights and sounds and smells seemed magnified a hundredfold. "Hattie."

"Tony?" She turned, gasped, clasped her hands to her face. "Oh, Tony!"

His age. His beloved appeared the same age as he, and she ran to him as he ran to her. Tears streamed down her cheeks, down his own. He caught her in his arms, clamped them tightly around her, smothered her with kisses; her face, her chin, her shoulder—wherever his lips deigned to touch. "Oh, God, Hattie."

She laughed through her tears and lifted her face for his kiss. "I prayed you'd come back to me. I prayed so hard."

He kissed her as if starved, unleashing the longing that had built inside him during their fifty-one-year separation. And when they paused to draw breath, he drew back enough to hand her the carnation. "I had to come walk with you on the cliffs."

"Just like we used to." She smelled the yellow petals that had been their link to each other for such a long time, her eyes sparkling with so much love. So much love, and so much joy.

Hand in hand, they walked together, across the craggy cliffs to the special oak where they'd first confessed their love; where Tony first had proposed, and Hattie had accepted; their arms entwined, their hearts beating contentedly as one; and, inside his mind, Tony heard Suzie's laughter, her voice. *If only one has the courage to believe, miracles can happen beside a dreamswept sea.*

"I believed, Suzie," he silently whispered to the child who'd taught him the power of faith and magic and love.

The power of Seascape Inn.

Don't miss *Tomorrow's Treasures* by Rosalyn Alsobrook—the next magical SEASCAPE ROMANCE. Turn the page for your sneak preview . . .

Why does life always have to be so complicated? Damon Adams wondered, dividing his attention between the old, worn maroon and white travel brochure open on his desk and the storm-cloud gray telephone receiver gripped in his hand. Quickly, he punched the lighted buttons in correct sequence with his pencil eraser. Planting his elbows on a note-stuffed, ink-scribbled desk pad, he listened for that first ring. Four rings later, Miss Hattie finally answered.

"The Seascape Inn, Hattie Stiliman speaking. May I help you?

Despite the purpose behind his call, Damon smiled at the natural warmth in Miss Hattie's familiar voice. How he loved that jaunty clip so characteristic of her fellow "Mainiacs of the mid-coast". Only someone as pleasant as Miss Hattie could make him grin at a time when what he would really rather do was pull out large hunks of his dark hair. Or better yet, pull out large hunks of Blair Brockway's short, transient-brown locks.

Some friend she turned out to be.

"I certainly hope so. This is Damon Adams. I know this is late notice, but I need to try to reserve a third room for ten of those twelve days Jeri and I will be there. You wouldn't happen to still have a vacancy during that time, would you?" *Please say, no.*

"I just might. Which ten days are you talking about?"

"Starting that Friday."

"Let me check." She clattered the phone, then leafed

through papers, probably the pages of her reservation book. After a minute or so humming the first stanza of *Amazing Grace*, she came back on the line. ''Aye, that's what I thought. You are in luck, Damon. The couple who had booked the Cove Room for the last two weeks in July called just yesterday to tell me they would be staying only through that first Thursday. Seems their younger son recently joined the Navy and the couple wants to be there when he graduates from Great Lakes that next day, much earlier than they'd thought. How nice for you because that room will give you the entire second floor right here inside the house. That will afford you a little more privacy than most guests have.''

Rats. ''Then add it to my reservation.'' Damon sighed. He wrinkled his nose beneath the bridge of the designer, gold-rimmed glasses he had slipped on to read the unreasonably tiny print on the brochure. Had there been no vacancy, he would have had a good excuse to forget the whole thing. After all, there was no way Jeri would allow anyone of the adult female persuasion to share her room. The kid was going to be furious enough just having one join them. Even though Jeri was destined to become one, his daughter did not yet trust anyone who was both female and over the age of eighteen. Of course, her own mother had had plenty to do with that. ''Do you need my credit card number again?'

''No, no, I still have that right here. Besides, I know I can trust you to pay your bill. You haven't failed me yet.'' She paused a moment. ''What name shall I put down as the occupant for this third room?''

''Paige Brockway.'' Nervously, he tapped the metal pencil band against the side of the telephone base. It looked like he would have to go through with it after all.

Drat.

''A close friend of yours?''

''No, she's more like a friend of a close friend.'' He cut his gaze to Blair seated primly on the only chair in his office not cluttered with paperwork. ''Or rather the sister of one. She should arrive sometime Friday to help keep Jeri entertained and out of trouble while I put together a bid for a very important contract. It's one of those unexpected last minute deals that can't be helped.''

"How old is she?"

If anyone but dear, sweet Miss Hattie had asked, Damon would have simply told her it was none of her business and been done with it. But Miss Hattie had a true interest in people, and liked knowing a little about her guests beforehand so she could to make them feel more at home.

"How old is Paige?" he repeated, and thought a moment. "She's twenty-three."

"No, twenty-*five*," Blair corrected. She leaned forward to be sure he heard her. "Paige is now twenty-*five*."

Damon frowned, distracted from the conversation with Hattie. "Already?" He pulled the receiver away from his mouth, but didn't bother to cover it "She can't be that old already. Why, it was just yesterday the little twerp was out riding that goofy looking white bicycle with the pink and purple tassels and—"

"That wasn't *yesterday*, Damon." Blair wagged a perfectly manicured nail in his direction. "Paige got rid of that old bike when she was thirteen and we had to move. Paige really is twenty-five now."

He groaned at the reminder. If Paige was twenty-five, that meant he was thirty-one. He didn't like being thirty-one. Scowling deeper, he jerked his reading glasses off and shoved them aside before talking again into the telephone receiver. "Ah, my mistake. Seems the years are getting by me without enough notice. It looks like little Sticks is now twenty-five. And to save you from your next questions, she's a women's fashion designer who I understand is very good at what she does. She lives in New York City for now but is about to move back here to Mt. Pine."

"No, Paige is *not* coming back to Texas!" Blair came out of her chair with a regal vengeance. "She's not throwing away her career like that. She is to stay right there in New York with me. You are about to make sure of that, remember?"

Damon didn't care to explain away another blunder so he simply went on with his description. "She's single, educated, and nauseatingly successful for someone so young—and most importantly—she is not coming because I have any sort of romantic interest in her. Got that? You are to do none of that matchmaking you're so noted for. This is strictly business."

"Mmmmm, strictly business?"

"Yes strictly business, " Damon repeated. There was something in Miss Hattie's tone that made him nervous enough to lie. He had seen Miss Hattie in action. "I'm dating someone else right now who would have a royal conniption if she thought I was up there fraternizing with the help. Please, keep that in mind while we are there."

"Oh? You have finally found enough time to date again? How nice. Why don't you bring your new lady friend with you, too? I'd truly love to meet the woman who finally made you realize what your life was lacking. What's she like?"

Not in a creative mood, Damon cut the conversation short. "I have work to do, Miss Hattie. I'll tell you all about her when I see you in a couple of weeks. Goodbye until then."

After he jabbed the off button, he set the handset down beside those fiendish eyeglasses as he rubbed the pad-dented bridge of his nose with a gentle finger and thumb.

"Okay," he muttered. Dropping his hand, he returned his attention to Blair, now seated again. "I did it. Your sister now has a room at the Seascape Inn." He slid the pencil into the empty pocket of his bright red cotton shirt. "But what makes you so all-fire certain she'll go to Maine with us?"

"Oh, she'll go all right," Blair replied with a slightly impish smile—the same sweet, dimpled smile that had made her famous world wide. It was also a smile Damon had learned to be wary of years ago.

"Don't you worry. My sister will be there. I'll see to it." Her smile deepened as she braided her slender hands together and rested them gracefully on a silk draped knee. "And she will loathe every minute she's there. *You* will see to that."

"If that's what it takes." Damon let out a tired breath then rolled his head back and rested it against the top of his worn, leather chair. "Then that's what I'll do."